Praise for the novels of Sherryl Woods

"Woods' amazing grasp of human nature and the emotions that lie deep within us make this story universal."

—*RT Book Reviews* on *Driftwood Cottage*

"Woods' emotionally intense story of loss and love will appeal to a broad range of readers."

—*Booklist* on *Willow Brook Road*

"Once again, Woods proves her expertise in matters of the heart as she gives us characters that we genuinely relate to and care about. A truly delightful read!"

—*RT Book Reviews* on *Moonlight Cove*

"Woods employs her signature elements—the southern small-town atmosphere, the supportive network of friends and family, and the heartwarming romance—to great effect."

—*Booklist* on *A Slice of Heaven*

"Woods…is noted for appealing character-driven stories that are often infused with the flavor and fragrance of the South."

—*Library Journal*

"Woods delivers a charming novel…[a] unique blend of sparkling humor and family drama."

—*RT Book Reviews* on *Midnight Promises*

Also by #1 New York Times *bestselling author Sherryl Woods*

Chesapeake Shores

Willow Brook Road
Dogwood Hill
The Christmas Bouquet
A Seaside Christmas
The Summer Garden
An O'Brien Family Christmas
Beach Lane
Moonlight Cove
Driftwood Cottage
A Chesapeake Shores Christmas
Harbor Lights
Flowers on Main
The Inn at Eagle Point

The Sweet Magnolias

Swan Point
Where Azaleas Bloom
Catching Fireflies
Midnight Promises
Honeysuckle Summer
Sweet Tea at Sunrise
Home in Carolina
Welcome to Serenity
Feels Like Family
A Slice of Heaven
Stealing Home

The Perfect Destinies

Treasured
Priceless
Isn't It Rich?

The Calamity Janes

The Calamity Janes: Cassie & Karen
The Calamity Janes: Gina & Emma
The Calamity Janes: Lauren

The Devaney Brothers

The Devaney Brothers: Daniel
The Devaney Brothers: Michael and Patrick
The Devaney Brothers: Ryan and Sean

Ocean Breeze

Sea Glass Island
Wind Chime Point
Sand Castle Bay

For a complete list of all titles by Sherryl Woods, visit sherrylwoods.com.

SHERRYL WOODS

Destiny Unleashed

Recycling programs for this product may not exist in your area.

ISBN-13: 978-0-7783-1889-7

Destiny Unleashed

For questions and comments about the quality of this book, please contact us at CustomerService@Harlequin.com.

www.MIRABooks.com

Printed in U.S.A.

Dear Friends,

The Perfect Destinies series was originally issued as three Harlequin Special Edition books (Million-Dollar Destinies), with a longer follow-up book written for MIRA Books. I'm so pleased to have all of them available in these new editions from MIRA.

As many of you know, I've always loved writing about families. And in this case three sexy, very different brothers were raised by their madcap Aunt Destiny, after the tragic death of their parents. Think Auntie Mame for those of you old enough to remember that wonderful movie. Or meddling Mick O'Brien, if you're a fan of my Chesapeake Shores series.

I hope you'll enjoy revisiting the Carltons, if you've read these books before. And if you're new to the series, I hope you'll welcome the family into your heart as you have so many of my other families.

All best,

Sherryl Woods

Destiny Unleashed

1

If she'd had any idea that reinventing herself would require so much self-doubt and soul-searching, Destiny Carlton might have left it for another day. Perhaps another lifetime.

Her agitated pacing slowed at last, and she turned to the woman who had been her personal secretary and confidante for nearly two decades.

"Am I crazy to even be thinking about this?" she asked Miriam Thomas. "Have I finally lost it completely? Give me your honest answer."

Miriam's lips quirked. She'd never been anything less than brutally honest. "You're the most sane person I know," she said loyally.

"But this," Destiny said doubtfully, "this is huge. It's not as if I want to get a little job in the corner card shop."

"Hardly," Miriam agreed wryly.

"I haven't worked in years," Destiny pointed out.

"Ha!"

"Okay, okay, I've run charity events and I've certainly kept my eye on all the decisions at Carlton Industries, but that's not the same as actually being in business. It's not the same as going in to my nephew and asking him to trust me to take over an entire division of the family company."

"Isn't that the point?" Miriam asked. "It *is* the family company and you're a very important part of this family, the matriarch, in a manner of speaking."

"True, but I turned my back on it years ago and left it to my brother. The only reason I gave up my art and my studio in the south of France was because of the plane crash that killed my brother and his wife. I couldn't leave Richard, Mack and Ben all alone. They were mere boys at the time. They needed me. Now they're grown men with wives of their own."

"Thanks to you," Miriam reminded her.

Destiny allowed herself a small smile. "Yes, all that meddling did work out rather well, if I do say so myself. There was no telling how long it would have taken them to get around to settling down if I hadn't given fate a bit of a nudge."

"So they owe you," Miriam suggested. "If you want to try something totally new, if you want to reinvent yourself completely at this stage of your life, why shouldn't you? And why shouldn't they give you their blessing?"

"It's not just their blessing I want," Destiny said. "I'm asking to take over the European division. Richard has me tucked into this nice, predictable niche in his life. I'm the doting, slightly madcap aunt. He doesn't see me as any kind of businesswoman. I'm partly to blame for that. I've never shown the slightest inclination to work for Carlton Industries before, at least not in any formal capacity."

"Sit down," Miriam ordered in one of her rare displays of impatience. She actually scowled until Destiny complied. "Bottom line, you know this company inside out, whether you've ever held an official job here or not. You're on the board of directors, for goodness' sake, and no one goes into those meetings more informed than you do. Am I right?"

"I try," Destiny agreed. It was a point of honor to her that she do her homework if she was going to hold a seat on the board.

"And you're uniquely suited to this particular job, isn't that right?"

Destiny thought of the problems in the European division. Most of them had been caused by the persistent stealth attacks of one man in particular, William Harcourt, the man she'd once loved with all her heart, the man she'd walked away from more than twenty years ago when she'd come back to the States to take care of her suddenly orphaned nephews.

"I do know how William's mind works," she agreed. "And the fact that he's become a threat to my family's company—perhaps because of me—makes me highly motivated to put a stop to it."

"Well, then, I don't see how you have any choice. You have to do this," Miriam concluded. "Not just for your own sake, but for the company."

"What if I botch it up?" Destiny asked, unable to shake her own self-doubts.

Miriam gave her a scathing look. "Don't be ridiculous. You won't." She grinned. "For one thing, you'll have me right there beside you."

Destiny stared at her. "You'd go to London with me?"

"I certainly wouldn't let you set off alone," Miriam said emphatically. "Besides, with Darryl dead and Dwayne in college, my life is as much of an empty nest as yours. It will be good for both of us to dive into something new and exciting."

Yes, Destiny thought, that was exactly it. She needed a challenge. Ever since the marriage of her youngest nephew, she'd been essentially at loose ends. If she wanted to go back to her house in France, she could. If she wanted to spend her time painting, she could do that, too. If she merely wanted to travel, that option was open as well.

But all these years of running a household, of overseeing her nephews' education, of taking a more active role on the Carlton Industries board of directors had given her a jaundiced view of idleness.

She wanted to be productive. She'd made the transition from eccentric artist to instant mother rather successfully. Now she wanted to reinvent herself yet again. There was someone inside her still to be discovered. She had a lot left to prove, not to her nephews, but to herself. Leading a wildly madcap lifestyle in her twenties or even at thirty had been one thing. It was quite another to consider going back to it in her fifties.

It wasn't too late to find an entirely new direction that suited her, she assured herself. At fifty-three, she was still vibrant, intelligent and capable. In fact, in no small measure thanks to her success in getting her nephews settled, she felt ready to tackle anything.

For months now this idea had been brewing in the back of her mind. She'd tossed out an occasional hint, just to see if Richard would jump at the bait, but he didn't seem to be taking her seriously. It was time he did. After all, he was the one who'd indirectly planted the idea in her head.

It was all tied up with William Harcourt, who had turned out to have an astonishing head for running his own family's business. In recent years he had made it his apparent mission in life to go after every European contract previously held by Carlton Industries. He'd won some, lost more, but there was no mistaking his use of inside information—her own pillow-talk revelations, damn him—to make her family's company pay dearly for every deal it made. Until very recently his actions had been more annoyance than threat, but lately his tactics had grown bolder and more damaging. It was time to put a stop to it.

Destiny had made a lot of impulsive decisions in her life, but she didn't intend for this plan for her future to be one of them. She'd given the matter of William Harcourt targeting Carlton Industries a lot of thought and finally concluded that she was the only one who could make him rue the day he'd decided to betray her and go after her family. Revenge would be so much more challenging—so much more *fun*—than going back to claim an idle life that no longer held any meaning.

She simply had to convince Richard—the entire family, in fact—that she was up to the task.

"You honestly believe I can do this?" she asked Miriam one last time.

"Without question," Miriam said confidently.

Destiny nodded. "Then it's time I get Richard on board with the idea. He is the CEO, after all. I don't suppose you have any idea how I'm going to accomplish that, do you?"

"Pull rank," Miriam suggested, the glint in her eye suggesting she wasn't entirely joking.

"I think finesse is probably a better approach," Destiny scolded mildly, then grinned. "I'll save pulling rank as a last resort."

"You want to do what?" Richard's head snapped up from the stack of papers on his desk. He studied his aunt as if she'd announced she intended to take up skydiving, though come to think of it that was something Destiny was entirely likely to do if boredom set in. This announcement was far more unexpected.

"Don't glower at me like that," she scolded. "It's not as if I haven't grown up around this company. I know its inner workings almost as well as you do. It was my grandfather who started it, after all, and my father who turned it into a worldwide conglomerate. I've held a seat on the board for years now, and believe me, I do not let the reports sit on my desk gathering dust. I may be the only person on the board besides you who actually reads them."

"But you've never shown the slightest interest in working for Carlton Industries," Richard said, totally perplexed. "When your father tried to groom you for a position here, you ran away to France. When you came back after my father died, you left it to his executive vice president to run things until I was old enough to take over."

"Because, just like you, your father lived and breathed this company. I simply let him have it because it was the sensible, fair thing to do. I had more interesting things to pursue. And when I came back, I had far more important responsibilities—you and your brothers. The company was running smoothly and you were already being groomed to take over. There was no need for my interference or involvement."

"Okay, I can accept all that," he said, still perplexed. "What's changed?"

"I've changed," she said simply. "Now I want to run the European division. If you agree to this, Richard, I can promise you won't regret it."

"But why?" Richard persisted.

"Because it's there," she snapped impatiently. "Don't be dense, Richard. I want to do it because now that you and your brothers are married, I need something to do. I want to find out what I'm really made of."

He was still bewildered. His aunt's days were jam-packed with things to do. "When was the last time your calendar wasn't crammed with foundation meetings, fund-raisers, luncheons and social engagements?"

Destiny waved them off as if they were of no consequence. "There was a time when that lifestyle suited me. Now it doesn't. I need a real purpose. I want to make a contribution to this family. I think I have something unique to offer Carlton Industries. All those years coaxing dollars out of tightwads for various charities ought to be good for something."

"Hold it right there," Richard said, regarding her with exasperation. "Don't you think you made an incredible contribution by coming back here to take over when Mom and Dad died? You gave the three of us a home and stability. You brought fun and adventure into our lives. Rosalind Russell in that old *Auntie Mame* movie you showed us had nothing on you. You saw that we became decent, well-educated men. Hell, you even meddled until we were married to women you approved of. There's a whole new generation of Carltons coming along, thanks to you."

"Exactly my point," Destiny responded. "You're all settled. You have your own families. You don't need me anymore."

"We'll always need you," Richard protested, indignant that she could think otherwise. "Have we not shown you that?"

"You need me as the doting great-aunt who spoils your children rotten, nothing more. I can't be content with that. I want more."

He decided to try another tack to dissuade her from this insane idea. "What about your house in France? I always thought you'd want to go back there someday to live, get back to your painting and your gardens. You always talk about that time in your life as if it were magical. Now's your chance. Go for a few months. Open your studio and paint again."

"All that's in the past," she said blithely, as if she hadn't talked incessantly about doing that very thing at some distant point in the future. "You can't recapture something that was lost. In fact, I'm thinking of selling the house."

Shocked by the blasé announcement, he stared at her. "Now I know there's something wrong. What aren't you telling me? You always swore you would never sell that house, that you wanted to know it was there for your old age."

She shrugged. "Times change. I was young and impetuous back then. While you boys were growing up, so was I. I have new dreams now."

Richard regarded her skeptically. "And one of those dreams is to run our European division?"

"Yes," she declared flatly, her gaze unblinking.

Truthfully, he didn't doubt for a second that she could do it. Destiny was an amazing woman. She had a huge and generous heart, an astounding zest for life, and a mind that could grasp the details of a business merger even more quickly than his.

In her fifties, she was still a beautiful woman, trim and lithe with a cloud of soft brown hair framing a face that time had treated kindly. Her generous mouth was usually curved in a brilliant smile and laugh lines fanned out from eyes that sparkled.

There was no shortage of available men to fill her evenings, and yet she kept most of them at arm's length. His wife said it was because Destiny still longed for the love of her life—whoever the hell that was—the man she'd left behind when she'd come home to take charge of her nephews. Maybe that was true, though Richard didn't like thinking that she'd sacrificed someone so irreplaceable that she'd spent the last twenty years yearning for him. It would be even worse if that man turned out to be William Harcourt, as he once suspected. Harcourt was the very man who'd become the bane of Richard's existence by mucking about in every deal Carlton Industries tried to make in Europe.

He pushed all of that from his mind and tried to view this request from Destiny's perspective. In all these years she had never asked for anything for herself. She'd thrown herself into sudden and unexpected motherhood with complete abandon, mastering it with her own unorthodox style. After all she'd done for him and his brothers, if she wanted this one thing from him now, how could he deny her?

Still, the decision seemed so impulsive, so out of

character, he had to be sure it wasn't a whim. Carlton Industries wasn't some playground for a woman who was simply bored with her life.

"Destiny, have you really thought this through?" he asked. "There are downsides. Serious downsides, in fact. Tackling such a huge job will mean long days in an office. There will be a lot of stress involved."

Her gaze narrowed. "Are you suggesting I'm not physically or mentally up to it?" she asked, her tone suddenly icy.

Richard knew better than to say any such thing. "Of course not."

"Well, then, why are you hesitating?"

"Because this is so unlike you. In fact, every time I've brought up the European division and the problems it was having, you've told me to deal with it myself."

She regarded him blandly. "But you haven't, have you?"

Richard sighed. She had him there. William Harcourt was still insinuating himself into every single negotiation Carlton Industries was involved in. Richard had managed to thwart most of Harcourt's attempts to steal business, but he hadn't really dealt the man a final, knockout blow that would end the nonsense.

He couldn't help wondering yet again if there was a link between Harcourt and Destiny he didn't know about. He'd asked Destiny before if she had known the man years ago, but she'd avoided giving him a direct answer. Ben had managed to finagle an admission that she'd known Harcourt, but had gotten nothing more. That rather incomplete acknowledgment had raised Richard's suspicions that there was more going on with

Harcourt than business, but without proof he hadn't been able to call her on it. He needed to try again.

"Does this have something to do with Harcourt?" he asked her.

"No, it has to do with me," she insisted, regarding him with an unblinking gaze that gave away nothing. "It's time to find out what I'm made of."

"You're an incredible woman!" Richard said impatiently. "Why are you questioning that now? Don't start spouting some nonsense about low self-esteem to me. I'll laugh you right out of here."

"Darling, it's not that I don't think I did a good job raising you and your brothers or that I haven't made a contribution to the community, but I don't know who I am, not really. I don't paint anymore. I'm not your surrogate mother. I'm bored by running events. Somewhere along the way I've lost myself."

Richard was completely bewildered by her claim. "That's crazy."

"Is it? I was very young when I first went to Europe. I had plenty of money and virtually no responsibilities. I painted because I enjoyed it, not because I was passionate about it. I was surrounded by people who were as irresponsible as I was."

"Including William Harcourt?" he asked again, wondering if she would finally give him an honest answer.

She gave him a sour look. "Yes, if you must know, including William."

When Richard began to press her on that, she held up her hand. "The point I'm trying to make is that when your parents died, I came back here and had the responsibility of a family thrust on me. I think I lived up to that responsibility reasonably well—"

"Of course you did."

"But," she added with a trace of impatience, "those years were a gift, something unexpected, that shaped my life for a time, but now I'm ready to move on. I need to find out who Destiny Carlton really is."

"And you think you could be a successful business-woman?"

"Why not?" she asked. "It is in my genes, after all." She gave him a hard look. "I honestly don't know why you're making such a fuss or why you're so surprised by this. I've been talking about it for months now, ever since Ben's wedding. I've been waiting for you to come up with this idea on your own, but you've ignored every hint I've dropped."

"I honestly didn't think you were serious."

"In other words, you were certain it was just another one of Destiny's flighty whims," she scoffed. "And that says it all, doesn't it? Is it any wonder I want my family to start to take me seriously?"

He could see that he'd hurt her, but he didn't know how else he could have reacted to this crazy idea. He couldn't just turn over an entire division to her because it was what she wanted. He had as much responsibility to the company as he did to her.

"Destiny, why don't you think it over for another day or two? Or take a vacation, go to France and see if that fits you the way it once did," he suggested finally, hoping to buy himself enough time to formulate a plan to steer all this energy in a different direction. Surely there was some other satisfying pursuit she could take up that would keep her right here at home. Maybe they could encourage her to accept one of the marriage proposals constantly being tossed her way by high-profile men in the region. The prospect of a little turnabout meddling struck him as a fine idea.

Meantime, though, he gave her a placating smile. "Think about it for a few days or even a few weeks and we'll talk again."

"Meaning you want to check with your brothers to make sure I haven't gone round the bend," she said dryly. "Okay, fine. I'll compromise, but I won't put this off for weeks. For one thing, William is nipping at our heels on another deal, and this time there's a good chance we can lose if we don't act quickly. I can wait twenty-four hours while you hold a family powwow, as long as it gets me what I want. Trust me, Richard, I won't change my mind."

It wasn't the delay he'd hoped for, but he could see she wasn't prepared to bend any further. "Fine. We'll get together at the end of the day tomorrow."

She gave him an innocent look. "I really do hope you'll see this my way."

"I promise to give it serious consideration," he told her.

"I know you will," she said cheerfully. "I'm sure you're aware that I'd hate to have to pull rank on you."

His gaze narrowed. "Meaning what, exactly?"

"Meaning that I'd prefer not to go straight to the board to explain that the European operation has been in a shambles for some time and that you haven't taken any definitive action to shore it up and turn it into the gold mine it could be."

As her words sank in, Richard stared at her. If he had ever doubted Destiny's business acumen or her ability to be a tough negotiator, he didn't any longer. She'd obviously done her homework rather thoroughly before coming to him. And she'd delivered that threat without so much as a blink of her steady gaze.

"You would do that?" he asked, stunned by her audacity.

She beamed at him. "I don't think it will be necessary, do you?"

With that, Destiny swept out of his office, looking as regal and smug as a queen.

Richard watched her exit and sighed. Heaven help the European division! There was little doubt that Destiny was taking over. He considered himself to be a tough-minded businessman and a seasoned negotiator, but she'd put him in his place in no time flat. He'd just have to find some way to keep her on a tight rein.

But even as he reached that conclusion, Richard had to laugh. Keeping his aunt under control was going to be a little like trying to contain a hurricane. It simply couldn't be done.

Destiny thought her meeting with Richard had gone rather well. There was little doubt that he would come around to her way of thinking, eventually, at any rate. It might take a bit more persuasion, but she thought that subtle threat at the end of their conversation had probably done the trick. He definitely hadn't been anticipating that. She had a feeling he'd been as impressed as he'd been shocked. Hard truths and uncompromising stands were something her nephew understood.

She poured herself a cup of tea and settled into a chair in front of the fire, her feet tucked under her, and thought about what she would do first when she got to London, where Carlton Industries was headquartered.

She'd been studying the reports for months now. Goodness knows, there was a lot to do and not all of it had to do with William. There were some very stuffy people in charge and the entire operation needed a good shake-up.

She was still happily contemplating all that when the front door burst open and Mack and Ben called out to her.

"In here," she responded, not the least bit surprised by their arrival. "Having tea by the fire. If you want some, get cups before you come in."

They came in a few minutes later, not only with cups, but with another pot of tea and a plate of the housekeeper's chocolate chip cookies, which were always on hand, especially for Ben. Not that there was any shortage of sweets in his life since he'd married Kathleen, who baked like a fine pastry chef, but he still loved Mrs. Darlington's cookies.

"I imagine you've been talking to your brother," she said when they were seated. "If you've come to change my mind, you can forget it."

"Not to change your mind," Ben said gently. "Just to see if we've done something to make you feel that you're not needed here."

"Don't be silly," she said at once. "Why can't any of you see that this isn't about you? It's about me and what I need to do."

"You really want to move halfway around the world?" Mack asked doubtfully.

"Yes. And it's not as if we don't own a corporate jet that can bring me home anytime I'm needed here." She reached for Ben's hand and gave it a squeeze. He was the real worrier, and she could see the concern in his eyes. "Darlings, this really is what I want to do. I'm looking forward to having a brand-new challenge in my life. Think how exciting that will be for me. If we don't take on new things once in a while, we stagnate."

"Is this really about a new challenge or an old love?" Ben asked directly.

"Perhaps both," she admitted. "But I'm not hoping to reignite an old flame, in case that's what's worrying you. If anything, quite the opposite. William has made a nuisance of himself in our company's business for far too long now. The fact that he has dared to become an increasingly serious threat to my family cannot be tolerated. I intend to see that he realizes that."

Mack regarded her intently, then slowly nodded. "You really are excited about this, aren't you? You're looking forward to busting some serious butt over there?"

"Excited, stimulated, determined," she said. "In fact, I haven't felt like this in years. I feel young again, as if there are endless possibilities spread out before me."

Her nephews exchanged a resigned look.

"I still don't like it, but I suppose we have no right to stand in your way," Ben said. "We'll talk to Richard and convince him that you know exactly what you're doing."

"Thank you, darling."

"Don't thank me," Ben said, his expression gloomy. "I still wish you weren't dead-set on doing this."

"Me, too," Mack said. "But I think I understand your reasons for wanting to. When that knee injury killed my football career, I was at loose ends for a while, too, until you and Richard convinced me that I could use my love of the game in a whole new way by buying into the team. If I could reinvent myself from a professional athlete into a businessman, then you can surely be anything you set out to be."

"Oh, Mack, what a sweet thing to say," she told him, her eyes misting up.

"Just one question, you won't leave before Beth has the baby, will you? She'll never forgive you," Mack said.

"Absolutely not," Destiny assured him. "And once Richard agrees to this, I'm sure it will take weeks and weeks for him to drill me on all the little odds and ends he thinks I must know to be successful. I would like to be over there before Christmas, though."

"Christmas?" both men said, clearly appalled.

"You could all fly over," she reminded them. "I was there for the holidays years ago. There's nothing quite like a Christmas in London."

Ben sighed. "I think we're getting a little ahead of ourselves here. Let's take one step at a time. Let's get Richard on board with this."

Destiny beamed at him. "Oh, I think once you two speak up, it will be a foregone conclusion."

"Oh?" Mack said. "He didn't sound so convinced when I spoke to him."

"Let's just say I left him with a little incentive to mull over," Destiny said coyly. "I'm not surprised he didn't mention it. I think he was caught off guard."

"An incentive? He didn't mention any incentive to me," Mack said.

"Nor to me," Ben agreed, giving her a sharp look.

"Was it an incentive or a threat, Destiny? What are you up to?"

"Nothing that an outstanding businessman like Richard won't understand," she assured them both.

Mack began to chuckle. "Oh, Destiny, something tells me Europe is not ready for you."

She laughed with him. "Well, darlings, ready or not, here I come."

2

William Harcourt was on a golf course in Scotland when he got word that the European office of Carlton Industries was soon to be operating under a new chairman. Sir Lloyd Smedley gave him the news just as William took his shot on the seventh hole tee.

"Is that so?" William asked, distracted. The seventh hole was a tricky one. It had gotten the better of him yesterday, but he'd be damned if it would again.

"Destiny Carlton is taking over," Lloyd added, his expression totally innocent. "Believe you knew her, didn't you?"

William's golf ball dribbled off the tee and died, which was precisely the result his sneaky companion had obviously been hoping for. Lloyd was losing today. He'd clearly intended his little bombshell to ruin William's concentration, not just on this hole, but for the rest of the round.

William felt a little *zing* in his blood, something that hadn't happened nearly often enough since Destiny had walked out on their relationship twenty years before.

Back then, he'd stubbornly resisted following her to

the States, deluding himself for the longest time that a love like theirs wasn't something she could possibly forget or abandon forever.

But she had. He'd totally misjudged her sense of family loyalty. The Destiny he'd known in France hadn't had a maternal bone in her delectable body. She'd been carefree, impetuous and a bit of a Bohemian. But to his shock, she'd thrown over all traces of her carefree ways to settle down and mother her three orphaned nephews.

After a time, when he'd heard barely a word from her, his pride had kicked in. She'd chosen children who were virtual strangers over him, the man she'd claimed to love. It had grated.

It had taken him a long time to catch on to the fact that nothing on earth was worse than a man more devoted to pride than common sense. If she'd abandoned those boys, as he'd anticipated, she wouldn't have been the kind of woman he wanted in his life. *That* was what he should have realized from the beginning. He was the fool who'd forced her to make an impossible choice, rather than going after her and being supportive when her entire world had been turned upside down. All these years, he could have had her love and the love of three stepsons, plus maybe some children of their own. Any children of Destiny's would have been astonishingly bright and handsome. Destiny hadn't cost the two of them a future. He had.

William had found his own shortsightedness to be so incredibly annoying, so completely perplexing, that he had spent the last ten years mucking up every business deal Carlton Industries set out to make in Europe. It wasn't something he'd done to get rich. Hell, he had more money than he could spend in ten lifetimes. It wasn't even the satisfaction of winning that had drawn him into the game. It was an idiotic, half-baked attempt to get Destiny's attention.

And now he had.

He grinned as he set his ball back on the tee and slammed it straight down the fairway toward the green, gazing at its trajectory with satisfaction. About damn time she got the message. He'd wasted a lot of years waiting for life to get interesting again.

Harcourt & Sons was one of those long-established London companies that dabbled in a wide variety of businesses, assembled over generations less with logic than with the various passions and needs of prior generations. William appreciated that aspect of the company's history. It made his own acquisition tactics in recent years seem perfectly fitting. His ancestors had acquired whatever companies appealed to them, just as he was intent on acquiring those most likely to annoy Destiny.

Harcourt owned a small chain of exclusive haberdashers, founded due to William's grandfather's girth and demand for excellent tailoring. The chain had begun on Saville Row, then spread through the countryside, thanks to his grandfather's contacts in Parliament who wanted the shops that specialized in personalized service conveniently located in their home districts. It was also a small way to support their local woolen manufacturers.

Another company was renowned throughout the country for its exotic selection of teas, acquired when William's grandmother had had difficulty obtaining the blends she wanted. Those shops had later been expanded to serve an elegant afternoon tea, when his mother had wanted a place to take her friends after a day's shopping.

The whole conglomerate had begun quite unexpectedly with an antiquarian bookshop, opened after his great-grandfather's bookshelves were filled to overflowing with leather-bound editions of the classics, as well as the lighter novels preferred by William's great-grandmother. This remarkable woman had not been content to sit idly in the country when her husband came to London. Far ahead of her time, she'd wanted something productive to do. She'd found a location and badgered her husband until he'd helped her to set up the shop. Their friends had been scandalized that Amanda Wellington Harcourt would ignore the family's noble heritage and go into trade.

To everyone's surprise, except her husband's, she'd made an enormous success of it. *She*, not William's great-grandfather, was the Harcourt of Harcourt & Sons. H&S Books now had stores all over Great Britain, still dealing primarily with rare books and first editions, though a rack of current bestsellers was beginning to appear in some of the stores along with important biographies and books on travel.

Recalling the oft-told tale now, William couldn't help being reminded of Destiny. She and Great-grandmother Amanda had a lot in common. Both were bold, strong women, who refused to be confined by society's constraints. They both had vision and the drive to succeed.

He'd been little more than a toddler when his great-grandmother had died, but he could still remember the fire in her eyes and the enthusiasm in her voice as she'd talked about books and read to him from the classics. She, more than any teacher he'd ever had, had taught him to love learning and to be open to new ideas. She'd been the one who'd made him into the kind of man who'd be drawn to an unconventional woman like Destiny.

Sitting behind the desk in his office, William pulled a signed volume of Charles Dickens's *A Christmas Carol* from the shelf behind him and rubbed his fingers over the fine, gold-embossed leather. This rare treasure had been a gift from Destiny when she'd discovered his love of old books. Inside, he found the card she'd written in her neat hand. "To my love. May you always know the true meaning of Christmas and feel the joy in my heart when I think of you. You, too, are rare and wonderful. Love, Destiny."

Carefully, he replaced the book in its place of honor on his shelf, then buzzed for his assistant. Malcolm Dandridge had been with Harcourt & Sons since William's father's day. There was little Malcolm didn't know about what went on inside the company and in corporate London. William counted on Malcolm's loyalty and his discretion. Over the years both had proved invaluable.

"Yes, sir?" Malcolm said, entering with pad in hand, ready for whatever business William needed him to tend to.

"Sit, Malcolm. Tell me what you've heard about Carlton Industries lately."

To his credit, Malcolm had never asked about William's seeming obsession with the American conglomerate. Nor had he criticized the sometimes inexplicable decisions William had made to go after companies that were ill suited for Harcourt & Sons. If he thought William's behavior was reckless, he was far too polite and loyal to mention it.

"It's been a bit quiet lately," Malcolm reported. "It's my opinion, sir, that the last negotiation rattled them. It proved rather costly, thanks to your clever strategy. I'm sure they're busy trying to conserve capital in order to offset that particular deal."

"Anything about the new chairman?" William asked, wondering if Lloyd had gotten it right and Destiny truly was coming to take over. "Has one been appointed?"

"Yes, sir. A Ms. Destiny Carlton, a rather surprising choice according to my sources."

William's heart did another little stutter step, even though it was old news to him. Having it confirmed made it seem that much more real.

"When will she be taking over?" he asked, hoping his expression was totally bland.

"I believe Ms. Carlton is expected in early December, sir."

"Not until then?" William asked, both surprised and more than a little disappointed. It was only the beginning of October now. "Any explanation for the delay?"

"None, sir, though it is my opinion that she's probably being groomed for the position. My sources tell me that she's had virtually no hands-on experience at the company. I believe that we will be able to make some solid inroads against them once she's on the scene."

"Don't sell her short," William warned.

Malcolm looked startled by his sharp tone. "You know her, sir?"

"Quite well, as a matter of fact. She might not have spent much time working with the company, but it would be naive to assume she can't handle the job. She's a Carlton, after all. I suspect we'll have our work cut out for us, if we intend to get the better of her." He was not about to admit how much the prospect excited him. There was a deal on the table right now for a group of faltering travel agencies. The notion of battling wits with Destiny to acquire it right out from under her was stimulating. This was one fight he intended to win at any cost, a metaphor of sorts for his intentions toward Destiny.

"As you say, sir. But as brilliant as she may be, she'll be no match for you. The nephew certainly hasn't been."

"Because his mind hasn't been on it," William guessed. "And the stakes haven't been high enough." He paused thoughtfully. "I imagine Destiny's going to come in and do something dramatic, if only to get our attention. She won't be satisfied to win this skirmish for Fortnum Travel. I wonder what her first target for acquisition will be?"

"Shall I see what I can find out?" Malcolm asked. "Perhaps there are rumors inside the company."

William nodded. "Yes, definitely, see what you can learn, Malcolm. A preemptive strike might be just the thing. We'll want to keep her on her toes."

In fact, he thought cheerfully, a preemptive strike might bring Destiny roaring straight into his office, eyes blazing and temper high. Now, there was a sight he'd been longing to see for far too long now.

Destiny was growing weary of all the admonitions and instructions and piles and piles of detailed reports, most of which she'd read long before she'd put her plan into play. She knew perfectly well that Richard was merely trying to overwhelm her with so much information, to make the task seem so daunting and formidable that she'd give up in frustration and declare herself no longer interested in taking over the European division. He still wasn't entirely reconciled to this whole idea of her as an integral part of the company.

She frowned as Richard went over ground he'd covered just last week…and the week before that.

"Do you truly believe that I am so forgetful that I don't know we've been over this twice before?" she asked finally, her voice filled with undisguised frustration.

He seemed startled by her question. "Have we?"

She rolled her eyes. "Either you're the forgetful one or you've gotten your strategy completely muddled."

"Strategy? What strategy?"

"To make me forget what you still believe is a crazy idea," she said mildly. "Mack and Beth's baby is due any day now. I'm leaving in two weeks, Richard. Get used to it."

"I just want you to be fully prepared to pull off this Fortnum Travel acquisition. We can't afford any missteps," he retorted defensively. "This deal will set the tone for everything you do from now on. After all, you're not just someone new coming in. You're a Carlton. How would it look if you're not on top of things?"

"I'm sure the earth would keep spinning," she responded.

"But you need to have everyone's respect from the moment you set foot into the building," he said. "You only have one chance to make a first impression. How many times did you drill that little maxim into my head?"

"A first impression is one thing," she responded. "Respect is something else entirely. No one gains respect just because they show up, I don't care what their name is. Respect is earned. I expect to pay my dues in that regard, which is why we will acquire Fortnum Travel. I won't let it slip away. I promise."

"I'm just trying to make it a bit easier," he grumbled.

"I know," she soothed. "And I do appreciate it, but this is getting old, Richard. It's not as if there aren't phones and faxes over there. I'll be able to reach you at a moment's notice if something comes up that I can't handle. I'm neither proud nor foolish. I'll ask for any help I need."

"Yes, of course," he said finally, his expression resigned. "Is there anything I can help with now?"

Destiny had been waiting for just this moment. She'd been toying with an idea for a few weeks now, something guaranteed to get William's attention and show him that she was about to make his life the same sort of hell he'd been trying to create for Carlton Industries. It would be solid proof that she was just as capable as he of capitalizing on the intimate secrets they'd shared all those years ago. She reached into her briefcase and pulled out a thick folder. She'd left absolutely no stone unturned in accumulating her research to make her case to Richard. The cover sheet was concise, but there were pages of backup material for every premise she'd stated.

"Take a look at this," she said, handing it to Richard. "Tell me what you think. I want your honest opinion. Don't sugarcoat anything."

Richard's eyes widened as he glanced through the detailed research. "You've spent a lot of time on this," he said eventually in a cautious tone that could only be construed as less-than-a-ringing endorsement.

"I wanted to be sure I could answer any questions you might have."

"The numbers make sense," he admitted.

"But?"

He gave her a perplexed look. "Why on earth would you want to acquire some nothing little bookstore? I don't get it. It's not the kind of business that's a good fit for us. It's too small. There's no real growth potential."

She smiled at his logic. It was exactly what she'd expected. Richard was very much a bottom-line kind of man.

"But it is the kind of business that fits quite nicely with Harcourt & Sons," she explained. "It's the only major antiquarian bookseller in London that's on a par with H&S Books. The owner is old. He wants to retire, but he doesn't want to sell to just anyone. He's been annoyed at Harcourt & Sons for some time now for the aggressive way they've gone after rare books. He finds it a bit unseemly. He's from an era that considered the pursuit of rare editions to be a gentleman's sport."

"So we help him to get his revenge," Richard said slowly. "And in the process, we annoy the daylights out of William Harcourt."

Destiny beamed at him. "Precisely. It's the last thing he'll be expecting. Right now all of his attention is on the Fortnum Travel deal."

"But will he really care? This is nothing to a man like Harcourt."

"In dollars and cents, yes," she agreed. "But not in

importance. H&S Books is the cornerstone of the company, their prestige division. It was William's great-grandmother's creation. It has huge sentimental value, if not financial significance. William won't be happy if he thinks we're about to invest major money in his competition and target it for expansion. And it will send a clear message that if he continues to go after us, we'll go after him, business by business, first books, then tea, then clothing, until we have competition not just in England, but all over Europe."

Richard regarded her with evident surprise. "You really do have a knack for this, don't you? And a rather bloodthirsty eagerness to go for the jugular."

"Well, of course I do," Destiny said impatiently. "Nobody messes with my family and gets away with it. Making William sit up and take notice will be my pleasure."

"It's not all about getting even with Harcourt," Richard warned. "We do have a company to run over there. Some of our existing businesses are not performing to our expectations. Those need to be addressed, too."

"I know that and I have plans for each and every one of them. This," she said, gesturing toward the folder, "is just for the fun of it."

Richard laughed. "Let me go over these figures again tonight."

"Don't take too long. I want to arrive in London with guns blazing."

"This is only a BB shot," Richard reminded her.

"Even a BB shot hurts when you're not expecting it and it hits you where you live," Destiny retorted.

"Remind me never to get on your bad side," Richard

said, regarding her with evident approval for the first time since they'd set off down this road.

"Darling, you could never get on my bad side," she assured him. "You're family, and no matter how annoying you might become, family always forgives and forgets."

"Good to know."

Even as she left her nephew to ponder her suggested strategy, she couldn't help wondering if William was going to be shocked that she could come after him the way she intended to, given the feelings they'd once shared. Probably. He seemed to have missed the fact that nothing was more important to her than family. He hadn't gotten it twenty years ago, and it was plain he didn't get it now.

That was just one reason she wanted to arrive in London with an unmistakable message. Apparently William wasn't too smart about subtleties and nuances. She was going to have to deliver a direct hit, then see to it that she kept them coming until he abandoned the fight and went crawling back to whatever country estate he was living on these days.

Richard had an odd feeling in the pit of his stomach as he reread Destiny's proposal for taking over the small but prestigious London bookseller she'd targeted. On the one hand, it didn't make a lick of sense to acquire Jameson's Booksellers. It would be a nuisance purchase, requiring them to track down or train someone with the necessary expertise to make a success of it, to make it a worthy rival for H&S Books. On the other hand, he could see precisely why Destiny thought it would be a nice opening salvo against Harcourt.

He tried to put his finger on what was really bothering him. It wasn't the cash outlay. That was peanuts to a corporation the size of Carlton Industries. It wasn't the energy likely to be expended on making and then following through with such an acquisition. So what was it?

Melanie came into his den after putting their daughter down for the night, took one look at him and murmured, "Uh-oh."

He met her gaze. "What?"

"I know that expression." She came and sat on his lap and traced the crease in his brow. "You're worrying about something. And since I recognize Destiny's handwriting on that file, I assume it has something to do with her."

"You're too smart for your own good," he murmured, breathing in the flowery scent she'd dabbed on while she was upstairs. It would be very easy right now to forget all about business and spend the rest of the evening in bed with his wife, working on the expansion plan they had in mind for their family. Maybe the prospect of another baby would cut short Destiny's European adventure and get her back home again.

"I have to be smart to keep up with you two," Melanie said. "What's Destiny done now?"

"Nothing yet," he admitted. "But she has an idea she wants to pursue the minute she gets to London."

"A bad idea?"

"Not really."

"An expensive idea?"

"Not at all."

"Is it dangerous? I mean to her, personally."

"No," he admitted.

"Then what's the problem?"

Richard sighed. "I can't put my finger on it. Maybe you can." He described Destiny's scheme, then asked, "What do you think?"

"I think it's ingenious," she said at once. "She's going to be an invaluable asset, you know. Is that what you're having trouble admitting?"

"Of course not. I've always respected her intelligence. And I've always known she was clever. She got the two of us together, didn't she?"

"Over your vehement objections, in fact," Melanie concurred. "And my somewhat less strenuous ones."

"Wise woman," Richard admitted, grinning.

"Her or me?"

"Both of you, in fact, but not half as smart as I was to go along with the plan in the end."

Melanie kissed him, which momentarily served as a rather effective distraction.

"Want to know what I think your problem is?" Melanie asked eventually.

"Sure."

"You don't like the fact that she's the one who came up with the idea."

Richard scowled at her implication. "Don't be ridiculous. I am not jealous of my own aunt. That would be childish and immature."

"Yes, it would," she agreed readily. "And I'm not suggesting that, but you can't deny that it is nagging at you that she apparently has enough insight into what makes William Harcourt tick to come up with a plot like this."

The explanation resonated with him a little too clearly. "You could be right," he admitted slowly. "I don't like anything I don't understand, and Destiny has never been forthcoming about just what this man meant to her. I'm beginning to get the nasty feeling that he was quite important to her once, more important than any of us have suspected."

"And if he was?"

"Then he's a real danger to her and to the company," he said.

Melanie regarded him with shock. "You can't honestly think she would ever betray Carlton Industries."

He heard her scandalized tone and tried quickly to explain that he didn't doubt Destiny's honesty or integrity. "I don't think she would do anything intentionally," he began carefully. "But people who think they're in love do all sorts of crazy things they might not do if they were thinking clearly."

"Like us?"

"This is nothing like us," he protested. "There was never any conflict of interest with the two of us."

Melanie stood up, her disapproval plain. "I suggest you not repeat your concerns to Destiny," she told him quietly but emphatically.

He stared at her blankly, not quite getting why she was suddenly seething. "I have an obligation to the company. Why the hell shouldn't I say something if I think she's putting our interests at risk?" he demanded.

"Because your implication is insulting, and frankly, if I were Destiny, I'd slap you silly. I'm very tempted to do it myself on her behalf."

She stalked off then, obviously every bit as insulted as she insisted Destiny was likely to be.

Richard stared after his wife in consternation. Give

him a complex business situation to resolve anytime, because if he lived to be a hundred, he would never understand the women in his life.

3

Malcolm's usually dour expression was downright grim when he walked into William's office at the end of the day on the last Friday in November. It was already well past quitting time, but William had lingered, not the least bit anxious to face the raw London night or his lonely flat. He'd been about to pour himself a glass of whisky when Malcolm appeared.

"Care for a drink?" he asked his assistant.

"Yes, sir, I believe I would."

William poured two fingers of whisky into each heavy crystal glass and handed one to Malcolm. "Why don't you tell me what has you looking so positively dire?" he suggested, sitting in the chair next to the one Malcolm had taken. Because William had known the older man since he was a boy, their relationship was far more informal than those William had with other employees of the firm. In many ways Malcolm still served as a surrogate father figure.

"You won't like it, sir," Malcolm announced gloomily.

"Bad news is usually best spoken quickly, man.

What is it? There's very little you and I haven't had to deal with over the years. We've managed most of it rather well."

"It's Jameson's Booksellers this time, sir," Malcolm said. "It's been sold."

William was obviously missing why this spelled catastrophe. "The old man has to be nearing ninety," he said. "Where's the shock in him selling now? In fact, if I'd known he was thinking of retiring, I'd have made an offer myself. It would be a nice fit for us, but it's no loss if someone else is taking over. Jameson's is very small potatoes in the world of London bookselling."

Malcolm took a devilishly long time replying. "That's the thing, you see. He sold it to Carlton Industries."

William choked on his whisky. That was the very last thing he'd anticipated. No wonder Malcolm looked so grim. There could be only one reason for Carlton to take an interest in such a small bookstore. The company intended to go after H&S Books.

"You're sure of that?" he asked Malcolm, though he already knew that Malcolm's information was always reliable.

"No question about it, sir." Malcolm handed over an item clipped from a London newspaper, one William had obviously missed. "It's all right here in black and white. I couldn't believe my eyes, frankly, so I called and checked it out myself."

"You didn't let on that you were calling on my behalf, did you?" William asked, frowning. He'd hate it getting around that this acquisition worried him in any way. It was never good business to show any hint of weakness.

Malcolm regarded him with a chiding expression. "Of course not. Just said I'd read about it in the news and wanted to offer congratulations. Told Jameson I was a long-time customer and hoped things wouldn't change too much." He shook his head sadly. "You should have heard the gloating in the old man's voice. Sounded like a boy again, he was so eager to tell me the details. He says they're planning a huge expansion, a catalog business as well as stores all over Great Britain. For a man once so set in his ways, he's embracing all the changes with astonishing enthusiasm."

William mulled that over. "I can see why he's glad to be rid of it, and probably at a tidy profit, but why the dickens would Carlton Industries be interested in books?" he muttered. But the answer dawned on him almost immediately. "This is Destiny's work, no question about it. She's the only one who would know how I'd feel about an attack on H&S Books, which is obviously what she intends to do."

For the first time since his game had begun, William started to wonder if he hadn't carried it too far. It was one thing to try to grab Destiny's attention. It was quite another to make an enemy of her.

Malcolm nodded. "I would say that has to be the case, sir, though her name never came up. It was all handled through a Carlton solicitor."

"And the papers are signed?"

"The deal is airtight, sir. Jameson was happy to tell me the money is in his bank and that he'd be leaving for his little stone cottage in Cornwall, once he's spent a few weeks consulting with the new company."

William sighed. So that was the way Destiny intended to play the game. This was meant as his wakeup call, a little greeting to let him know that she was on her way and that she didn't intend to sit idly by while he wreaked havoc on her family's business. He glanced at his assistant and saw that, if anything, Malcolm was taking the news even harder than he was.

"It's nothing to worry about," William reassured him. "Jameson's has always been more like a gnat than any real threat."

"Because he didn't have Carlton capital behind him, sir. I know that you can handle whatever they're up to, but I also know how much H&S Books means to you. I'd have to say this particular strategy was personal, wouldn't you?"

"Definitely," William agreed. In fact, it was the one bright aspect of the entire mess. It proved that Destiny's coming to London wasn't just about business. She was coming not just to shake up her own company, but him.

And in that regard at least, Malcolm's news couldn't have been better.

Destiny would have given anything to have been a fly on the wall when the news about Jameson's Booksellers was given to William. Ah, well, she supposed she'd have a reaction from him soon enough.

In fact, he might not even wait for her to arrive in London, where she was due in a few days. William was not the sort of man to waste time when he had something on his mind. That was one of the things she'd most admired about him when they'd first met so many long years ago. He'd been forthright and candid from the outset.

He was also a man who knew his own mind. Though he'd paid precious little attention to the family business back then, and had, in fact, renounced it to be with her, she saw now that her belief that he had no head for it had been foolish. Once William had turned his attention to the family business, he'd obviously been quite capable of running Harcourt & Sons with cutthroat intensity and skill. Just as he'd startled her, she intended to surprise him with her own level of expertise and dedication.

All of that meant that she could expect some sort of reaction, and perhaps retribution, for her daring purchase of the rival bookstore.

When the phone rang, she jumped, her nerves jittery with anticipation. It was a letdown to hear Ben's voice on the other end of the line.

"You don't sound especially thrilled to hear from me," her youngest nephew teased. "Should I be insulted or were you hoping to hear from someone else?"

"I am always thrilled to hear from you," she said, avoiding the trickier question. "What's going on in your life? How's Kathleen?"

"You could see for yourself, if you'll join us for dinner."

"Not tonight, darling. It's been a long day."

"The first of many, I imagine. Are you sure this new adventure isn't going to be too much for you?" he asked worriedly.

"Absolutely not," she said emphatically.

"Then it must be that you really want to sit by the phone in case it rings," he said knowingly. "Expecting to hear from William, now that you've fired the first shot?"

"You heard about that?" she asked, surprised.

"Richard filled me in. He seemed quite proud of

you, actually. Have you heard anything from the enemy camp?"

"Not even a moan," she told him. "And it's far too late now in London for William to be calling, so don't think I'm sitting around here hoping to hear from him so I can gloat a bit. I'd just like a good night's rest so I'll be ready for anything in the morning."

"Okay, then," he said, giving up. "But we're all having dinner at the farm on Sunday, so we can wish you bon voyage. No excuses, okay?"

"Not a one," she promised. "I'm looking forward to it."

After they'd said goodbye, she sat back and closed her eyes, her thoughts drifting to when it had all begun with William. Fate had definitely had a hand in things that night.

Paris, 1980

It had taken the considerable wiles of Madame Grégorie to convince Destiny that her paintings were worthy of a showing, even in such a small gallery on the Left Bank. Now that the doors were about to open, Destiny's stomach was filled with butterflies. She grabbed a glass of champagne from a passing waiter and drank it down.

"Such a terrible waste of fine champagne," Violetta Grégorie scolded, giving Destiny's hand a squeeze. "You do not need it, *ma chèrie.* The critics will love you."

Destiny appreciated the attempt to reassure her, but she knew better. She understood the art world almost as well as Violetta did, knew that critics were ready to pounce with savage cruelty on a newcomer, especially a young American woman with little formal training and only modest talent.

Violetta disagreed, of course. The gallery owner said Destiny's work was fresh and innovative, while being extraordinarily commercial. That, of course, was precisely what the critics would find most offensive—that her paintings would sell like crazy to tourists because they were pretty, not to serious collectors because they were exceptional. Her work wasn't pretentious, nor was she, but having a formal showing in a well-respected French gallery certainly was.

She'd held out as long as she could, but from the moment Violetta had discovered her art in a small shop near Destiny's home in Provence, she'd been relentless. The dark-haired, dark-eyed whirlwind of energy had barraged Destiny with persuasive arguments. All of Destiny's protests had fallen on deaf ears. Finally she had been forced to give in, if she was ever to have any peace again. And, truthfully, she'd been flattered that Violetta was so passionate about her work.

Destiny told herself that if she could get through tonight, the worst would be over. She could be back at home before the dreaded reviews even appeared. Violetta wouldn't be insensitive enough to send the worst ones to her, and few of Destiny's friends in Provence paid attention to such things.

What Destiny feared most about this night wasn't the embarrassment and humiliation of a bad show. Rather, she was terrified that any criticism that *did* reach her would destroy her pleasure in painting, that the critics would undercut the passion she felt every time she put brush to canvas. She should never have agreed to the showing. She could have gone on for years, quietly selling her paintings, living in her studio in the south of France surrounded by the people and things she loved.

But this… She heaved a sigh. This was asking to be flogged in public.

Assaulted by another wave of butterflies, she went in search of more champagne and a secluded nook to hide in until she could gather her composure to face the invited guests, who were just now starting to arrive, a glittering assortment of French society and the Left Bank's art and literary crowd.

Standing in the shadows, she assumed a cool, bored expression, a haughty look she'd perfected at social events back home in Virginia to cover for her innate shyness. Few people had any idea just how self-conscious and uncertain she was, because she masked it so well. This particular look kept people away, which was something she devoutly hoped to do tonight.

She spotted the man coming toward her only an instant before he arrived in her secluded corner. He was her own age—close to thirty, most likely—with the athletic build of a polo player and the tanned complexion of a man who spent much of his time outdoors. The tan made his blue eyes the same brilliant shade as the turquoise sea. Sun had streaked gold through his light brown hair. His clothes fit in a way that screamed expert tailoring, rather than off the rack.

Not a critic, she concluded with relief. More likely, one of the many rich, available men Violetta tried to lure to these events to make the occasions that much more attractive to the women most inclined to come and spend money on the art. Champagne and flirting tended to loosen their purse strings.

The stranger slid into the shadows beside her and whispered, "Mind if I try to be unobtrusive with you?"

She found his conspiratorial tone amusing and the glint of mischief in his eye alluring. One on one like this, she could handle almost anyone. It was crowds she found daunting.

"Who are you hiding from?" she asked, matching his confiding tone.

"Violetta, of course. She's dead set on me meeting the woman of the hour. She says I'll be fascinated. What she really means, of course, is that she hopes I'll become so infatuated I'll spend a bloody fortune buying these paintings."

"Do you have a bloody fortune?" Destiny inquired, only mildly curious since she had more than her own share of inherited wealth. It was his casual mention of money that spoke volumes. Only the very rich had that careless air.

He shrugged. "And then some, I suppose."

"Then why not spend a bit of it on art?" she challenged. "Would it cut into the funds available for polo ponies?"

"I have enough for both, but this art?" he asked with a shudder. "Too saccharine. There's talent there, of course, but it's being wasted."

Destiny's temper stirred. "Is that so?"

He gave her a sharp look. "You like it, I imagine. I suppose it does suit a woman's romantic sensibilities."

"It certainly suits mine," she said. She gave him her most chillingly polite smile and held out her hand. "Destiny Carlton."

He blinked and a dull red flush crept up his neck. "The artist," he said.

"Indeed."

"Though I probably should slink away without admitting it, I'm William Harcourt," he said, giving her an abashed look even as he took her hand and held it long enough for her blood to stir as heatedly as her temper had moments before. "And I'm dreadfully sorry. I usually don't set out to jam my foot in my mouth so quickly."

Destiny hid her hurt pride. He had taken only a tiny nip, after all. "Why be sorry? You were being honest. And art is subjective, isn't it? There are very few, I imagine, who fall in love with both Monet *and* Jackson Pollock." She surveyed him. "I would guess Pollock is more to your taste."

When he realized that she hadn't taken serious offense, that she could talk calmly and reasonably about the pros and cons of various works of art—including her own—he gave her a considering look that made her pulse hum.

"Perhaps Violetta wasn't so far off the mark when she said she wanted to introduce us," he said with a quiet intensity that shook her. "Would you care for coffee after this affair is over? I imagine we can find any number of topics to pursue without me tripping all over myself to offend you."

Destiny gazed into his fathomless, sea-green eyes and found herself intrigued, too fascinated to write off the encounter and head immediately home as she'd planned. There was more than a simmering attraction she didn't want to ignore. She liked his directness, even when it came at her expense, and the promise of challenging, witty conversation. He would fit quite nicely into the assortment of friends she'd found since settling in France.

"Coffee would be lovely," she said, impulse overruling whatever qualms she might have had. Violetta would never have invited this man here tonight to meet her if she hadn't believed him to be respectable. And Destiny trusted her own judgment, too. Even as she voiced the mundane words, she knew that the end of the evening was going to be so much better than its start. It was going to be the beginning of something extraordinary.

Anxious to begin, she smiled up at him. "Why wait?"

William's eyes lit up. "No coy games?"

"I don't believe in them," she told him. "Neither, it seems, do you."

"No," he agreed. "When I see something I want, I go after it. Let that be a warning to you."

She smiled. "Well taken," she said. "But just so you know, I'm no amateur at getting what I want, as well."

William laughed. "Then it seems we're a perfect match. We'll have to thank Violetta one day."

"Perhaps we will," Destiny said. "When we're much older and spending a holiday in Paris."

She was only partially joking. Somewhere deep in her soul she already knew that William was going to be an important part of her life, perhaps the best part.

Twenty-five years later as Destiny walked off the plane in London ready for battle, she looked back on the young, naive woman she had been when she'd first met William with something akin to pity. Back then she had been so certain that William was the man of her dreams, an equal with nothing to prove, nothing to gain from a liaison with a Carlton. She'd thought their love was not only inevitable, but invincible.

As she waited at Heathrow for her luggage, she recalled that, to her shock and dismay, William had been damn quick to let her go after her brother's and sister-in-law's tragic deaths. He'd sent her back to the States with a kiss and a promise to be waiting for her when she returned. She should have seen the handwriting on the wall when he'd refused to come with her.

"It's a private time for your family," he'd said, his tone perfectly reasonable, even considerate. "I don't belong there. I'd only be an unwelcome distraction."

Destiny hadn't begged. She'd been too grief stricken and too proud to waste the energy. If there was one thing she knew with certainty by then, it was that William rarely changed his mind once it was set. It certainly hadn't changed once he'd set his sights on her that night at Violetta's gallery. His attention had been unwavering despite the very significant price he'd had to pay for choosing her over his own family.

At first, back home in Virginia and facing the unbearable grief of her nephews and their need for all of her attention, it had been easy for Destiny to accept that William had been right to stay behind, that he was sincerely trying to be thoughtful, even if she felt the attempt was misguided. Their phone calls were brief and hurried and lacked the kind of detailed, intimate conversation they had shared for the three years they had been inseparable.

But as time passed, even those contacts had dwindled and fury had set in to fill the void. She had needed him so desperately and he hadn't been there for her. She'd lost respect for him—or told herself she had—because it was the only way to bear that loss on top of everything else. Changes were flying at her too fast for her to absorb them all.

As yet more time passed and she realized the enormity of what was being expected of her, she'd had little time to waste on a man who didn't seem the least bit interested in pursuing their relationship now that it was no longer uncomplicated.

Destiny moved on to Customs and another wait. It have her more time to think about how she had continued to mourn his loss as she had her beloved brother's. She'd missed what she and William had had together—the meeting of minds, the exuberant passion, the teamwork, the idle hours spent wandering the beach or flower-strewn fields, stormy nights in front of a cozy fire, the sudden spark of lust while sipping wine at a sidewalk café. She'd been desperately and completely besotted by him, then wildly disappointed to discover how flawed he was.

Obviously he hadn't shared that same depth of feeling. She'd had to accept that eventually and move on. There were too many crises in the present to squander time on memories or old emotions.

Even now, all these lonely years later, she didn't hate him for fooling her or for letting her go, she realized as she sat in the taxi that would take her from the airport to her new home. She merely wanted a chance to show him what he'd given up. She'd taken to heart an old Dorothy Parker adage. Living well was, indeed, the best revenge. And she intended to show William that she had lived an extraordinarily rich and challenging life without him. She intended to take on London in a way that would dazzle him and make him rue the day he'd crossed her or her family.

That alone wouldn't be enough, of course. She also intended to use this time in London to teach him a lesson or two about business. She might be newer at it than he, but she was confident that she was as quick a study as he'd ever been. The Jameson's acquisition was merely a beginning. She had quite a few tricks left up her sleeve. She doubted William would be expecting any of them, much less be ready to counter them effectively. Ever the gentleman, William might not be prepared for the kind of down-and-dirty warfare she had in mind.

He'd surprised her by ignoring her opening salvo. There was no way that he hadn't gotten wind of it by now. For several years, it seemed, he'd known what Carlton Industries intended to do even before the ink was dry on their plans. Whether he had a source inside the company or a clever outsider, Destiny intended to find that person and deal with him or her, as well.

She caught a glimpse of her reflection in the taxi's rearview mirror as they drove through the London mist toward the flat that had been rented for her. She couldn't seem to stop smiling. Nor could she prevent the rush of anticipation that filled her now that she was finally here.

It was going to be a magnificent battle, and it would all begin tomorrow.

4

Destiny was at her desk just after dawn, eager to put things into motion for her debut as the new chairman of the Carlton Industries European division. She'd dressed carefully for the occasion, knowing that first impressions were important if she expected to be taken seriously. Just being here so early would put to rest any notion that she was merely a figurehead, who would be seldom seen and whose imprint on the operation would be minimal.

She'd chosen a dark brown suit, severely tailored, and added a gold silk blouse and discreet gold jewelry. She'd spent a lot of time on her hair and makeup, going for a look that was understated and businesslike. Not that her hair was happy with the attempt to tame it. Several strands had sprung free on the brisk walk to the office in the misty morning air. In retrospect, she probably should have taken a taxi, but she enjoyed walking and liked the natural color it put into her cheeks. And at her age, she'd take any chance she could to catch a few minutes of exercise. Since she loved good food and absolutely hated going to a gym, walking was her primary way to battle the effects of a slowing metabolism.

She'd arrived at the Carlton Industries headquarters feeling invigorated and maybe just a little noble for having gotten her day off to such a healthy start. Now for the real challenge—making this office and this assignment into her own.

She'd already spent an entire evening planning changes to her rented flat so that it would be more of a reflection of her personality and taste. At the moment it was elegant and entirely too dull, but she would have to wait until after the holidays when the decorations came down to start a complete makeover. For now, she would devote her attention to the office and work.

In the middle of the great mahogany desk, which was far too masculine for her taste, she had placed her agenda for the day, along with personnel reports on all of the company's key executives. She intended to meet with every one of them to establish the new goals they were going to accomplish together, beginning the first of the year. Richard had looked over and approved her strategy, but cautioned her against moving too quickly.

"This isn't the States. London moves at a slower, more resolute pace," he'd warned.

She'd regarded him evenly. "Not anymore, it doesn't. Not at Carlton Industries, at any rate."

"If you try to shake things up too quickly, you'll meet resistance," he'd insisted.

"Not for long," she'd assured him, her voice filled with determination.

Richard had regarded her with dismay. "Destiny, you can't steamroll over everyone there, the way you do over Ben, Mack and me. It simply isn't done. You'll offend the very people you need as allies."

She'd laughed at him. "I do know other tactics, darling. Surely you don't think all those women who've served with me on various charity boards take kindly to steamrolling."

"No, I imagine not, but sugarcoating it is not the same as using a different tactic altogether. Are you even familiar with the term consensus-building? Or a win-win strategy?"

She bit back the sharp retort that popped into her mind at his patronizing tone. "Will you just leave all of this to me?" she'd pleaded. "I promise I won't uproot the entire staff the first week I'm there. Nor will they leave in droves because I'm such a tyrant."

He'd finally taken her at her word, but she knew he continued to have his doubts about the wisdom of this entire assignment. Richard was just one more person she intended to prove wrong. It was annoying, but not entirely unexpected.

The door to her office swung open suddenly and a rather bland-looking man, dressed all in gray, appeared. When he saw her, shock registered on his face, immediately followed by alarm.

"Ms. Carlton, I had no idea you would be here so early," he said. "I apologize for not knocking. You should have let me know when you were coming in. I would have been here to greet you. And I'd planned on having flowers delivered later this morning."

"No problem," she said. Flowers were the least of her concern. Better to do something about the dreadful furniture and heavy, dark draperies. "I assume you're Chester Sandhurst."

"I am," he said, coming forward to grasp her hand. "It's a pleasure to meet you."

Destiny sincerely doubted that. In essence, she'd taken the man's job. He would continue to be the chief executive officer, but she had been installed over him as chairman, a newly created position that clearly held all the power and authority he'd once had. Still, she went along with the polite charade. Better to have him as an ally than an enemy.

"I'm sure we'll work very nicely together," she said to him. "May I offer you some tea? I brought along a teapot and made some when I got here. Then we can have a little chat and get better acquainted."

He looked taken aback by the invitation. "Now? You want to meet now?"

"We're both here. I don't see why not. Do you have anything more pressing on your calendar?"

He blinked at the subtle hint that there couldn't possibly be anything more important. "No, of course not."

Destiny rose and poured him a cup of tea, then retreated behind her desk, keeping the balance of power solidly on her side. Richard wasn't the only one in the family who understood the subtle dynamics of the business setting. She'd never liked such formality, but it suited this situation. Perhaps one day soon she'd be able to let down her guard and relax with her staff, but not just yet and not with a man who needed reminding that she was in charge.

She met Chester's gaze, saw the hint of concern he was trying with some difficulty to conceal. "Have you scheduled all the meetings I requested when I faxed you my arrival schedule?"

"Most of them, yes. They'll begin at ten."

"So late?" she questioned.

"I wasn't sure what office hours you planned on keeping."

"I like to get an early start on the day. I'm sure you'll take that into account from now on. Why weren't all the meetings scheduled as I requested?"

"A few people are out this week," Chester responded, beginning to sound just a little defensive. "Some had previously scheduled vacation times and I hesitated to disrupt their plans. There's also a nasty flu traveling through the city."

Letting go of her annoyance, Destiny tapped the folders in front of her. "Then let's go over the list of those who will be in. I'd like your perceptions before I meet with them."

Chester seemed to relax at the suggestion that she intended to defer to his opinion. In fact, he became downright chatty, offering glowing reports on the executives he'd assembled during his ten lackluster years at the helm.

"David Perkins is an outstanding chief financial officer. We're lucky to have him. And Edward Wildemon is considered tops in the marketing field," he summarized. "You'll find all the others quite competent, as well, I'm sure. I'm sorry you won't be meeting Edward today. He's one of the ones on vacation, but David will be here. If you have any questions at all about the bottom line, he's your man."

Destiny refrained from responding. If all these people had been so blasted competent, there would be no need for her to be here. And at least one of them had to be knowingly or unwittingly leaking inside information to William.

"I'll certainly look forward to speaking to each of them," she said. "Now, then, have you ordered the invitations I requested?"

Chester's pallor returned. "It's a busy time of year at the printer's," he told her evasively. "Christmas card engraving, you know."

"But they will be on my desk this afternoon?" Destiny persisted. "You explained that this is a rush order and that the printer will be paid handsomely for the accommodation?"

"I'm not sure why you even feel the need to have a party," Chester said, still not giving her the direct answer she'd requested. "You've just arrived. It's the holiday season. You should be enjoying London."

"I'm not here to enjoy London," she informed him coldly. "I'm here to do a job."

Chester was undaunted. "But a party? When you've just arrived? No one expects it, I'm sure."

She was tiring of his attitude. "Then won't it be lovely when I surprise them?" she responded. "I'll expect the invitations this afternoon, along with the list of addresses I requested. I'd like everything addressed and sent out by courier first thing tomorrow. My secretary will be able to handle that."

His obvious discomfort deepened. "I'm afraid we haven't assigned you a secretary just yet. We thought you'd like to interview the candidates for the position, perhaps after the holidays."

"Then isn't it lucky I've brought my own from home," she said cheerfully, relieved that she'd had the foresight to do just that. Miriam was as eager as she to get started. Thrilled to have an opportunity to live in London for a few months or longer if Destiny required it, she would do her part to whip the office into shape in no time.

"Thank you, Chester." She handed him a paper. "Can you please see that these people come to see me at the times I've indicated. Hopefully my changes haven't disrupted your schedule too much. Those who aren't here today can be scheduled with Miriam as soon as they've returned to the office."

"You don't wish me to sit in on the meetings?" he asked, clearly dismayed.

"I'm sure you have far more important things to attend to, such as getting those invitations printed. I wouldn't dream of tying up your entire day like that," she told him. "It was good meeting you, Chester. I'm sure I'll have a million and one questions once I'm finished interviewing everyone. Why don't we plan on meeting at this time every morning for the foreseeable future?"

He paled at that, but nodded. "As you wish."

He left then, closing the door behind him. Destiny could almost hear him uttering a sigh of relief on the other side. She'd shaken him up, no question about it. In fact, she found that a bit promising. If Chester was intelligent enough to see that she was quite clearly in charge now, then perhaps they could find some way to work together, after all. She hadn't relished the idea of firing him before her first day on the job was an hour old.

"She's doing what?" Richard asked, not entirely certain what the fuss was about, but there was no mistaking the alarm in the voice of his CEO for European operations.

"Barely here and she's throwing a party, sir. A few hours from now, in fact," Chester Sandhurst informed him in a hushed tone, as though he were terrified of being caught betraying the new chairman of his division. "I tried to steer her away from the idea, but she was adamant. Had to rush the invitations to satisfy her. It's costing a bloody fortune to do all of this in such a hurry."

"Is this party for the staff?" Richard asked, thinking that wasn't so bad. A nice holiday celebration might be just the thing to get Destiny off on the right foot with everyone in the London office. She'd always been a fabulous hostess. It would also explain why she'd been so hell-bent on getting to London before Christmas despite his pleas that she wait until the New Year to tackle her new assignment.

"The executives," Chester told him. "And the heads of most of the companies with which we do business. It's an impressive guest list and most have accepted, despite the last-minute invitation. It's evident they all want a look at her."

Two birds with one stone, Richard concluded, ignoring the surprise in Chester's voice. That seemed perfectly sensible to him. "Why are you so worried about this?" he asked Chester.

"I didn't see the complete guest list until after the fact, otherwise I could have prevented this, I'm sure," Chester said.

"Prevented what?" Richard asked, impatient with all the dancing around.

"The inclusion of this one particular guest," he said, then added in that same dire undertone, "William Harcourt."

Richard's blood froze at the mention of Harcourt. Why would Destiny invite the man who had been a thorn in Richard's side, a man who'd been pecking away at their business like a particularly pesky pigeon? What the hell was Destiny thinking by giving him an opportunity to mingle, not only with Carlton executives, but their key business associates? He knew she had something up her sleeve, but this was a dangerous game she was playing, no question about it. Add a little alcohol into the mix and who knew what corporate secrets were likely to be spilled? He'd obviously been right when he'd expressed concern to Melanie about just this sort of thing a few weeks back. Her outrage over his concerns had lulled him into ignoring them.

"I'll talk to her," he reassured Chester. "Thanks for the heads-up, but a word of advice, Chester. Don't come running to me behind my aunt's back again. She'll have every justification she needs for firing you and I'll applaud her for it."

Chester's gasp was audible. "Of course, sir. I realize that she's a bit inexperienced at this sort of thing, and, well, I just thought you should know that she might be getting in over her head."

Richard bit back a sigh. If he'd ever doubted that sending Destiny to take over the helm of the European division was wise, listening to Chester just now confirmed it. He might not understand what his aunt was up to with this party, but whatever it was had to be better than relying on a man who jumped at shadows. Sandhurst's overly cautious attitude was precisely the reason Carlton Industries was underperforming in Europe.

"I'm sure your intentions were honorable, Chester,

but my aunt is in charge now. It is not my intention to second-guess her at every turn," he said, determined not to undercut her authority when she'd barely gotten started. "If I'd felt that was necessary, I would never have sent her in the first place. I'm sure you'll find some way to work with her and see that she has whatever information is necessary for her to succeed."

"Absolutely," Chester said, sounding more resigned than enthusiastic.

Ten minutes later, Richard was on the phone to Destiny, not to second-guess her, he reminded himself, but to find out what the dickens she thought she was doing. He kept Melanie's warning in mind, though. The last thing he wanted to do was insult his aunt and get her dander up.

"Having fun yet?" he inquired lightly.

"Settling in," she corrected her.

"Any plans in the works now that you're on the scene?" he asked. "Any strategy you perhaps forgot to mention before you left?"

She heaved a sigh. "You've heard about the party."

"And the guest list," he admitted.

"Chester, I imagine. I know he was snooping around Miriam's desk while she was addressing the invitations."

"I'm not telling," Richard replied. "I assume you have a reason for including Harcourt."

"I do."

"Mind sharing?"

"As a matter of fact, I do," Destiny said. "I'll let you know how it turns out, though. I'll give you a call first thing tomorrow."

"Damn straight you will," Richard groused. "You

do still answer to me, you know." It was something that bore repeating with his headstrong aunt.

Destiny merely laughed. "Don't get all huffy with me, Richard. I know exactly what I'm doing."

"I just wish I did."

"It's nothing illegal or immoral, nothing that will reflect negatively on Carlton Industries. That's all you need to concern yourself with. You know the old adage about keeping your enemies close, don't you?"

"I do."

"Well, then, think of it that way. I intend to keep William Harcourt very close. He won't make a move from now on without me catching wind of it."

All of which struck Richard as a somewhat risky but reasonably fine idea until later that evening when his wife reminded him over an early dinner with his brothers and their wives that they were all but certain William Harcourt was not just some casual acquaintance from years ago, but the important man in Destiny's life when she'd lived in France.

"Whoever that man was, she was deeply in love with him," Melanie said. "In fact, she once called him the love of her life. Sounds to me as if she has a very different agenda in mind."

"She never admitted that that man was Harcourt," he grumbled, knowing that he was splitting hairs. Destiny had conceded that she'd known William back then and she'd also acknowledged that there had been an important man in her life. The likelihood that they were one and the same man was fairly high, especially given her eagerness to take on this assignment. Richard might not like it, but the coincidences were too obvious to ignore. Wasn't that the very thing that had him so worried about all of this?

"But I picked up on it," Melanie said.

"So did I," Kathleen added.

Richard looked at his brothers. "Did you guys get all of that from whatever Destiny said?"

"Pretty much," Ben said.

Mack merely shrugged.

"You really should pay more attention to what people tell you," his wife scolded. "She laid all the clues out there."

He stared at his brothers in complete bewilderment. "Okay, let's say she was in love with Harcourt at one time. They haven't had any contact in a couple of decades now. She did say that, right?"

"Yes," they all agreed.

"Then what on earth is Destiny up to over there?"

"Sounds to me like she's out for blood," Mack said.

"I don't think so," Ben said, his expression thoughtful.

Though Ben refused to accept it, he was Destiny's favorite and he was closest to her in temperament. Richard knew if anyone could see into her heart, it was Ben.

"She might think that's what she's after," Ben continued. "But I think it's something else."

Richard's heart drummed slowly. "What?"

All three women and his youngest brother stared at him as if he were totally dense. "The man who got away," they chorused.

"She took this job because she wants William Harcourt back in her life?" he asked, astonished and suddenly more worried than ever. Destiny's remark about keeping the enemy close echoed dully in his head. "Then what was all that garbage she fed me about finding herself, about taking on new challenges and reinventing herself?"

"A smoke screen," Mack suggested.

Beth regarded him with pity. "Don't be absurd. Destiny wants to do all of those things. I'm sure she wants to become a powerful business executive *and* William's lover. The two things are not mutually exclusive."

"What's more, I'd say he's after the same thing," Kathleen added.

"Dear God in heaven," Richard muttered. "I've got to get her back here."

Mack laughed at that. "How do you propose to do that?"

"I'll fire her," he said grimly.

"That won't bring her home," Ben told him. "It'll just infuriate her. Besides, right now you've got her in a place where you can keep an eye on her. Old Chester the blabbermouth will alert you if she gets in over her head."

"Actually, I warned him to stop tattling on Destiny before she caught on and fired him with my blessing."

"Well, that was shortsighted," Ben told him with a dismayed look.

"If I'd had any idea what she was really up to over there, believe me, I would have handled things differently," Richard replied defensively.

"Maybe we're worrying over nothing. Maybe Harcourt won't even show up at the party," Mack suggested. "Maybe he got over his personal interest in Destiny years ago."

All three women hooted at that.

"The man has been bidding huge amounts of money on companies he probably didn't even want just to get Destiny all worked up and lure her over there," Kathleen said. "Trust me, he'll be at the party."

Richard gaped at the comment. "You think that's why he's been mucking about in our business, just to get Destiny's attention?"

"That's been my theory all along," she said. "If we're right about their involvement years ago, it's obvious he still knows her very well."

Richard groaned at the implication.

"When is this party, by the way?" Ben asked. "Is it too late to fly over? I wouldn't mind getting a look at this guy myself."

"Too late," Richard said bleakly, glancing at his watch. It was midnight in London. Then he brightened. "Actually, the party was probably a crashing bore and is over by now. Harcourt's probably gone. And Destiny's safely tucked in her own bed, exhausted by all her machinations."

"Or they're sharing a private moment with some brandy in front of a cozy fire, discussing the past," Mack suggested.

Richard shot him a sour look. "Bite your tongue."

"Well, I think it's romantic," Kathleen said staunchly. "Destiny has spent years and years catering to your every whim. She deserves to have some romance in her life, if she wants it."

"Not with a man who's out to destroy an entire division of Carlton Industries," Richard retorted.

"I'm telling you he doesn't give a damn about Carlton Industries," Kathleen responded. "This has been about Destiny from the very beginning. If it hadn't been, you would have lost more of those acquisitions than you won."

"Kathleen could be right," Mack said slowly. "The man always seemed to know just when to pull out of the bidding. You've said yourself, Richard, that it was almost uncanny how he backed down, just when you were about to concede defeat."

"All that tells me is that someone was leaking our final offer to him, and he was smart enough to see he was out of his league," Richard said. "That's not much comfort. And this Fortnum Travel acquisition that's coming up is critical. Destiny's there and he's showing no signs at all that he's going to stop fighting us for it. This time he seems determined to win."

"Really?" Kathleen said, obviously surprised. "Then he could be a real threat on this one?"

"Yes," Richard said succinctly.

"But he could still back off at the last second, right? He's done that before," Ben said. "He might make some gallant gesture for Destiny's benefit."

Richard glowered at him. "I don't know about you, but I can't take a lot of comfort in the notion that a man that sneaky and underhanded is after our aunt."

"Oh, please," Mack said. "When it comes to being sneaky and underhanded, Destiny's a match for any man. All you have to do is look around this room to see the evidence of that."

Richard sighed at that. It was true. All three marriages were the result of Destiny's clever schemes. If she could handle the three of them, William Harcourt would be a piece of cake. Richard just didn't want Harcourt to be the piece of cake that wound up giving Destiny—or Carlton Industries—food poisoning.

5

Destiny's only regret about arranging this party before she lost her nerve was that it hadn't given her much time to get over her jet lag and assure herself that she looked like a million bucks. Still, a glance in the mirror told her she looked more than respectable in an emerald satin cocktail suit that matched her eyes and showed off plenty of pale-as-cream skin.

Her London flat had been decorated for the holidays in advance of her arrival. The sparkling decorations were the only thing that had kept her from gasping with dismay at the sight of the dull furnishings. Once she'd seen her office, she recognized Chester's taste reflected in both places. The man obviously had no imagination. Thankfully, Miriam had had the foresight to track down a decorator to handle the holiday preparations.

The tree shimmered with tiny white lights and golden ornaments, echoing the diamond-and-gold sparkles at Destiny's neck and ears. The large rooms were filled with flattering, romantic candlelight. The buffet table set for the late-evening gathering glistened with silver and crystal and a centerpiece of holly. The bar shimmered with rows of Waterford champagne flutes and bottles of Dom Pérignon. Soft Christmas music and the scent of bayberry filled the air. She'd deliberately chosen a late start for the event, hoping that anticipation would add an extra element to the occasion.

She gazed around in satisfaction. The scene had been properly set, worthy of a spread in some slick magazine. Best of all, it was a far cry from the simpler, more casual style of her holiday entertaining years ago. Then she had prided herself on outrageous decorations and an eclectic assortment of guests. Tonight spoke of a woman of taste, elegance and substance. Those parties had been fun. Tonight's was meant to impress—one man in particular. If Richard had suspected as much when they'd spoken earlier, his panic level would have increased tenfold. In fact, now that he'd had time to think, she imagined he was working himself into a frenzy over his own dinner.

Chester, an unaccompanied bachelor, was the first to arrive, obviously in a misguided attempt to forestall the mistake he thought Destiny was intent on making. Other Carlton executives and their wives were right on his heels, probably at his command. Destiny did her best to make them feel welcome, all the while keeping one eye on the door.

It was after ten, beyond fashionably late, when William finally appeared. Her heart immediately did a little flutter-step, which she promptly and viciously tried to regulate. Only when she had her emotions firmly in check did she go to greet him.

"William," she said, pressing a kiss to his cheek, a kiss no more intimate than those she'd bestowed on all the other guests. It was the little jolt to her senses that made this greeting different. "How lovely that you could come."

He regarded her with amusement. "You knew I wouldn't stay away. It's been a long time, Destiny. Far too long."

"Has it?" she asked, as if his absence had barely registered. "Yes, I suppose it has been. The years have flown by."

She regarded him more intently. He was as handsome as ever, his complexion tanned even in December from recent rounds of golf, no doubt. There was no softness to the line of his jaw and few signs of aging beyond the laugh lines at the corners of his eyes and a trace of gray in his hair.

"Yet you've hardly aged a day," she added appreciatively.

"And you not a moment," he said, surveying her with equal approval. "You're every bit as beautiful as I'd remembered. Perhaps more so. There's a glow about you. It must be the excitement of your new challenge."

"And you have the same glib charm I remembered," she said lightly.

He laughed, obviously aware that she'd meant it not as a compliment, but as a subtle dig suggesting total insincerity.

"Tell me, Destiny, how are your nephews?"

For the first time, her smile came easily. "Wonderful. They've grown into extraordinary young men. I'm very proud of them."

"I shouldn't be surprised. With your influence, how could they have turned out any other way?"

She laughed at the continued flattery. "Oh, there

are some who despaired at me being in charge of shaping their lives. They thought I'd ruin them. What sort of mother would a madcap, gadabout like me make, after all?"

"An amazing one, I would think," he said, his expression solemn. "Those boys couldn't have been any luckier than to have you come to pick up the pieces after their parents died."

She didn't want to feel anything at the total sincerity in his voice, but she did—another of those traitorous flutters in the region of her heart. To cover for it, she glanced around quickly for an escape. Better not to linger when her defenses were so clearly down. Better to escape while this first meeting was going so well. There was an art to captivating a man. It was essential to leave him wanting more.

"Do you know everyone here?" she asked. "Let me introduce you around."

She hurriedly parked him with Chester, a safe-enough bet, then made her way to the balcony off the living room for a quick breath of air. All of the oxygen seemed to have been sucked from her lungs at the sight of William. It wasn't fair that he could still affect her so deeply, not fair at all.

The London night was raw and damp, but the air served its purpose. It wiped away the warm and fuzzy feelings that had resurfaced the instant she'd laid eyes on William. She'd told him the truth inside. The damn man had barely changed at all. Those few distinguishing streaks of gray in his thick hair, the laugh lines on his tanned face only added character.

She had to keep reminding herself that he was a snake, a snake who meant to do her family harm. That wasn't bitter resentment talking, but truth. He'd proved his intentions time and again. He hadn't been targeting a million and one different companies for acquisition in recent years, only those in which Carlton Industries had expressed an interest. There was no mistaking that his business actions were directed her way. It would take longer to figure out why he was so intent on creating problems for her family's company. But she would, and no matter the lingering attraction she felt, she would make him pay.

Still, it was hard, if not impossible, to keep the flood of other, kinder and gentler memories at bay.

And so, forgiving herself in advance for the indulgence, she let them come.

Provence, 1981

The fields were alive with poppies, bright red flags waving against a sky of purest blue. Destiny had glimpsed the glorious sight from her window not ten minutes before. Captivated, she ran down the stairs, grabbed easel, canvas and paints and ran barefoot through the field across from her house to a vantage point that showed a tiny patch of sparkling sea in the distance. While the light was still exactly right, she set to work.

"How many times are you going to paint this same scene?" William inquired, appearing behind her an hour later with a cup of coffee in hand, an amused expression on his face.

Destiny barely spared him a glance. "It's different every time. The light is never the same," she murmured absently, already lost in her work. "I'll never tire of it."

William sighed. "I suppose it's the same way I feel about you."

Something in his voice caught her attention. She turned slowly and put down her brush. "Oh?"

"I don't think I shall ever tire of you," he said, reaching for her, his hands skimming her breasts, covered only in the soft white cotton of the gown she wore to bed. "God, you're gorgeous. You make me wish I could paint so I could capture you looking just as you do now, all rosy and rumpled and sexy."

"Perhaps one day I'll put myself in a painting and give it to you."

He stroked her belly, starting a fire that couldn't be ignored.

"It won't be the same," he said. "You don't see yourself as I do. You still think of yourself as the American runaway, a shy girl escaping the demands of her family. I see you as a woman with so many facets, I'll never know them all."

At his touch, his words, Destiny gave up all thoughts of painting. "Will you try?"

"Always," he said, scooping her into his strong arms and carrying her back to the house, to the bed they'd been sharing for almost a year. "When I found you, I truly found my destiny."

Destiny fit her body to his, reveled in his touch, and wondered if it was true, if they would be like this always.

But, of course, they hadn't been, Destiny reminded herself sadly, shivering in the chill of the London night. Their magical time together had been cut short by the tragic deaths of her brother and his wife. And even though she'd felt an instantaneous connection to William tonight, he wasn't the same person he'd been back then. Neither of them were. Sentiment and nostalgia had no place in their relationship now. They were business enemies. It would be wise to remember that and keep her defenses solidly in place.

It was also important to remember the reason she'd thrown this party in the first place, then added William to the group. It hadn't been merely to catch a glimpse of him while surrounded by other people. She'd wanted to see if there was anyone here tonight who seemed especially friendly to him or, possibly, someone he was careful to avoid. She couldn't detect any of that from her safe spot on the balcony, and it was time she got to work.

When she opened the door, the sounds of a successful party spilled out. The faint strains of music were overshadowed by laughter and conversation. Sometimes all it took to make a success of an evening was the right mix of champagne, good food and people with something in common. Over the years, she'd also learned it was good to throw a little something extra into the mix, someone to create a bit of controversy and keep the conversation lively.

Whatever whispers had been stirred by William's arrival into the midst of this Carlton event, he'd clearly overcome the initial suspicion and distrust. He was chatting with two couples now, her director of finance and her marketing expert, and their wives, as Chester stood grimly by, his expression still registering his disapproval. If he kept it up, he was going to put a real damper on things.

Destiny plucked two glasses of champagne from a

tray and went to join them, handing one to Chester. She tapped her crystal glass to his. "To a successful partnership," she said quietly.

Chester stared at her in surprise. "Yes, of course," he said, then took a polite sip of the champagne.

"Could I see you for a moment?" Destiny asked, coaxing him away from the others. David Perkins and Edward Wildemon would have to fend for themselves with William. And if one of them happened to be William's spy, it was unlikely he would reveal himself in front of the other. At the moment, though, the conversation seemed focused on the current season of London theater.

"Is there a problem?" Chester asked at once.

"You need to cheer up," she chided. "You're giving everyone the impression that William needs to be watched like a hawk."

"And well he does. Have you forgotten what he's been up to?" Chester demanded. "It was a mistake inviting him. I don't intend to let it turn into a disaster."

"Then perhaps you should spend your time appeasing some of our neglected business associates," she suggested.

His gaze narrowed. "You wanted Harcourt here for a specific reason, didn't you?"

"Of course."

He studied her intently. "Surely you don't think he'll give himself away. He's too smooth for that."

Destiny couldn't deny that William was a slick operator. She'd alluded to that very thing when she'd spoken to him earlier. "But perhaps his inside source will not be quite so clever," she explained.

"I'll keep an eye on him. I'll keep a close watch to

see who he spends time with," he said more eagerly. "But from a discreet distance."

Destiny beamed at him. "I knew you would understand."

He gave her an apologetic look. "Perhaps I misjudged you," he said.

"It happens," she said blithely. "Usually never more than once."

For the first time since they'd met, Chester actually laughed. "Something tells me that working with you is going to be a revelation."

She patted his hand. "For both of us, Chester. It can be a good partnership, you know. You have much-valued expertise in business and in the European market. I am rather clever with people. Together, I think we'll be quite formidable, if you'll give it a proper chance."

"I most certainly will," he said at once.

"And no more calls to my nephew. Understood?"

He blanched at that. "Richard told you?"

She laughed. "After promising he wouldn't? Never. He didn't have to. As I said, I understand people."

"It won't happen again, I assure you."

Destiny nodded. "Then go and mingle. This is as good a time as any to prove to everyone that you and I intend to run this company as a team, rather than being at odds."

When the obviously relieved Chester had gone off to talk with her other guests, Destiny turned her attention back to William. He was alone now, standing off to one side, almost in the shadows, his hooded gaze watching her. It reminded her all too vividly of the night they'd met, when he'd sought a hiding place where he could observe rather than participate in the gathering.

She made her way across the room in his direction. It took some time, because with the champagne flowing, her guests were suddenly eager for a moment of her time, anxious to share ideas in a way they hadn't been during the first tense meetings in her office.

When she eventually reached William, he grabbed her hand and pulled her into the kitchen, which was a beehive of activity as the caterer and his staff readied more hors d'oeuvres to keep the tables overflowing with food. William clearly saw his mistake at once and grimaced.

"There doesn't seem to be anyplace where I can have a moment alone with you," he grumbled.

Destiny laughed. "The bedroom's probably free, but I imagine that would be a serious mistake. It might be misconstrued by my other guests." Worse, she could just imagine how Richard would interpret it, if he heard about it, and there was little question that he would, despite Chester's reassurances.

William's gaze clashed with hers. "Would it really? It seems forever since I've held you in my arms."

"Then you should be over the desire," she said tartly, refusing to be swayed by the hunger in his eyes. "I am."

"Are you really, Destiny?"

"I was over it in months," she lied. "After more than twenty years, those days we shared in Provence are merely a small blip in my memory. A regret."

His eyes turned dark and dangerous. "You can't mean that."

"I can and do," she insisted.

"Perhaps I can remind you," he said, touching a finger to her cheek, tracing the delicate line of her jaw.

Her pulse jumped and skittered wildly, but she kept her gaze steady and, hopefully, disinterested. She thought she was making a success of it, until he lowered his head, his intention to kiss her clear. She couldn't mask her reaction to *that* and she knew it. She made a timely move, jerking her attention away from William and toward the caterer, who looked at her with surprise when she nearly bolted in his direction.

"Is there a problem?" Harold inquired, his eyes filled with alarm.

"No, actually everything is perfect," Destiny reassured him smoothly. "I was just hoping that there are more of those delicious crab puffs. People are raving about them."

"There are more in the oven. They'll be out in a few minutes," he promised.

"Wonderful," she said. "I'll tell the others."

She brushed past William, anxious to make her escape from his disconcerting presence, but he caught her hand.

"I'd like to see you again, Destiny. Perhaps we can have dinner."

"I've just arrived and my schedule is packed until Christmas," she told him. Her plan to keep him close now struck her as far too dangerous. Arm's length was better, after all.

"Will your family be joining you then, or will you fly home?" he asked.

"Neither. I intend to put my feet up and catch my breath over the holidays, so that I can hit the ground running after the first of the year. I've barely settled in and there are a million things to do to make this place my own."

"Then we'll see each other during the holidays," he said. "I'll be in touch to arrange it."

She regarded him curiously. "Why, William? Why, after all this time, would you want to see me again?"

"We're old friends," he said. "At least I like to think we are."

"We were much more than friends, William. That's the problem. What we had is not something that can be recaptured. Nor is it something I really want to reminisce about. In case you've forgotten, it ended rather badly."

"Whose fault was that?" he asked, a surprising edge in his voice.

"I can't believe you need to ask," Destiny said tightly.

He searched her face, then sighed. "Then we'll have a fresh start," he said.

She shook her head. "That's not possible, either. Some things are impossible to forget."

His expression brightened a bit then. "Then you do remember," he said quietly.

Destiny steeled herself and looked directly into his eyes. "That you abandoned me when I needed you most, that you've systematically gone after my family? Yes, William, I remember. I remember all too clearly."

She left the kitchen then, leaving him staring after her, the waiters dodging him with their trays of food. It was unfortunate that the servers were very agile. At that moment, she wouldn't have minded seeing William covered with seafood dip and crackers. In fact, if she hadn't been trying very hard to make a dignified impression tonight, she might have tossed them at him herself.

It was beyond annoying that the man thought he could waltz into her party, say a few sweet words and charm her right back into his bed. There was little question in her mind that that had been his intention. Either he had a very high opinion of himself or a very low opinion of her. Maybe a combination of the two.

Okay, maybe it was a tiny bit flattering. Despite her age, there were still many men who regarded her with evident fascination, but she'd grown increasingly cynical about their interest. Many were far more intrigued by the Carlton name and wealth than by her. But there had been real heat in William's eyes, the kind with which she had once been intimately familiar. To her discredit, for a moment, she'd let herself revel in it, allowed herself to feel like a desirable woman.

But if those men back home had ulterior motives, how could she doubt that William's motives were equally impure? No, she simply could not permit herself to be distracted for a second from her suspicions about him and the harm he meant to do to her family.

Besides, she hadn't come to London to have herself a midlife fling, as attractive and exciting as the possibility might be. She'd come here to prove to herself that she had the talent and ingenuity it took to be a powerful businesswoman in her own right. *That* was her mission, and she couldn't lose sight of it, certainly not with the real game just beginning.

6

Destiny had changed. William had recognized it the moment he'd looked into her eyes and seen not the shyness and vulnerability of the girl he'd first met, but the steely resolve of a woman who'd matured, a woman who was icily furious with him.

He'd fallen in love with the girl all those years ago, but the woman excited him in a whole new way. He'd anticipated winning her back with a first glance, perhaps a touch. Instead, she was going to be a challenge, perhaps an impossible one, but he'd never avoided something merely because of the uncertainty of the outcome. Seemingly insurmountable odds were his favorite kind.

No question, this was going to take some cunning on his part. He refused to consider that it might also take time. They'd wasted enough of that, thanks to his own foolishness. He didn't intend to lose a moment more than necessary. It was a good thing he had an excellent head for strategic planning. He'd gotten Destiny over here, hadn't he?

Of course, that, too, had taken time and patience

and an ever-escalating campaign against Carlton Industries. Now, with the Fortnum Travel acquisition on the horizon, the fight continued. He could give up as a gesture of good will, but more than any of the other companies he'd sought to steal out from under Carlton, Fortnum was a perfect match for Harcourt & Sons. Destiny wouldn't be pleased when she discovered he was dead serious about this one.

"How was your first meeting with Ms. Carlton?" Malcolm asked when he joined William in his office the next morning. "Did things go as you'd expected?"

Had they? William gave the question some real thought. In some ways they'd gone better. There had been a lively spark in Destiny's eyes that had given lie to all of her claims to have forgotten what they'd once meant to each other. But there had also been a hard, unforgiving edge he hadn't entirely anticipated.

Not only had Destiny revised history and blamed him solely for their separation all those years ago, but she'd apparently taken his attacks on Carlton Industry to heart, even though he'd been deliberately unsuccessful in most cases. He'd succeeded from time to time, only to keep the threat legitimate and to raise the stakes in the hope of getting her to London to retaliate. He should have guessed that the mother-hen protectiveness that had taken her back to the States all those years ago would be more powerful than ever by now. Perhaps he *should* reconsider the Fortnum acquisition, but that would be a risky business, as well. How much respect would Destiny have for him if he gave up suddenly or too easily?

Returning to Malcolm's question, he said finally, "It was an interesting evening." It was the best he could do.

"Any idea why you were included in a Carlton event?"

William laughed. "Oh, I think that was clear enough. Destiny wants me to know she's keeping an eye on me. In fact, she had Sandhurst watching me all evening long in case I gave away my inside contact."

Malcolm permitted himself a rare smile. "Then it's a very good thing that you don't have one, isn't it?"

"Indeed. And just as well you haven't told me yours," William replied. "There was no way either of us was likely to give ourselves away."

"What's your next step, sir?"

"I'm thinking about that right now."

Malcolm studied him soberly. "Sir, if you don't mind my asking, what exactly is your goal? I've never been entirely clear on that."

"To be honest, there have been a few moments when I've lost track of it myself," William admitted.

"And now?"

William smiled. "Now that I've seen her again, it's all perfectly clear. I want Destiny Carlton back in my life. And this time, I don't intend to let anything stand in my way until she's my wife." Not even Fortnum Travel, if it came down to that.

Malcolm nodded slowly. "I thought it was something like that. If there's anything I can do to help, it will be my pleasure."

"You've done more than enough," William told him. "I think the rest is up to me."

"Will you be needing more inside information, sir?"

"Quite likely," William said. "I can't have Destiny thinking that she's scared me out of the game merely by showing up. We need to keep the pressure on. Line up another meeting for me with the Fortnum executives so I can press our case."

Malcolm nodded. "Things will be quiet during the holidays, but I'll schedule it for the first of the year. And I'll get back to my source at Carlton then, as well, and see if there's any indication what Ms. Carlton's strategy will be now that she's in charge."

"And meantime, why don't we get together with Langley as soon as possible? Perhaps he'll have some ideas about how H&S Books can make Ms. Carlton rue the day she decided to buy Jameson's Booksellers."

"There are only a few days left before Christmas, sir. I doubt we can have much impact on their holiday sales," Malcolm said.

"We can if we increase advertising and undercut their prices," William suggested, his expression thoughtful. "And I believe it's time to announce our own mail-order catalog, don't you? Should have done it years ago."

"Isn't slashing prices a rather shortsighted strategy, sir?" Malcolm asked, clearly scandalized by the thought of taking losses. "We can't go on in such a way, not without destroying our own business. And won't a catalog cost a pretty penny?"

"Not if we do it on the internet, rather than printing and mailing it. As for the holiday sale, I'll discuss it with Langley, of course, but it seems to me we only have to slash the prices on certain books to get people through our doors and away from Jameson's. And it will send a clear message to Ms. Carlton that we intend not only to stay in the fight, but to up the ante."

Malcolm's aristocratic brow rose slightly. "Poker, sir?"

William hadn't thought of the connection himself, but it was accurate. "Yes, it is a bit like poker," he said. "But in this case, we're not bluffing, Malcolm. We have the hand it takes to win."

Malcolm still looked distressed and unsettled. "If you say so."

William laughed at his sour expression. "Buck up, man. I have no intention of driving us into bankruptcy simply to win Ms. Carlton's heart."

"Good to know, sir," Malcolm responded, though he didn't look entirely convinced.

"Will you get Langley in here? We have to put this plan into motion at once. Even a few days of eating into their sales at this time of year can have a huge impact."

"Yes, sir. Right away."

As William waited for the head of his book division, he leaned back in his chair and closed his eyes. He felt more energized than he had in years. He'd always thought attending to business was a rather mundane necessity, but he was discovering it could be intellectually stimulating with Destiny now a factor.

A gentlemanly attempt to win Destiny back would probably allow her her little victory with Jameson's, but he knew her too well to play it that way. She would relish the challenge and, in the end, would respect him for it. At least, he hoped he wasn't misreading the situation as he'd misread things so badly years ago.

Time would tell.

Two days after her party, Destiny opened her paper as she drank her morning tea and very nearly choked. Running a full-page ad this close to Christmas had to have cost H&S Books a fortune. It featured the latest bestsellers at prices with which Jameson's couldn't possibly compete, something William had obviously known when he'd devised the sneaky strategy.

He'd taken his own sweet time coming up with a response to her purchase of Jameson's, but she was forced to concede it had been a good one. The clever little line on the bottom of the ad about watching for their new online ordering service was brilliant, as well. He'd gotten a jump on her plan to open a catalog business. Now H&S Books would look as if they'd thought up an entirely fresh idea for expanding sales and taken it a step further by utilizing the internet and saving on printing and mailing costs. Her own plans would seem old-fashioned at best and a weak counterstrategy at worst.

After allowing herself a moment to admire William's audacity, she picked up the phone and buzzed for Chester.

"I need to see you in my office at once," she said tersely.

"Is there a problem?"

"I'll explain when you get here."

Chester arrived within minutes. He saw the paper on her desk and paled. "What is it?"

She shoved the advertisement toward him. "What do you think?"

Chester scanned the paper, then sank onto a chair. "He's one step ahead of us, isn't he?"

"The question is, how did he know about the catalog plans? We've discussed them with no one."

"Perhaps it's coincidence," Chester suggested.

Destiny scowled at him. "Don't be ridiculous. William knows. It's obvious. We have to find the leak. It's more critical than ever."

"But as you just said, we've discussed those plans with no one inside the company. Only you and I were aware that it was part of the strategy when we acquired Jameson's. I certainly haven't spoken to Harcourt or anyone else about it. Have you?"

Destiny watched him closely and sighed. If he had given away the secret, he was covering it well. He sounded totally sincere.

"No, I've spoken to no one since we concluded the negotiations," she said. "It certainly did not come up when I spoke with William at my party."

Chester's expression turned thoughtful. "One of the solicitors, perhaps?"

"In violation of their ethics?"

"No, no, of course not. Can't imagine what I was thinking."

"Who else is there?" Destiny asked.

Chester's expression turned thoughtful. "It could be Jameson himself, I suppose. I never thought to speak to him about confidentiality, and he was awfully excited at the prospect of our expanding his business. It's entirely possible he's told all of his customers by now, including someone close to Harcourt."

Destiny nodded slowly. "That has to be it. Well, it's spilt milk now. What do we do about the price cuts?"

"Nothing," Chester advised. "If they want to incur huge losses in these last days before Christmas, let them."

"I suppose, but it doesn't feel right to sit by and do nothing." She considered the problem from several angles, while Chester regarded her with obvious dismay.

It seemed to her that it was essential to act quickly and decisively. She didn't want William to have the upper hand, even for a minute. He needed to know she was as skillful as he at adjusting to changing circumstances.

Suddenly inspiration struck.

"Find me a wholesale source of fine tea, Chester."

He regarded her with a totally perplexed expression. "Tea?"

"Yes. Those tea shops of William's must do a booming business this time of year."

"I don't understand," Chester said.

"We'll have a campaign in the paper starting tomorrow, something along the lines of relaxing with a cup of tea and a good book during the holidays. We'll give away a gift packet of tea with every purchase, something everyone will want for themselves or as a treat to go along with a present. We'll serve tea, as well. We'll make Jameson's *the* place to go to get away from holiday stress."

"You can't mean it," he said, clearly stunned. "You want to do this by tomorrow?"

"Yes. How difficult can it be? It's not as if we have an entire chain of stores. We have just the one, and it shouldn't be any more difficult to stock it with tea than it was to start bringing in new books," Destiny said blithely, eager to get on with it. "I'll set up the advertising and I'll call and speak to the manager about getting the tea brewed and ordering cups. China, I think, so the atmosphere is right. Jameson's has such a traditional feel to it, doesn't it? Those throwaway cups would never do."

"You're making a snap decision, one you're likely to regret," Chester warned her. "It can't possibly be wise to make such an investment on the spur of the moment. There are procedures. This venture is too new to be pouring resources into it without thorough consideration."

"Procedures be damned," Destiny said. "We have to be innovative and responsive. We can't do that if we're worrying about dotting every *i* and crossing every *t*."

"Perhaps you should speak to Richard. See what he thinks about all this," Chester said.

Destiny sent him a piercing look. "I imagine if I don't, you will."

"I feel it's necessary," Chester said stubbornly.

She met his gaze. "Do whatever you feel is necessary, by all means," she said coldly. "But market situations call for quick thinking, Chester. You won't be doing yourself any favors by turning to my nephew every time you doubt one of my decisions."

Chester blanched at that. "No, of course not. It's your call."

"Thank you. Now, can you arrange to have the teas delivered this afternoon?"

"You can't possibly expect to do something like this in a day," Chester protested. "We'll manage it in two, if we're lucky."

"I'd like to know why we can't do it in one," Destiny responded. "A defeatist attitude isn't acceptable, Chester. Nor are we going to be complacent or traditional. From now on, we both need to think outside the box."

"Outside the box," he echoed weakly. "I'll do my best."

Destiny beamed at him. "I knew you would. Now, let's get busy. As you said, we don't have much time if we intend to pull this off. If worse comes to worst, we'll simply buy the tea at the market and pay full price until we can arrange for a wholesale delivery."

An hour later, Destiny had done her part. She'd scheduled the advertising in several papers, spoken to Jameson's manager—a bright young woman who was refreshingly eager to try something innovative—and Destiny had ordered some simple but elegant china cups to be delivered before the end of the day.

Satisfied with her morning's work, she picked up the phone and dialed William's number.

"It's not going to work, you know," she said cheerfully when he got on the line.

He laughed. "Is that so? I understand people are coming into our stores in droves today. Best holiday business we've done in years."

"Then I suppose you should thank me. Obviously it took a bit of a challenge from me to get you out of your stodgy ways."

"Thank you," he said dutifully.

"I hope you enjoy today's success," she said. "Tomorrow's another day."

"Oh? What have you got up your sleeve now, Destiny?"

"Something rather clever, if I do say so myself."

"No hints?"

"No. I don't want to give you enough time to try to counter my strategy. You'll see in the morning. Hope it doesn't spoil your breakfast."

"Why not join me and you can judge my reaction for yourself?" he suggested.

Destiny considered the invitation and decided it might be fun to watch William's face when he realized she was after not just one of his key businesses, but two of them now. Maybe that would be enough to convince him to stay away from Carlton Industries projects.

"A triumph might be just the thing to whet my appetite," she said. "Will seven be too early? I like to be in the office early."

"Seven will be fine. Where shall we go?"

"Your choice. After so many years away, I don't know London as well as you do."

He suggested a small restaurant in her neighborhood.

"That will be perfect," she said at once. "And William, don't spoil this for me by looking at your morning paper before you come."

He laughed. "I promise. Shall I bring one with me?"

"If you wish."

"Any particular paper?"

"No, any paper will do."

"Gone all out, have you?"

"And then some," she assured him breezily. "After all, when you're doing something brilliant, you want everyone to know about it."

"You're really enjoying this, aren't you?" he asked, his tone more serious.

"Actually I'm having the time of my life," she agreed. "And in a way, I have you to thank."

"How so?"

She considered her response thoughtfully. From the moment this plan of hers to compete with William and save her family business had been formulated months and months ago, she'd been making new discoveries about herself and her abilities. To realize that she'd had hidden talents all these years was remarkable at her age. She was thriving on the excitement and challenge. She woke up each morning eager to begin the day. Since Ben's marriage, she'd been far too bored. It wasn't a state that was good for anyone, especially someone with her energy.

"Intentional or not, you provided the incentive for me to get into business," she said eventually. "Until now, I'd had no idea how much fun it could be. No wonder my grandfather, father and brother loved it so much."

"And your nephew? Does Richard love it, too?"

"Of course. He also loves to win. And just so you know, that's a trait we share."

"Warning duly noted," he said solemnly. "But just so *you* know, I don't intend to lose."

He'd hung up before she could come up with an adequate response to his very confident declaration. Just as well, Destiny concluded. Maybe by morning when she saw him, she'd have one.

William strolled to the restaurant in the morning, eager to get on with things with Destiny. Whatever plot she had up her sleeve wasn't nearly as important to him as the fact that she'd agreed to meet him for breakfast. He remembered a time when they'd shared rich coffee, croissants and fresh fruit every morning at a sidewalk café near the sea. They'd lingered long after their food was gone, caught up in some lively debate or another to the amusement of the waiters.

They'd rarely agreed on anything, not art, certainly, nor books or films or world affairs. Even when they had, William had always taken an opposing point of view just to see the quick rise of color in Destiny's cheeks and the fire in her eyes. She'd never ceased to enchant him with her lively mind and tart tongue. And everyone at their favorite restaurant had enjoyed their passionate exchanges as if they were witnesses to some sort of live theater.

William could already tell that in that regard, at least, she hadn't changed. There was still nothing she enjoyed more than a good battle of wits.

When he walked into the restaurant, she was already waiting for him, engaged in a conversation with the waiter, whom she'd clearly charmed.

"Ah, here is my guest now," she said when she spotted him.

William bent down and kissed her cheek, then grinned at the waiter. "Nice to see you, George. And just so there's no mistake, Ms. Carlton is my guest this morning."

Destiny began to protest, but George nodded. "As you wish, sir."

William sat down as George went off to get his coffee. "It pays to know the staff," he told Destiny. "And you need to know that not everything is going to go your way this morning."

She gave him a serene smile. "Then I shall give in gracefully on that point, since everything else is so obviously going to go my way." She glanced pointedly at the paper he was carrying. "Have you looked?"

"I told you I wouldn't. Shall I scan through it now?"

"Perhaps we should wait till after you've eaten. I'd hate to spoil your breakfast."

"I doubt whatever scheme you've come up with is going to destroy my appetite, despite your very apparent hope for that." In fact, he found her eagerness delightful.

"Then by all means, have a look," she said. "I think the ad turned out rather well. It's on page—"

William cut her off before she could say it. "The only way to judge an ad's true effectiveness is to see if it catches a person's attention, don't you think? Let me put yours to that test."

He opened the paper and slowly turned the pages. It didn't take long for the ad to pop out at him with its picture of a stack of books topped by a steaming cup of tea. Tea, dammit! He recognized the ploy at once, even before he read the details. She was going after two businesses now, no more than an annoyance in either case, but clever, just the same. She was good at this, better than he'd expected, in fact. It would keep things between them lively, no question about it.

He worked to keep his expression neutral as he lowered the paper and faced her expectant look. "You're going into the tea business now?"

"As an experiment," she said happily. "If it's as successful as I anticipate, then it could make quite a nice expansion for Jameson's, don't you agree? We'll provide a lovely, cozy place for people to enjoy a good book and a refreshing cup of tea. I can see it becoming a gathering place for those who love literature."

"You'll never know for sure, if you begin by giving the stuff away," he said more testily than he'd meant to.

"But it's the perfect way to get people to form a habit that will bring them back into the store," she said. "Just as cutting the cost of your books is something I'm sure you have no intention of sustaining forever."

"Not necessarily," William said. "If it's successful, we'll certainly keep it going after the New Year, and based on yesterday's sales, I'd have to say it looks like a winner."

"Perhaps you should wait till you see how things go today," Destiny responded.

He heard the challenge in her voice and looked into her flashing eyes. "We can always walk over to one of the shops after breakfast and you can see for yourself," he countered. "We're opening at eight so people can shop on their way to work."

She paled a bit at that, but rallied quickly. "What a marvelous idea!"

He bit back a grin. "I imagine you'll be opening at seven starting tomorrow."

"No need," she said at once. "We believe most people would rather shop on their lunch hours or after work, so we've added more extended hours till Christmas. Wander by on your way home tonight and see for yourself how successful it is. Our customers have been wildly enthusiastic, and now that they'll be able to get a cup of tea and perhaps a bite to eat, as well, I'm sure it will go over better than before."

William regarded her with new respect. "You really do have a knack for this sort of thing, don't you?"

"I like to think I come by it naturally," she said.

"Have you worked for Carlton Industries all these years?"

"Heavens, no," she said at once. "Raising Richard, Mack and Ben was more than enough to keep me occupied. Now, though, I'm eager for new challenges."

"It wouldn't have been enough for you to take up your painting again?" he asked.

For an instant, he thought he detected a trace of sadness in her eyes, but she shook her head.

"I haven't picked up a brush in years except to dabble a bit," she said.

"You can't be serious!" he said, genuinely taken aback by that. "Your art always meant so much to you."

"It was part of the life I gave up when I went home," she told him. "There was no room for that kind of self-indulgence once I became a surrogate mother to those boys. That was a full-time job. They required all of my attention to make up at least a little for what they'd lost."

"Oh, Destiny, I'm so sorry," he said with total sincerity. It made his heart ache to think that she'd felt the need to give up something that had once brought her joy. "I should have been there to help."

Her gaze met his. "But you weren't," she said quietly. "So I had to do what was necessary on my own."

There was no hint of self-pity in her voice. Indeed, what he heard was the kind of strength and determination that must have gotten her through the turmoil of those days when her life had been turned upside down. His admiration for her grew.

"You're a remarkable woman," he told her quietly. "But then I always knew that."

She frowned at that. "Did you really?"

"Well, of course I did," he said, surprised that she needed to ask. "Why would you say such a thing?"

"Because you let me go," she said, her eyes filled with emotion. Then she looked away, and when she turned back, her face was as expressionless as if they'd been discussing the weather. "Well, that's neither here nor there."

"Destiny, please, let me explain," he began. They'd each played a role in the way things had turned out. The fault wasn't only his, though he bore the lion's share of it. That made it his duty to set things right between them.

"There's nothing to explain," she said curtly. "We can't change the past. Rehashing it is a waste of time. I made a choice back then. So did you. All either of us can do is live with the decisions we made."

"But I want you to understand," he said, feeling helpless and frustrated because he knew that no matter what he said, no matter how sincere the explanation he offered, it would never be enough to change what had happened.

She looked him in the eye, her own gaze steady and unyielding. "I do understand," she said quietly. "I really do, William. I just can't forgive you."

7

Destiny's declaration lingered in William's head long after they'd parted. Her insistence that she couldn't—or wouldn't—forgive him had shaken him more than he wanted to admit. The woman had a stubborn streak, and if she'd made up her mind to keep him at arm's length, it was going to take a monumental effort to change that.

Years ago, he'd been daunted by her stubbornness. He'd given up in the face of her silence, rather than fighting for her. He didn't intend to make that mistake again. The keys to a successful campaign were going to be seeing her often, surprising her frequently and never again letting her think for an instant that she wasn't the most important person in his life.

En route to his office, he stopped by a florist's and picked up an enormous bouquet of red poppies. On the card, he wrote, "When you see these, think of me and summer in Provence. William."

When he reached his office, he gave the flowers to Malcolm and asked him to personally deliver them to Destiny. "I know I could have had the florist do it, but

I wanted to get your impression of things over there. You'll be able to tell me if everyone's in a frenzy now that she's shaking things up."

"I'll see what I can discover, sir. Anything else?"

"No. That will be all. I'm taking the rest of the day off. Why don't you do the same? Finish up your Christmas shopping. We'll talk again tomorrow."

Malcolm nodded. "I do have a few last-minute holiday purchases to make. Thank you, sir."

Satisfied with his morning's work, William set out to do a little Christmas shopping of his own. He'd already bought gifts for family members, staff and friends. Destiny was the only person left on his list. It was essential that he find the perfect present, something that would be a constant reminder of the past, as well as a hint of how enduring his love had been. It was a lot to expect from one little gift, but it wouldn't be the first time he'd relied on a present to say what he hadn't been able to put into words. He'd often done it in those blissful years when she'd kept him tongue-tied.

Provence, 1982

William had never been so totally beguiled by a woman. He'd been with Destiny for more than a year now and he was still enchanted. She was like the sunset, reliable, yet ever-changing, always magnificent.

He'd ignored all of the entreaties from back home to return to London and take over at the helm of the family's businesses. His father's health was good. There was no reason for him to give up the reins at Harcourt & Sons, and William would never have been content as second fiddle.

In fact, he was more than content right here, in an odd little stone farmhouse with few amenities. His basic needs were being met, which didn't seem nearly as important as the fact that his heart was overflowing with unexpected joy. He'd tried to explain that to his father over the phone just the week before.

"You must know," he told his father. "You and Mother have been together for years. Surely you understand what it's like to wake up each morning with the one person you were meant to spend the rest of your life with."

His father's dry bark of laughter had surprised him. "Is that what you think? Your mother and I are together because we were a suitable match. It's worked out well enough and it resulted in you, but if you're caught up in some crazy idea that there's romance involved, you're wrong. Harcourts are driven by duty, not impulse."

William had been shocked and more than a little dismayed. "If that's so, then I'm sorry for you both," he'd told his father. "But I can't live that way."

"I'll cut you off," his father had threatened.

"Do whatever you feel is necessary," William told him. "I'll manage."

"How? Will you live on this woman's charity?"

"Absolutely not," William replied fiercely. "I'm not without contacts and resources of my own."

"Then I suggest you make use of them," his father had declared bitterly, clearly infuriated with William's refusal to comply with his wishes. It was a power struggle they'd been engaged in for years.

"You'll not get another tuppence from me," he warned.

"As you wish," William said quietly.

Despite his calm tone, William had been shaking with outrage when he'd hung up. He'd turned and found Destiny watching him, worry etched on her brow.

"Oh, William, you can't cut yourself off from your family like that," she said sorrowfully. "It's wrong. I won't be responsible for it."

"You've cut yourself off from your family," he reminded her.

"Not like that. Not forever."

"Darling, don't worry. We'll mend fences eventually," he assured her. "It's not the first time we've fought. Nor is it likely to be the last. For a stuffy pair, Father and I can be quite volatile from time to time." He changed the subject, refusing to dwell on the bitter exchange. "Now, what shall we do to celebrate your birthday? Do you want a party? A trip to Paris?"

"I don't need anything," Destiny said.

William frowned at her. "Is that because you think you've just cost me all my money?"

"Well, haven't I?"

"Hardly. But even if you had, I'd find a way to make your birthday special."

"But I really don't need anything," she repeated. "Just you."

"That you have, always," he promised her.

She smiled at him, but there was no mistaking the worry shadowing her eyes. She was afraid for him, afraid of the price he was paying to be with her. He could see that she feared one day he'd wind up resenting her, but that would never happen, not when she was the best thing to ever come into his life.

That afternoon, when the hot summer sun was beating down and Destiny was napping in the shade in the garden, he slipped into town and used the phone at their favorite restaurant to make arrangements for a surprise party the following night. Nearly everyone in the small village was invited, invitations spreading by word of mouth after those first few strategic calls.

When he'd made all the arrangements, he went shopping for something that would prove to Destiny how much he loved her. It wasn't easy finding something in such a small town, but it seemed everyone he spoke with had a suggestion. Destiny had made herself a vital part of this community during her time here, and they all loved her as much as he did.

Nothing he came across seemed exactly right. Not the jewelry. Not the glamorous beachwear. Her studio was already stuffed with books. The counters overflowed with art supplies. She was not the sort of woman who prized material possessions, anyway. Her life was built around her painting, her friends and him, and made more enjoyable by simple, delicious food and good wine.

He finally returned to the little café where the party was to be held and sat at one of the outside tables.

"No purchases?" François asked, regarding him worriedly.

William shook his head dejectedly.

"She is a woman who requires something from the heart, something lasting," François said.

William agreed. "But what?"

"Perhaps I should not speak so plainly, but is money an issue?"

"No." William had enough to manage something extravagant in spite of his father's threats.

"You know she has been teaching art classes for the children here, *n'est-ce pas?*"

William nodded.

"There is not sufficient room in her studio for all who want to attend. It seems everyone who adores Mademoiselle Destiny would like to be an artist now. Not that so many have talent, but a few do, and even the others enjoy themselves. All over town there are paintings by her students decorating kitchen walls."

William chuckled. He'd seen many of them. "What are you suggesting, François?"

"A small school, perhaps, with another room as a gallery. I know it is extravagant, but I know someone who has just such a place. Because of their love for Destiny, the cost wouldn't be too great, I think. And the size would be just right."

"A Destiny Carlton School and Gallery," William murmured, intrigued. It would be perfect. It would be something lasting, as enduring as his feelings for her, a reassurance that his life was here with her.

"Can you contact this man? I'd like to see him at once."

"I can have him here in a few moments," François assured him. "He will show you the property and you can decide." He frowned. "It is not too much? I have not overstepped?"

"No, you're a genius," William assured him.

For a village that tended to thrive on a leisurely pace, things had moved with astonishing speed after that. He saw the property, closed the deal and had an entire team of willing workers paint the faded exterior by the following afternoon. A simple sign was created by the most talented of Destiny's students.

That evening the entire village was jittery with anticipation. When William and Destiny arrived at the café, she was stunned by the sight of so many people there to celebrate her birthday. She turned to him with shining eyes.

"You did all this for me? I told you I didn't need anything."

"Perhaps you didn't need it," William told her. "But I needed to give it to you. And everyone wanted to share in the occasion."

For two hours in the waning sunlight, they ate and drank wine with their friends. There was plenty of laughter and lively conversation and even a bit of dancing. Destiny sat back with a sigh.

"It's been an absolutely perfect evening."

"It's not quite over," William said as everyone watched them with barely suppressed excitement. "Let's go for a walk. There's something else."

"Something else? I thought the party was my present."

"Just the beginning," William told her. He held out his hand. "Come along."

"But we can't leave our guests," she protested.

He laughed. "They'll be coming, too. I doubt we could keep them away."

It was only a few blocks to the new school, and they turned the walk into a joyous parade. When they were almost there, he told her, "Close your eyes."

"So I can trip and break my neck?"

"No, so I can save the surprise till the very last second."

She trustingly tucked her hand in his and let him lead the way.

"Now," he said at last, when he was sure the angle was just right for viewing the building with the last of the orange sunset's glow falling on the newly white-washed stucco walls.

He held his breath as Destiny slowly opened her eyes. At first, she seemed merely puzzled, but then her gaze fell on the sign.

"A school?" she whispered. "You've bought me an art school?"

"And a gallery, for your work and for your students'."

Her eyes brimmed with tears as she turned to the others who were waiting for her reaction. "And you knew? You were all in on it?"

"But it was Monsieur William who did it," they told her. "It is his gift."

William studied her intently. "Do you like it? I wanted you to know how much I respect your talent, how much I want to be a part of this place with you."

"Oh, William," she said, then burst into tears.

Panic spread through him. "You hate it, don't you? It's all wrong."

"No, no, it's the sweetest, most generous gift anyone has ever given me. I just can't believe you would do such a thing, not when you've just..." Her voice trailed off.

"Just been disinherited?" he asked wryly. "Darling, I told you that didn't matter. Not compared to you. Nothing compares to you."

And it hadn't. Not then. Not ever again, William thought as he wandered the boutiques of London looking yet again for the perfect gift for Destiny.

He was counting on quite a lot from this gift, as well. It needed to remind her of the past, yet promise the future. He supposed another building was out of the question. He hated to repeat himself.

Besides, she would quite likely throw the deed back in his face at this point.

No, this needed to be something smaller, something more personal, an everyday reminder of him that she couldn't easily ignore.

It was late and he was beginning to despair when he finally spotted it in a shop window. He smiled the instant he saw it.

Five minutes later it was tucked in his pocket, and he was thinking ahead to Christmas Day. It was the first time in years he'd actually looked forward to the holiday, the first time in ages he'd had someone special he wanted to impress.

Of course, it was also the first time ever that a woman was likely to regard his offering with suspicion and distrust. But perhaps, just perhaps, it would create a tiny chink in Destiny's armor, a hole large enough for him to steal back into her heart.

"Don't blow a gasket," Ben announced when he strolled into Richard's office two days before Christmas and tossed several newspapers onto his desk.

Richard moaned. If his laid-back baby brother was already warning him not to get upset, then whatever was in those papers was going to set his teeth on edge. And it obviously had to do with Destiny, who'd been amazingly adept at ducking his calls in recent days. Since he'd instructed Chester never to tattle on her again and since her personal secretary was as tight-lipped as anyone on earth, there was no one in London he could call to ask what she was up to. Maybe his brother had the answers he'd been seeking.

"What is it?" he asked.

"Take a look at the papers and see for yourself," Ben suggested.

"Maybe you'd better just tell me. Use Destiny's favorite tactic and sugarcoat it."

Ben grinned. "Can't be done this time. It's all there in black and white. She's obviously taken this assignment to heart. She's going after Harcourt with a vengeance."

Richard gave the papers a wary glance. "Oh, God, not in the media. Please tell me she is not attacking him in the London press."

"Not the way you mean," Ben reassured him. "She's got more class than that. And this is definitely all about business."

Richard reached gingerly for the first paper and spread it open on his desk. It didn't take long to find the full-page ad heralding the opening salvo from Harcourt, a slashing of prices on bestsellers.

"I suppose it could have been worse," he muttered. "I'd expected something like this. I knew he wouldn't take our acquisition of Jameson's lying down. If that little store turns out to be a nuisance or a distraction, we can get rid of it."

"Then you'll be happy to know that Destiny's not sitting back and taking it lying down, either," Ben said cheerfully.

Richard opened the second London paper and found the full-page ad for Jameson's, "Now offering tea in elegant surroundings while you browse."

"She's gone after his tea business," he said weakly. "That's the heart and soul of his company, aside from books. He'll bury us. What was she thinking? She's only tossing fuel on the fire."

"I imagine she was thinking that she couldn't let him get the better of her," Ben suggested. "You have to admire her gumption. She's a lot like you in that regard. She doesn't like anyone getting the better of her."

"You admire her," Richard said grimly. "I'm going over there to strangle her."

"No, you're not," Ben said fiercely. "You gave her this assignment—"

Richard cut him off. "Unwillingly," he reminded his brother.

"Nevertheless, Destiny's there and she's in charge. You can't second-guess her at every turn."

"I most certainly can," Richard said, then sighed. Ben was right. Even if she weren't his aunt, he couldn't do that to her. It would destroy company morale, undermine her and give Harcourt way too much satisfaction. He had to let this play itself out.

"I need a drink," he told his brother.

"Let's go," Ben said at once. "But I promised Melanie I'd have you home in time for dinner."

"You saw her before coming here?"

"Who did you think gave me the London papers?"

"Why the hell didn't she give them to me herself?" Richard grumbled.

"I believe that was in the interest of marital harmony. She doesn't care if you shoot the messenger as long as it's me."

"Am I that predictable?" Richard asked.

"And then some," Ben told him. "But we love you, anyway."

Richard sighed. It wasn't much comfort.

On Christmas Eve Destiny stayed on at the office long after everyone else had gone home to celebrate the start of the holidays with their families. Even Chester had taken off to visit friends in Devon for a week, and Miriam had flown back home to see her son after assuring herself that Destiny would be all right on her own.

And she was. She was alone with her sales reports, eager to see how her strategy had paid off.

The figures weren't bad. Sales were definitely up over a year ago, even without today's last-minute purchases figured in. The tea strategy had worked. The manager at Jameson's told her that the customers were anxious that the experiment continue after the New Year and perhaps be expanded to include some sort of food service, as well.

"And newspapers for the customers to read, while they linger over tea," Jillian had suggested. "It will be a place for people who love books to gather and to meet one another. I think we'll do a brisk trade with single young professionals who don't like hanging about in pubs. I've been thinking of a series of events, as well. We could do author signings, but I'd like to offer more than that—speakers, perhaps."

Destiny had promised to consider the idea and to discuss it further after the holidays. She would have to move cautiously. As Chester had reminded her, Jameson's was a new acquisition and a relatively unimportant one. She couldn't devote too many resources to it, even if its competition with H&S Books did make it more valuable in her mind. There were a dozen other fires that needed to be put out to get the European division onto solid ground, and she needed to start paying attention to them. She'd asked for reports from all of her key managers and anticipated that they would make dull reading for quiet holiday afternoons. The stack had been sent over by courier this morning and was awaiting her in her apartment.

In the meantime, though, not every hour of the week that stretched ahead of her needed to be devoted to work. She intended to use at least some of that free time to refurnish her dreadful apartment and make it her own. Browsing for a few paintings and a new sofa would fill some of the empty hours. Once the Christmas decorations came down, she wanted the dreary fabrics replaced by bright chintz and airy draperies that would let in the rare London sunlight.

She'd heard nothing from William since they'd had breakfast. He was probably somewhere licking his wounds. Or perhaps off visiting some country estate with a houseful of friends. She tried not to be envious, but she couldn't deny that a part of her wished she'd had time to acquire her own circle of friends here.

That would come, though, she told herself briskly, impatient with herself for displaying so much as a hint of self-pity given the richness of her life.

Tonight she would have a lovely dinner, a glass or two of an excellent Bordeaux, then sit quietly in front of the fire and savor this time on her own. Tomorrow there would be calls home and presents to open, followed by an excellent holiday feast already delivered by the same caterer who'd done her party. And there were stacks of new books she'd been dying to read. She would be alone, but not lonely.

It had been a long time since she'd been so completely and totally on her own. Since before she'd met William, in fact, and even then she'd been surrounded by friends in Provence, an eclectic mix of visiting artists and writers, as well as the locals who'd befriended her.

Back then, if she'd faced the prospect of more than a few days alone, she would have packed her bags and taken off for some livelier setting, sometimes Paris, sometimes London or even the casinos of Monte Carlo. She'd been a gadabout with few responsibilities and boundless energy. There was always a house party somewhere where she would be welcome.

Once William had come along, though, she'd settled into a kind of domestic bliss. They'd seldom traveled except to Paris, content to spend their days with long walks, companionable meals, an occasional concert and impromptu gatherings of friends. He'd filled not only her heart, but every waking hour of her day.

For a time, she'd thought of what they had as an informal marriage. Perhaps if they'd ever formalized it and taken the vows, they wouldn't have been so quick to throw it all away when the tragedy back home had struck.

Ah, well, water long since under the bridge, she concluded. There was no point in dawdling in her office on Christmas Eve, wondering if they could have changed what happened.

She gathered up her things, wrapped herself snugly in her cashmere coat and bright red muffler, then struck out for home, hoping the walk would chase away the last of her ridiculous blues.

The night was clear with stars shining and a waning slip of a moon. The air was crisp and invigorating, rather than damp, as she joined a parade of weary last-minute shoppers, laden down with packages.

Seeing them, she imagined the frantic rush back home, where none of her nephews ever gave a thought to presents until the last possible second. They were probably desperately fighting their way through the crowded aisles of Alexandria's boutiques at this very moment. Later they'd be haphazardly slapping paper, tape, tags and ribbon on the purchases, which despite being bought in haste, were always exactly right.

Missing that scene—missing them—she went into her flat and straight to her phone, only to find the message light blinking.

"Destiny, it's William," the first message began. "I'll try to catch you later."

And then, "Destiny, it's me again. Perhaps you're out for the evening, so I'll wish you a happy Christmas and speak to you tomorrow."

Hearing his voice, she sat down, her knees suddenly weak. Blast it all, how could the mere sound of his voice still get to her all these years later? She couldn't possibly still be in love with him, could she?

No, she told herself emphatically. Absolutely not. It was impossible. He was the sworn enemy now. Even if her heart wavered, there was Richard to think of and the company. She couldn't betray either one by getting entangled with a man who was a threat to them.

And yet, rather than calling home as she'd intended, she played the messages one more time, then went and crawled into her bed and fell asleep, knowing that tonight she would dream of the way they'd once been when life had been far simpler and love was all that mattered.

8

William had his solitary cup of strong tea, a boiled egg and toast on Christmas morning. There was a stack of unopened presents under a tree in his living room, but he had no particular interest in determining their contents. The only gift he truly cared about was being delivered right about now. The piece of jewelry hadn't been outrageously expensive, but he'd known that anything more would be rejected out of hand. This, however, Destiny might accept, might wear and think of him.

It was a small artist's palette made of gold. The colors on it were chips of jewels—a patch of emerald, a tiny ruby, a bit of sapphire, and a slash of rare yellow diamond. The moment he'd seen it, he'd known it was meant for Destiny. He'd been anxiously awaiting the right moment to give it to her.

Now that he'd sent it over by courier, though, he was having second thoughts. What if she'd really meant it when she'd said her painting no longer mattered to her? What if he was trying to remind her of a time she truly did prefer to forget? After all, she was here as a prominent businesswoman now. Clearly times had changed.

Even so, he found it difficult to accept that she could have tossed aside something that had once been so intrinsic to her being. He'd been counting on that when he'd chosen the pin. To him their past would be forever linked to her paintings, to the aroma of oils on her palette and the scent of turpentine cleaning her brushes. It saddened him to think that she'd given it all up, had begun to think of it as an indulgence rather than a life-affirming passion. He wanted her to see it that way again.

In fact, in some odd way, he was hoping that if he could coax her back to art, he could also persuade her to come back into his life. He'd even managed to convince himself it wasn't a fool's errand. He'd seen a spark in her eyes at her party and again at their breakfast a few days later that hinted that she was still the same lively, adventurous woman he had known. Of course, there was always the chance that the spark in her eyes had to do with their business competition and had nothing to do with him. She'd felt victorious over that tea business, no question about it.

Whichever it was, he hadn't been deceived by her generally cool demeanor into believing that the old Destiny was gone forever. He wanted her back and he intended to get her, making use of fair means or foul to do it. The present was just the beginning of the campaign.

He calculated the time it would take for the courier to reach her flat, then watched the clock nervously as the minutes ticked by. Was she opening it now? Was her face alight with pleasure? Or had she merely opened the card, seen his name and tossed the gift aside unopened?

Dammit, why hadn't he taken it to her himself and avoided all this damnable waiting? He was no good at waiting. He certainly hadn't demonstrated any patience when they'd met. He'd followed her to Provence after that first night and had never left. Now he was leaving things to chance. He'd made that mistake once before and look at the years it had cost him.

He was about to dress and head on over to her flat when his phone rang. His voice was gruff, filled with irritation when he grabbed the receiver. "Yes?"

"Merry Christmas, William, and thank you."

At the sound of Destiny's soft, musical voice, his impatience died. "You like the brooch?"

"You knew I would. You always gave the most thoughtful gifts."

"Did I? I was afraid I might have lost the knack for it where you're concerned. You said the other night that you rarely paint these days."

"I do when I have the time and only for myself. My nephew Ben is the painter in the family. He's better than I ever was. He's become quite a critical success."

"I always thought your paintings were wonderful."

She laughed. "Who's revising history now? You thought they were too saccharine and had no hesitation at all about saying so."

William groaned. "You'll never forget how I insulted you on the night we met, will you?"

"Obviously it didn't crush me. I fell in love with you, anyway."

His heart stumbled. "Yes, you did. And I with you."

Destiny cleared her throat. "Yes, well, that was a long time ago. We're older and more sensible now."

"Older certainly," he agreed. "But more sensible? I hope not. I'd like to think there are a few madcap adventures ahead of us yet."

Silence fell. Destiny, never without words, seemed to be speechless at the suggestion he was looking ahead into the future.

"Will you have Christmas dinner with me?" he asked, pressing this tiny advantage. "Or have you been deluged with invitations?"

"There's a pile of them on the hall table," she said, then added, "but I turned them down."

"Oh?"

"I wanted a quiet day to myself."

"That doesn't sound like you."

"I've changed, William. Settled a bit. We all do."

"Not everything changes. I'm sure there's an impetuous streak still buried inside you. Be brave and have dinner with me. I'll cook here. You can come whenever you're ready. No need to dress up. We can talk about old times."

"I think that's precisely the topic we should avoid," she said.

"Then we'll talk about whatever you like—the weather, American football, business."

She laughed at that. "I think business is another of those topics that ought to remain off-limits."

"You don't trust me?"

"With good reason," she replied tartly.

"Then there will be no talk of business," he said readily. "You can brag all about your nephews, instead. Bring pictures, whole albums, in fact."

"Be careful what you wish for," she warned.

"No need. I promise you won't bore me."

"And what will you tell me about?" she inquired. "All the women in your life?"

It was his turn to laugh. "Only if you insist, since I'm afraid it would make a rather boring tale."

"I doubt that."

"Then I'll tell you everything and you can decide for yourself whether or not my life has been dull without you in it. Will you come, Destiny? It's just two old friends sharing a holiday. No one can make too much of that."

"And your family?"

"All gone now. You've nothing to fear. Not even a ghost."

Again there was silence, and he thought for sure she was going to turn him down.

Then at last she said, "Will three o'clock be all right?"

He bit back a sigh of relief. "Three will be perfect."

"Don't go to any trouble. I'm not expecting a feast. Tea and sandwiches will do."

"It's Christmas, Destiny. I think can do better than that. Let me surprise you by demonstrating how domesticated I've become."

In fact, if he had his way, there would be many surprises before the day was done.

She didn't trust him. She *couldn't* trust him. Destiny repeated that refrain to herself on the taxi ride to William's house on Cavendish Square. It had been years since she'd been there, but she remembered it well, remembered the oppressive sense of family history she'd felt walking through the wrought-iron gates and up the wide, impressive steps to the double front doors with their gleaming brass lion's head knockers. It had made the long history of the Carltons in their lavish town house in Alexandria, Virginia, pale by comparison.

Inside, William's family home had been filled with dark, forbidding portraits of past generations, as well as heirlooms that were both priceless and ugly, far too massive for the small rooms. She'd hated it on sight and wondered how anyone could survive in such dreary surroundings, much less cultivate any liveliness or sense of humor. That William had thrived and prospered there and turned into a man of wit and intelligence with a zest for life made him seem all the more remarkable.

Destiny lifted the heavy knocker, then let it fall. A doomsday knell? she wondered.

William was there in an instant, as if he had been waiting nearby. When he threw the door open, the first thing she was struck by was the unexpected light pouring through the foyer. The heavy tapestries that had hung on the walls were gone, replaced by paint in a pale shade of blue with white trim. The ugly portraits were gone, as well. In fact, over a delicate antique table hung one of her own paintings…that poppy field in Provence that had always enchanted her in the ever-changing light, the field he'd sought to remind her of with his bouquet a few days earlier.

Inexplicably, Destiny's eyes stung with tears. She couldn't be sure if they were for that carefree, magical time in her life, or for the hint of sentimentality the painting's presence suggested. She quickly busied herself with removing her coat so that William wouldn't see how shaken she was. She was totally composed by the time she met his gaze.

"You've made changes," she said, understating the obvious.

"I think every home should have a good shaking up every century or two, don't you?"

She smiled. "At the very least."

"Are you starving? Would you like to eat right away or would you care for a glass of wine first?"

"Wine would be nice." It would steady her nerves, which were more jangled than they'd been in years. All the self-confidence she'd gained over the last two decades seemed to have vanished, leaving her feeling like the awkward, shy girl she'd been before she'd learned to mask it with brazenness.

"You know the way to the drawing room," he said, gesturing down the long hall. "Right through there. I'll fetch a bottle and be right with you."

There were more surprises in the drawing room, at one time the dreariest of places. Now another of her paintings hung over the mantel. This one had come from the gallery on the Left Bank, the one where they'd met. Destiny recalled packing it up and sending it to Violetta just before she'd gone back to the States for her brother's funeral. It had been the last one she'd painted in France.

It wasn't one of her favorites and she couldn't imagine that it was to William's taste. She'd been experimenting with a still life, playing around with the bolder strokes of van Gogh just to see how it felt. The result had been vivid splashes of color, but little more. Oddly enough, it seemed to suit this room, which had been redecorated in the same bold colors. The heavy drapes she remembered had been stripped away and light poured through the tall, mullioned glass windows. With a fire in the grate, it was a welcoming room now, and the small Christmas tree in the corner with its multicolored lights gave it an even more festive air.

When William returned and caught her staring at her own painting, he gave her a vaguely chagrined shrug. "It was a sentimental purchase. I bought it when I began to miss you, when I realized you were never coming back, that our time together was truly over. I bought it to remind myself of all the color that had gone out of my life the day you left."

Destiny felt the tears well up again. She hadn't expected the sentiment, the open display of vulnerability. "William, you shouldn't say things like that."

"Why not? I'm being honest here. I'm baring my soul. Some would say it's past time I did that."

Was it belated honesty or was he cleverly trying to manipulate her? She wished she could be sure. For all she knew, he'd acquired the paintings only after learning she was on her way to London, a gesture meant to impress her. But, despite all the anguish he'd caused her years ago, despite the more recent attacks on her family, some traitorous part of her wanted to believe in him.

"If you missed me so dreadfully, why didn't you get in touch with me?" she challenged. "You knew where I was. You called often enough at the beginning. And then, nothing."

"It took a while, but I finally understood that you had made a choice, one that didn't include me."

She met his gaze, saw with some surprise the hurt in his eyes. She hadn't intended to be led down this particular path, but she owed him the truth. "You always seemed so content with the way things turned out. I thought our time was simply over for you."

"It's never been over, not for me," he said quietly.

"Oh, William, didn't you understand that I would have made room for you, if only you'd asked?"

"How could I? I always thought you were so wise. I imagined you were doing what you thought was best."

"I was, for Richard, Mack and Ben, but not for me." She looked away because the raw emotion in his eyes made her feel guilty for something that had never been her fault, not entirely, anyway. Half to herself, she added, "And then, in time, it became what was best for me, too. They brought so much into my life, William, things I'd never expected, small joys at first, then unimaginable satisfaction. I was good at motherhood."

"Of course you were," he said, as if there had never been a doubt about it.

Destiny laughed and the moment was broken. "If only I had shared your confidence. For such frightened young boys, they scared me to death when I first arrived, especially Richard with his stoic determination to become the man of the family."

"Tell me about them," he said with an eagerness that caught her off guard.

"Are you sure you know what you're asking? I could talk about them all day and into the night. They're very accomplished young men."

"I have time. And I meant what I said on the phone, I would love to see pictures."

"We'll save those for another time, I think." Then she told him about how it had been when she'd gone back to Virginia. She told him about the three terrified, lost boys she had found on her return home, about the struggles to adjust to an entirely new way of life for all of them, about the mistakes she'd made trying to do what she thought her brother would have wanted, rather than what her heart told her was in their best interests.

"Eventually we settled for something more in the middle, a path that included duty and responsibilities, as well as quite a lot of spontaneous fun. In the end, we all seem to have survived," she said with pride and not a small amount of amazement.

"And what now, Destiny? Now that they're grown, what will you do?"

"Isn't that obvious? I'm here with the rather huge task of running our European division."

He gave her a knowing look. "Then you've developed a head for business."

She shrugged off the vaguely insulting remark. Once it had been true, she'd had no inclination toward business at all. "I'm smart enough to know when someone is making a concerted effort to destroy us."

"And to foil those efforts?"

She leveled a steady look straight into his eyes. "Yes, absolutely. I think you've already seen a glimmer of just how determined and competitive I can be."

He nodded, unsuccessfully trying to hide the grin tugging at his lips. "Good. Then our cards are on the table."

"I'd say so."

He lifted his glass of wine. "May the better man—"

"Or woman," she corrected.

"Indeed. May the better man—or woman—win."

Destiny studied the unnerving glint in his eyes and had a sudden flash of insight. Despite what he'd have her think, despite the very aggressive forays into Carlton Industries' business, it was entirely possible that she and William weren't after the same stakes, after all. How absolutely fascinating.

"Where the devil can she be?" Richard grumbled after hanging up the phone. It was the fifth time he'd tried to reach Destiny on Christmas Day, only to get her damnable answering machine, instead. He could have sworn she'd told him she intended to spend a quiet day on her own.

"Have you ever known Destiny not to manage some sort of holiday celebration wherever she is?" Ben remarked. "Remember the time we got caught in a blizzard after going off on impulse on Christmas Eve to see the tree at Rockefeller Plaza in New York? Where did we wind up?"

"Somewhere off the New Jersey Turnpike," Mack said.

Richard groaned. "In what had to be the worst dive with the worst food ever set on a table."

"But it had a tree," Ben remembered. "And a packed house. By the time the storm ended the next morning, we had dozens of new friends and had spent the whole night singing Christmas carols. Destiny absolutely refused to let us feel sorry for ourselves that our presents were back home. She'd even charmed that awful owner into letting her make pancakes, so the entire crowd had an edible Christmas breakfast."

"Any chance that she's off somewhere making the holiday cheery for the downtrodden this year?" Richard asked without much hope.

"No, I suspect she's celebrating with friends," Melanie said.

"Or one friend in particular," Kathleen chimed in.

"Bite your tongue," Richard groused. "I wish all of you would stop acting as if she's off on some romantic lark over there. Am I the only one who considers Harcourt to be the enemy?"

"Yes," his sisters-in-law said at once.

His wife grinned at him. "Sorry. I'm with them."

Richard turned to his brothers. "It's been days since I've been able to reach her. If I don't get her on the next try, I swear to you that I'm going over there to see for myself what's going on."

"No, you're not," Melanie said just as emphatically. "At least not right away."

"Why the hell not?"

"Because for the foreseeable future, you are a stay-at-home dad," Melanie declared. "You promised that this holiday season you were spending time with your family."

He stared at her blankly. "Isn't that what I'm doing today?"

"*Season* was the operative word there," Melanie said. "That's one whole week, minimum. Don't even think about trying to get out of it."

He heard the finality in her voice and knew that she was perfectly capable of making his life hell if he tried to renege on some promise he didn't even remember making. She'd probably wheedled it out of him when he was in the middle of a conference call and not paying attention.

Suddenly his mood brightened. "We could all go to London," he suggested.

"Not a snowball's chance in hell," Mack said. "In case you've forgotten, my football team is heading for the play-offs. None of you are going anywhere unless you're back in time for the games."

"Play-offs?" Ben asked. "I have a dim recollection of what those are. It's been a while, though, hasn't it? Are they important?"

"Go to hell," Mack retorted. "We're there now. That's all that matters."

Resigned to staying put to pacify his wife and support his brother, Richard looked at his watched and calculated that it was nearly 10:00 p.m. in London. "I'm calling again," he announced. "If she's not there by now, I'm calling Harcourt."

Beth chuckled.

"What so damn funny about that?" Richard asked.

"I was just picturing Destiny's expression if she does happen to be there when you call to check up on her," she said, her grin spreading.

"Oh, yes," Mack said. "I can see it, too. Why don't you do it, bro? Call Harcourt."

Richard regarded them all sourly. "Don't think I won't," he muttered even as he dialed Destiny's London flat.

When she picked up on the second ring, sounding perfectly healthy and cheerful, he snapped irritably, "Where the hell have you been?"

Silence greeted him.

Richard finally took a deep breath. "Sorry. I've been trying to reach you for hours. I was worried."

"That's much better," Destiny said happily. "Merry Christmas, darling. Is everyone there?"

"We're all here," Richard confirmed, relieved to

hear her in such good spirits and forcing himself to ignore the nagging suspicion he had about why she was so cheerful. "We miss you, though."

"Oh, and I miss all of you. Thank you so much for the lovely presents. You all went overboard."

He laughed at that. "You can thank Melanie, Beth and Kathleen for those gifts. The ones from Mack, Ben and me didn't get in the mail until yesterday."

"Just last night I was imagining all three of you rushing around with your last-minute shopping," she said, a surprising hitch in her voice.

"Destiny, are you okay?" he asked, alarmed.

"Fine, darling," she said with a faint sniff. "Sorry. I suppose I'm just a little emotional. It's been years and years since we haven't been together for the holidays."

"Since we were boys," Richard said quietly. "I wish you'd waited to go to London."

"Right this instant, so do I," she said. "But I am having a wonderful time. The work is a real challenge. I have so many plans we need to discuss, but we'll save all that till after the first of the year. We're both on holiday now, unless you've reneged on your promise to Melanie."

"You know about that, too?"

"Of course. She told me herself when we spoke the other day."

"You've talked to my wife?" he asked, shooting a fierce look in Melanie's direction. She merely shrugged, her expression totally innocent.

"It's not a crime, is it?" Destiny asked lightly.

"No, of course not. You never did say how you spent your Christmas," he said.

"I had a lovely dinner with a friend," she said.

"You're being evasive," Richard accused. "That can only mean one thing."

"Oh?"

"Was Harcourt the friend?" he asked.

"If you must know, yes."

"Dammit, Destiny! I will not allow you to consort with the enemy."

Behind him he heard a chorus of "uh-ohs." In fact, there was an immediate warning din in his head, as well.

"I beg your pardon," Destiny said icily.

He ignored his family, the warning clamor in his head and her tone. "I mean it," he said stubbornly. "The man is not to be trusted."

"I didn't say I trusted him. I said I had Christmas dinner with him."

"Did you at least get him to back off the Fortnum Travel acquisition?"

"The subject never came up," she told him.

"Why the hell not?"

"Because it's Christmas, in case you've forgotten. Now, I think you'd better let me speak to the others. Perhaps they're in a better frame of mind."

Richard bit back the retort that was on the tip of his tongue. "Merry Christmas, Destiny. I do love you, you know."

"I know," she said softly.

Richard turned and handed the phone to Mack, then crossed the room to stare out the window. Melanie came up behind him and put her arms around him. "She's an intelligent woman, Richard. Stop worrying. I'm sure she knows what she's doing."

"How can she? If she was in love with the man once,

then she's vulnerable to him. She could get her heart broken if she discovers he's only using her."

"You're forgetting something. She's also a Carlton, and nothing is more important to her than family loyalty. He tried to hurt you and the company, Richard. She won't forget that. Her guard is up. You've told her how important this travel company deal is to you, right?"

"Yes."

"Then you have nothing to worry about."

"I suppose."

Melanie gave him an impatient shake. "You *know*," she said emphatically. "Now, come along and let's get dinner on the table before it's all ruined. I want you well fed and strong for tomorrow."

He gave her a questioning look. "What's happening tomorrow?"

"The holiday sales," she said cheerfully. "We'll need to be there early."

"Oh, no." He trailed behind her to the kitchen to help get dinner on the table. "No sales," he added emphatically in case she'd missed his point. "Not a chance. There is not enough money on earth to get me into a store tomorrow."

She stopped in her tracks, turned and stood on tiptoe to kiss him, rather thoroughly, in fact. He was a bit dazed when she finally pulled away.

"No fair," he muttered, then gave her an indulgent look. The woman could twist him around her finger and she knew it. She was watching him expectantly. "Okay, okay. What the hell time do we have to go?"

"Just think of it as another workday," she told him

cheerfully. "I'll get you up around five-thirty. You'll need time for a hearty breakfast."

"I suppose this is one more thing I can thank Destiny for," he grumbled. "She's usually the one you go with, isn't she?"

"But having you along will be so much better," Melanie told him.

He gave her a doubtful look. "Why is that?"

"You're bigger and stronger."

"And that's an advantage?"

"Darn straight. Some of these people are crazy. Besides, you'll be able to carry more packages."

"Why do we even bother shopping before Christmas, if the sales are so much better afterward?"

"Trust me, if you and your brothers get much more last minute with your shopping, you will be buying things after Christmas." She gave him a considering look. "I think next year we'll work on that."

"Haven't you reformed me enough already?"

She patted his cheek. "Oh, sweetie, please. I've barely gotten started."

To his dismay, Richard was pretty sure she meant it.

9

The morning after Christmas, Destiny was still indignant that Richard had ordered her to stop seeing William. How dare he? Did he think she was some foolish girl who couldn't be trusted to keep corporate secrets? Nobody knew better than she did what was at stake. The fate of the entire European division, to say nothing of her own self-respect, hinged on her making a success of this assignment. She wasn't going to mess that up over a bit of nostalgia for what had once been. Perhaps her nephew would finally believe her once she pulled off this Fortnum Travel acquisition.

Fortnum was a relatively small, but very prestigious, travel agency specializing in luxury tours and cruises. With most major airlines and hotels offering online ticketing these days, Fortnum had found a niche for itself that kept its customers coming in and its bottom line solid. It also promised to provide Carlton Industries with an in-house travel division to book the extensive amounts of travel its executives were required to do. Richard really wanted this company, and Destiny intended to see that he got it.

She absentmindedly fingered the pin on her sweater as if it were a talisman. But was it lucky? Or had accepting it been the first step down a dangerous slope, after all? And if so, had sharing Christmas dinner been the second? Was she even now in danger of losing her footing and sliding straight into disaster, as Richard believed? If only she could know for certain.

No, she thought fiercely, she knew exactly what she was doing. And, more important, she was confident she could pull it off. William was the one in danger of hitting an icy patch that would put him—and his company—in jeopardy. She intended to use every occasion she spent with him trying to learn his corporate plans so she could counter them effectively. There would be surprises aplenty for him by the time she taught him what it felt like to be on the receiving end of betrayal.

When her phone rang, she almost ignored it. She wasn't in the mood for more of Richard's nagging and that's what any call home was likely to be. She knew him well enough to know that he hadn't really given up after her outburst the day before.

Another insistent ring and she finally braced herself and picked up the receiver. "Hello," she said cautiously.

"Destiny?"

Relief nearly overwhelmed her at the sound of William's voice, when quite the opposite should have happened. He was second on the list of people she really didn't want to speak to this morning. She was feeling unsettled and vulnerable and yes, dammit, lonely. The novelty of having time to herself had already worn off.

"William," she said a little too cheerily as guilt over her happiness immediately kicked in. "You're up bright and early."

"A habit I picked up years ago," he said quietly.

There was no need to add a comment about where or when. Those simple words were enough to remind her of how many early mornings they'd spent watching the first rays of sun spill into their bedroom, wrapped in each other's arms and half asleep from making love.

"Yes, I know," she said softly, then caught herself and determinedly sought to achieve a less intimate connection. "Anyone in business knows that dawn is the best time to get anything done at home or at work. Once the phones start, control of the day shifts to other people."

He laughed, clearly understanding why she'd so deftly turned the topic to something less personal and risky. "So, my dear, what are you up to this morning, then? Planning your takeover of my company?"

"I am giving that some thought," she told him. "When I have my strategy formulated, you'll be the first to know. I believe in giving fair warning."

This time his laugh wasn't quite so lighthearted. "Yes, I imagine you would. You always believed life should be fair, didn't you?"

"Yes, I did," she admitted. "Even after I'd learned the bitter lesson that it usually wasn't."

"Because of your brother's and sister-in-law's deaths," he said.

"And you," she reminded him. "Let's not forget about your role in my awakening to reality."

"We talked about that, Destiny. I thought we'd decided that we both shared some of the blame for not adequately communicating in the days and weeks after the tragedy struck your family."

"But it was so much easier when I could lay all the

blame at your feet," she said plaintively. Then there had been no conflicting feelings churning inside her to keep her safely immune to him.

He laughed. "Yes, I imagine it was. You never liked being in the wrong. You certainly never liked admitting to it. In fact, you always went to great lengths to avoid acknowledging a mistake."

"Few people like admitting they've made a miscalculation about something important."

"And some of us wait entirely too long," he said candidly. "But I'm admitting it now, Destiny. I was wrong back then. I was stupid and stubborn and far too proud. I won't make that mistake with you ever again."

Her heart flipped over, the wall around it cracking just a bit in the process. Because she recognized the danger in that, she said briskly, "I really must go, William. I have things to do."

"Then you're too busy for a drive in the country?"

It was tempting, and because of that, she knew she must decline. "I'm afraid so. Another time, perhaps."

"I'll count on it, Destiny. We'll do it before the start of the New Year."

"Yes," she said, happy enough for the delay. It would give her time to shore up her defenses, as well as time to formulate a long string of satisfactory excuses that wouldn't suggest for a second that she was running scared.

In the meantime, she needed to do some thoughtful reevaluation of her plan to keep the enemy so close. Much as she hated to admit it—William had been on the mark about her aversion to making any such admission—she could see now that Richard was right. She'd been setting herself up—if not the company—for disaster.

With the whole day stretching ahead of her and way too many uncomfortable thoughts tumbling around in her mind, Destiny decided it was time to do a little firsthand market research. She would pay a visit to the nearest H&S Books and then, perhaps, stop for afternoon tea at one of the Harcourt Tea Shoppes, which could generally be found in the same neighborhood. There was nothing like a little snooping to get her juices flowing.

The original H&S Books was on Charing Cross Road. Since the morning fog had yet to burn off and she had no desire to get lost in the pea-soup atmosphere, she found a taxi to take her. Deposited at the curb a half-hour later, she paid the fare, then stood on the sidewalk to study the bright window display. It featured piles of books, in no discernable arrangement. There was nothing cohesive about it, no theme. Cookbooks were jammed up against children's storybooks. Novels had been stacked next to political nonfiction. The only qualification for being granted such a prime showcase seemed to be quantity. There were no fewer than a dozen copies of any of the books displayed.

Inside, the aisles were wide, the bookcases well lit, but the displays practically begged for a knowledgeable person to make sense of them. In fact, Destiny found herself so annoyed at being unable to determine where to look for any particular genre, had she been the average busy customer, she would have left in dismay. Perhaps some of the confusion could be blamed on post-holiday chaos, but she doubted it. It looked more as if the books had never been properly sorted and displayed in the first place.

She would have left then, content that Jameson's could make better sense of its stock than H&S Books ever would, but her eye was suddenly drawn to an art book of paintings featuring scenes from Provence.

She plucked the book from the shelf and stood leafing through it. When she came upon a scene of an outdoor café, one she'd been to many times herself, she paused, suddenly lost in memories once more.

Provence, 1982

The young woman in the café was blatantly flirting with William. In fact, she'd been trying to make eye contact ever since he and Destiny had sat down. It was beginning to get on Destiny's nerves. She'd never thought of herself as a possessive woman, but apparently she was. It was quite a rude awakening to discover she was capable of pea-green jealousy.

"You needn't shoot daggers at her," William said, clearly amused by her reaction.

"And why shouldn't I?" she groused defensively. "Can't she see you're taken?"

"If you're confident that I am taken," he said mildly, "then what is it you're afraid of?"

She sipped her wine and thought about that. What was she worrying about? In the time they'd been together, William had never so much as glanced at another woman with interest. He'd given her no reason whatsoever to doubt him. If he'd done nothing to earn her distrust, then it must have something to do with her and her own self-doubts. It was an embarrassing thing to have to admit, so she didn't.

"Perhaps I'm merely sending up warning flares," she said. "I can't have you or some indiscreet stranger thinking I won't mind if you stray."

His smile spread. "Really?"

Something in his tone caught her attention and suddenly she was riveted on William's face, the woman forgotten. "You seem surprised."

"I am. It's the closest you've ever come to admitting your feelings for me."

She stared at him, truly shocked. "Don't be absurd. I tell you all the time how I feel."

"You do," he agreed. "You tell me how you feel about the weather. About local politics. About the latest gallery showing. Not about what's in your heart."

"But I've told you I love you," she argued. "I've said the words."

"In passing, yes, as if they meant no more than 'how are you?' or 'what's the weather like?'"

The accusation stung, but she couldn't immediately deny it. She did tend to say the words casually, dropping them in at the least intimate moments. As well, she scattered them thoughtlessly around with her friends.

"Love you. Bye," was her ready line whenever she ended a phone call, whether to family, a neighbor or the friendly owner of their favorite restaurant. No wonder William considered the words alone to have little meaning.

Filled with chagrin, she met his gaze. "I'm sorry. I never realized how it must appear to you. I never made it seem as if there was any distinction at all between you and the butcher."

He laughed then, breaking the somber mood. "Trust me, I know that I hold a different place in your heart than the butcher."

She grinned at him. "Not when he's offering a special on lamb chops. Then I truly do adore him."

"Adore, perhaps, but not love, Destiny. Not the kind of love I'm beginning to believe you feel for me."

"No, not that," she agreed, leaning forward and putting a hand on his cheek. "I'm sorry I'm so careless about your feelings. I suppose it's because I'm still scared that I've got this all wrong, that it's too good to be true."

"Even after all this time?"

"Even now," she confirmed.

"What will it take to convince you that I will never even notice another woman if you are in the room?"

"Time, I suppose."

"Then isn't it lucky that we have years and years ahead of us?" he said.

But they hadn't had years and years, of course, Destiny remembered as she closed the book and returned it to the shelf. They'd had barely another twelve months, as it had turned out.

She traced a finger along the spine of the book, tempted still to buy it, but filled with misgivings over the memories it was likely to dredge up.

"I'll buy it for you," William said quietly, coming up behind her. "I have a copy on my shelves, as well. The first time I saw it, I knew I had to have it."

Destiny didn't turn around. She didn't want him to

catch the flush of embarrassment in her cheeks over having been caught indulging in pure sentimentality.

"No, thanks. I was just browsing and noticed the title."

"Oh? It looked more as if you were lost in thought, perhaps remembering another place, another time."

She did face him then. "Please don't make anything of this. You'd be mistaken."

He nodded slowly and the spark in his eyes dimmed just a bit. "Were you here spying on the competition, then? Checking out our extensive inventory to see what Jameson's is missing?"

"I could spend all day and not know that," she said tartly. "You could use some organization in here, William. Not that I'm trying to tell you how to run your business, of course."

"Of course," he said solemnly, even as the corners of his mouth tilted up in a barely suppressed grin. "I know you would never dream of doing such a thing."

He gave her a knowing look. "Since you're in the neighborhood, would you like to come along with me for tea? There's a Harcourt Tea Shoppe in the next block."

Destiny feigned amazement. "Really? How perfectly lovely! As a matter of fact, I would love a cup of tea."

He laughed, obviously not buying the act. "I suspect you have the address jotted down on a paper in your purse," he chided. "And if I hadn't come along to invite you, you'd have gone there on your own."

She shrugged. "It does pay to know the competition."

"When it comes to books and tea, you're no competition for me, Destiny. Accept that, why don't you?"

"Perhaps we aren't," she conceded. "Not yet, anyway, but we will be, William. Make no mistake about that. It's one of the goals I've set for myself for the New Year. I promised you fair warning, so there it is."

"Then I'll be sure to keep my guard up."

He guided her out of the store, waving to the clerk behind the desk as they went. Something in the girl's expression made Destiny instantly suspicious.

"You knew I was in the store, didn't you? This wasn't a chance meeting at all."

"And if I did?"

"Did you give all of your clerks my photo like some sort of wanted poster and tell them to call you at once if I crossed the threshold?"

He laughed. "You don't worry me that much, Destiny. Not when it comes to business, anyway. When it comes to a few other areas of my life, you worry me quite a lot."

She studied him with a narrowed gaze. "Meaning?"

"Best not to go there," he said. "Not just yet, anyway. You're still skittish." He stopped in front of the tearoom. "We're here. Do you want to step back and get a first impression before we go inside?"

She gave him a sour look. "As a matter of fact, I do," she said, taking a good long look at the friendly facade, gilt lettering on the window and the well-nurtured pots of plants outside the doorway. They were evergreens now, lit with tiny white lights, but she imagined in summer those pots would be filled with colorful flowers. There was a bright blue-and-white awning over the window, as well, to give customers a place to wait in the rain for a passing taxi. All in all the effect was charming and cheerful.

"I like it," she admitted. "I'd want to come here often."

"Most of our customers are regulars," he said. "We make it a point to know them by name and preferences."

"That is the mark of an outstanding retailer, isn't it? It's all about excellent customer service."

"I always thought so," William agreed. "But in this day and age, it's becoming more and more of a rarity." He grinned at her. "Now, if you've had enough of a first impression, shall we go inside and have tea?"

"You're not absolutely terrified that I'll steal your list of suppliers?"

"Not in the slightest," he said easily. "I intend to steal your pen, if I catch you trying to take notes."

"And you think I don't have sufficient memory left to keep it all in my head?" she asked with a hint of indignation.

"I'm sure your memory is quite adequate," he soothed, his eyes twinkling. "I merely intend to keep it focused on other things."

"Such as?"

He bent and kissed her then, the touch of his lips so wonderfully familiar, so wickedly persuasive, that all thoughts of tea did, indeed, vanish.

He stood back eventually and studied her, then gave a little nod of satisfaction. "I think that accomplished what I set out to do," he said, his expression entirely too smug.

"Orange pekoe, Ceylon, Darjeeling," Destiny immediately recited. "English breakfast, Earl Grey."

William laughed. "Lucky guesses," he said easily. "No respectable tea shop would be without those."

Destiny grinned, despite herself. "You can't spend the whole time we're in here kissing me," she reminded him. "And I see the selections are posted in rather large lettering behind the counter. I won't even require my glasses."

"Don't tempt me to try to prove you wrong," he warned. "It seems like a fine idea to me, to say nothing of a rather clever strategy."

"I won't allow it," she said simply. "We can't have people all over London talking about us. How would it look if someone spotted us and spread the word that two business rivals were kissing like crazy in plain sight of God and everyone?"

"Perhaps it would look as if we'd finally come to our senses," William said.

Destiny stared at him, taken aback. And then she couldn't seem to stop herself from laughing. Perhaps it would at that.

"Sir, I know you told me not to call again about anything having to do with your aunt, but I felt I must," Chester said, his tone more dire than ever. "If I heard about this all the way in Devon, then who knows what's being said around London."

"Said about what?" Richard asked reluctantly. He knew that Chester was not a stupid man. If he was taking the risk of ignoring Richard's warning, then the news was bound to be upsetting.

"It's your aunt and Harcourt, sir. They've been seen about town together."

Richard bit back the desire to curse. "So?" he asked

mildly, not wanting to let on to Chester, of all people, how disconcerting he found the news.

"In what some might consider to be a compromising situation," Chester went on boldly.

"Are you certain this is something more than idle gossip?" Richard asked, almost terrified to hear just what Chester considered to be compromising.

"Absolutely, sir, or I wouldn't be calling. The person who called me saw the two of them together yesterday."

"Where?"

"In one of Harcourt's little tea emporiums."

"And they were together?" Richard asked. "They didn't just happen to bump into each other there?"

"There was a kiss that suggested they were very much together," Chester reported. "Quite steamy, if you know what I mean."

Richard knew exactly what he meant. "I'll deal with it," Richard said tightly.

"I hope I did the right thing by calling, Mr. Carlton."

"Yes," Richard said grimly. "In this instance, you did exactly the right thing."

After he'd hung up, Richard sat staring at the phone, trying to make himself pick it back up to call London and give Destiny the blistering lecture she deserved. Keeping the enemy close, indeed! She'd crossed a line, dammit! Pretty soon, she'd make herself the laughingstock of London, if people got the idea that a Carlton executive was quite literally sleeping with the enemy.

"What on earth is wrong?" Melanie asked, regarding him worriedly. "You look furious enough to commit murder."

"I am, but how the devil can I, when it's Destiny who deserves killing?"

"Uh-oh. Tell me what's happened."

Richard gave her the condensed version, which was really all he had, anyway.

"Leave it alone," Melanie advised.

He stared at her. "How am I supposed to do that?"

"By packing up the baby, getting in the car with me and going out to the farm to see Ben," she suggested.

"And letting him deal with Destiny?" he inquired hopefully.

"No, you idiot. Using that time to forget all about it."

"I can't do that," he said bleakly.

"Oh, yes, you can. If Destiny wants to kiss William or be kissed by William, there is not a blessed thing you can do to stop it. If you try, you'll only insult her and alienate her."

He considered his wife's advice. He knew she was right. Making a huge deal out of this would only make Destiny more determined than ever to follow whatever insane course she was on with Harcourt.

"You're absolutely certain that I have to let this go, pretend I never heard about it?"

"That's what I would do," she said flatly.

"And if she gets in over her head?"

"She'll figure that out and extricate herself. Give her a little credit, Richard. She did a pretty good job of managing to get you, Mack and Ben to adulthood, and she was flying by the seat of her pants then, too."

"I suppose."

She laughed and nudged him in the ribs with her elbow. "You *know*."

He pulled her onto his lap. "What would I do without you?"

"You'll never have to find out," she assured him.

"Do we have to go to Ben's?"

"I told him and Kathleen we'd be there," she said.

"Too bad."

She grinned. "Not as bad as you're thinking. I'd say we have at least an hour till our daughter wakes up from her nap."

Richard grinned. "Hooray for naps! Want to take one?"

Melanie gave him a wicked smile and took his hand, already heading for the stairs. "Not exactly."

He laughed. "I really do love the way you think."

Suddenly all thoughts of London, the European division and even Destiny and that snake Harcourt were the furthest things from his mind. To accomplish all that, he was pretty sure his wife had to be a magician. But then he'd known all along how remarkable she was. He was just beginning to see, though, how her clever talents could make all the stresses in his life miraculously vanish.

10

After the kiss, William had been all but certain it would be easy to persuade Destiny to spend New Year's Eve with him. In fact, he'd been counting on the occasion to remind her that they, too, could have a fresh beginning. But rather than accepting with the expected alacrity, she'd flatly turned him down. Several times, in fact.

She'd made no excuses, no apologies. She'd simply said no. He'd finally concluded it was precisely *because* of the kiss, a defensive reaction he hadn't anticipated at all. Years ago, she would never have been thrown off kilter by a kiss. He should have taken heart at that and counted himself lucky, but he was annoyed, instead.

It wasn't that he minded spending the evening without a companion. There were parties all over town where he'd be welcomed as an available man to balance out the numbers. Nor did he really object to being at home on his own. The point was that he wanted more than anything to start this new year with Destiny, the way he intended to finish it and every other year from here on out.

He sat around most of the morning mulling over his options. The only one that appealed to him was the one least likely to appeal to Destiny: him turning up on her doorstep uninvited. She would be furious, no question about it. Unless, of course, she wasn't even home. His ego was secure enough for him to believe, though, that if she wasn't with him, she wasn't going out with anyone.

So, perhaps there was a way, he finally decided after long and careful thought. As soon as the idea formed, he was on the phone making the arrangements. Heaven help him if it was all a wasted effort and she truly was spending the evening out, but he was convinced the gamble was worth the expense.

By eight he was dressed in his tuxedo. By eight-fifteen, he was outside her flat, ready for the first arrival, a florist laden down with bouquets of spring flowers. He'd had to move heaven and earth to find them and to get them delivered at this hour.

When the deliveryman came out of the building five minutes later, he gave William a nod. "She loved them. Took her by surprise, you did. I imagine it was worth the pretty penny you had to pay."

"Let's hope so," William said, knowing that the battle was far from over.

The musicians arrived next, a trio who'd come with flutes and an eclectic repertoire of Destiny's favorite Mozart sonatas and lively Irish tunes. He spoke to the singer, Ian, whom he'd known for a number of years, then sent them inside and waited. When they hadn't come scrambling right back out after fifteen minutes, he breathed his first sigh of relief. So far, at least, Destiny hadn't rejected anything out of hand. He took that as a promising sign.

Yet another delivery van pulled up then, ready with the five-course meal William had ordered from one of Carlton Industries' own restaurants. There were bottles of iced champagne, as well. He paid the driver and told him, "I'll take it from here."

This was going to be the tricky part, getting inside her apartment with limbs intact, rather than having the door slammed on his leg. He doubted she'd bother to call an ambulance.

Inside the building, he rode the elevator to her floor, then rolled the cart down the hall. He could hear the flutes playing inside and hoped she was being soothed by the concert. It might make the rest easier.

He set the food-service cart up outside her door, rang the bell, then stood just out of view and waited until the door finally opened. He heard her muted gasp when she saw the lavish display of sterling and crystal, as well as all the tempting covered dishes.

"You might as well come on in, William. I know you're out there lurking in the shadows somewhere," she said.

She was obviously trying hard to sound more resigned and annoyed than pleased. Even so, she hadn't entirely been able to mask her delight. At least one thing about her hadn't changed. She still loved surprises.

William stepped out of hiding, then had to bite his tongue at the sight of her. She was in her bathrobe, fuzzy slippers on her feet, her face devoid of makeup. It was testament to her maturity and self-confidence that she didn't look the least bit embarrassed to be caught at less than her best. Personally, this was the look he liked best, a bit rumpled and sexy and approachable. He'd had a hard time getting used to his once-carefree Destiny in the prim power suits she'd been wearing since her arrival in London.

"You look beautiful," he said.

"Ha!"

"You do," he insisted. "I always loved you in your nightclothes."

"And out of them," she murmured, even as color promptly flooded her cheeks. "Come on in and you can tell me what possessed you to do something this insane."

"It's not insane to want to surprise you, especially on New Year's Eve."

"Even after I'd repeatedly turned down your invitations?" she asked. "For all you knew, I could have had a hot date here tonight. It takes a certain amount of insanity to ignore the message, don't you think? Or wouldn't you have minded if I'd shared all this with another man?"

"I prefer to think of it as determination," he responded. "And, yes, I most definitely would have minded if you'd shared it with anyone other than me."

"Determination?" she echoed, obviously amused. "Yes, that makes perfect sense. It shows you in a better light."

He laughed. "Well, it's evident that you don't have a date lurking in the bedroom, so will you accept my company, after all?"

She met his gaze, indecision written all over her face. "Will you take me as I am?"

"The fuzzy slippers don't scare me," he said wryly.

"What were you doing before I interrupted your evening?"

"Listening to this lovely, unexpected concert," she told him.

"And before that?"

"I was curled up with a good book, if you must know. The days are long past when I felt the need to be out reveling till the wee hours of the morning on New Year's Eve."

He smiled at the obvious attempt to prove she was succumbing to middle-aged stuffiness. "That must be because there's no one around stimulating enough to keep you awake," he teased.

"And you intend to change that?"

"Absolutely."

"I'm not a girl any longer, William. I'm a mature woman. I don't have to be on the go constantly or surrounded by people to feel alive."

"Not people, Destiny. One person," he said lightly, holding up the champagne. "Would you like some?"

"One glass," she said, her expression filled with caution.

He lifted a brow. "Are you afraid I intend to ply you with champagne and steal corporate secrets?"

She shrugged. "It wouldn't be the first time."

Filled with a sudden surge of anger at the injustice of the accusation, William set the bottle down carefully. He waited for an entire minute, pretending to concentrate on the music, before he finally looked her in the eye. "You can't possibly believe that," he said quietly.

"Why can't I?" she retorted, her jaw set stubbornly. "It's true, isn't it? You used things you learned from me to hurt my family."

"That's absurd," he said furiously. "It's been years since we've even seen each other, Destiny, and how often did we ever discuss business back then? Beyond knowing that Carlton Industries was in your family, I knew nothing of its holdings then. Nor did you, for that matter."

She kept her gaze steady, obviously intent on not backing down even when confronted with the facts.

"Come on, Destiny, answer me," he insisted. "And be honest. Did we ever once lie awake nights while you poured out Carlton secrets? Who's revising history to suit them now?"

"We must have," she said, though her voice lacked conviction. "Otherwise you couldn't have pulled off half of the sneak attacks you've made on the company."

He stared at her, nearly struck dumb by the fact that she actually believed that she was somehow responsible for leaking information to him. "Have you been blaming yourself all this time for the actions I've taken in recent years against Carlton Industries? Is that what brought you charging over here?"

Her eyes flashed dangerously. "Yes, if you must know. The constant disasters in the European division are making people question my nephew's leadership. Since everything that's happened over here has been my fault because of my connection to you, it's up to me to make it right."

William had to fight the hysterical laughter that was bubbling up inside him. "Destiny, it wasn't like that. Not at all."

"Words, William. Just words. Your actions speak loudly enough to the contrary. You're simply not to be trusted. I must remember that."

He could see that she honestly believed what she was saying. "Okay, let's get to the bottom of this. I won't let you make yourself out as some sort of traitor," he said. "Sit down."

She sat primly on the edge of the sofa, her hands folded in her lap, her entire demeanor radiating skepticism. William sat next to her, close, but not so close as to make her more skittish than she already was.

"Now, look me in the eye," he commanded, and waited until she did. "Have you ever known me to lie to you?"

The answer was a long time coming, but Destiny was too honest to tell anything less than the truth, or at least the truth as she saw it. "No," she finally admitted. Her eyes flashed with barely banked anger as she added, "That only means I never caught you."

William choked back an exasperated retort. "I have *never* lied to you," he said emphatically. "And I never will."

"But you *have* attacked my family's business," she said. "You can hardly deny that."

"No," he agreed calmly. "I can't deny that. Do you know why I've done that?"

"Because you're a typically greedy and vicious businessman and you wanted to get back at me."

The accusation stung, but he could see how it would seem that way to her. "I understand why that would be your interpretation," he said.

She gave him a scathing look. "Is there any other?"

"Yes, as a matter of fact."

"Then, please, enlighten me."

"This had nothing at all to do with retaliation. I simply wanted to get your attention, Destiny. I wanted you mad enough to come over here and confront me. I wanted to get everything out in the open between us, to say all the things we should have said years ago and didn't."

She stared at him with openmouthed astonishment. "This was some sort of game? All of those bids were simply meant to get my attention?"

He nodded. "It's been a rather successful game, as it turns out."

The first hint of doubt flickered in her eyes. "Why should I believe you?"

"Because if you search your heart, you'll know I'm telling you the truth."

"Wouldn't it have been easier just to come to the States and see me?"

William shrugged. "Probably. And if I'd come to my senses years ago, that's what I would have done. Since I didn't, this seemed to make more sense."

"But why, William? Why did it even matter after all this time?"

Now it was his turn to look astonished. "I thought that was obvious."

"Not to me."

He hadn't intended to get into this yet. He'd wanted time to woo her, to show her how he felt, not just say the words. Unfortunately, it seemed he didn't have a choice, if he wasn't to derail his whole plan right here and now.

He looked her directly in the eyes and reached for her hands, holding them tightly so she couldn't immediately pull away. "Because I'm still in love with you, of course. Never stopped loving you, to be brutally honest about it."

Her mouth gaped. "You're still in love with me," she echoed weakly, then blinked as an odd flash of light lit the room. "What on earth was that?"

He nearly laughed at her astounded expression. "What?"

"That light."

"It was nothing, I'm sure. Now, stop trying to change the subject. You asked why I did everything I've done and I've told you. I love you," he repeated.

"But that's not possible," she said flatly.

"Of course it is," he said, annoyed.

"No, no, it isn't." She stared at him, obviously flustered. "I think you'd better go, William. Now."

He stared at her, but she was obviously serious. "You actually want me to leave now?"

"Yes."

"Why?"

"Because this is all wrong. You almost had me believing you, but then I remembered one thing."

"What? What on earth could you have remembered that would make you question my sincerity?" he asked, exasperated by her attitude. "We're two mature adults who've wasted far too much time as it is. We've both been alone because we were too foolish and filled with pride to reach out to the one person we loved."

"Speak for yourself," she muttered.

He ignored her. "It's time to get our cards on the table, Destiny. It's time to move forward to claim the happiness we deserve."

Destiny looked as if he'd suggested sunbathing nude in Hyde Park. "Absolutely not," she said fiercely.

"Why are you fighting this?"

"Because…" she said, looking miserable. "Because

I can't risk trusting you. Not for a minute. Have you forgotten Fortnum Travel, William, because believe me, I haven't. If you have your way, you'll steal it right out from under us."

That said, she ran from the room. A moment later, William heard her bedroom door slam shut. He sighed. Oddly enough, he had forgotten about the blasted travel agency. If David Fortnum hadn't been so intent on a merger with Harcourt & Sons, rather than a takeover by Carlton Industries, he would let it go. Fortnum was a friend, and William had little choice but to honor his promise to the man. He might have explained all that to Destiny if she hadn't run off, but he doubted she'd believe him, and he honestly couldn't say he blamed her.

The last notes of a flute sonata faded away and the musicians looked to him for some direction. "Go," he said wearily. "Thank you, but I think the evening is over."

They nodded.

"Happy New Year, sir," they murmured as they left, but they obviously knew, as he did, that there was nothing happy about it.

Destiny knew she'd behaved appallingly by running out on William, but it had suddenly been too much for her. The admission that he'd lured her to London deliberately, the announcement that he still loved her, the suggestion that they merely pick up things where they'd left off years ago, the convenient lapse of memory about his ongoing attempts to interfere in Carlton business—it was all too much.

There had been a time when him wanting her back would have meant everything to her. Now it was merely a taunting distraction. Perhaps that was what he was after, a way to get her thoughts so scrambled that she couldn't effectively counteract whatever sneaky plot he had planned to ruin Carlton Industries.

If only he hadn't sounded so sincere, if only her heart hadn't taken in every word, every declaration, and slowly but surely softened toward him. Which was, no doubt, exactly what he'd been counting on, the dirty scoundrel. If Richard had been a fly on the wall during this scene, he'd have been laughing his head off at her gullibility.

It had been some time now since she'd heard the music end and the front door close. She was alone again and her eyes were dry. She felt a little foolish for having run away, but it wouldn't be the first time she'd taken the coward's way out of a sticky situation. If she'd stayed in that room with him another second, there was no telling what she might have done. She might have launched herself straight into William's arms, Fortnum Travel and Carlton Industries be damned. It was exactly the kind of impetuous thing she would have done years ago. William had probably been counting on that.

Her stomach growled insistently, reminding her that they'd never gotten around to eating so much as a bite of that delicious dinner he'd sent over. She wondered if he'd left it. Without bothering to wash her face or put some drops in her red and stinging eyes, she walked into the living room and stopped dead.

William sat where she'd left him, leafing through a magazine, looking as at ease as if he were in his own home. He'd taken off his jacket and loosened the tie of his tux, which gave him a rakish, far too approachable look. How could a man his age look as attractive and as exciting as he had at thirty? It didn't seem fair. Even if she'd scrubbed her face, spent hours on her makeup and clothes, she never looked anything other than what she was—a fifty-three-year-old woman who worked to stay presentable. Oddly enough, she felt better than that when William's appreciative gaze was on her.

"Ah," he said when he saw her, immediate warmth lighting his eyes. "Just in time."

She scowled at him. "Why are you still here?"

"I came to celebrate New Year's with you. I waited to do just that."

"What if I'd stayed in my room?"

He grinned at that, mischief written all over his face. "Then I would have joined you."

She could see he meant it. She hugged her robe a little tighter and tried not to think of what a sight her tear-streaked and swollen face must be. "I thought I'd made it clear that I wanted you to go."

His gaze never faltered. "And I thought I'd made it clear that I don't intend to be put off this time. I'm not giving up, Destiny. Not again. No matter what it takes, I will win your trust back."

"Just give up for tonight," she pleaded, desperately needing time to regain her equilibrium, time to sort through the priorities she'd set for herself when she'd come to England. Allowing herself to succumb to William had not been on the agenda.

He shook his head. "Not even for tonight."

She regarded him with irritation. "You always did insist on having your own way."

"As did you," he said mildly. "Perhaps it's time we both learned to compromise. Share a glass of champagne with me. Greet the New Year. And then I'll go. There's nothing too scary about that, is there?"

"I'm not scared of you," she said sharply.

He laughed. "Sorry. My mistake. It must be your feelings for me that scare you, then."

She felt her lips twitch, despite her annoyance. "You never did lack for ego, did you?"

He winked at her. "Never saw any need to." He stood up. "Champagne, Destiny?"

If it would get him out of here sooner, then she would drink the entire bottle. "Yes."

He handed her a glass, then glanced toward the clock. "Eleven-thirty. We've just enough time to eat before the clock strikes twelve."

"Isn't it all ruined?"

"I moved most of it into the kitchen. The salads are chilled and still crisp, I imagine. And the prime rib is warming in the oven. Shall I bring it in here?"

"Let's eat in there," she suggested. Perhaps the informal setting and the stark, uncomplimentary lighting would take the romance out of things, though if her attire and her blotchy face hadn't accomplished that for him, nothing would.

"Fine with me," he said agreeably.

Destiny led the way and saw why he'd been so amenable. He'd already set the table, anticipating her choice. He'd added candles, as well, and he promptly lit them and cut off the glaring overhead lights.

Sighing, Destiny helped him put the food on the table without comment.

When he'd graciously pulled out her chair and seated her, she took the first bite of salad—a mix of field greens, pears, walnuts and blue cheese—and her appetite returned. She ate the rest ravenously, then eyed his untouched plate.

"A good cry always did make you hungry," William noted as he gave her his salad. "It always shocked me that you could be so emotional one minute and starving the next. Maybe that's what passion is all about."

She regarded him curiously. "How so?"

"Everything is approached with total abandon—emotions, work, food." His gaze caught hers. "Sex."

"Don't go there," she admonished.

He grinned. "If you say so. Are you ready for the prime rib now?"

She nodded. But after he'd placed it in front of her, she couldn't seem to make herself cut into it. William regarded her with concern.

"Too rare? Too well done?"

"No, nothing like that."

"Do you no longer eat beef? It used to be your favorite."

Destiny sighed. "That's it, actually. The fact that you remembered that it's my favorite. It's caught me by surprise that you still know me so well."

"Those were memorable times, Destiny. At least for me."

The clever words slipped past her defenses and snuck into her heart yet again. She'd never been a silly, sentimental woman, or at least she didn't think she had been, but she was succumbing far too easily to every charming word William uttered.

Determined not to let him see her vulnerability for an instant, she picked up her fork and knife and savagely cut into the tender meat.

"Pretending that's me?" he asked dryly, laughter dancing in his eyes.

"As a matter of fact, yes," she responded.

"Ah, Destiny, how am I going to win your trust again?"

"I'm not sure you can," she admitted with an unmistakable hint of sorrow in her voice.

"I will," he responded, undaunted.

Just then the clock chimed midnight. William stood and rounded the table, even as Destiny's heart thumped wildly in her chest. When she didn't look up, he waited and waited some more.

"Destiny," he said quietly, a chiding note in his voice.

She stood and faced him then, reminding herself that it was only a New Year's kiss he was after, at least for the moment.

His mouth covered hers and she knew in an instant that she'd been right to hide from the kiss. Because in that sweet moment, with his lips hard and persuasive against hers, with their breath tangling and her pulse racing, she knew with absolute certainty that he was after more. He wanted her heart.

And if she didn't maintain the most rigid self-control, she would very likely give it to him.

11

William returned to work after the holidays feeling more upbeat than he had in years. Everything was going according to plan. Not that Destiny was exactly falling straight back into his arms, but her resolve to fight him was weakening. That much had been evident in the kiss they'd shared on New Year's Eve.

Well-satisfied with the several successes of his plan over the holidays, he whistled as he poured his first cup of tea of the morning. He was startled when Malcolm knocked and then entered his office without waiting for an invitation. Not that William stood on formality, but it was rare that Malcolm didn't. He regarded his assistant warily.

"Everything okay?" he asked.

"I suppose that depends on your point of view, sir." Malcolm held out one of the London tabloids. He gripped it by its corner as if he feared contamination, then dropped it gingerly on William's desk. "If you'll look at page three, sir, I think you'll see the problem."

Page three of this particular paper was filled with the latest gossip making the rounds in London. It relied on rumor and half truths, often skirting libel. Because of its generally lascivious tenor, respectable members of London society preferred not to be mentioned, even in the most innocent way.

"Just tell me," William said impatiently.

"I'd rather you see for yourself."

Scowling in Malcolm's direction, he picked up the paper and opened it, only to see a shocking photo of himself and Destiny on her living room sofa, her in her robe and those silly slippers, him in his tuxedo, her hands in his. There was no question in his mind that it had been taken New Year's Eve, sometime at the height of their argument if her distressed expression was any indication of the timing.

"What the devil?" he muttered as his temper kicked in. "Who took this?"

"Anticipating that question, I made several calls in an attempt to discover that myself, but the paper's executives are falling back on the usual evasion," Malcolm said with undisguised disgust. "They merely cited the confidentiality of their sources, which they were happy to remind me is one of the first canons of journalistic ethics." He shook his head. "As if they truly give a damn about that."

"It is a handy catchphrase, though, isn't it?" William responded.

Whether the paper acknowledged it or not, the source had to be one of the musicians he'd hired. They were the only ones in the apartment at the right time that evening and they'd definitely been close enough to get this particular shot. It wasn't grainy enough to have been taken by a telephoto lens from some distant balcony.

"I'll deal with this, Malcolm," he said, resolving to call Ian Whitcomb immediately. Ian was as trustworthy as they came, but William had known only one of the two musicians Ian had brought with him. He'd never considered him to be particularly shady, but the third one was a total wild card.

"I was certain you would want to," Malcolm said. "I'm sorry, sir."

"So am I," William responded grimly.

He was also furious, but he suspected his own high emotions were nothing compared to the outrage Destiny was probably feeling about now. This disaster couldn't have come at a worse time. Given how suspicious she was of his motives, there was little question that she was going to turn this into a deliberate betrayal, an attempt by him to weaken her position in European business circles, to make her an object of ridicule just when she was trying to establish herself as a credible businesswoman.

Worst of all, he was damned if he could blame her. If the shoe had been on the other foot, if she had appeared unannounced on *his* doorstep and this had been the result, he would have suspected the same thing himself.

"Mr. Harcourt is here," Miriam announced in a low voice when Destiny responded to her secretary's buzz. "Shall I send him in?" There was a note of indignation in her voice that suggested she would much rather stick a knife in his heart.

Destiny felt a chill go down her spine. "No, you can tell that low-down, scheming scoundrel to go back to whatever rat hole he climbed out of."

The words were scarcely out of her mouth when the door to her office burst open and William strolled in.

"Get out!" Destiny said, seething at his audacity. Not that it surprised her. William had always had confidence enough for ten men. New Year's Eve had been reminder enough of that. "Leave at once or I will call security and have you tossed from the premises. Perhaps I'll call the media first, so they can get a good shot of it for tomorrow's editions. Then they'll know exactly what I think of you and your low-class activities."

William had the grace to grimace. "You've seen the paper, then. I was hoping you hadn't."

"Yes, I imagine you were."

"I understand why you're upset," he began.

"Upset," she nearly shouted, as furious about his patronizing tone as she was about that ridiculous photograph. "That doesn't begin to cover it. I could strangle you right now with my bare hands and do it without a twinge of conscience. I'm sure Miriam would be happy to swear that she never saw a thing. In fact, she'd probably happily help me dispose of the body."

He winced at the certainty in her voice. "Yes, well, I'm not all that happy myself at the moment, but your fury is misdirected. I had nothing to do with that photo in the paper. I'm as much a victim as you are."

She couldn't believe he thought her to be so gullible. "Yes, men are always ruined when it appears they've made a conquest, aren't they?" she asked with a real bite of sarcasm.

"The picture is not my doing," he repeated.

"Do you deny that it was taken inside my apartment?"

"No."

"And that people you hired must have taken it?"

"There's no proof of that, but, yes, it certainly looks that way."

She blinked at his ready agreement. "Then why shouldn't I blame you? Do you think one of those musicians brought along a little throwaway camera just on the off chance something fascinating might happen? Perhaps it's a little sideline one of them has developed over the years—scandal and blackmail. How lovely of you to make it so convenient for them."

"Perhaps," he said. "More likely, someone else put them up to it. I'd like to find out who, wouldn't you?"

"I already know who did it, dammit! Now get out."

"You're repeating yourself, Destiny. Worse, you're showing an uncharacteristic lack of open-mindedness."

"If I'm repeating myself, it's because you're obviously not listening. As for open-mindedness, I think there's little evidence that it's called for in this case."

"You're the one who's not listening," he said quietly. "I had nothing to do with that picture. Which means someone is out to catch you or me or maybe both of us in a compromising position."

"Well, they certainly accomplished that, didn't they?" She stared at him and waited for her temper to cool. When she could speak calmly, she asked, "Do you honestly expect me to believe it was someone else?"

"Yes."

"Why?"

He smiled slightly. "Because I've never lied to you."

"You keep saying that," she said with exasperation. "Yet the evidence to the contrary keeps piling up."

"Only if you choose to believe it."

Destiny sighed. "To tell you the truth, I don't know

who or what to believe anymore." She picked up the shredded newspaper from the waste basket beside her desk. "Except for this. My God, William, what are people going to think of me now? There I was, sitting in my rumpled bathrobe, looking for all the world as if I just crawled out of bed, with you sitting beside me looking like the cat that swallowed the Carlton Industries canary. It's humiliating."

"Or you can view it as a call to arms," he suggested lightly. "It's time to take a good look around, Destiny, and see who'd like you to fail here."

"Besides you?"

"I don't want you to fail," he said fiercely. "Why the devil would I want to do anything that might drive you away from London? It took me too damn long to get you here."

He had a point…if, of course, he was being honest. Damned if she could tell anymore. She'd been wavering until she'd seen this morning's paper.

If there was a chance, though, that it *was* someone else, she needed to look into it and prepare for battle. William wouldn't be a bad ally, if that turned out to be the case.

"Say I believe that you weren't involved, where do we start to find out who *was* behind it? The newspaper?" She knew from planting a few clever items in the past herself, though, that no one there would ever admit to a thing.

"No, I've already had someone go that route. The editors are tight-lipped. But as you suggested, those musicians are my prime suspects. I'm going to have a chat with the man I hired when I leave here. Would you like to come along?"

She stood at once. "Just try to stop me."

He laughed as she strode past him and out of the building at a brisk clip. "Out for blood, are you?"

"No more than you must be, if you're as innocent as you'd have me believe," she said. On the assumption that William hadn't hired the musicians to do more than play their flutes, she asked thoughtfully, "Did you know these men before you hired them?"

"Two of the three, yes. I can't imagine that Ian's involved in something this underhanded. His friend always seemed a stand-up man, as well, but I know nothing about the third one."

"Are we starting with him, then?" she asked as she stepped into the car William had waiting at the curb.

"No, we'll go to the one I know best," William said decisively, already giving instructions to his driver. "Ian should prove more open. I send a lot of business his way."

They found Ian Whitcomb half asleep in a two-room flat in a seedy part of London inhabited by struggling musicians, actors and artists. He brightened when he saw the two of them on his doorstep.

"You've made up, then," he said enthusiastically. "Good show!"

"Save your excitement," William said. "The truce is in danger, thanks to someone who has it in for one of us."

Ian stared at him blankly. "You'd better come in. You're not making sense, bloke." He gave Destiny a winning smile as he swept a pile of sheet music off of a chair and offered it to her. "So, what's up?"

William handed him the paper.

"Blimey, who did this?" Ian asked, looking genuinely shocked. "It looks as if the picture was taken on New Year's Eve."

"It was," Destiny confirmed. "And the only people around were you and your friends."

"You can't think it was one of us," he said indignantly. "We wouldn't get many jobs if it got round that we'd sell gossip or photos to the highest bidder."

"What other alternative is there?" William asked.

Ian seemed stymied by the question, but then his expression suddenly brightened. "Wait a minute! I remember now. The two of you were having your argument and we were playing right through it, when there was this bright flash of light. About blinded me, it did. I looked at my mates and said something about the fireworks starting early. You can speak to 'em yourself, if you doubt me, but that must have been it. It must have been a flashbulb going off just outside."

Destiny looked at William. "I remember that flash," she said slowly. "In fact, I asked you about it, but you hadn't noticed it at all. Could there have been someone on my balcony? How would they have gotten there?"

William's expression turned grim. "Let's go and have a look, shall we?" He glanced at Ian. "I hope you're telling the truth."

"I've no reason to lie to you," Ian insisted. "And Ms. Carlton just said she saw the light herself. If you doubt me, then you have to doubt her."

Back in William's car, Destiny looked at him. "Do you believe him?"

"Let's just say I'm reserving judgment until I see what the outside access is like to your balcony."

"But, William, how would anyone else have known that you and I were together that night? We never made any plans. The only people who knew were those you hired."

"And the doorman of your building who let me in," he said slowly.

"But why would he…?" Destiny's voice trailed off. "Chester."

William stared at her. "What the devil does Chester Sandhurst have to do with this?"

"He saw to the rental of that flat for me. It would be easy enough for him to bribe the doorman into reporting back to him about your presence. He's suspicious of my friendship with you, and he's not especially happy about answering to me."

William looked skeptical. "But Chester as a spy? Really, Destiny, I don't think he has the ingenuity, much less the gumption for it."

She gave him an impatient look. "I doubt he was out there personally leaping from balcony to balcony, but he has the motive and wherewithal to hire somebody more daring to do his dirty work."

"But all of this had to be accomplished on very short notice," William reminded her. "The night of your party, I'm almost certain he told me he was going to Devon for the holidays."

"There are phones in Devon," Destiny said. "And it's easy enough to have people on standby even on holidays, if you pay them enough. A call from the doorman to Chester, another from Chester to his sleazy photographer. How long could that take?"

"Not that long, but what about access?" William asked, his expression thoughtful. "He couldn't have gotten out there through your apartment and waited, since as you say we hadn't made the plans ahead. He would have to have been provided a key to a neighboring apartment, then climbed across. Is that feasible?"

"I honestly don't know," Destiny said. "It never occurred to me to check to see if one could leap about out there."

They were still debating the matter when they arrived at her building. Inside, they fell silent as they rode the elevator and walked to her door. No sooner had she opened it than the phone started ringing.

Destiny grabbed it as William went straight to the balcony. "Yes, hello," she said distractedly.

"Dammit, Destiny, what are you up to now?" Richard demanded.

She sighed heavily. Only one thing could have put him in this foul humor this early in the day back in the States. "You've seen the picture," she guessed.

"Yes, I've seen the blasted picture. Why was that man in your apartment while you were dressed in nothing but a bathrobe? My God, you might as well advertise that the two of you are sleeping together."

Destiny hadn't been any happier about the picture than Richard was, but she resented his attack and his ready assumption that she was having an affair. Of course, if her own nephew didn't believe there could be an innocent interpretation of that picture, who would?

"Stay out of this, Richard," she said tightly. "I'm dealing with it."

"What exactly are you dealing with? The negative publicity or Harcourt?"

"Both," she said.

"Well, pardon me if I find your tactics a bit unorthodox."

"That's me, isn't it?" she retorted. "Unorthodox is my middle name. You used to find it charming."

She could practically hear him grinding his teeth.

"Darling," she said, softening her tone. "It really is going to be all right. Nothing happened in my apartment. I'm okay. So is Carlton Industries. We'll weather this storm. It's little more than a tempest in a teapot, anyway."

"Have you considered the likelihood that your good friend William is the one behind this embarrassment?"

"I'm not dense, darling. Of course I've considered it. In fact, I'm investigating the whole thing right now, so you'll have to excuse me. I need to go and see what my…" She hesitated, searching for the right description. "I need to see if my partner has learned anything new from his search of the balcony."

"You hired a private investigator? Good. That's the first sensible thing I've heard."

"Yes, well, I do have my sensible moments," Destiny said blithely. "Goodbye, darling. Love to everyone."

She hung up quickly, scowling. That call had been the most serious warning yet. She'd heard it in Richard's voice. He was worried about her and about the company, and if one more thing happened that he didn't like, he was going to take action. She didn't think he'd yank her out of the job, but he might come charging over here to fix things. That was the last thing she wanted. In fact, if she had her way, her nephew and William wouldn't be on the same continent, much less in the same city, until she could get this mess straightened out herself. There was nothing worse than a couple of territorial, testosterone-driven males fighting for supremacy.

* * *

William came back into the living room, triumphantly holding the end of a cardboard film packet. "Found this on the balcony next door," he told Destiny.

She immediately paled. "You went scrambling over to another balcony?"

"I wanted to make sure it could be done," he said. "Nothing to it."

She sank down on the edge of the sofa. "I think I feel faint."

William took heart at her reaction. "Brace up, Destiny. I'm here and in one piece."

"Minus only your good sense, it seems," she muttered.

William laughed. "Don't tell me you'd have cared if I fell to the ground."

She flashed him a hard look. "I'd have been upset only about the waste of time all the explanations would have taken."

"Too late now. The truth is out. You do still care about me, just a little, anyway."

"So, maybe I do," she finally conceded. "As I would for any old friend."

"That's something at least. Now, what do you think of my find?"

"I think it raises more questions than answers, and I can't face them on an empty stomach. There's enough beef left for sandwiches. Would you like one?"

He nodded. "In the meantime, why don't I go down and try to find out a little something about your neighbors and about the doorman on duty that night?"

She seemed relieved to have him go, William decided, again considering that a sign of progress. In his possibly twisted view, it suggested that she was growing too comfortable having him close at hand and that she regretted it.

Downstairs he found a chatty doorman, who was only too happy to tell him that Destiny's neighbors—the Hyde-Lewises—were away, that, yes, the security staff had access keys to all of the flats in case of emergency, and that the doorman on duty that night was now off with a worrisome cold that had come up rather suddenly, right after New Year's, in fact.

William slipped his source a hefty tip and went back upstairs. He found Destiny in the kitchen, a cup of tea and an untouched sandwich in front of her. She looked up at his arrival.

"I don't like this, William," she said somberly.

"The sandwich?"

She frowned at his attempt at levity. "No, this whole situation, people sneaking around on balconies and peering in windows. It's given me the creeps."

"Would you like to move?"

"I wonder if that wouldn't be a good idea," she said. "Though I'm not accustomed to running from trouble. That leaves a bad taste in my mouth, as well."

"You could have someone here with you," he suggested.

"A bodyguard?"

"In a way."

She gave him a piercing look. "You're not applying for the job, are you?"

"Who better?" he asked, watching her closely. "We know each other's habits, good and bad. We'll be less likely to be in each other's way."

"A bit convenient for you, isn't it? Careful or I'll go

back to thinking this whole plot was dreamed up by you for just this purpose."

He frowned at her. "As eager as I am to have you in my life again, my dear, I'd prefer it to be on terms other than as roommates. My offer is purely honorable, I assure you." He grinned. "Not that I don't intend to try a different angle when the timing is more opportune."

"I'm delighted you're finding so much humor in this," Destiny retorted.

William frowned at the criticism. "I find nothing in the least humorous about any of this," he assured her. "We have what could turn out to be a rather serious situation on our hands. I'd like to get to the bottom of it as much as you would."

"Then let's stop worrying about who's going to live where and concentrate," she suggested. "Where do we go from here?"

"Do you want to go sleuthing around London like Miss Marple, or shall I hire someone?" William asked.

Destiny regarded him with a thoughtful expression. "Why not a combination of the two? Let an investigator look into whether that doorman is really sick or at home with a guilty conscience."

"While you and I do what?" William asked warily.

"While *I* pay a surprise visit to Chester in Devon," she said. "He's there till the weekend."

William stared at her. "On your own? Definitely not," he said flatly.

"What do you think he's likely to do if he is behind this? Bind and gag me and toss me into some lake?"

"Why take chances?"

Destiny regarded him incredulously. "You don't seriously think he'd do me any harm, do you?"

"To tell you the truth, I never thought he'd hire a sleazy photographer to spy on you, so now that he's quite possibly proved me wrong on that count, I no longer know what to believe. If you go to Devon, I go with you."

She gave him an impatient look, but William refused to back down. Eventually, she muttered, "Oh, suit yourself. Hire that investigator while I make a few calls to free up the rest of my day."

"Better free up tomorrow, too," William advised. "We might not be back by tonight."

She studied him suspiciously. "Another ploy to get me all alone, William? I'm disappointed in you. It's a little obvious, don't you think?"

"The only thing obvious to me at this point is that we're going to get a rather late start. It will take us time to get there and time to track down Chester. Once we've spoken to him it could lead to other lines of inquiry."

"Such as?"

"His alibis," William suggested. "If there are any delays, it will be far too late to think of driving back."

Destiny nodded slowly. "I suppose that makes sense."

"Thank you," he said wryly. "I do try to employ a bit of logic to things from time to time."

"William, did you always have this sharp edge?"

He laughed. "What can I say? The new Destiny inspires me."

"You say that as if it's a good thing," she responded. "To tell you the truth, I'm not sure I like it."

He laughed. "Stick around. It could grow on you. I did once, after all."

She gave him a vaguely bewildered look. "So you did. Right at the moment, though, I can't imagine how that happened."

12

Finding Chester Sandhurst proved to be trickier than Destiny had anticipated. On the drive to Devon, she called all of the contact numbers Chester had left for the office, but either there was no answer or whoever answered had no idea where he might be at the moment.

"Expect him later," several people assured her. "Shall I pass along a message?"

"No. No message." Destiny frowned. This was working out exactly as William had predicted, which she found mildly annoying. Did the man have to be right about absolutely everything? Why couldn't Chester have obligingly picked up on the first ring at the first place she called and set up a meeting time and location?

Probably because that would have helped her to avoid this fluttery little hint of anticipation in her stomach when she contemplated being tucked away in a country inn with William just down the hall. Despite her rather emphatic protests, she was no more immune to his charms now than she had been years ago. Perhaps the fates had concluded it was time for her to face that fact and deal with it. If only the trust issue could be overcome as easily as her years of carefully nurtured antagonism.

Well, the stupid fates didn't know everything, she thought heatedly. She had more important fish to fry at the moment. Finding out if Chester was responsible for the photo for starters. Then, if it turned out he was, his head on a sizzling skillet held an astonishing appeal. If that happened to give her the excuse she needed to avoid dealing with her renewed attraction to William, so much the better.

"Want to give up and turn back?" William asked, a knowing glint in his eyes.

Naturally, since he seemed so smugly certain about what she was thinking, she was forced to say no. "We've come this far. We must follow through," she said decisively. "Besides, whatever he thinks of me, Chester won't stay out of touch with the office for long. I've instructed his secretary to patch the call through to me the instant she hears from him."

"Good show," William said. "What shall we do in the meantime? Would you like to see the sights? Have a cozy dinner in front of a fire at a local pub?"

"I think the less the two of us are seen together in public, the better," she said wryly. "We can't afford to give the tabloids any more fodder."

"Innocent public appearances are far less likely to be subject to misinterpretation than intimate tête-à-têtes," he retorted.

He was right…again. "Okay, you have a point," she conceded, reconsidering her stance. "A lively pub seems to be just the thing. It's been years since I've been to one."

William glanced at her. "Was it the one I took you to when we came to England to visit my family?"

Reluctantly, Destiny nodded. It had been another memorable night, one she'd tried unsuccessfully to forget over the years. Even when she'd brought her nephews to London, she'd avoided taking them to any of the local pubs, fearful that even at their innocent young ages they would pick up on her nostalgia and ask questions she hadn't been prepared to answer.

"Destiny?"

She blinked and met William's gaze. "What?"

"Shall we go to a pub or would you rather not? If it brings back too many memories, I'm sure we can find a more sophisticated restaurant that's to your liking."

The vague hint that she was scared to dredge up old memories grated, as did the suggestion that she'd turned into some sort of snob.

"A pub will be fine," she said tightly, then closed her eyes and leaned back against the car's soft leather upholstery. Let the blasted memories come. Maybe if she faced them, she could purge them at last. Maybe it would even be the end of William being able to use them against her at every turn as he had just now.

London, 1982

The trip to England to visit William's family had been an unmitigated disaster in Destiny's opinion. His father was still filled with fury and resentment toward her, blaming her for keeping William from coming home to claim his rightful place in the family business. He'd barely spoken a civil word to her the entire week they'd been in London.

William's mother, with her lovely peaches-and-cream complexion and soft-spoken manner, had tried to smooth things over, but there was no disguising the chill in the atmosphere. Destiny was convinced she'd have frostbite before they finally got away.

Alone with William and feeling thoroughly defeated, she admitted, "We shouldn't have come."

"I'm sorry he's being such a stubborn old goat," William apologized. "I warned you, though. My father doesn't want fences mended except on his own terms."

"I was so sure that once the two of you talked face-to-face, when you'd explained your position, things would be different. I can't imagine anyone in my family holding a grudge for so long."

"Welcome to the Harcourt tradition. Family feuds are our forte. Some lasted generations," William said wryly. "Now, I have a suggestion. Why don't you and I get out of here tonight? I'll take you to my favorite pub, buy you a ploughman's dinner and teach you how to throw darts. You need to have at least one adventure with the local culture while you're here. Not everyone is as stuffy and unbending as my father."

"Anything that will give us some time on our own is fine with me," she said, though she was unconvinced that the evening he described would be much of an improvement on the chilly atmosphere around the ancestral home. Despite William's disclaimer, she couldn't help envisioning a place filled with more stuffy, disapproving old men.

The second they walked through the door of the lively pub, however, she knew she'd been wrong. The air was thick with smoke and filled with music and laughter. In fact, the din was quite incredible, the music promising.

"I'll see if there's a table to be snagged," William said. "Wait here by the door, so I can find you again."

As he'd pushed his way through the crowd, Destiny looked around her at the working-class patrons and the obvious assortment of tourists who'd come to absorb some of the local color. It was exactly the kind of eclectic mix of people she adored. It was yet more evidence of just how well William understood her needs. He'd brought her here knowing she'd fit right in and be totally comfortable for the first time in days.

"Over here, luv."

She heard William's voice, the accent thicker than she'd ever noticed before. In France, he usually sounded more urbane, a citizen of the world with smooth edges on his voice, making it all but impossible to discern his real roots. She could see from the broad grin on his face when she finally spotted him, though, that he was as much in his element here as he was in the upper-crust Paris art gallery where they'd met.

She worked her way in his direction, laughingly apologizing to the waitresses and customers she accidentally jostled en route.

"How did you manage this?" she asked, when she found that their table was right beside the musicians.

"I know one of the lads playing. This is their table. They said they'd be happy to have us make use of it while they play and join them on their breaks."

"Perfect," she said, accepting the pint of dark ale he handed to her, then wincing at the first bitter sip.

William chuckled. "Would you rather have wine?"

"Absolutely not. I want to drink what the locals drink."

"Have I ever told you how much I admire your adventurous spirit?"

"From time to time, but I never tire of hearing it." It made her feel as if she'd made a success of something important. She'd chosen her nomadic life to keep from settling into a dull routine back home. She'd also wanted her brother to have a clear shot at the family business, because it meant the world to him. Had she stayed at home, her determinedly fair parents would have insisted on dividing things up equally, despite her repeated insistence that the business meant nothing to her, that her talent lay in another direction entirely.

Though she'd left home for one reason, it had proved to be an astonishing triumph in other ways. She'd learned that she could live quite nicely on her own, that she loved getting to know people of all kinds, that she was strong and capable, rather than the shy little wallflower she'd convinced herself she was when living in the shadow of her bolder, more outgoing brother.

When the music began, it was a lively Irish jig, and a number of people flocked to the minuscule dance floor to dance. As Destiny watched the intricate steps, William stood and held out his hand.

"Come along. I'll teach you how to do it," he offered.

She realized then that they'd never actually danced together, and here he was wanting her to try a complicated dance that was likely to result in her feet becoming impossibly tangled.

"I don't know," she said doubtfully.

"You've taken far more dangerous risks," he reminded her.

"No, I haven't," she protested.

He laughed. "You got involved with a disinherited Englishman, didn't you? Now, come on. I can see you want to try it."

When they reached the dance floor, people made room for them. William demonstrated the steps, and as others applauded and cheered encouragingly, Destiny tried to follow.

She'd never been an especially graceful dancer, and because she'd been shy, she'd usually lacked for partners, but in no time at all, none of that seemed to matter. Caught up in the music and emboldened by the onlookers, she managed to keep up with William, who was surprisingly energetic and talented. By the end of the song, she was breathless and exhilarated. She fell into his arms, laughing.

He gazed at her, his eyes filled with amusement. "Now, that wasn't so bad, was it?"

"It was wonderful. Let's do it again."

He turned and winked at his friend in the band. "How about something slow and romantic?" he called out. "So I don't collapse in a heap and prove that I'm no match for her, after all."

"Right-o," his friend replied, and the band began to play the golden oldie, "Smoke Gets in Your Eyes."

Destiny moved into William's arms and rested her cheek against his chest. She realized it was the place she felt safest, the place she always longed to be.

But with his father so disapproving of their relationship, how could it last much longer? She believed too wholeheartedly in the importance of family to willfully destroy William's ties to his parents. And though he'd claimed that the family business meant little or nothing to him, she wondered how much longer he would be content to go on living idly with her in France. He'd been brought up for another life entirely.

As if he sensed the sadness building in her, William held her away and met her gaze. "Where have you gone?" he asked. "Just a moment ago, your cheeks were flushed and your eyes were sparkling. Now you look as if you've lost your best friend."

She touched his cheek. "I'm very much afraid I will," she said.

"Who?" he asked, his expression filled with dismay, and then, as understanding dawned, he added incredulously, "Me?"

She nodded.

"Never, darling. You can't lose me."

"It's already happening," she insisted. "Don't you think I can see how this visit is tearing you apart?"

"If I'm upset, it's only because I can see how my father's attitude is hurting you," he said fiercely. "His actions toward me mean nothing."

"You can't mean that," she protested. If her father had behaved so abominably toward her when she'd decided to leave, it would have cut her to the quick. She might very well have stayed and acceded to his wishes. Fortunately her father had never been the controlling type.

"I do mean it," William said emphatically. "Destiny, my happiness lies with you, wherever you are. I can manage all the rest."

She wanted so desperately to believe him. In fact,

she did believe that he meant what he was saying. She just wasn't convinced he could live with it.

Worse, she was beginning to see that she couldn't, not without denying one of the things she valued most in her own life—the ties to family.

Destiny awoke with a start, the dream—or memory—lingering in her head. How had she forgotten that bittersweet night in London and the realization she'd come to that she and William were destined to part? Perhaps it was because it had been months and months before she'd had to put her resolve to the test and when that time had come, it was hard to separate all the emotions. One day, though, she would, she concluded with a soft sigh. It was long past time to examine her role in the actions that had robbed them of a future. William had hinted at as much, but she'd been too eager to heap all the blame on him.

"You're finally awake, then?" William said from the driver's seat beside her, giving her an indulgent smile. "We're almost at that pub I promised you."

"I wasn't sleeping," she mumbled halfheartedly.

"Made a good show of pretending, then," he countered. "I've been talking to you for miles now and getting no response." He grinned. "Made it easy to believe I was going to have my own way, for once."

Destiny chuckled. "Not likely, but you might as well tell me what you were hoping for."

He glanced at her as he pulled up to the curb. The corners of his mouth twitched ever so slightly. "Not just yet," he said finally, after searching her face for some sign he apparently didn't find. "I don't think you're quite ready to hear it."

For some reason, his words made her pulse skip a beat. Or perhaps it was the heat in his eyes that caused her heart to race and her skin to flush. She hadn't felt this way in years and never with any other man. She wondered if William had guessed that and intended to capitalize on it, not for pleasure, but for business.

As soon as the thought occurred to her, her anticipation dimmed. She reminded herself sharply that she was here in search of a potential backstabber, not to recapture a lost passion, especially not with a man whose own motives might not be beyond reproach.

William was right…again, dammit. She wasn't ready to hear whatever he'd been about to say. There were too many unanswered questions yet to be resolved.

Suddenly she wanted to get them answered and over with quickly, so she could move on. Whether that meant moving toward something—or someone—or running away was yet to be determined.

William was struck by the fact that Destiny had gone quiet on him. Usually she wasn't one to sit silent for long, but she was definitely brooding about something now.

"Are you worrying about Chester's reaction to finding us chasing after him?" he asked.

She looked startled by the question. "I don't give two figs whether he's furious or not. If he's innocent, he'll be as indignant as we are about what's gone on and ready to join in the hunt for the guilty party. If he's the guilty one, he won't be able to hide it."

"Then if it's not Chester on your mind, what has you looking so glum?"

She shrugged, idly pushing the last of her food around on the plate. She was barely aware of the pub's music or the lively chatter around them.

"Destiny, if something's bothering you, especially if it has to do with me, then by all means get it out in the open. Let's deal with it."

"I'm thinking what a muddle we made of things years ago," she admitted at last.

William laughed. "Yes, we did. I think we should chalk it up to being young and foolish and start over."

She regarded him incredulously. "Just like that?"

"Is there any reason we shouldn't?"

"Dozens," she said at once. "Possibly more."

"Name one."

"You've tried to destroy my family's business," she said at once.

He frowned at that. "I thought we'd established that I had my reasons," he chided. "And, moreover, that I hadn't done a very good job of it, anyway."

She waved off the explanation. "I doubt that will wash with Richard. An attack is an attack. He's furious enough that I'm even speaking to you. Anything more would bring him charging over here to save the day. I won't do anything deliberately to upset my family."

"Would it help if I swore that the competition, such as it was, is over?"

"Your credibility is a little low right now."

"With you or your nephew?"

"Both of us, I suppose, especially with this Fortnum Travel deal in the works. I'm as determined as you to have it."

William nodded. "So noted. As long as nothing

sneaky or underhanded is involved in the outcome, we should be able to live with whatever happens."

"Why can't you simply drop it?" she asked.

"Because I made a promise," he said.

"To whom?"

"David Fortnum."

She stared at him with obvious shock. "You can't be serious."

"Oh, but I am. He wants a merger with Harcourt & Sons, not a hostile takeover by an American company."

"I don't believe you. This is just another of your annoying moves to challenge us."

"I swear to you that it's not. I would be doing the same thing if any other company were involved."

"Ha!"

Her blatant disbelief irked him. He gave her a piercing look. "Look into my eyes and tell me that you don't trust me on this," he said.

She lifted her gaze and met his. "I don't trust you," she said flatly. "Not entirely, anyway."

Her last comment offered a small spark of hope, but William's spirits sank, anyway. Perhaps he'd gone a bit too far in his zeal to snag her attention. He hadn't thought it through to the end, hadn't considered how he was going to convince her he wasn't out to steal her company's business after working so hard to convince her of precisely the opposite. Walking away from the Fortnum Travel situation would do it, but that was impossible.

"Don't spend too much time worrying about me being a threat to Carlton Industries," he said eventually. "There's someone else who's a far more serious threat."

"You're talking about Chester," she said at once.

"Possibly. We don't know that for sure yet. Frankly, I still have my doubts."

"Who else could it be?" she demanded. "He has the most obvious motive."

William thought for a moment before responding. "Sometimes it's the person who appears to have the least motive," he said slowly. "He tends to get overlooked and can get away with far more damage before he's discovered."

She seemed startled by his observation. Obviously, it wasn't something she'd considered.

"Do you think we're wasting our time here?" she asked.

"I didn't say that. I merely said it's important to keep an open mind. Why not try to call Chester again? You'll sleep easier if you've spoken to him tonight and at least arranged a meeting."

She handed him the list of numbers as she retrieved her cell phone. "Read me the number for his cell phone," she said. "It'll save me digging around for my reading glasses. They're forever getting lost in the depths of my purse."

"Reading glasses?" he echoed, amused. "You haven't used them all day."

She scowled at him. "I was being vain, dammit. And now my eyes are tired. Just stop chuckling and read the number."

"Happy to," he said at once, and reeled it off. Still scowling at him, she punched in the number rather forcefully, then waited. Suddenly her expression brightened.

"Chester, is that you? I've been trying to reach you all day."

Whatever Chester said in response must have included a lengthy explanation, because Destiny stayed silent, nodding from time to time.

"Yes, well, I'm sure you had a wonderful time, but I need to see you," she said at last. "No, not in London. I'm here in Devon. It's rather urgent, you see. It couldn't wait for you to get back."

William watched as her expression transformed into a look he'd never seen before. There was a glint of steely determination in her eyes.

"Yes, tonight," she said flatly. "Tell me where you are or you can come to me."

William jotted down the name of the inn where he'd made reservations for them and passed it to her.

"The Devonshire Arms," she told Chester. "In an hour. We'll meet in the lobby."

She hung up slowly. "He's in a state," she told William.

"What do you mean?"

"I could hear the panic in his voice. I don't like it. What if he runs?"

"Then you'll know he's both a traitor and a coward," William told her. "If he's any kind of a man, if there's a shred of loyalty to you or Carlton Industries left in him, he'll be at the hotel in an hour."

"Then I suppose we should be getting there, as well," she said, a bit more color rising in her cheeks.

"Destiny, you're up to this," William said. "I know you think you're not—"

"I've never had to confront someone about betraying me before," she said, her expression glum. "I don't want to get it wrong. We need answers, not defensive evasions."

William tucked a finger under her chin and waited until she met his gaze. "You had no qualms dealing with me, did you?"

"That was different."

"How? Because you knew me? If anything, I would think that would have made it all the harder to accuse me of betraying you. Yet you didn't hesitate."

She nodded slowly, her expression brightening. "Of course you're right. I can do this. I'm very good at reading people." She gave him a wry look. "Most of the time, anyway."

"Always, I suspect. It's just that sometimes you don't want to deal with what you're finding."

She gave him a puzzled look. "Meaning?"

"That you don't really want to believe that Chester is a traitor, so it may take you a bit to accept it, even if the evidence is plain as day." He grinned. "And you're not ready to believe you can trust me, even though that evidence is as plain as day as well."

"Maybe it's plain to you," she said tartly. "But you're correct. As far as I'm concerned, the jury is definitely still out."

"Maybe we should stick to Chester for the moment," William suggested.

Destiny laughed. "Probably best," she agreed. "At least from your point of view."

"Best all around," he said. "You can't afford to be distracted going into a meeting as important as this one." He gave her a deliberately long, lingering look that brought some color into her cheeks. "Too bad, too, because right this second I would love to kiss you."

She swallowed hard, and it took a long time for her to tear her gaze away. That told William all he needed to know and then some. Destiny might not entirely trust him, but the attraction simmering between them was about to reach a boiling point.

13

Destiny chose a comfortable wing chair in a secluded corner of the hotel lobby and waited for Chester to appear. Then she braced herself for an explosion when she told William she intended to handle this entirely on her own, that it was a company matter.

"It's not a company matter," he retorted indignantly. "I was in that picture with you. I should be here. Besides, there's no telling what Sandhurst might do if he's cornered. You said he sounded panicked on the phone and that's even before knowing what you want to see him about."

"If he's guilty, he knows precisely why I want to see him. Besides, he's not going to murder me in cold blood in the hotel lobby," Destiny responded. "I'll be safe enough." She looked into his turbulent eyes. "I need to do this, William, on my own. It's my first real test at the helm and I need to prove I'm up to it. I've flung myself into what appears to be a shark tank. I need to see if I can swim."

He regarded her with a troubled expression, but Destiny refused to back down.

"Fine," he relented at last, "but I'll be in the bar. If you need me, all you'll have to do is call out."

"Thank you," she said, unable to deny him that. Besides, much as she hated to admit it, it was reassuring to know that he was within earshot if something should go dreadfully awry. At this late hour, there were few people in the lobby who could rush in to help her.

William had been gone only a few moments when she looked up and spotted Chester striding across the lobby, his expression harried, his tie askew, his shirt buttoned so hastily, it was misaligned. It was that as much as anything that gave away his distress. In the few weeks she'd known him, he'd always been impeccably turned out for every occasion.

"Destiny, what on earth is this all about?" he asked, looking as though he might bolt at the first sign that he was under siege. "You're carrying on as if there's been some sort of calamity. Surely there's nothing that couldn't have waited until I get back next week."

She bristled at the attempt to characterize her as some sort of hysterical female. "It might not be a calamity, but it's close enough," she said, barely managing to stay calm. "Sit down, Chester. I need your input on something that's come up."

"And it couldn't have been discussed on the phone?"

"No, I needed you to see this." She slowly pulled the newspaper from her purse. "And to see your reaction to it."

She handed the paper to him, then watched closely as he opened it and saw the incriminating photograph, then finally sat down as if his knees had given way.

"Blast and hell, what is this?" he demanded with suitable indignation. "How did it happen? Who took it?"

"That's what I'd like to know," she said mildly.

He blinked in confusion, but as understanding dawned, his complexion turned ruddy. "You honestly think I had something to do with this?" he demanded heatedly. "Do you truly think so little of me?"

"I think you might be able to point me in the right direction," she corrected him mildly. It was a very tiny distinction, but to an innocent man it would be an important one.

His gaze narrowed. "Then you're not actually accusing me?" he asked.

"I know you don't believe I have what it takes to run this division," Destiny told him. "You have to admit that something like this would bolster your opinion, especially if it's seen by the right people."

"Meaning Richard, I suppose," he said, his expression grim. "Someone sent this to him? You think I'm devious enough to try to discredit you in such a way?"

"Someone is. Richard received it first thing this morning," she confirmed. "Needless to say, he's not very happy with me at the moment."

"I imagine so," Chester said, then regarded her earnestly. "But I wasn't behind it. Not the picture and not sending it to your nephew. I could never do such a sleazy, traitorous thing."

"Oh?"

"It has the potential to hurt not just you, but the company," he explained. "I've spent my entire career with Carlton Industries in one capacity or another. I won't betray it."

"Even if you feel its betrayed you?"

He seemed startled by the question. "Because Richard sent you over here?"

Destiny nodded. "It was a slap in your face. Not that it was meant to be, but it would be understandable if you felt that way."

Chester stayed silent for several minutes. "If I'm to be totally honest, yes. I wasn't happy about this turn of events, but I'm a realist, Destiny. I can't deny that the company needed someone else to take charge. We're not growing the way we should be. In some measure that's due to Harcourt, of course, but some of it was my own tendency toward caution. I never liked putting other people's money at risk, which is what Harcourt was forcing us to do with his shenanigans. Richard convinced me that you were a person of great vision and that we would complement each other. You said much the same thing yourself."

"And I meant it," Destiny assured him.

"It's only been a few weeks since your arrival, but I've come to believe that, as well," he said. "If I hadn't hoped it would work out, I would have quit, not done something like this to get even. I've had other offers through the years, some quite recently, in fact. I could have taken any one of them. So you see, I have no reason to plant some ugly little photograph in a tabloid."

To her surprise, Destiny believed him. She wasn't sure why it was so easy to trust Chester and so difficult to trust William, but there it was. She believed everything Chester was saying.

"Any idea who might have been behind it?" she asked. "Someone inside the company?"

"Or Harcourt himself," Chester suggested.

"Trust me, I've been over that ground," Destiny assured him. "It wasn't William."

"How can you be so sure?"

She thought of William's determination to get her to London and his desire to keep her there. Whatever else might be in doubt, she didn't question his sincerity about that. It was, however, not an explanation she cared to share with Chester. He might view it as yet more evidence of her own divided loyalties.

"Instinct, I suppose," she said eventually. "I know that must not be a very satisfactory answer to someone who prefers facts and figures, but it's the best I can do. I've known him a very long time, and I believe I know what he is and isn't capable of doing."

Chester nodded slowly. "Then for now, we'll work on the assumption that your instinct is to be trusted. I'll come back to London first thing in the morning and we'll do some digging inside Carlton Industries."

Destiny viewed him with surprise. "Is there someone you suspect?"

"Several people were hoping to move up if Richard fired me," he admitted. "None of them were overjoyed to hear not only that I was staying, but that you were taking charge in a newly created position above me. So, yes, there are resentments." He patted her hand. "Don't worry, though. We'll narrow the field of possibilities down together. I think we can make quick work of it, in fact."

To Destiny's amazement, he sounded downright eager to get started. In fact, he sounded more energized than he had at any time since she'd arrived.

"You're going to enjoy this hunt, aren't you?" she asked, not even trying to disguise her surprise.

He looked vaguely chagrined at having been caught taking pleasure from a task born out of someone's act of betrayal. "A very long time ago, I toyed with the notion of becoming a detective and trying to root out those engaged in corporate espionage. This will be a bit like that, don't you think?"

"A bit," she said, laughing. "If there's one thing we both seem to be learning these days, it's that it is never too late to go after an old dream."

He gave her a worried look. "As long as that dream doesn't include Harcourt," he said. "No offense."

"None taken," Destiny said. "Leave William to me, Chester. You find whoever's out to get me and the company."

"I'm not convinced it's not one and the same," he said, suddenly dire again.

"Keep an open mind, Chester, or you'll be defeated before you get started."

"You do the same," he advised. "I hate to think of the consequences if you've gotten it all wrong about Harcourt."

Destiny sighed heavily. "So do I," she murmured. "Given the stakes, so do I."

"Thanks for leaping to my defense," William said, startling Destiny when he appeared at her side within seconds of Chester's departure.

"Is that what you heard me doing?" she asked irritably. "I thought I was merely leaving room for doubt."

"I prefer to take a more optimistic view of your words," he countered. "Now, shall we have a drink and toast the success of your first confrontation with the old Carlton management?"

"It wasn't a success. I still don't know who was behind that photograph."

"But you do know one person who wasn't behind it, and it seems you've found a real ally in the process."

She regarded William with surprise. "You felt that, too?"

He nodded. "Yes. I think Chester's exactly what he claims to be, a man who's a pragmatist, loyal to a fault and not quick to retaliate for hurt feelings."

"That was my impression precisely," Destiny admitted.

William's expression turned oddly nostalgic. "Remember how we used to do this after every gathering we had in Provence? We'd stay up late, after everyone else had left or gone to bed, and compare notes. We always agreed, always had the same impressions of the newcomers."

Destiny smiled at the memory. "So we did." Sometimes those quiet, late-night postmortems on the parties had been the best part. They'd shared gossip they'd picked up, laughed at the often drunken foibles of some of their guests, and a time or two commented on the vibes they'd gotten about a marriage in trouble or an affair about to begin.

She glanced at him. "Have you ever been back?"

He shook his head, his expression sad. "Not since I closed up the house for you. Have you?"

"Never."

"Why? Somehow I envisioned you taking your nephews there for summer vacations. I almost went in August one year in hopes of running into you by chance."

"I never took them," she told him.

"Not even once?"

"Never."

"But why? You loved it so."

"I suppose I was afraid they'd see how sad it made me and blame themselves."

William smiled. "Boys are rarely as intuitive as that."

"You're right, of course. But there was another reason," she admitted.

"Oh?"

"I didn't want to be there without you. I think that would have been the most painful thing of all. Even though I'd lived there on my own before we met, once you became a part of it, it would never have been the same. I would have felt your presence in every room, seen you every place I turned in town. I've actually thought of selling it in recent years just to avoid all those haunting memories."

"But you haven't?" he asked.

She gave him a rueful look. "No. I couldn't bring myself to do that, either. I've paid for the upkeep on the house and for the gallery. It seemed important to me to know they'd be ready if I ever chose to go back."

"Perhaps we can go back together one day," he said. "I'd like that."

Destiny hesitated, conditioned not to bare her soul, but at last she took the risk. "I'd like that, too," she said softly. "Someday."

Back in London, William considered the trip from every angle and pronounced it a success. Destiny's attitude was softening, no question about it. And she now had an ally within Carlton to help in the hunt for whoever was intent on betraying her. He wanted her to succeed at that, to discover for herself that he was in no way involved. Perhaps then she could make the final leap of faith toward trusting him enough to let him back into her life in the intimate way he wanted.

Of course, he could not ignore the power of Richard Carlton's objections, which would only become more strenuous once William succeeded in taking over Fortnum Travel as he intended to do. Destiny, he suspected would not be able to overlook those objections, even as she resented her nephew's interference. William couldn't help wondering if it wasn't time he made some sort of overture in that direction.

He was still pondering that when Malcolm knocked on his door and came in, his expression glum.

"Not another photograph?" William asked.

"No, sir, nothing like that. But I met with my source inside Carlton Industries last night. There are some rumors about a more aggressive campaign to compete with us."

William scowled. "Good grief, man. We're no competition for them. It would be a waste of their time to bother with any more of our enterprises."

"They've been making inquiries about haberdasheries for sale," Malcolm said. "Why else would they do that, if not to challenge Harcourt & Sons?"

"Let them," William said. "A little healthy competition never hurt anyone."

Malcolm looked scandalized. "But, sir, you can't just give them the field and let them run all over it. Their resources are far greater than ours. They'll bury us."

"No," William said with certainty. "They'll tire of the game eventually and get back to chasing after the kind of mergers and acquisitions that are their real strength."

"Are you still prepared to annoy them on that front, at least?" Malcolm asked. "Perhaps if they're distracted with all these petty games, we can steal some desirable firm right out from under their noses."

"We could," William agreed. "But with the exception of Fortnum Travel, I made a promise not to try."

"A promise to whom?"

"Destiny, of course. I've sworn to her that the games are over beyond that one situation in which I gave my word to an old friend."

Malcolm's frown deepened. "Is that wise, sir, especially in light of the evidence that she doesn't seem inclined to return the favor?"

"Calm down, man. I'll point that out to her and that will be that."

"You think so?" his assistant asked doubtfully. "I would have thought that photograph I brought you would have hardened her resolve."

"It might have, if the wound had been allowed to fester, but I took care of that."

"How, sir, if you don't mind me asking?"

"She's going after the real culprit, someone who's most likely inside her own company. I pity the poor soul when she finds him. She's not happy, Malcolm. Not happy at all. And when the full fury of Destiny's temper is unleashed, all hell is likely to break loose."

For the first time since he'd come into William's office, Malcolm's lips twitched. "I believe I'd like to see that, sir."

"It'll be a show, all right," William said. He had to admit, he was looking forward to it himself.

Before he could say anything more, his intercom buzzed. "Sir, it's Richard Carlton on line two," his secretary announced. "He's been calling since yesterday."

"Thanks," William said. He glanced at his assistant. "I think I'll need some privacy for this, Malcolm."

"Certainly. If you need me for anything, let me know."

"Right. And thanks for passing along the latest information on Carlton Industries."

When Malcolm had gone and closed the door securely behind him, William picked up the phone. "Harcourt here."

"About damn time," Richard said angrily.

William tamped down his own temper. "I've been expecting your call," he said mildly. "I'm surprised it took so long."

"What will it take to get you to stay away from Carlton Industries?" Richard asked bluntly.

"Your aunt's already seen to that," William responded. "Perhaps you should have checked with her before you called."

"Excuse me?" Richard said, as if William had presented him with some impossibly complicated scenario rather than a simple declaration that the war between their companies was over.

"With one exception, the game's ended, at least on my side," William explained. "It's your company that seems intent on extending it, if the rumors I hear are to be believed. Don't get the idea that I won't change my mind and come after you again, if attacked."

"What the devil are you talking about?"

"Again, I think I'll refer you to Destiny. She's the one you should be talking to."

"She'll only tell me to butt out," Richard muttered, sounding exasperated.

William couldn't stop the laugh that bubbled up. "Yes, I imagine she will. She seems quite capable of running things on her own, if you want my opinion."

"Actually, I don't give a damn about your opinion," Richard retorted.

"Perhaps you should. It seems there are certain aspects about your aunt that I understand better than you do."

"Not possible," Richard stated flatly.

"If you go on believing that, it will only harm your relationship with her in the long run. Now, I believe I've given you something to think about, so I'll say goodbye."

He hung up before Richard could respond, then leaned back in his chair, well satisfied with the way the conversation had gone. First he'd gotten Destiny's attention and drawn her over here. Now it appeared he had the attention of her oldest nephew. The only thing left was luring the whole lot of them to London, so he could move forward with his master plan to win Destiny's heart. Without their blessing, she would never agree to the future he had in mind for the two of them.

"And then he had the audacity to tell me that I was about to spoil my relationship with Destiny if I didn't leave her alone and let her run things," Richard grumbled, pacing from one end of Ben's study to the other. Ben and Mack were both observing him with a certain amount of undisguised amusement.

"Which part of that annoyed you the most?" Ben inquired lightly. "The implication that Destiny is capable of running things without your input or the fact that Harcourt seems to understand her better than you do?"

"Don't be absurd," Richard responded. "Harcourt doesn't know a damn thing about Destiny. We lived with her for more than twenty years. He was with her how long? A year or two, maybe?"

Mack nodded. "Just a year or two? Say, about the length of time Ben and Kathleen have been together? Not much less than the time I've been with Beth or you've been with Melanie?"

Richard paused in his pacing and glared at his brother. "Okay, I see your point. You're taking into account the whole love factor."

Ben bit back a grin. "Yeah, that love factor is a killer, all right. Teaches you all sorts of things."

"Do you have to enjoy this so damn much?" Richard asked.

Ben and Mack nodded.

"Yep. It's the most fun we've had at your expense in years," Mack said. "The only thing more fun would be having our wives around to add in their two cents."

"Which is precisely why I didn't tell them about this little meeting," Richard said.

"Maybe you should have," Ben said. "I think a woman's perspective might be in order, don't you?"

"So now you're saying that, not only does Harcourt understand Destiny better than I do, but our wives do also?" Richard asked, beginning to feel besieged from every direction.

"That's about it," Mack agreed.

Richard sighed. "I still say it's time for me to fly over there and straighten this whole mess out once and for all, face-to-face."

"No," Mack said emphatically.

"Absolutely not," Ben added. "That's the worst thing you could do."

Richard scowled at the pair of them. There had been a time when they'd both paid a lot more attention to his opinions. Now they didn't hesitate to criticize and question him at every turn. "What do you suggest, then?"

"Sit tight. Let it play itself out," Mack advised. "Let Destiny get her feet under her and run the division. She's obviously craving the sense of accomplishment that will give her."

"And that's what you would do if some part of your football franchise was in trouble?" Richard demanded.

"No, of course not," Mack said, grinning. "But I wouldn't have put Destiny in charge of any part of the franchise in the first place."

"Oh, really? How would you have stopped her, once she got the notion in her head?"

Ben laughed. "I'd like to hear the answer to that one myself."

Mack frowned, clearly unhappy at having the tables turned. "She's a reasonable woman."

"Ha!" Richard and Ben said in unison.

"I would have told her no," Mack said emphatically.

"Oh, yeah, that would have done it," Richard said. "She'd be coaching the offense by now."

Mack sighed heavily. "You're probably right." A grin tugged at his lips. "I guess it's a good thing she has a better head for business than she does for football, then."

"That remains to be seen," Richard responded. "Are you sure going over there is a bad move?"

"Oh, yes," Ben told him.

"But," Mack began, his expression thoughtful, "that doesn't mean we couldn't send our wives over."

Richard opened his mouth to dismiss the idea out of hand, but the logic of it finally hit him. Destiny wouldn't be nearly as defensive with Melanie, Beth and Kathleen. And the three of them could get a good, unbiased read on Harcourt and his intentions.

"I like it," he said finally. "How soon could they go?"

"A week from now? Two weeks?" Mack suggested. "As soon as they're certain the nannies can take care of the kids to their satisfaction. Right now, Beth's not likely to let the baby out of her sight for more than a couple of days, though."

"Hold on," Ben said quietly, putting a damper on their enthusiasm. "Destiny's not stupid. She'll see through it in a minute if they turn up right now with virtually no warning. Nobody drops everything and goes to London on the spur of the moment, not with kids to worry about, anyway. It'll take some planning."

"Then let's start making those plans," Richard said at once.

"No," Ben said. "That's the thing. We can't make the plans. We have to get Melanie, Beth and Kathleen to make the plans. They have to think it's their idea. They're no happier about our meddling than Destiny is, so the trip definitely has to be something they devise completely on their own."

Ben's strategy was a little convoluted and sneaky for Richard, but it made a weird kind of sense. Still, it would take time, time he didn't want to waste.

"How the devil do we make them think it's their idea?" he asked.

"The same way they get us to do stuff. Drop a few hints about Destiny sounding lonely," Mack suggested.

"Mention that things seem to be heating up with Harcourt and we're worried that she's going to get her heart broken," Ben said. "It shouldn't take much. Take home a copy of one of the London papers with the theater and gallery schedules. That'll get Kathleen's attention, I know."

Richard regarded his brothers with renewed admiration. "You guys are as sneaky as Destiny."

They laughed.

"Hey, we learned from a master," Mack reminded him. "I'm sure if you dig through that stuffy, straightforward philosophy that guides you, you'll find a sneaky gene or two buried in you, as well."

Richard shrugged. "Maybe so, but who has time to go digging right now? I'll just follow your lead. We ought to be able to get them over there by when? February?"

"March," Ben said. "We don't want to seem too anxious. Besides, you need to let things simmer down on Destiny's end. If they arrive too soon, she'll see straight through it, too, and trust me, bro, none of our lives will be worth living after that."

Richard nodded, reluctantly accepting the fact that Ben had a valid point. "I suppose I can stave off disaster till March. This Fortnum Travel deal should be decided in April. Once our wives report back, I can go over there and see that it goes our way."

"Not your job," Mack reminded him. "It's Destiny's."

Richard grimaced. "Don't remind me. That's precisely why we're in this mess."

"Hey, don't look so glum," Ben told him. "The way your wife tells it, there's no such thing as bad PR, as long as the papers get the name right. Destiny's keeping Carlton Industries in the news."

"Oh, that's a real comfort," Richard responded. "Did you see that picture? Destiny was in her bathrobe, for God's sake. Her old one."

Mack chuckled. "Would you have been happier if it had been some slinky silk robe?"

Ben fought a grin.

Richard stared from one to the other. "If you two aren't going to take this seriously, I'm going home to start working on Melanie."

"Subtly," Ben reminded him. "Remember, bro, you have to be subtle."

Richard frowned. "I can be subtle."

His brothers hooted.

Richard stalked out of the house without a backward glance. He was beginning to get the distinct impression that not one damn soul in his whole family had a shred of respect for him anymore. If the voters in Alexandria got wind of that, his career in politics was going to be the shortest on record.

14

William had been careful to stay away from the Carlton Industries offices since he and Destiny had returned from Devon. He figured the internal gossip was bound to be active enough after he'd attended her party. And following that revealing photo in the paper, if anyone found out they'd gone chasing after Chester together, it would only double the speculation about their relationship. He had too much respect for her to put her in that position when she was trying so hard to establish herself as a capable businesswoman.

But after his conversation with Richard and Malcolm's announcement that Carlton was looking at making other forays against Harcourt & Sons, he decided it was time to break the rule he'd set for himself. He needed to get a few things straight with the chairman of Carlton Industries' European division. He just had to do it without offending Destiny in the process. The fact that they were the same person was beginning to muddy things up a bit.

He found Destiny closeted in her office with Chester. Miriam had put up token resistance to William barging in, but he was in no mood to follow orders.

"William!" Destiny exclaimed when she saw him. She cast a worried look toward Chester and quickly added, "I had no idea you were coming by."

"Really?" William asked. "Then you thought I wouldn't find out about your attempts to acquire a haberdashery to go head to head with my company? What's next? Will you take over the woolen manufacturing company with which I deal exclusively?"

She paled at that and again looked toward Chester. "I thought I told you to call off that purchase. It's time to stop escalating the tensions between our companies."

Chester gave her a stubborn look. "I thought it best not to be too hasty."

Destiny frowned at him. "William and I have come to an agreement, Chester. He won't interfere in our business as long as we leave his alone. We need to honor that agreement. I'm sure there's enough business in Europe that we needn't compete for the same markets."

"And Fortnum Travel?" Chester asked. "Have you made an agreement on that, as well?"

Destiny gave William a sour look. "No, that's still up for grabs, apparently."

"What other exceptions might come along?" Chester demanded, scowling at William with suspicion. "Do you actually trust him to stick to this so-called agreement?"

"I do," Destiny said firmly.

"Is it in writing?" Chester asked.

"William's word is enough for me," she replied.

Chester looked resigned. "You are far too naive, my dear."

William waited for an explosion. Destiny surprised him by going the icy-disdain route, rather than fiery fury. He watched as she regarded Chester like a queen about to order a subject's head to be chopped off.

"I would advise you against declaring something like that again," she told him coldly.

"We can only work together if I'm permitted to be honest," Chester said, undaunted.

Destiny seemed surprised by his refusal to back down. She nodded slowly. "A valid point. Next time, try to inject a diplomatic note into the criticism, though, will you? It will make things go much more smoothly. I get enough of the other from Richard."

Chester laughed and the tension was broken. "I suppose I can do that much at least. I'll speak to you later about the rest of this. I think we're making excellent progress, Destiny. You've done a fine job of streamlining things throughout the division."

William waited until he had gone, then turned to Destiny. "You two seem to have formed some sort of mutual-admiration pact all of a sudden."

She regarded him with curiosity, then laughed. "My goodness, William, don't tell me you're jealous?"

"Of Chester? Hardly."

"Really? It sounded that way to me."

He tried to contain his amusement at her interpretation of his reaction. "Perhaps I might be, if I thought you were his type."

A touch of purely female indignation flared in her eyes. "Why wouldn't I be?"

"You're a woman."

She stared at him blankly, then gasped. "Oh, my. Chester's gay?"

William nodded. "Well-known around town. He's been with the same man for some years now."

She shook her head. "I don't know how I missed that one. Why on earth didn't Chester bring his partner to my party?"

"Perhaps he didn't want to offend you, in case you objected."

"I'm far more broadminded than that," she said. "Unorthodox relationships are nothing new to me."

William barely contained a smile, knowing that she was lumping their relationship in with Chester's in an odd sort of way. "I'm aware of that," he said agreeably. "But he didn't know that, did he? That could also explain his panic when you turned up in Devon. I'm sure they were on holiday there together."

Destiny frowned. "I'm not sure I like the fact that you seem to know more about my personnel than I do."

"Have lunch with me and you can pick my brain for any other tidbits I know. You might find it illuminating."

"You didn't come over here to ask me to lunch," she reminded him. "You came to accuse me of going back on our deal."

"True enough, but we've taken care of that, and now that I'm here, I find I haven't seen quite enough of you yet. Are you free?"

She regarded him thoughtfully, then finally nodded. "I can be. Give me a couple of moments to rearrange a few things."

After she'd spoken to Miriam, she grabbed her coat

and allowed William to help her into it. He let his hands rest on her shoulders when he was done.

"I've missed being able to do this," he told her quietly.

She turned and faced him, her expression quizzical. "What? Helping me on with my coat?"

"No, being able to touch you, smelling that wonderful, sexy scent you wear."

"You remember my perfume?" she asked incredulously.

He laughed. "Wasn't it Proust who wrote an entire book based on the memories that are stirred by aromas that once meant something to us? Nothing is more evocative than scent." He winked at her. "Besides, I must have bought you gallons of the stuff. How could I possibly forget it? At the time it was the most expensive perfume on the market, I'm sure."

"But surely you've bought perfume for many women since then," she said.

He shook his head. "Never."

Again, surprise lit her eyes. "Please don't try to convince me that you've lived a celibate life since we parted, William. You're far too attractive and virile to have gotten away with that. I suspect women were falling all over you from the moment you returned to London."

"Well, of course," he teased, knowing it would bring a flash of annoyance to her eyes. He wasn't disappointed. Satisfied, he changed his tack. "But there have been far fewer women than you might imagine, and none of them ever touched my heart or lingered in my memory."

She blinked back the sudden dampness he could see in her eyes.

"Oh, William, you mustn't say things like that."

"Even if they're true?"

"Even then," she said fiercely.

"Why? Because they might soften your heart toward me?"

"Yes, that's precisely the reason."

He searched her face, wanting her to admit the truth, that she still cared for him, as well. "Would that be so awful, Destiny?"

"Not awful," she said. "Dangerous."

"I won't hurt you," he promised.

She regarded him sadly. "You can't be sure of that. You did once. And if me being with you threatens to cause a rift for me with my family, I'm afraid we'll face the same fate a second time, only this time with me to blame."

"We both had our hearts broken, Destiny. I'd say we're even and it's time to think of starting over with the slate clean. I'm going to keep telling you that till I've convinced you. In the end, this will be your decision, not Richard's."

She looked torn. "If only that were true," she began, then shook her head. "But it's not. Let's not discuss this again, William. It's pointless."

"Love is never pointless," he said. "Didn't you once tell me it's the most important thing of all? I imagine that's what you taught your nephews, too."

She laughed, her eyes suddenly alight with some memory. "Indeed, I did. Come, let's go to lunch and I'll explain."

The moment was broken now, so William relented. "What are you in the mood for?"

"Italian, I think. Something robust."

"Then I know the perfect place," he said, tucking her arm through his. "I hope you cleared the entire afternoon, because once we're there, you won't want to leave."

She frowned at him. "I do have work to do, you know. I'm not idle, as I once was."

"But you're the boss now. You can indulge yourself from time to time."

"Why, so I am." Her expression brightened. "The boss," she echoed with a shake of her head. "Amazing. Who would have thought it?"

"I would," William said at once. "I always knew you could do anything you set your mind to."

"But to take on such a challenge at such a late date," she said. "It's really rather astonishing."

"Late date? Oh, my dear, don't you know that the best years are yet to come?"

Excitement sparkled in her eyes when she met his gaze. "You know, William, I do believe you're right."

A bottle of excellent red wine and a huge plate of a spicy vodka penne left Destiny feeling pleasantly full and quite mellow.

"That was delicious," she told William. "But now I think I need a brisk walk in the cold air if I'm to get any work at all done this afternoon. I've some hard decisions to make about staffing in one of our departments. I can't put off meeting with the people involved."

"No dessert? No coffee?" he asked.

"We have an outstanding crême brûlée, ma'am," the waiter said. "And excellent espresso."

Destiny laughed. "I don't know," she protested.

"Just a taste," William taunted. "I know crême brûlée is your favorite."

"Next to chocolate mousse," she said.

The waiter's expression brightened. "We have that, as well."

"We'll have one of each and two espressos," William said, taking the decision out of her hands. "Let me indulge you just this once."

"Just this once," she agreed. "Otherwise, I won't be able to fit into that new wardrobe of suits I bought for work."

She met William's gaze and thought she spotted a shadow in his eyes. "What is it? Is something wrong?"

"There's something I've been debating telling you," he admitted eventually.

"Just say it."

"I think I will. I don't want there to be any secrets between us, but I worry that it will upset you."

"William!"

"I spoke to Richard earlier today."

She frowned at him. "You spoke to my nephew? Why?"

"Actually, he called me to warn me away from Carlton Industries."

Destiny felt her heart begin to pound. She was going to wring Richard's neck the first chance she got. "How dare he!" she muttered. "What did you tell him?"

"That the game was over and that he should be talking to you. I said you'd handled the situation."

She regarded him with surprise. "You said that?"

"Of course. It's the truth. The situation is in hand, at least as far as Harcourt & Sons is concerned. The only competition between us now is the travel company. I don't expect you to give in on that and I think I've made it clear to you why I cannot."

She was surprised that he'd given her the credit for settling most of the differences between the two companies, though she doubted that Richard had been convinced. "Thank you. Did he believe you?"

"Hard to say. Since he obviously didn't call you straight away, I'd say he's probably still miffed at my suggestion that I understand you and respect you far more than he does."

Destiny bit back a chuckle. "Yes, that would annoy him. Since he hasn't called, I wonder what he's plotting over there."

"You don't think he'll just take my word that there's no longer anything for him to worry about and let it drop?"

"Now who's being naive?" she said. "No, Richard won't let this drop. He doesn't trust you, and to be perfectly honest, he's not too sure about me."

"Don't you find that vaguely insulting?"

"*Vaguely* insulting? I find it infuriating," she said tightly. "But I'm prepared for anything now. Thank you for telling me he's now going behind my back to take care of things. I believe dealing with Richard will be my next challenge, and frankly, I'm looking forward to it."

"A little too eagerly, if that glint in your eyes is any indication."

She grinned. "You read me so well."

"Perhaps we should change the subject," William

said. "I didn't want to upset you and yet that's precisely what I've done."

"No, you've forewarned me. That's something else entirely," she said as the waiter set their desserts on the table.

Destiny absentmindedly picked up her spoon and took a bite of the chocolate mousse. Light and rich, it was almost delicious enough to distract her from the problem of her nephew's interference. She tasted the crême brûlée next with its crisp, sugary topping and delicate orange-flavored custard, and sighed with pleasure.

"Your mood seems to be improving," William noted with amusement.

"For the moment," she agreed, focused on the desserts. It was hard to say which was better. She couldn't possibly eat both of them. It would be too decadent. "Don't you want one, or some of each?"

"I'll eat whatever you don't finish," William said.

"Now, there's a risky approach," she teased. "You might wind up with nothing at all."

"I'll take my chances," he said, sipping his espresso and looking thoroughly content.

"How do you do it?" she asked.

"Do what? Ignore dessert?"

She made a face. "No, of course not. How do you run a company and make it look so easy?"

"I'm not sure what you mean."

"I know you're more focused than you seem. Harcourt & Sons has grown since your father's day. He would be proud of what you've accomplished. Yet you seem to take it in stride, as if you handled it all before ten in the morning and had all the time in the world left for other things."

"Maybe because I've surrounded myself with competent people I trust," he said. "My assistant could probably run it quite nicely without me ever setting foot in the office, but he's been there since my father's day. He knows all the ropes. You're basically starting fresh, even with Chester on board. It takes time, Destiny, but you'll accomplish it, too. There's a great deal of delegation and trust involved in running a company, unless you anticipate doing everything yourself. And that course will send you to an early grave."

"I hope you're right," she said plaintively. "Right now, it seems so daunting. I'm not sure I'll ever get it all sorted out."

"You will. Chester himself said you've already made great inroads. And once things are running like a well-oiled machine, you'll be able to prioritize and do the things outside of work that matter to you." He gave her a rather lascivious look. "Have a relationship, perhaps."

She felt the heat climbing into her checks. "Let's not go there."

"Once our relationship was your top priority," he reminded her.

"Yes, but times change. I came here to accomplish something, to prove something to myself. I think I rather like being hands-on at Carlton Industries," she said. "I feel useful. It's a challenge. I never expected to be excited by business, but I am. I was never prouder than I was when I saw the sales figures for Jameson's during the holidays and could show Richard that our investment was going to pay off. You, of all people, must know how that feels."

William nodded. "I suppose I felt a bit of that excitement when I first came home and went to work for the company. After my initial reluctance, I found I was eager to prove myself and win back my father's approval." He gave her a look filled with sorrow. "And I was eager to forget, as well. I needed to keep my mind occupied twenty-four hours a day."

Destiny nodded, recognizing that he'd gone through much the same thing she had when she'd arrived back in the States all those years ago.

She pushed that aside for the moment and concentrated on William. "Did you make peace with your father?"

"Eventually," he said.

"I'm glad. That's what I'd hoped for."

"It was at a terrible cost, though," he said, his gaze on her. "I'd lost you."

Once again, Destiny compared their situations. Had the price of caring for her nephews and giving them a secure life been too high? How could she say that? Yes, she'd lost something precious, a love she had treasured with all her heart, but she'd gained so much. Putting the two on a ledger and trying to make them balance was an impossible task.

"We both did what we had to do," she told him, sure of that much at least. And though she didn't want to say it, didn't want him to realize the deliberate decision she'd made back then, part of what she'd had to do was give William back to his family.

"I suppose," William said, clearly skeptical.

"Darling, it's water under the bridge, anyway. It's useless to live with regrets. All that counts is the here and now."

"Then I shall count myself lucky to be blessed with your company right here and right now," he said, then grinned. "But I won't stop looking toward the future, Destiny."

Destiny felt a long-forgotten twinge of excitement. What a perfectly delightful warning!

Richard was impatient to put his plan into motion, despite the warnings Mack and Ben had given him. Sitting at dinner with Melanie, he pushed his food around on his plate and kept a worried expression on his face. Eventually his wife took the bait.

"Is something bothering you?" Melanie asked. "You've hardly touched your dinner. I thought you loved my pot roast."

Now, there was a minefield, Richard thought. He'd made the mistake once in the full heat of romance of praising her dried-out pot roast. Now she fixed it at least once a week and he was forced to go along with that original pretense.

"Dinner's fine," he said. "I'm just thinking about Destiny."

"Oh?"

"Have you spoken to her?" he asked.

"Not for several days," she said. "Why?"

Relieved that she'd have no recent comparison with which to challenge his fibs, he said, "She sounds really down. I think the work's getting to her. Or maybe she's homesick."

Melanie's expression turned thoughtful. "Isn't that natural? She's been so close to you, Mack and Ben for all these years and done very little on her own. It makes sense that she'd be missing you."

"And the babies," Richard added. "Plus, I think she's gotten used to being around you, Beth and Kathleen. After having nothing but boys around, it's been great for her to have women friends. I know she says stuff to you that she'd never say to us. She probably misses having someone to confide in. With so many new things going on in her life, she must regret not having anyone she trusts to talk to."

"I suppose," Melanie said, giving him an odd look, as if she didn't entirely buy his sensitivity to Destiny's moods. "If you're really worried, I'll give her a call in the morning. It's too late now."

He nodded. "Good idea. Maybe you can get to the bottom of her mood. I don't want this job to put too much pressure on her."

"Oh, I'm sure she's up to the challenge," Melanie said at once. "She's probably thriving on it. If anything, she might be a little homesick."

"What do we do if she is? If I suggest she come home, she'll think I'm calling her back here because I disapprove of the way she's handling things."

Melanie gave him a wry look. "Which, of course, you do."

"That's not the point. I would never do anything to hurt her."

"I know you wouldn't mean to," she agreed. She regarded him with a narrowed gaze. "What's really going on here, Richard? What are you up to?"

He worked hard to plaster what he hoped was an innocent expression on his face. "Me?" he asked, barely able to mask his exasperation with himself for blowing things. "I'm not up to anything. You asked me what was on my mind and I told you."

"Uh-huh," she said, her skepticism plain. "I'm not buying it."

"You don't think I'm capable of worrying about Destiny?" he demanded.

"Sure you are, but if you were really worried about her, you'd hop on the company jet and go over there. You're being subtle and trying to get me involved, instead. It's totally out of character."

Richard bit back the groan that would have given him away for sure. Obviously he was totally lousy at subterfuge. He hoped to hell Mack and Ben were having better luck if they'd been stupid enough to try this particular, clearly doomed tactic.

"Just call her, okay?" he said irritably.

"First thing tomorrow," Melanie promised. "And then we'll finish this conversation and you can tell me what's really going on."

Richard wondered if this had been part of Destiny's scheming intent when she'd handpicked Melanie for him. Had she realized that Melanie would see straight through him in the same way Destiny had always done? He'd found it mildly annoying in his aunt. Living with it day in and day out, and knowing that it was the way things were going to be between him and Melanie till the day he died, was daunting.

Surely a man ought to be able to slip something past his wife from time to time. God help him if he was ever insane enough to try to keep anything important from her. Melanie would have the secret out of him before he'd had time to construct any sort of positive spin.

"I have no idea why you think there's something going on," Richard grumbled, making a halfhearted attempt to divert her. "It's a phone call. If you don't want to make it, don't. It's not a big deal."

Melanie merely rolled her eyes. "Tell me something. If I were to call Beth and Kathleen later this evening, would they have had similar conversations with Mack and Ben? Are they planting similar seeds of worry in their wives' minds?"

"No," Richard said with confidence. *They* probably hadn't been stupid enough to get into this without giving it more thought. *They'd* probably stuck to the plan to build up to all of this slowly.

"Really?" Melanie asked, looking surprised. "You won't mind, though, if I call them to check?"

Richard shrugged, envisioning the whole scheme going up in smoke thanks to his precipitous actions. "Whatever."

Melanie laughed. "You are so bad at this," she told him, coming around the table to snuggle onto his lap.

"Bad at what?"

"Trying to be devious."

He sighed, accepting that any further denials were totally pointless. "You'd think I'd have learned better from Destiny."

"Frankly, I'm grateful you didn't," she told him. "Now, come on and tell me what's really going on. I'm on your side. You know that."

"You might not be when you hear the whole story," he warned her.

Then he told her everything that had happened in London and explained that he, Mack and Ben thought their wives ought to go over and get a firsthand look at the situation.

"Let me see if I understand this," Melanie said slowly. "You want us to spy on Destiny for you?"

"Pretty much, yes."

"Okay."

He stared at her in shock. "You're agreeing? Just like that?"

"You want us to go to London, not Siberia. It sounds like fun to me. I'm sure Beth and Kathleen will agree."

He studied her with a narrowed gaze. "And the spying part?"

She laughed. "That all depends."

"On?" he asked suspiciously.

"Whether or not we can wheedle something even more intriguing out of Destiny for keeping quiet."

"You intend to play us off against each other?" he demanded indignantly.

"Why not? You're the one who's relying on sneakiness to get what you're after, Richard. She ought to be able to play the same game."

"Oh, God," he whispered. "What the hell have I done?"

"Started something you don't know how to finish?" Melanie suggested cheerfully.

Richard nodded glumly. "I'd say that about covers it."

15

Richard had suddenly taken a decidedly hands-off approach to managing the European division. Destiny had grown so used to having him looking over her shoulder, she didn't quite know what to make of this new tactic. She probably should have been relieved, but instead she was becoming highly suspicious. It wasn't like her nephew to let days pass without checking up on her, much less two entire weeks. It was the beginning of February, and she'd hardly heard from him since he'd made that call to William.

When she couldn't stand the silence another moment, she picked up the phone and called him.

"What are you up to now?" she demanded.

"What the devil are you talking about?" he retorted with suitable indignation. "I'm not up to anything."

"You must be. You've left me alone for days and days now. Are you hoping if you give me enough rope, I'll hang myself and you'll be justified in firing me?"

"I wouldn't do that," he said, sounding genuinely shocked that she would even suggest such a thing.

"Then it must be something else," she said suspiciously. "Have you got someone over here spying on me?"

"I told you way back in December that I'd informed Chester I didn't appreciate him doing that and that I'd back you up if you fired him for it."

It wasn't exactly a direct disclaimer, but Destiny was stymied. If Richard did have a spy, he wasn't going to admit to it. Even so, she refused to let the matter drop so easily.

"Then I'll ask again," she said. "What are you up to?"

"Have you ever considered that I might simply be gaining faith in your abilities?"

"No," she said without the slightest hesitation. "Even if you were, you'd still be watching me like a hawk. You micromanage everything, Richard. It's the way you operate."

She noticed that he didn't rush to deny that. Inspiration finally struck. "You have someone dogging my every action, don't you? He's not spying and reporting back to you, but if I do something he doesn't think you'd approve of, he's to jump in and save the company from ruin."

"Destiny, that logic's a little twisted even for you."

He had a point, but she wasn't prepared to admit it. "Well, I know you're up to something. Trust me, sooner or later, I'll figure it out."

He laughed. "I'll consider that fair warning, then. Bye. I love you."

"I love you, too," she responded distractedly.

She didn't buy his innocent act for one second. Richard didn't sit back and wait for disaster to strike. He was the kind of businessman who tried to foresee potential problems and nip them in the bud. He had a spy on the premises. She would bet her prized chintz teacup collection on that.

Determined to figure it out, she picked up the phone again and called Chester. Perhaps he knew what was going on.

"I'd like a meeting with you," she said unceremoniously.

"Now?"

"Yes."

"Destiny, is something wrong? You sound rather peculiar."

"We'll discuss it when I see you."

Chester was in her office in less than two minutes. The man could move when he had to. She admired that.

"Have you spoken to Richard lately?" she asked without preamble.

"Richard? No, of course not. He made it quite clear that you're in charge. And I assured you that I would no longer go behind your back. If I have a problem with one of your decisions, I'll bring it to your attention."

"Humph!" she said skeptically. "Is there someone else who could be reporting to him?"

Chester regarded her with obvious bemusement. "What on earth makes you think someone is speaking to your nephew behind your back?"

"The fact that's he's not calling me every ten seconds to see what I'm up to. That tells me he already knows every move I'm making."

"Perhaps he's beginning to trust your decisions," Chester said. "Or perhaps it's the fact that you've been inundating him with reports on the progress we're making in all areas. He must be pleased by that."

"He said something like that himself," she admitted.

"Well, then, you should be proud of yourself for winning him over."

"I would be, if I thought that was it, but I don't."

"Destiny, I think you're worrying about nothing."

Destiny didn't believe that for a minute, but it was obvious Chester wasn't the person involved. She changed the subject. "How are you coming on discovering who might have hired that photographer who took those pictures outside my apartment?"

"If I were you, I'd have a talk with Perkins and Wildemon."

David Perkins was her chief financial officer and Edward Wildemon was head of marketing. She'd been impressed with both of them when she'd first met them. They were experts in their fields and they were quick-witted and filled with fresh ideas. She'd hate to think either of them was involved in something so sleazy. Still, the possibility had to be considered.

"They'd both hoped to move up if you were fired?" she asked Chester.

"Yes, and frankly, I'd start with Wildemon. He's the one with the media contacts. I doubt it would take much for him to locate a sleazy photographer and then to get the pictures placed in that newspaper."

"You haven't talked to him?"

"No, I thought you'd prefer to do that yourself. I didn't want to tip him off that we were even looking into the matter."

"But you have nothing on either of them beyond suspicion, is that right?" she asked.

"Yes," he admitted a bit defensively. "I can't very well go through their bank records to see if they made payments to a photographer, and they're certainly not bragging about this around the office. It is common knowledge around here, though, that they're still resentful of the way things turned out."

Destiny nodded slowly. "Okay, then. Thank you, Chester. I'll take it from here."

After he was gone, she wondered if he realized how terrible he was when it came to detective work. It was just as well he'd chosen a different career path.

The only problem with taking on the assignment herself was that she was equally stymied about how to carry on from here. She'd never once fancied herself to be at the center of an Agatha Christie mystery. Nor had she ever compared herself to Jessica Fletcher on *Murder, She Wrote.*

Ah, well, wasn't she the one who'd said not too long ago that it was never too late to tackle a new challenge? Perhaps she'd turn out to be a clever sleuth, after all.

William knew that Destiny wanted Chester to handle the search for the person responsible for planting that incriminating photograph, but he wasn't entirely sure Chester could be trusted. Perhaps Chester had made peace with Destiny's presence at Carlton Industries, but for an ambitious man to give up so easily struck William as highly unlikely.

Fortunately, he belonged to the same men's club in London as several people who traveled in Chester's social circle. At the end of the day, he decided a cup of tea or perhaps a glass of whiskey would be just the thing to stave off the night's chill.

The club to which Harcourt men had belonged since William's great-grandfather's day was every bit as staid and dreary as the men who belonged to it. The wallpaper was a muted stripe of burgundy and cream, the drapes a heavy burgundy velvet. Huge wing chairs and mahogany side tables were grouped around a stone fireplace in the lounge. The roaring fire and the excellence of the whiskey were the primary comforts on the cold, raw night.

William spotted Sir Lloyd Smedley when he entered and figured he would be the best place to start. Lloyd was, after all, the one who'd told him all those months ago on a golf course about Destiny taking over at Carlton Industries. He obviously had some sort of pipeline into the company's internal politics.

William crossed the room. "You waiting for someone, Lloyd?"

The man glanced up from his paper, his expression brightening at once. "William. Haven't seen you in ages. Have a seat and tell me what you've been up to."

William sat down and beckoned to the butler for a drink. Ignoring Lloyd's question, he said, "You're looking fit. Have you been playing golf since we were in Scotland?"

"Every chance I get," Lloyd said. "Winds and cold are the very devil this time of year, though."

"Still cheating to win?"

Lloyd choked on his sip of whiskey. "The devil, you say. Never cheated in my life. Another era, I'd call you out for saying such a thing."

William chuckled at his indignation. "You forget I've been on the greens with you. In fact, last time we were out, you did your best to rattle me and put me off my game."

Lloyd looked vaguely abashed. "You mean that business about Destiny Carlton? Just passing along a bit of gossip. Imagine you've seen her by now," he said, his expression sly.

"I think everyone in London knows about that."

"Can't fathom what you mean. Are the two of you carrying on in some sort of public spectacle?"

He managed to sound innocent enough, but William wasn't convinced. "You didn't see the picture in the paper?"

Lloyd's high color gave him away. "Didn't see it," he claimed, then admitted, "It was the talk of this place, though. Must say, your stock rose quite a bit."

"Really? Anyone seem especially delighted about it?"

Lloyd might have a single-track mind, occupied mostly by golf scores and the hunts still held on his country estate, but he wasn't a fool. "You looking for the person responsible?"

William nodded. "Any ideas?"

"Let me think a minute." Lloyd's expression turned thoughtful. "That chap, what's his name?" He frowned. "You know the one I mean, goes around with Chester Sandhurst."

William's pulse began to race. "Oliver Diggs?"

"That's the one. He seemed delighted about it. Couldn't wait to show it round. Didn't have a look myself. Told him I thought it was unseemly to take such interest in someone else's private business."

"What did he say to that?"

"That I wouldn't be so stuffy if one of the two people involved had done me the kind of wrong done to Sandhurst."

"Is it possible Diggs himself was behind the picture?" William asked. It made a certain amount of sense. If Diggs felt Chester had been wronged, he might have gone behind his back to seek revenge. And Chester might have inadvertently given him the way to gain access to Destiny's flat. Perhaps he even had his own ax to grind after being excluded from Destiny's party.

"There was definitely satisfaction in his expression," Lloyd said. "Thought at the time he was just gloating about another's misfortune, but it could have been something else entirely. Pride over a job well done, perhaps."

"Is he around here much?"

"Haven't seen him since, as a matter of fact. He's not a member himself. It's Ridgely who brings him and Ridgely's been off on a vacation to some warm island in the Caribbean since just after the holidays."

"Thanks, Lloyd. You've been a big help. Next round of golf's on me. Might even let you increase your handicap by a shot or two."

"No need to do me any favors," Lloyd retorted. "I can win on my own."

"Yes, but it's your tactics that worry me," William said. "I'll sign for the drinks on my way out."

Lloyd nodded. "Never say no to that. Good to see you."

"You, too."

Lloyd gave him a sly look. "You making progress with the Carlton woman? Looked for a time before Christmas that she might be getting the better of you."

"If you're talking about the competition between H&S Books and Jameson's, don't believe everything you see in a newspaper ad."

"Seldom do, but those ads gave me a good chuckle. Couldn't decide which bookstore to give my business to."

"Which did you choose?" William asked curiously.

"Divided it up," Lloyd said. "Had to get a look at what was really going on."

"And? Will you go back to H&S Books or Jameson's?"

"Have to wait and see what lures the two of you come up with, don't I?"

William sighed. He and Destiny had clearly started something that was going to be hard to put a stop to now that they'd declared their personal truce. If there were more people around London who felt as Lloyd did, the bookstores would remain empty until they came up with whole new marketing campaigns.

Ah, well, he'd known having Destiny back in his life was going to be a challenge one way or another. He just hadn't expected the challenges to be coming at him from every direction.

The first wave of assault from across the sea came in the form of all three of Destiny's nieces by marriage. Melanie, Beth and Kathleen descended on London on a cold March day with blustery winds blowing in from the north. They appeared in Destiny's office without warning.

"Darlings," she said, delighted and wary at the same time. "Why didn't you tell me you were coming?"

They gave one another wry looks.

"We didn't know ourselves until a few days ago," Melanie said.

Destiny regarded her suspiciously. "Did you fly over on the company plane?"

"No, we came on a commercial airliner," Beth said, and earned a poke in the ribs from Kathleen for her candor.

Destiny smiled. "Paid a pretty penny, did you? Or have you had those tickets longer than a few days?"

Melanie gave her sister-in-law an aggrieved look. "We made the reservations a while back, but we weren't entirely sure we'd be able to come until a few days ago. We had to make arrangements for the time off, and Beth wanted to be sure her new nanny could handle things for several days. As it is, she'll be fussing and calling home every ten minutes."

"Nice save," Destiny complimented her. "So, are you here for shopping, the theater, sightseeing?"

"All of that," Kathleen said, when neither Melanie nor Beth could find their tongue.

Destiny regarded them with a resigned look. So, this was Richard's scheme. "And a little spying, I imagine."

Only Beth and Kathleen blushed. Melanie regarded her with a brazen look and never even blinked.

"Richard's worried," Melanie admitted.

"Richard's always worrying about one thing or another. What is it this time?" Destiny asked, even though she knew the answer.

"He thinks you're getting too chummy with William Harcourt," Beth told her. "Mack's concerned about the same thing."

"As is Ben," Kathleen added.

"None of them are buying that you're seeing him entirely for the sake of the business," Melanie added.

"So what? Are they afraid I'll sell all our trade secrets?" Destiny asked. "Surely they know me better than that."

"No," Melanie insisted gently, coming over to give her a fierce hug. "They're afraid you'll get hurt."

Destiny squeezed her hand. Melanie was a wonderfully sensitive woman, which was one reason Destiny had handpicked her for Richard. "You may be worried about that, but I guarantee you that Richard is not. I love him dearly, and I've had high hopes for him since he was wise enough to marry you, but he's a single-focus, bottom-line kind of man."

"Not where you're concerned," Melanie countered. "He knows that you and William have a history. He doesn't know the details, but he suspects that William has already hurt you once."

"History is exactly what William and I have," Destiny claimed, determined not to suggest for a second that she'd been unsettled ever since she'd laid eyes on him again. "It's old news."

Beth gave her a penetrating look. She was a doctor and scientist. She had an uncanny knack for diagnosing what was at the heart of things. "Then what are all the cozy dinners about?"

"Good food, friendly conversation, spying," Destiny said blithely.

They laughed. It was Beth who sobered first.

"You're trying to steal *his* trade secrets?" Beth guessed.

"Why not?" Destiny replied without the slightest hint of guilt. "It seems only fair since he's used things I told him in confidence years ago to try to steal business from us." It was a believable spin, she thought.

"Learn anything valuable?" Melanie asked curiously.

"Not a blessed thing," Destiny grumbled. "He seems to be on to me. Besides, we've called a truce and he's sticking to it. I'm not sure I want to do anything that will spark another attack. We're in the thick of the Fortnum Travel negotiations right now, and I know William intends to swoop in and save David Fortnum's hide. I'm doing all I can to make it difficult for him. I know if we lose, Richard will be furious. He's determined to have that company."

"Just how does William intend to beat you?" Melanie asked.

"Out of loyalty to Fortnum, I suspect he'll do whatever it takes to make an offer that's more attractive to the shareholders than whatever we come up with," Destiny explained. "I just wish I knew how far he's willing to go."

"Perhaps you've been skimping on the wine. Invite him over and let us go to work on him," Beth suggested. "We'll find out for you."

"I'll bet we can wrangle all sorts of juicy tidbits from him," Kathleen added eagerly.

Destiny frowned at the idea. "You just want to get a good look at the two of us together so you can report back."

"That, too," they admitted candidly enough now that the cat was out of the bag about the real reason for this supposedly impromptu visit.

Destiny shook her head. It was definitely a bad idea to put these three in the same room with William. "I don't think so."

"We'll find him on our own, you know," Melanie

reminded her. "We can't go back home laden down with nothing but shopping bags and theater stubs. We have to go back with some news that will reassure our worrywart husbands."

Destiny smiled. That was true enough. And better to let them meet William and go home with some nice, dull report, than to have Richard charging over here. Compared to Richard when his ire was up, these three were capable of being friendly enough.

"Fine," she relented. "We'll all have tea. Someplace public, so William won't fear a lynching."

"Your place," Melanie insisted with a grin. "Let him squirm a little. All things considered, that's more than fair, don't you agree?"

Destiny wasn't entirely sure her worst enemy deserved to have these three turned loose on him, but she was sure William was up to the challenge. And maybe he did deserve to have to answer to someone other than her. She certainly didn't seem to be intimidating him in the slightest these days, not even with her rather clever business tactics.

Besides, Melanie, Beth and Kathleen were bright and intuitive. Perhaps they could decipher whether William's claim that he still loved her was sincere or just some plot to trick her into trusting him for his own devious reasons.

"Okay, then," she agreed eventually. "My place, but we'll wait until tomorrow. I need time to prepare."

"What's to prepare?" Melanie demanded. "I'm sure the three of us can rustle up an appropriate tea by late afternoon today. No point in dragging this out. Once we've done our duty, we can settle down and do some serious shopping."

"I agree. If it seems as if we can't pull it off, I'm very talented at finding excellent carryout," Beth said.

"Forget that," Kathleen said decisively. "Destiny, is your kitchen well stocked with the basics?"

Destiny's head was spinning. On their own, she was a more-than-even match for her nephew's wives. Now that they'd ganged up on her, the odds had definitely shifted in their favor. "Well, enough for my needs, but I doubt the pantry will have what you need if you intend to start baking."

"I'm thinking scones and little tea sandwiches with some bits of cake and tarts," Kathleen said. "That's what my customers love when I have teas at the gallery."

Melanie and Beth stared at her.

"How had I forgotten that one of us actually knows her way around a kitchen?" Melanie said. "Come on, Beth. Let's get Kathleen to the nearest store so she can get to work." She turned back to Destiny.

"Call William," she said briskly. "And don't take no for an answer."

Destiny gave them a key to her apartment and the address, then watched the whirlwind leave her office with the same energy with which it had entered. She sank back in her chair, exhausted by it all. When she'd caught her breath, she picked up the phone and dialed William.

"You're never going to believe it," she told him. "Guess who's turned up in London."

"Your nephews' wives," he said at once.

"How on earth did you know that?"

He laughed. "I'd like to tell you that I'm psychic or that it was totally predictable that they'd turn up sooner or later, but the truth is I called your office about an hour ago and Miriam told me."

"Did she also tell you you're invited to tea at my flat at five?"

"I don't believe she mentioned that," he said.

"Good. Then at least she isn't listening at the keyhole," Destiny said tartly. "Will you come?"

"Of course," he said eagerly, then hesitated. "Unless you'd rather I came up with an excuse."

She debated how to reply in a way that wouldn't get his guard up. Better to let him think their curiosity was purely personal, an inspection tour so to speak, rather than any sort of attempt to dig into his business plans.

"Unfortunately, I don't think there's an excuse you could manufacture aside from being on your deathbed that would get you out of this," she told him truthfully. "Even then, I'm not sure they wouldn't insist on bringing tea to you. They've heard a lot about you and they intend to have their curiosity satisfied."

He laughed at her obvious dismay. "Not to worry, darling. Charming suspicious women is something I do rather well."

"Yes, well, it hasn't worked on me yet, has it?" she retorted. "I'll see you at five."

She hung up and closed her eyes, trying to imagine how this encounter was likely to go. The only image that came to mind was of total disaster.

16

William had a few hours to kill before tea with Destiny's family, so he went looking for Oliver Diggs. It was something he'd been debating for some time now. If Diggs was somehow involved with that photograph, there was no telling what he might do if William cornered him. If he was innocent, then being questioned might make him angry enough to get Chester all stirred up in a way that would become a problem for Destiny. After weighing all the risks, William finally concluded it was something that had to be done. Better to know if Diggs was the enemy than to be blindsided by another surprise attack.

He tracked Chester's partner to an exclusive gym known to be favored by London's elite gay men. Since William doubted he could disguise himself as any sort of member in the establishment, he opted for waiting across the street in a small coffee shop.

He was sipping his second cup of coffee when Diggs emerged, his complexion ruddy from his workout. A good decade younger than Sandhurst's fifty, Diggs clearly prided himself on staying fit. His shoulders were broad, his hips lean and his step jaunty.

William crossed the street. "Oliver, fancy seeing you here," he greeted the man, as if it were nothing more than a casual encounter.

Diggs's gaze narrowed. "Harcourt, isn't it?"

"Yes, William Harcourt. We've met at my men's club. Believe you go as Ridgely's guest," he said, trying not to make an immediate connection to Chester. Better to reveal himself slowly.

"Brutal day, isn't it?" William added. "Haven't felt the wind like this in an age. I was thinking of a cup of coffee. Care to join me?"

The man immediately regarded him with suspicion. "This isn't a chance meeting at all, is it?"

Caught, William didn't waste time denying it. "No. Actually, I was hoping to have a word with you."

"About?"

"Would you mind discussing it once we're out of the cold air?"

"If you're hoping to pump me for inside information about Carlton Industries, I'll tell you right now, I don't have any. Chester doesn't bring his work home with him."

"Why would I want to do such a thing?" William asked. "If I were after inside information, the last person I'd choose to ask would be someone whose first loyalty is to a member of the Carlton executive team."

"Perhaps, but everyone in London knows there's a feud in the wind between Carlton Industries and your firm. Chester natters on and on about it. Gets bloody tiresome to be perfectly honest."

William grinned. "Yes, I imagine it would. Business

is seldom all that interesting to people unless they're involved in it. Now, about that coffee?"

Diggs finally relented. "I have a few minutes to spare, I suppose."

"Excellent," William said a little too heartily.

Thankfully the waiter in the coffee shop didn't acknowledge by so much as a blink of an eye that William had left the very same table not five minutes before. He brought their coffees, then discreetly disappeared.

"You and Chester enjoy yourselves in Devon over the holidays?" William asked.

For the first time Diggs's expression registered real surprise. "You knew about that?"

"Ran into someone who mentioned it at the club," William said evasively. No point in stirring up speculation by mentioning that he'd been there with Destiny when she'd turned up and brought their vacation to a sudden end. "You have family there?" he asked instead.

"No, no family. The truth is, neither of our families approves of us, so we rarely see them, and never together."

"Too bad."

Diggs shrugged. "To be expected from conservative old sods, I suppose. Wouldn't have expected it from Ms. Carlton, though. Thought all Americans were more liberal-thinking than that."

"Oh? What makes you think she doesn't approve?"

"It's not me, so much as Chester. He didn't want me anywhere about the place when she had her fancy holiday party." He gave William a speculative look. "Heard you were there, though. How did that happen?"

"We're old friends, as a matter of fact," William

said. "To tell you the truth, you should be grateful you weren't forced to attend. It was more of that business talk. You'd have been bored."

"Can't imagine they were talking too much business with you underfoot."

William laughed. "Yes, the key people did tend to clam up whenever I got near. Still, I can see your point about being excluded. Must have made you angry."

Diggs shrugged as if it were no longer of any consequence. "Not angry. Just a bit disappointed. Blamed Chester mostly. He's not the kind who likes to take chances. One of his flaws. He admits it himself. Says that's why Carlton sent Destiny over here to take charge."

"How do you feel about taking chances? Are you more of a risk-taker than Chester?"

"No. I just believe it's pointless to try to hide the truth." He shrugged. "Water under the bridge now."

"Then you and Chester have made peace?"

"Of course."

"So you wouldn't have any reason to want to get even with Ms. Carlton?"

Diggs looked genuinely shocked by the suggestion. "Get even? And risk Chester's job in the process? May be an enigma to me, but he loves that company and his work. Why the hell would I do something to put that in jeopardy?"

"Retaliation for a snub," William suggested. "Or resentment over the way they treated Chester."

"Wasn't her snub, more than likely. It was probably Chester doing what he thought was best without giving a thought to my feelings. As for the other, if Chester can live with it, so can I."

William nodded, certain that Oliver had it pegged exactly right. "Then as far as you're concerned, dealing with Carlton Industries is Chester's call? You wouldn't go round him with your own agenda?"

"Absolutely not." He regarded William curiously. "Why are you so interested in this?"

"Just making conversation," William said.

"Thought maybe you were hoping to find a rift between me and Chester that you could exploit," Diggs said, proving he had the kind of devious mind it would take to plot revenge, even though he'd claimed he had no reason to.

"Nope. Ms. Carlton and I have worked out a truce," William said, preferring not to admit it was a rather tenuous one at this point.

"Wonder if Chester knows that? He still seems to think of you as the enemy."

William laughed. "Some people require more convincing than others."

"Chester's a cynic, all right," Diggs agreed. "But that's because he's loyal to Carlton Industries. He'll always be alert to potential trouble. Finds it lurking in every shadow. Must get tiresome, if you ask me."

William thought about it before nodding. "You have a point, Diggs. All that intrigue does get tiresome."

In fact, if William could get rid of this one nagging concern that someone else wasn't ready to let it go, he'd be happy to move on himself.

When Destiny got to her flat, she found it filled with the most amazing scents. Kathleen had obviously found everything she needed and was intent on putting on quite a show for William. Or maybe they were hoping to lull him with food, so he'd be more inclined to give himself away if he still harbored any devious intentions.

Whatever they were scheming hardly mattered. It was the tantalizing aromas she was drawn to now, that and the laughter emanating from the kitchen. For once the dreary decor, which she still hadn't remedied, didn't seem quite so boring. All the flat needed was real life breathed into the place.

Destiny pushed open the door and smiled at the sight that greeted her. Though she was loathe to admit it, she'd missed this kind of family commotion since coming to London. A part of her was almost grateful to Richard and his ridiculous suspicions for getting Melanie and the others over here.

She surveyed the spread Kathleen had assembled, as if the task of afternoon tea were second nature to her. Plates were laden down with little sandwiches, tarts and cakes, far more than the five of them would require. It appeared she was mixing the batter for the scones now.

"Haven't you gotten a bit carried away, darlings?" Destiny asked, her voice filled with amusement.

They turned to her, still laughing.

"That's what I said," Melanie replied. "But Kathleen is used to preparing food for a hundred. She didn't know quite how to quit once she got started. Besides, we're all famished. Will William be here soon?"

"A half hour," Destiny promised.

"No problems getting him to agree?" Beth asked.

"Actually, I think he's looking forward to it," Destiny admitted. "William has always loved being surrounded by women. He considers it his natural element."

"Quite a ladies' man, then?" Melanie asked casually.

Destiny gave her a sharp look. "Never that. Not when he was with me, at any rate."

"And since then?"

"He assures me he's never found anyone else as special to him as I was." She managed to say it in an offhand tone, as if it weren't something she was beginning to believe, much less count on.

Melanie's eyebrows rose. "Really?"

"Sounds romantic." Beth's comment drew a scowl from the others. "What did I say? It does. Here he is a duke, isn't that right?"

Destiny nodded.

"That must make him quite a catch, yet all these years he's been pining for Destiny," Beth continued.

"So he says." Melanie sounded as unrelentingly skeptical as Richard would under the same circumstances.

Destiny gave her a hug. "Darling, you're beginning to sound far too much like your husband."

"Uh-oh," Kathleen said, grinning. "I think Destiny's gotten to you just in time, Melanie. One Richard in the family is enough."

Melanie frowned, then laughed. "Okay, okay. You're right. Enough of the doubts. I'll reserve judgment. Besides, we're supposed to concentrate on prying business secrets out of the man, not passing judgment on his suitability for Destiny."

"A refreshing change," Destiny told her. "Now, unless you need me to do something, I'll go and freshen up a bit."

Beth winked at her. "Go along. Wouldn't want you to have to face William at anything less than your absolute best, though it was clear in that newspaper photo that he wasn't put off by your old robe and slippers. Not that any of that matters to you, of course."

Destiny frowned at her. "Barely here and you're already starting to get on my nerves," she said lightly.

Kathleen stared at her. "I almost think she means that."

Destiny nodded in satisfaction. "Good. I wanted to give you something to think about. When William arrives, I expect all three of you to mind your manners."

Melanie gave her a fierce hug. "Best behavior, we promise."

"That will do, then."

But just in case they forgot their promise, when the doorbell rang at precisely five, Destiny intended to be there first.

Even had he not been forewarned, William would have known he was under a microscope the instant he set foot inside Destiny's flat. All three nieces by marriage regarded him with caution. Their greetings were polite, but distinctly cool. They were definitely withholding judgment, but one misstep on his part could easily swing the pendulum against him.

There were a few pleasantries exchanged before they ushered him to the living room, where tea with a formal silver service had been set up on an antique tea cart. Once he'd accepted a cup of tea from Destiny, he gazed at each woman in turn. Even without introductions, he would have recognized each of them from what Destiny had told him about them and their husbands.

He turned first to Melanie. As Richard's wife, she was most likely the one who'd require the most convincing that his intentions toward Destiny were honorable. "I understand you're quite a talented public relations expert," he said.

She seemed vaguely startled that he knew that. "My business has done nicely," she agreed, "though I have less time for it now that Richard and I have a little one at home. I still consult for Carlton Industries."

"Have anything to do with the Jameson's campaign over here before Christmas?" he asked with a pointed look toward Destiny. "It was rather clever."

Destiny chuckled. "That was my doing, William. Don't blame Melanie for cutting into your business and causing your holiday profits to fall below expectations."

He grinned at her. "Actually, we had our best season ever, thanks to you. Curiosity drove a lot more people into the store."

Melanie gave them each a piercing look. "What's he talking about, Destiny?"

Destiny waved her off before William could respond. "Let's not get bogged down in business talk."

William laughed. "Probably a good idea. Sorry I brought it up." He turned to Beth, who had the quiet demeanor he would have expected from a dedicated physician and scientist. "How is your pediatric-cancer research progressing?"

Beth gave him a startled look. "You know about that?"

"I made it my business to learn everything I could

about the people who are important to Destiny," he said.

Melanie's gaze narrowed. "So you could use us against her?"

Destiny scowled. "Melanie!"

"Sorry," Melanie apologized, without much sincerity.

William chuckled. "Destiny, you can't blame her for being suspicious. She is Richard's wife, after all, and it's plain what he thinks of me. Can't really blame her for taking sides." He met Melanie's gaze. "But I do hope you'll give me a fair chance for Destiny's sake."

Melanie's expression softened a bit. "I can try."

"That's all I ask," William told her. "It's all I ask of any of you."

"They're usually quite open-minded," Destiny claimed, giving them each a chiding look. "Right now they've been influenced by Richard, and he obviously doesn't believe me when I tell him that the competition between our two companies has ended."

"Except in one instance," William reminded her. "I don't want you to forget that I've given you fair warning on Fortnum Travel. I intend to have it."

"Oh?" Melanie queried. "Will you throw all your resources on the line to get it?"

William gave her an admiring look. "Nice try, my dear, but I think I'll keep my approach to myself for now."

"So, William, why don't you tell us how you and Destiny met?" Kathleen suggested, clearly anxious to make peace. She'd apparently concluded that the past was a safer topic than the present.

William smiled. "Now, that's a story that should

appeal to you especially, since you run an art gallery, right, Destiny?"

Destiny's expression turned nostalgic. "Yes, absolutely."

"Do you want to tell them?" he asked, wondering what spin she would put on the evening that had forever changed his life.

"No, I believe you should," she said at once.

William set his tea aside and reached for Destiny's hand. It was icy enough to tell him that she was far more nervous about this meeting than she'd let on. "It was a lovely spring night in Paris and I had been lured to this very prestigious gallery on the Left Bank for a showing by a young American artist," he began. "Violetta Grégorie, the gallery owner, was a dear friend and she was insistent that I would adore her latest discovery." He winked at Destiny. "Naturally, I was just as determined to avoid falling into that particular trap, so I ducked into a corner to hide out. I explained my sad plight to a young woman also hiding from the other guests."

Destiny grinned at him. "And then he had the audacity to insult my art."

"Oh, no," Kathleen said. "You didn't."

"I'm afraid so. I said it was...what was it, Destiny? I know you remember every word."

"You said it was too saccharine," she said tartly. "But you graciously conceded that you could see how it might appeal to a woman's romantic sensibilities."

"And yet you lived to tell the story," Kathleen said. "You must have done some fancy footwork."

"How could I with my foot planted squarely in my

mouth?" William asked. "Fortunately, Destiny has a very forgiving nature."

"Humph!" she said. "Not forgiving at all, just far too infatuated to let your bad artistic judgment interfere with getting to know the most fascinating man I'd ever met."

William smiled at her, enjoying the sparks flashing in her eyes at the memory of that night even after all these years. "We spent the rest of the evening together, talking about art, our families, our travels. I fell head over heels for her on the spot and then I followed her back to Provence. We were inseparable from that moment on."

"Love at first sight," Kathleen said dreamily. "How romantic!"

"Yes, it was," Destiny said quietly, her gaze locked with his, her hand in his much warmer now. "But some things were never meant to be."

"We were," he responded.

She shook her head. "Not us. Even if my brother and sister-in-law hadn't died, it wouldn't have lasted, William. You know that."

"I know no such thing," he said fiercely. "How can you possibly say that?"

"Because it's true." She regarded him with a sorrowful expression. "If it hadn't been for fate intervening, I would have ended it."

William couldn't have been more shocked if she'd told him that the sky was green and the moon made of tinfoil. But one look into her eyes told him she meant every word. How the hell had he missed that all those years ago?

Provence, 1982

From the moment she and William had returned from London, Destiny had felt they were living on borrowed time. It was a feeling she couldn't seem to shake. She knew what she had to do. She simply wasn't quite courageous enough to do it.

"Why so pensive?" William asked, joining her in the garden just before sunset.

Destiny had been weeding for the past hour, trying to find the words to explain to William why they had to break things off, why she couldn't live with herself if she kept him from his family for a moment longer. She gazed up at him, her hands deep in the dark, warm earth she loved, and felt her heart swell at the sight of him.

He was lean and tanned from all their walks by the sea. Laugh lines were forming at the corners of his brilliant blue eyes. Even at thirty, there was so much character in his face. Anyone who met him knew he was a man of honor, integrity and abiding love. That's why it was all the more impossible to keep him from doing what he knew was right, what they both knew was right.

"I love you," she said, tears damp on her cheeks. She hoped he wouldn't notice, that he'd attribute the moisture to the late-afternoon heat.

He hunkered down beside her and took her filthy hands in his, studying her with a worried frown. "Darling, what's wrong? You're crying."

"No, I'm not," she insisted, swiping at the telltale dampness and, no doubt, leaving streaks of dirt in her wake.

He gave her a look of tolerant amusement. "Let's not argue over that, since it's hardly the point. Tell me what has you so upset."

This was her opening, her chance to say that it was over between them. Of course, coming right on the heels of having said she loved him, she doubted he'd understand. Quite honestly, she wasn't sure she understood it herself. She was not the least bit noble. In fact, she'd often been accused of being quite the opposite, of being a bit selfish and spoiled, always insistent on getting her own way. She was living in France, on her own, after all, having abandoned her own family and the obligations back home.

It was different for her, though. She wasn't the only son, as William was. If her father had hoped she would play a role in the family business, he hadn't been relying on it. He'd been perfectly content to pass on the reins to her brother. He'd died content, knowing the company would be in excellent hands. William's father had no such reassurance.

"Destiny?" William said worriedly. "Talk to me. You know there's nothing we can't discuss."

"I know."

"Then what is it?" He studied her, as if trying to puzzle it out for himself. "Are you pregnant?"

"Good heavens, no!" she said. Even as the shocked disclaimer left her lips, though, she knew she would have given anything for the opposite to be true. Having William's child would have ended this torment. There would be no question of her letting him go, then. He would never have allowed it and she wouldn't have argued.

But there was no baby. There was no reason at all

for not ending it between them right this second, except for her own cowardice, her own reluctance to put an end to the most important relationship of her life.

She touched his cheek. "I'm sorry. I didn't mean that the way it sounded," she apologized. "Having your child would be amazing, but I'm not pregnant."

"Maybe we should consider doing something about that," he suggested. "But in the proper order. Marry me, Destiny."

"What?"

"Marry me. You know I love you with all my heart. We'll have a good life together, complete with a houseful of gorgeous, suntanned babies who'll romp in this garden and play havoc with your flowers."

Once again, her eyes turned watery as she envisioned the idyllic scene he'd described. Oh, how she wanted just that, but it couldn't be. One look at his hopeful expression, though, and she couldn't tell him no.

"Oh, darling, nothing would make me happier, but are you sure? There are so many things to think about."

"What's more important than the fact that we love each other?"

She regarded him sadly. "There's your family to consider."

"They don't matter."

"Yes, they do. Inevitably, it would become a problem. You'd resent me for coming between you."

"How could I, when they're the ones who are being impossible? You've done more than your share to make things right with them and they rebuffed you. You endured that tedious visit with a smile on your face every moment."

"I know how it would work out between us eventually," she insisted, then sighed because she knew she couldn't counter his proposal with a rejection that would sever all ties. Not tonight. "Let's go on as we are."

"It's not enough. You deserve more."

"I have everything I need," she said. "Honestly, William. I never expected any more than this. What we have has been a gift. Let's not spoil it by asking for more."

Eventually he nodded. "For now, I'll let you have your way, as always. But the topic's far from done."

But it was, Destiny thought wearily. She might not have gotten out the words, but her mind was made up. She would let him go…as soon as she found the strength.

17

Destiny had forgotten all about the fateful decision she'd made all those years ago until just recently. It had been a few more months before the tragedy in Virginia had intervened, taking the decision of whether to stay with William or leave him out of her hands.

At that point, separation had been inevitable, but she'd been so grief-stricken at the time, had needed William so desperately, that she'd turned things completely upside down. She'd blamed him for not being at her side, when she herself had believed it was right to end their relationship only a few weeks earlier.

Perhaps on some subconscious level, she'd used her brother's death as the excuse to do what she knew she had to do without ever being responsible for the decision. Considering that possibility put an entirely new spin on what had happened. Perhaps William had never abandoned her at all but had been inadvertently driven away, responding to signals she hadn't even realized she was sending. It was something she needed to consider. Perhaps she'd been struggling all these years to forgive something that hadn't in fact required forgiveness from him, but rather an apology from her.

"Destiny?"

The concern in Melanie's voice caught her attention and brought her back from the long-ago past. Destiny faced her, faced all of them with a smile firmly plastered on her face.

"Sorry," she apologized. "How rude of me. William, would you like more tea?"

"Love some," he said, regarding her curiously.

As she handed it to him, he murmured, "I think there are some things we need to discuss privately."

"Another time," she said firmly.

"Of course, but I won't forget."

She gave him a wry look. "Believe me, I'm aware of that. You always did have a memory like an elephant."

He laughed. "It made it hard for you to put me off, didn't it? I always brought the topic you were intent on avoiding around again."

"Yes. It was a most annoying habit."

"Better than most men, who can't remember so much as a birthday," he countered.

"Amen to that," Kathleen said, proving that most likely all three women had been listening intently to every word of Destiny's exchange with William. "Ben can't recall anything five seconds after I've told him."

"Neither can Richard," Melanie agreed. "Unless it has to do with business. Then he can recall every detail of the fine print in a contract."

"Mack must be the best of the lot, then," Beth said. "He usually remembers things I'd prefer he forget."

Destiny noticed that William seemed fascinated by the talk of her nephews.

"I'm anxious to meet your husbands," he told the women.

Melanie regarded him with obvious surprise. "Really? I would have thought you'd prefer to avoid them at all costs. Richard, especially."

William laughed. "Because of the adversarial business relationship we've had in recent years?" He waved it off. "With that one notable exception, it's a thing of the past. Destiny's seen to that."

Kathleen regarded him with curiosity. "You didn't stir up all of that merely to bring Destiny rushing over here to save the day, did you?"

Destiny waited to see if he'd own up to it. It was one thing to confide in her. It was quite another to admit the tactic to virtual strangers, especially to these women he was so obviously trying to win over.

He gave them a rueful grin. "I've already told Destiny as much, so I might as well admit it to you. It seemed my best bet at the time," he conceded. "Of course, I hadn't counted on it making an enemy out of Richard. That does complicate matters. He'll never believe that my efforts to get Fortnum Travel are based on a promise to an old friend and have nothing to do with Carlton Industries. I'd do the same if any company were trying a hostile takeover of Fortnum."

"What exactly does it complicate?" Melanie asked suspiciously. "Your negotiations for Fortnum?"

"No," William said at once. He glanced at Destiny, heat in his eyes. "I think that's something I should be discussing with Destiny before I get into it with the rest of you."

Destiny blushed. Because she didn't want any of them to know how easily he rattled her with his casual hints about the future, she reached for her teacup, only to have it tremble in her hand, splashing tea over the side.

"Are you okay?" Beth asked worriedly.

"Fine," Destiny said. "Just a bit clumsy."

"Perhaps I should be going," William said. He gave her nieces a warm smile. "I hope we can get together again before you go home. Would you like to go to the theater one night? Perhaps tomorrow? I'm sure I can get tickets and we'll find someplace wonderful to have supper after."

The three women looked to Destiny for some sort of signal. Though she wasn't anxious for another repeat of this nerve-racking evening, she smiled brightly. "The theater would be lovely, William. I know Melanie, Beth and Kathleen were looking forward to seeing a show while they were here. In fact, I haven't been myself since my return."

"Then I'll arrange it and call you," he said. "Ladies, I'll see all of you tomorrow."

Destiny walked him to the door.

"I think that went rather well, don't you?" he asked, clearly pleased.

"I suppose it depends on what they're after," Destiny said, thinking that he'd revealed precious few business secrets.

"Surely you don't think I gave them any evidence to take home that I'm a cad and a bounder, who should be banished forever from your life."

She smiled. "Hardly that. You were charming, the perfect gentleman."

He frowned at the description. "Is there some flaw in that that I'm missing?"

"Only that they may spin this into some sort of love affair," she said. "They're romantics at heart."

His gaze narrowed. "Would they be getting it entirely wrong, Destiny?"

"Of course they would," she snapped. "We agreed—"

"You *insisted,*" he corrected. "There was no such agreement, Destiny. I think my intentions have been clear from the beginning."

"Were they really?" she inquired tartly. "Would that be the intention to steal Carlton Industries' business? That's the one I seem to recall."

He frowned at her. "There's no need to keep reminding me of that. It's over. You put a stop to it."

She laughed, despite her annoyance. "Only because it was a ploy in the first place. It's not as if I launched some sort of retaliation that scared you into submission."

"Oh, really? You did launch a rather effective campaign against H&S Books. Destiny, you have a clever business mind. Please don't think otherwise, just because I never meant to be a serious competitor. Don't diminish your accomplishments since coming here. You've taken a firm grip on things. In fact, I've heard quite a bit of talk in the business community about how well you're getting things in hand."

She regarded him with surprise. "People are really saying that. And you believe it?"

"Yes, I do. If running this operation is something you really want to do, then don't let anyone tell you you're not up to the task, not even that nephew whose opinion you respect so much."

Impulsively, she stood on tiptoe and kissed him.

"Thank you. You have no idea how badly I needed to hear that. Richard's constant skepticism is draining."

He touched her cheek. "Admiration for you comes easily, my dear. Now, I'd better get going if I'm to snag five excellent seats for tomorrow night. I want your young friends to be impressed."

"I suspect you've already accomplished that," she told him.

When he was gone, she leaned against the door for a moment and closed her eyes. The truth was, he'd impressed her, too, and that scared her to death.

She gathered her composure at last and went back into the living room. All three women immediately fell silent.

Destiny regarded them impatiently. "Oh, go ahead with whatever you were saying. I can take it."

"I like him," Kathleen said, her tone gentle.

"So do I," Beth said.

Melanie was uncharacteristically quiet. Destiny studied her. "And you? What did you think of William?"

Melanie's torn expression gave her away.

"Are you afraid that admitting you liked him will be disloyal to Richard?" Destiny asked.

"It's not that entirely," Melanie said, looking dreadfully unhappy. "He's so smooth and polished and charming. What if it's an act, meant to take us all in?"

"That's Richard talking," Destiny said impatiently.

"Then you trust him?" Melanie asked. "Deep down, you really trust him?"

Did she? Destiny couldn't help wondering if she was as vulnerable and gullible as her nephew feared she was. "I want to," she finally admitted with candor. "I want to more than anything."

"Then do it," Beth advised. "Isn't that what you told each of us at one time or another, to trust our hearts? What's the worst that can happen?"

"I'll discover I'm a silly old woman?" Destiny suggested.

"Never that," Melanie said fiercely. "Whatever you do, even if it turns out to have been a mistake, it won't be because you're a silly old woman. You're the most intelligent woman we know. It won't be about you at all. It will be about William not being the man you believe him to be. The fault will be his."

"That will be small comfort, if he hurts the company," Destiny pointed out. "Richard would never forgive me if I put the family business in jeopardy, which is precisely what he thinks I'll be doing if I get involved with William again."

"Then you'll go forward cautiously," Beth said. "You didn't make mistakes when it came to us. Your instincts about us being the perfect matches for your nephews were right on track. Trust them now."

"Maybe it's easier to see clearly when it's not your own heart that's involved," Destiny said.

"I don't believe that for a minute," Kathleen said. "Not where you're concerned. Besides, I'd say the three of us have good instincts and we see what you see."

"Which is?" Destiny asked.

"A man who's been totally and thoroughly besotted by you for years," Kathleen said at once. "Right, girls?"

"Right," Beth said at once. She patted her heart in a dramatic gesture. "The way he looks at you…oh, my!"

Melanie was slower to answer, but eventually she

nodded, as well. "That's the way it seemed to me. And he does appear to be trying to be candid about his intentions where Fortnum Travel is concerned. He's not hiding that or sneaking behind your back. Just don't rush into anything," she pleaded. "Take your time. Be sure, not only of his feelings, but your own."

If only she had all the time in the world to do that, Destiny thought. Leave it to the young to imagine that life went on forever. She'd already wasted more than twenty years of hers. If William was still the man she thought he was, if he still loved her as deeply as he once had, how could she waste another minute of whatever time they had left?

Still, Melanie was right. She needed to proceed cautiously. Now was not the time for soul-searching, though. She forced herself to beam at her guests.

"What would you like to do tonight?" she asked them. "It's your first night in London. We can't spend it sitting around here like a bunch of old fogies. Would you like dinner? A club? Shall I call for a driver and have him take us on a moonlight tour of the major sights?"

"A tour, definitely," Kathleen said eagerly. "Buckingham Palace, Parliament, Big Ben. I want to see all of it." She looked at Melanie and Beth. "Is that okay?"

"Well, I certainly can't eat another bite," Beth said. "We probably should make it a walking tour."

"Then that's what we'll do," Destiny said decisively. "Let me put on my walking shoes and get a warm coat and I'll show you everything."

She was halfway across the room when she was met by Melanie, who suddenly threw her arms around her.

"We love you. I hope you know that. We honestly didn't come here just to make trouble for you."

Tears pricked Destiny's eyes. "I know, darlings. And I couldn't love the three of you more if you were my own. I'm delighted you're here."

"Even if we came as spies?" Melanie asked.

"Even more because you cared enough to spy," she reassured her. "Now, stop worrying. Let's have ourselves a night out and forget all about the frustrating men in our lives."

"Deal," Melanie said eagerly.

She stood watching as the three women, suddenly chattering like magpies, cleared away the debris from their tea. Her family, she thought happily. All because of a choice she'd made years ago to be a mother to the men who'd eventually become their husbands. Her life was rich. She shouldn't let herself forget that. Not for a minute.

William thought he'd passed muster. There hadn't been a single second, though, when he'd been unaware that he was being assessed. He was actually relieved that Richard Carlton had sent the three women to see how he measured up. They were far more likely to give him a fair chance and more likely yet to be on Destiny's side when it came to a matter of the heart. He'd predict smooth sailing if it weren't for the Fortnum matter. That was going to stick in Richard's craw no matter how William handled it.

In fact, Richard was going to find it all but impossible to forget the whole business rivalry and move past it. In retrospect that had probably been a bad tactic to use, but it was the only one William had been able to come up with that could accomplish what he'd hoped for.

Sitting in his office the morning after tea with the four impressive Carlton women, he buzzed for Malcolm.

"I need you to do me a favor," he said when his assistant arrived. "I need five of the best seats in the house for the theater tonight. Cost is no object, so find me the hardest-to-get tickets to the hottest, most critically acclaimed play. I'm out to impress some people."

"Who would that be, if you don't mind me asking?"

"Destiny and her nephews' wives."

Malcolm regarded him with dismay. "Is that wise, sir? You know how paparazzi love to hang around outside the theaters. A picture of all of you together would be bound to make it into the tabloids."

William groaned. He'd forgotten all about that. Well, it was unfortunate, but he wasn't going to back out now. He'd made a promise and he intended to keep it. "Get the tickets," he said succinctly.

"As you wish," Malcolm said, his disapproval plain. "By the way, you might want to take a look at the final December sales figures for H&S Books. Shall I bring you the report? It's on my desk."

William nodded. "How are they? The preliminary figures looked promising."

"Actually they're excellent," Malcolm said. "Apparently stirring up a bit of a rivalry brought enough people into the stores to counteract the discounts you were offering."

"I'll have to thank Destiny again when I see her. Something tells me that having her around will keep us on our toes."

"It could at that, sir." His dour expression returned. "A word of caution, though. There's a rumor circulating that a woolen mill that's been a favorite of ours is about to be purchased."

William stilled. "Carlton?"

"It would seem so, sir."

"Get me every bit of information you can find on that," William said tightly. He didn't believe for an instant that Destiny had gone back on her word and set out to do something so underhanded. Not after they'd discussed this very thing. "Something tells me the offer didn't come from Destiny. I'll wager it came from Virginia."

"Entirely likely, sir."

William stared after his assistant, his temper stewing. Damn Richard! He could handle the man if it came down to a fight. Whatever the manufacturer, the owner was likely someone William had known for years. It wouldn't take much to counter whatever offer Richard had put on the table. That wasn't the problem.

What William couldn't believe, what he found so blasted infuriating, was that the man was sneaking around behind his aunt's back. If William found that to be the case, there was going to be hell to pay. And once Destiny found out about it, he had a hunch he wouldn't be the first in line to get a crack at the man.

Destiny cast a concerned frown in William's direction. He'd been worried about something from the moment they'd all met outside the theater. When she'd asked about it earlier, he'd forced a smile and lied through his teeth that she was imagining things. Well, she'd just see about that, she resolved, sitting back to wait for intermission.

The instant the curtains closed to thunderous applause after act one, she grabbed his hand. "I'd like to speak to you," she said. "Now!"

He gave her a startled look. "What's wrong?"

"In the lobby," she said, determinedly tugging him past her curious nieces. "Excuse us, girls."

The instant they were out of earshot, she folded her arms across her chest and scowled at him. "Tell me," she said.

He regarded her blankly. "Tell you what?"

"Oh, stop it. You're not very good at dissembling, William. Something's on your mind and I have a hunch it has to do with me."

He sighed. "You see too blasted much," he grumbled.

She frowned and waited.

"Oh, all right. I'd hoped not to get into this tonight. I learned something today, something I suspect you know nothing about."

"Which is?"

"Carlton Industries has made an offer to buy my primary woolen manufacturer in Scotland."

Destiny felt faint. "That can't be. Nothing like that could happen without my knowing about it, and I can assure you I don't. We've already canceled the misguided purchase of the haberdashers, so what would we need with a woolen manufacturer?"

"I suspect it's being done merely to annoy me." He regarded her with something akin to pity.

"But I'm not behind it," she repeated. "No one else could authorize such a thing."

"No one except Richard," he said quietly.

She gasped. "He didn't," she said, then realized it made total sense. It was exactly the kind of thing Richard might do to send a message to a business rival. That he had done it without consulting her was proof of just how little respect he had for her or her position in the company. Didn't he see that it would be impossible for her to continue running the European division if he was going behind her back in such a way? Or was that precisely what he intended?

Barely containing her temper, she met William's gaze. "You're sure?"

"I spoke to the owner. He's been dealing directly with Richard. I'm sorry, but there's no question about this."

"And the outcome? Did Richard get his way?"

"Of course not. I discovered his plan in the nick of time and formed a lucrative partnership with the firm myself. Richard won't get his hands on it now."

"Good. Do you have your cell phone with you?"

He nodded.

"I need it, if you don't mind. I need to make a call to Carlton Industries. I suspect Richard will be expecting it."

William took his cell phone out of his pocket, but he held it out of reach. "What are you going to do?"

"I'm going to quit, of course."

"Destiny, you can't do that," he protested. "I know how much you want to prove yourself in this job."

"How can I, if my nephew is going to go behind my back and sabotage me? I made a commitment to you, and if you didn't trust me, you could easily have assumed I was behind this and launched an all-out assault against the company."

"But I do trust you and the matter is handled," he said. "Think about this. Wait and call him in the morning, when cooler heads will prevail."

"I don't want a cooler head when I talk to him," she insisted fiercely. "I want to tear him limb from limb. How could he do this? I've never been so furious and disappointed in my entire life."

"He's worried about you," William said quietly. "He wants you to quit and come home. I think that message is plain. Whatever he's heard from Melanie and the others since their arrival has obviously only fueled his concerns."

Destiny stared at him. He was absolutely right. That was Richard's intention. He knew she would find his actions intolerable, and he expected her to call and quit or at the very least to bolt home to confront him in person. There was a third alternative, though, one she doubted he'd considered.

"Give me the phone," she said quietly.

"Destiny, please, are you really sure about this?"

"Just watch and listen," she said grimly, punching in the numbers for Richard's private line. It was no surprise that he answered on the very first ring. He'd probably been sitting there on pins and needles all day long waiting for her call.

"Hello," he said, sounding a little too cheerful.

Destiny couldn't wait to spoil his mood. "Hello, darling," she said just as cheerfully. "Make any big deals today?"

"You heard about Scotland, I imagine," he said, still sounding surprisingly upbeat for a man whose deal had been foiled by William. "Sorry, but I did what I had to do."

"Too bad it didn't work out."

"Obviously William got word of it," he said.

"Even without me knowing a thing about it," she pointed out. "I assume you thought I was the one you couldn't trust with the information."

"Not under the circumstances, no," he admitted, though he was beginning to sound slightly less confident. "I know you're upset—"

"I was at first," she conceded. "In fact, I was mad enough to quit, which was precisely what I intended, until I thought it through."

"Oh?"

"William made me realize that quitting would be the worst decision I could possibly make."

"Oh," he said, his voice filled with resignation.

"Instead, I'm calling to warn you that if you try a stunt like that again, I will go to the board of directors and see that you're removed."

"What?" The word exploded from him. "You wouldn't dare."

"Try me," she said softly. "Just try me."

And then she hung up and handed the phone to an openmouthed William. "Let's get back inside. I'd hate to miss the second act."

Before she could take a step, though, he pulled her into his arms and gave her a hard kiss. "Have I mentioned how absolutely astonishing I think you are?"

She smiled at him. "You ain't seen nothing yet. And neither has my nephew."

18

Her nieces regarded her with obvious concern when Destiny and William slipped back into their seats a moment after the second-act curtain had gone up.

"Everything okay?" Melanie whispered as the orchestra began to play the overture to the first song.

Destiny forced a brilliant smile. "Fine. Nothing to worry about," she said, even though she still felt sick inside at what Richard had done and what she'd felt forced to do in response.

The threat she'd made months ago back in Virginia had been idle, something meant only to capture his attention and make him take her seriously. She was so furious now that she'd meant every word of this one. There was no telling how Melanie and the rest of the family were likely to react once word got around about her heated exchange with Richard. In fact, on second thought, she wasn't sure that she wouldn't have regrets herself.

Well, there was nothing to be done about it now, she thought, settling into her seat and trying to focus on the play. It was a wonderful musical, and on another occasion she would have been thoroughly entertained, but tonight it could have been a bunch of rank amateurs performing in a second-rate production of some ridiculous farce for all the attention she paid it. She was almost relieved when it ended.

"I've made reservations for supper," William said when they finally stepped out into the refreshingly balmy night air. He regarded her with worry. "Are you up to it?"

Beth immediately stepped to her side. "Destiny, aren't you feeling well? You do look a little pale."

"Oh, stop making such a fuss. I'm fine. And I am not going to spoil our evening out." She managed what she hoped was a reassuring smile. "Where are we going?"

His worried frown was still firmly in place, but William let the subject of her mood go. "It's a new place, all the rage, I hear."

"And you managed to get reservations at the last minute?" she asked. "Aren't you clever?"

"Actually it's my assistant, Malcolm Dandridge, who's clever. The man could wrangle an invitation to tea at Buckingham Palace if I asked him to. He has connections everywhere. Knows every maître d' and butler in town."

Destiny gave him a piercing look. "Oh?" she said, instantly suspicious. A man who knew so many people certainly bore closer scrutiny. Why hadn't she considered that before? "Who does he know at Carlton?"

William had the grace to look vaguely guilty at that. "No idea, but it wouldn't surprise me at all if he knew a few people there."

She frowned at him. "We'll discuss that later, I think."

He grinned, clearly undaunted by the warning note in her voice. "I'm sure we will."

They walked to the restaurant, which had been getting rave reviews in the papers for its Asian-Pacific cuisine. The decor was a little stark for Destiny's taste, but the menu looked promising, especially a grilled mahi-mahi with a mango-papaya chutney.

As soon as they'd all ordered, Melanie regarded her with a penetrating look. "Okay, what's up? What were the two of you huddling about during intermission and why did you both look upset when you came back? Maybe Beth can be put off with a few platitudes, but I can't."

"Just a minor annoyance," Destiny insisted. "Nothing worth discussing."

William regarded her evenly. "I think you should tell them."

"Tell us what?" Melanie pressed.

Destiny could see she wasn't going to get any peace, so she relented and gave them a condensed version of Richard's actions and her response to it. She gazed at Melanie. "I'm sorry, darling. I felt I had no choice. What he did totally undermined my authority over here. No one in my position would have found that acceptable."

"Of course you didn't have a choice," Melanie said, her expression grim. "I don't blame you a bit. What on earth was Richard thinking?"

"That he had to do something to force my hand, I imagine," Destiny said. "Or something to prove that I couldn't be trusted."

"He knows better than that," Melanie said fiercely. "My God, you're as much a Carlton as he is. I'm so furious I'm tempted to call and tell him off myself. I've told him before what I think of his ridiculous doubts about your loyalty to the company. He's convinced you can't separate your professional life from your personal feelings. It's been nagging at him from the beginning."

Destiny frowned. She didn't want Melanie, Beth and Kathleen drawn into this any deeper than they already were. "Don't get involved in this, any of you. This isn't your fight. I can handle Richard."

"That's obvious," Beth said. "Do you suppose Mack and Ben were in on it?"

"I doubt it," Destiny said honestly. "When it comes to Carlton Industries, they're not that interested."

"But this is about you," Beth reminded her. "Not just the company. I can't imagine that they would approve of what Richard did. It was a direct slap in the face."

Destiny gave them all a fierce look. "We are not going to get into some sort of family feud over this. Not if I can help it. It's strictly business. I don't want the rest of you taking sides. Is that understood? Please listen to me. If that happens, I will have no choice but to quit and come home. I will not be responsible for some huge family rift."

"But, Destiny," Kathleen protested, "what Richard did was wrong. He needs to know how we feel about his total lack of respect and consideration for your feelings, to say nothing of his disregard for your position in the company."

Destiny reached for Kathleen's hand and gave it a squeeze. "I suspect he understood the risk before he did it," she said quietly. "Richard always considered himself to be the man of the family after his parents died. Even though he was only twelve, he assigned himself the job of looking out for everyone's best interests, mine included. He's always taken everything to heart. He obviously thought this situation required drastic action. Believe me, I didn't cut him any slack. I'm sure he can already see how wrong he was to choose this particular course."

"I can attest to that," William said. "I heard every word she said. No intelligent man would take her lightly."

Melanie suddenly stood up. "Will you excuse me? I need to talk to him. I won't be a moment."

She rushed from the dining room before Destiny could stop her. Destiny stared after her, filled with misgivings. "Oh, dear, I hope I haven't made matters worse by getting into this with all of you."

"It's okay. Richard deserves what's coming to him," Kathleen said. "Maybe if he hears it from his own wife he'll wake up. This nonsense has to stop."

"Perhaps," Destiny said, but she was suddenly beginning to wonder if the price for her independence wasn't getting to be too high. The last thing she wanted was to be as alienated from her family as William had been from his all those years ago.

William wished he could turn back the clock. Oh, he'd been wishing for some time now to go back to the uncomplicated way things had been two decades ago in Provence, but right now he would settle for going back twenty-four hours to before he'd told Destiny about her nephew's sneaky attempt to buy the Glasgow woolen manufacturer. He'd handled the matter with no harm done. Perhaps he should have left it at that with Destiny being none the wiser.

He was sitting at his desk, staring morosely at the gray morning skyline, when Malcolm came in.

"How was the theater, sir?"

"Fine."

Malcolm frowned. "And dinner?"

"Fine."

"You told Ms. Carlton about her nephew, didn't you, sir?"

William wasn't surprised that Malcolm had guessed. They'd known each other too long and too well. "Yes."

"And now you're regretting it," Malcolm concluded.

"Yes, as a matter of fact, I'm regretting it deeply."

"I don't believe you should. If she's serious about making a success of this job, she needed to know what he's capable of doing behind her back."

"But she loves her nephew," William protested. "This must be tearing her apart. It's not as if she was betrayed by someone whose only connection to her was business." He turned slowly and met his assistant's gaze. "How did you happen to come upon that information, Malcolm?"

Malcolm regarded him with dismay. "You want me to reveal my source, after all?"

"Perhaps it's time I knew," he said. "This person has proved to be a godsend to us, but I'm not sure I like that Destiny has someone she trusts who's betraying the company so readily. Perhaps if she can show Richard who's been behind all the leaks, he'll finally let her do her job in peace."

Malcolm's expression filled with alarm. "You'd give this person away?"

William considered that, then sighed. "No, of course that's impossible. This person dealt with you in good faith. Damn, this has gotten complicated. I thought it would all be over once Destiny got to London."

"Perhaps it's time you and Mr. Carlton have a talk and settle this, then," Malcolm suggested. "He's the fly in the ointment now, isn't he? In the end, she could well be torn between her loyalty to him and her affection for you."

"You think I should go behind Destiny's back and speak to her nephew directly? Impossible," he said at once. "I won't undercut her authority in that way."

"As you wish, sir. It was just an idea."

"I know, Malcolm. I appreciate everything you've done. I couldn't have gotten her over here without you."

"Do you regret that, as well, sir?"

William's expression brightened. "Not at all. In fact, that's the first sensible thing I've done in years."

Now he simply had to figure out a way to straighten the rest of it out before Destiny regretted ever setting eyes on him again. For one thing, it was time to settle things with David Fortnum and his board of directors, so that matter could be put behind them all, as well.

Destiny was lingering over her morning tea, hoping for a word with Melanie before leaving for the office. She was on her third cup of Earl Grey and it was beginning to make her jittery by the time Melanie finally appeared, looking as if she hadn't slept a wink.

"I thought you'd be gone," Melanie said, pouring herself some tea and sitting down opposite Destiny.

"Is that what you were hoping?"

"Of course not," Melanie replied at once, then added. "Maybe."

"When you came back to the table last night, you never said a word about your conversation with Richard. How did that go?"

"He's beside himself," Melanie admitted. "He began by ranting on and on about your threat, then finally conceded he would have done the same thing had he been in your shoes. He truly regrets what he did, I think. In fact, he almost sounded as if he admired your audacity."

"But he would do it again," Destiny guessed.

Melanie nodded, looking miserable. "He's determined to protect you from William, to show him for the kind of man he is."

"Is it truly me he thinks he's protecting or the company?" Destiny asked dryly.

"You," Melanie insisted. "I couldn't get through to him. He didn't want to hear my impressions of William. In fact, he was furious that we'd gone to the theater together. That set him off all over again."

Destiny regarded her with amusement. "I thought Richard wanted you to spy on the two of us. How did he expect you to accomplish that without ever setting eyes on William?"

Melanie grinned for the first time. "I don't think he was inclined to be logical last night."

"If I ask you something, will you give me an honest answer?"

"Always," Melanie promised.

"Given everything you know about the possible repercussions, do you think it's crazy for me to want a second chance with William?"

"Absolutely not," Melanie responded fiercely. "If you love him and he loves you, then nothing should stand in your way, not even my stubborn, bullheaded husband."

"But look what it's doing to the family," Destiny said. "We haven't even declared an intention to get back together and Richard is in an uproar."

"Perhaps if William had come to him—or even to you—with hat in hand and expressed an interest in marriage, this wouldn't be so problematic," Melanie pointed out. "Instead, he attacked Carlton Industries to trick you into coming over here. I can see why Richard might be wary of his true intentions."

Destiny laughed ruefully. "Yes, that did muddy the waters, didn't it? Well, perhaps in time, everyone will meet and we can put all of this behind us."

"Maybe that's the answer," Melanie said thoughtfully. "If Richard actually met William face-to-face, I think he'd feel better about everything."

"But he's far too stubborn to come here now," Destiny said. "He'll only be happy if I come home."

Melanie's expression brightened. "You forget that I learned a few tricks from a master not that long ago. Leave Richard to me. I might not be able to pull it off overnight, but I think I can get him over here eventually. It'll just require putting a bit of a spin on things once I get home."

Destiny chuckled. "How perfectly lovely, then, that spinning a story falls right within your area of expertise."

"Exactly."

"Darling, just promise me you won't do anything

to jeopardize your relationship with Richard over this, okay?"

"I won't," Melanie reassured her. "Despite his very impressive list of flaws, I love your nephew. He's not going to shake me loose anytime soon."

Destiny nodded, satisfied. She'd done well in choosing this woman for Richard. Melanie had warmth, love, a generous heart and, best of all under the circumstances, she had staying power. Given the bumpy ride they were embarking on, she was going to need it.

"Destiny, is something wrong?"

Chester's voice broke into her reverie. "I'm sorry, Chester. What were you saying?"

"It's not important," he said, regarding her with concern. "You don't seem to be yourself this morning. Is there something I can do to help?"

"Not unless you have a potion for someone who stayed out too late and got up too early," she said, making light of her distraction.

"Yes, I'm aware of the late night," he said. "I imagine half of London knows about it."

She stared at him. "What on earth are you talking about?"

"The papers," he told her. "Several of them are running a picture of you and Mr. Harcourt at the theater with your nieces." His disapproval was plain in his expression.

Destiny sighed. "I should have expected something like that."

"It is a risk, if you intend to continue being seen with him," Chester said. "I might as well tell you that people here are starting to ask questions."

Her gaze narrowed. "What sort of questions?"

"They're wondering if you were the one leaking information to Harcourt all along," he said.

"That's absurd," she said indignantly. "I hope you set them straight. Most of that information was leaked long before I was even on the scene."

"I told them that, but some are wondering if you weren't in contact with Harcourt even back then."

"Oh, for heaven's sake," Destiny said impatiently. "I suppose what this means is that we'd better figure out who the real mole is before I lose everyone's respect. Send David Perkins in here, would you? I've put off speaking to him about this, but it seems I have no choice."

"I'll send him in at once," Chester said. "Be careful how you handle him, though. We need his financial expertise."

"Not if it's been compromised," she reminded Chester.

"You have a point."

A few minutes later the chief financial officer came into her office. "You wanted to see me?"

"Yes, David. Have a seat." She waited, then looked him directly in the eye. "I'm sure you're aware that someone in this company has been leaking confidential information. Someone has also hired a photographer to take pictures of Mr. Harcourt and myself during a private meeting at my apartment. It's my belief that this person is one and the same."

"A logical conclusion," he said, frowning. "Any idea who it might be?"

"I was hoping you would have some."

"Not a clue," he said smoothly. "Certainly no one

on my staff. And only certain people would have been privy to the information in question, anyway."

"A valid point," Destiny said. "You, Chester, Edward Wildemon. Anyone else?"

"Yourself, of course."

"I wasn't directly involved with the company in any capacity at the time of the leaks," she reminded him. "And I can't think of a single reason why I would invite a photographer to take compromising photos to be printed in the most sensational newspaper in London. Had I done it, I can assure you I would have been dressed in a more flattering outfit." She met his gaze. "Can you think why I would want to sabotage myself in such a way?"

He faltered a bit. "No, of course not."

"Well, then, I think we can eliminate me. Any other ideas?"

He shrugged. "None offhand."

"I gather you were hoping to move into the CEO position if Chester left."

"That's no secret," he conceded.

"Were you disappointed when he stayed and I arrived to serve as chairman of the division?"

"A bit," he admitted candidly. "But I'm young yet and I'm a patient man."

She was suddenly struck by an inspiration. "Do you know Malcolm Dandridge?"

He stared at her blankly. "Who?"

His reaction seemed totally genuine to Destiny. "Never mind. I thought perhaps you might have met, but it's not important. Thank you, David."

He stood up and started for the door, then turned back. "Ms. Carlton, do you trust me?"

She returned his gaze evenly. "You've given me no reason not to, have you?"

"No," he said emphatically. "I wanted to be sure, though. If my loyalty is in question, then it would be better if I left."

She understood his need for reassurance and made a snap decision. "I'd like you to stay, David. But if anything comes to mind about who might be behind this, please let me know."

"Of course."

After he'd gone, she waited a few minutes before calling for the head of marketing. She wondered if David would rush straight to the man's office to warn him or leave Edward Wildemon to be taken by surprise.

She had her answer when Edward appeared in the doorway of her office without her even picking up the phone.

"I imagine you want to speak to me, as well," he said, coming inside without waiting for an invitation.

"David spoke to you?"

He nodded. "But I've been expecting this for some time."

"Why?"

"Because it's obvious that there's been a serious leak in the company and it's most likely someone at the top."

"True enough," Destiny agreed. "Any ideas?"

"I know you've concluded that Chester is beyond reproach, but I think your faith in him might be misplaced."

"You think that or you know it?"

"Who knows what he confides to his *companion*," he said with obvious distaste.

Destiny bristled on Chester's behalf. She didn't like prejudices of any kind. "Do you suppose he says any more to Oliver Diggs than you do to your wife?"

Edward blinked at that. He was savvy enough to interpret the disapproval in her tone. "No, I suppose not."

"Then I think we can eliminate that as a reason to suspect Chester," she said decisively. "Anything else?"

He leaned forward, his expression earnest. "Look at how the man dresses. He can't buy clothes like that on his income. He must have some other source. And I'll wager those suits of his are from Harcourt's haberdasheries. A quid pro quo, perhaps."

Destiny was liking Edward Wildemon less and less. "Suspicion, not fact," she chided. "I need facts, Edward. Perhaps we should concentrate on you for a moment, since that's the one topic about which you can speak authoritatively."

He blushed furiously.

"Do you resent the fact that Richard chose to keep Chester on?"

His chin jutted up stubbornly. "I thought it was a mistake, yes."

"Then you thought you should have that position?"

"Yes," he said, then quickly added, "or perhaps David. He has the financial background to make a go of things."

"Yes, I'm sure he does," Destiny admitted. "And what would your qualifications be, should there be a change down the road?"

"I know how to sell this company, how to get it recognized as a leader in Europe. We've been far too cautious in our approach up to now."

"A vitally important task," Destiny agreed. "But

do you have any management experience outside of marketing?"

"No," he conceded.

"Then wouldn't it be asking quite a lot for Richard to put you in charge?"

"No more than having him put you in charge," he retorted, then blanched at his lack of discretion. "Sorry. I shouldn't have said that."

Destiny bit back a sharp retort and managed to keep her tone perfectly even. "I appreciate your candor, Edward. That will be all for now."

As he headed for the door, she said, "By the way, that suit you're wearing, isn't it custom-tailored?"

He stared at her, his expression vaguely stunned. "Yes, but—"

Destiny cut him off. "No need to explain. You can see, though, how jumping to conclusions cuts both ways."

"It won't happen again."

"See that it doesn't."

After he'd gone, Destiny muttered the soft curse she'd been holding back during the entire encounter. She believed with everything in her that Edward Wildemon was the culprit, but as she'd so firmly told him, she needed proof, not suspicions. How the devil was she supposed to get that?

When inspiration struck, she grabbed her coat and headed for the door.

"Where are you going?" Miriam called after her.

"To see William."

Miriam regarded her with undisguised dismay. "Do you have an appointment? It's not on your calendar."

"No appointment."

"Should I call and make sure he's in his office?"

"No need. I want the element of surprise on my side."

"I'm sure Mr. Dandridge would be discreet," Miriam said. "It seems to be his nature."

Destiny regarded her with surprise. "You know Mr. Dandridge?"

"We've spoken once or twice," she said, blushing. "He's very charming on the phone."

"So I've heard," Destiny said. "But let's not involve him in this. If William's not in his office, I'll track him down." In fact, if he wasn't there, it would make her day. It would give her a chance to meet the incomparable Malcolm Dandridge and see for herself how far he might go to assist his boss.

19

William heard a commotion outside his office. If he wasn't mistaken, Destiny was right in the thick of it. He nearly knocked over his chair in his haste to intervene.

In the foyer he found Malcolm, arms folded across his chest, blocking Destiny's path. His forbidding expression would have daunted a lesser person, but as William knew all too well, there was nothing timid about Destiny when she was on a mission, and clearly some unpleasantness had brought her charging over here this morning.

"What's going on?" he inquired politely, taking both of the combatants by surprise.

Destiny whirled on him. "Your bodyguard says I can't see you without an appointment."

William bit back a grin. "Those are his instructions," he explained mildly.

"Well, there must be exceptions," she said. "Are you suggesting that I need to go away, call and then come back?"

"No, I think now that you're here, we can make an exception for you," William said. "It's okay, Malcolm.

Ms. Carlton will always be an exception to any rules we have around here."

"As you wish, sir," his assistant said, his spine stiff with disapproval. Clearly, he'd not come to terms with William's involvement with Destiny any more than Chester Sandhurst had.

"I think perhaps Malcolm should sit in on this meeting," Destiny said.

William frowned at her. "Then this is a business call?"

"Absolutely."

He was beginning to regret breaking the rules quite so quickly. "Then by all means, Malcolm, please join us."

"I'd rather not, sir. I have things to do."

"They can wait," William told him firmly.

Malcolm dutifully, if reluctantly, followed them into William's office. He perched on the edge of a chair as if he might bolt at any second. He continued to regard Destiny as if she were a coiled serpent.

"I've had a chat with some of my executives this morning," Destiny began, her gaze not on William, but on Malcolm. "It's proved rather interesting."

"Oh?" William said. "Sleuthing, were you? I thought you'd intended to leave that to a professional or at least to Sandhurst."

"Yes, well, things change, as you well know. I've discovered it's sometimes necessary to be a bit flexible in business."

"True enough," William agreed. "So, what did you discover?"

"Interestingly enough, Malcolm's name came up."

Malcolm had been staring past Destiny until that

moment, but his head snapped around. "I beg your pardon. In what context did my name come up at Carlton Industries?"

"Actually, my assistant has told me she finds you quite charming on the phone. It's the accent, I'm sure," Destiny said, as if she could find no other plausible explanation for such an analysis.

"Very kind of her," Malcolm said, looking vaguely embarrassed.

"Perhaps too kind, since I'm beginning to suspect you were the go-between speaking to one of my executives on behalf of Harcourt & Sons," Destiny said without the slightest hesitation. Her gaze never wavered. "Is that possible?"

Malcolm remained stoically silent. William could see that his assistant wouldn't say a word to give himself or William away, but William had lost patience with the entire game. Destiny already knew he'd been the beneficiary of inside information. There was little point in denying that Malcolm had had a hand in providing it. William would take full responsibility and handle whatever repercussions there might be. Besides, he was all but certain that Destiny merely hoped to get to the bottom of things, not to press charges of corporate espionage.

"Malcolm is my most trusted employee," William told her. "He does hear things from time to time that can benefit this company. As I told you last night, he has sources everywhere."

Malcolm stared at him. "You said that, sir? Why would you reveal such a thing?"

"Actually, it was in the context of singing your praises for acquiring those theater seats and dinner reservations," William told him. "But you also need to understand that Ms. Carlton and I are no longer engaged in any kind of subterfuge, Malcolm. I want her to be clear that anything you do, you do at my behest."

"Including buying information from Carlton insiders?" Destiny inquired.

"I've never paid anyone so much as a dime for information," Malcolm said indignantly.

Destiny waved off his claim. "To be honest, I don't give two bits what you do or don't do. You're William's concern, not mine. But I do need to know which of my employees is not to be trusted."

Malcolm's complexion turned pale. "I can't say, ma'am."

"Can't or won't?"

"Won't, if you're putting that fine a distinction on it."

"David Perkins claims he doesn't know you," Destiny said.

William was watching her intently, trying to figure out her game. Her gaze never left Malcolm's face.

"I don't recognize the name," Malcolm said without the faintest hesitation.

"That helps me eliminate one possibility, then," she said. "Of course, I imagine you're acquainted with Chester Sandhurst."

"By reputation only," Malcolm said calmly.

William was beginning to catch on. Destiny was going to throw out the names of those she didn't suspect to see if anything in Malcolm's demeanor changed when she finally mentioned the person she thought responsible for the leaks.

Destiny frowned a bit. "So Chester is off the hook,"

she said, her expression thoughtful. "Just as well. I was certain it was Edward Wildemon, anyway."

"Oh?" Malcolm said.

William saw a flicker of satisfaction register in Destiny's eyes and wondered what she'd heard in Malcolm's voice that he'd missed. Obviously she felt she'd confirmed her suspicions without Malcolm having to admit to a thing.

"Destiny, is that the last of your questions for Malcolm?" William asked, anxious to get to the bottom of what had sent her flying over here. Something must have happened at Carlton Industries this morning to trigger this interrogation.

"I believe so. Thank you very much, Mr. Dandridge."

"Yes, madam."

William gave the man's shoulder a squeeze as he passed. "It's okay, Malcolm."

"Oh, Mr. Dandridge," Destiny called after him.

"Yes."

"Please do not call Edward and warn him."

"I wouldn't dream of it, ma'am."

Once they were alone again, William met Destiny's gaze. "So, you think you have your spy?"

"And the man who planted that photograph," she said.

"Enough to convict him in court?"

"Probably not," she admitted. "But enough to see to it that he's never in a position to betray the company or me again."

"You'll fire him?"

"And have him sue us for wrongful termination and bloody our name in the press for months to come?"

she asked. "No. I'll just deny him access to sensitive information from here on out. Eventually he'll get the message that his ambitions will never be fulfilled at Carlton Industries and he'll move on."

She met his gaze. "I'm sorry I came here without warning and put Malcolm on the spot. I couldn't see another way to go about it."

"You didn't feel you could take me into your confidence?" Her silence was answer enough. "Will we ever get past this, Destiny?"

She gave him a sad look. "I want to."

"But the doubts keep nagging at you, don't they?"

"The doubts and Richard's reaction and the entire complicated mess that's been created."

"By me," William said.

"Not just you," she insisted. "I had a share in it, too."

"You?"

"Yes, years ago, if I'd been honest and insisted on sending you back to your family, perhaps it would have been best. Instead, I waited for the perfect excuse to come along, then ran myself. It left us both with too many unanswered questions."

He wasn't sure he understood her convoluted logic. "You'll have to explain that."

"I felt this incredible guilt over keeping you from your family. When my family needed me, it seemed like the perfect time to sever all ties. I don't think I consciously intended to use the tragedy that way, but it kept me from having to fight with you over it, especially when a very big part of me wanted so badly for us to go on just as we had been. I was afraid I'd never stand up to your persuasiveness, so I simply left."

She gave him a sad look. "When you told me recently that you would have come to me, if only I'd asked, I believed you. I think I always knew that. I think it's why I didn't ask, because a part of me believed you needed to be with your own family and that, until you'd made your peace with them, you and I could never be truly happy."

William's head was spinning. "You deliberately shut me out because you wanted me to come back to London?"

Destiny nodded. "And I was right. You came back here and took your rightful place in the family company. You made peace with your father."

"And it cost me the only woman I've ever loved," he said, unable to keep a trace of bitterness from his voice. "Who said you were the one who got to choose for me, Destiny?"

"I knew you could never make that choice for yourself," she said.

"Because it was the wrong choice," he told her emphatically. "There were other solutions."

"How can you say that? It was the only choice."

"Perhaps it wasn't wrong for you," he said then. "But it was for me and you had no right to make it."

"I made it because I loved you enough to let you go," she insisted.

He stared at her, still not comprehending how she could have ripped them apart without once discussing it with him. Maybe she and her nephew were too much alike, after all. Making unilateral decisions seemed to be at least one trait they had in common.

"I think you should go," he said quietly.

She stared at him, looking miserable. "William, please, don't be furious with me. I acted without thinking it through. In fact, I was so grief-stricken at the time I was barely thinking at all."

"I'm not furious," he said. "In fact, I'm having a very difficult time feeling anything at all."

Well, she'd certainly made a muddle of that, Destiny thought as she stood on the sidewalk in front of the Harcourt & Sons headquarters, shivering in the icy wind. Why hadn't she been able to make William see that she'd done what she'd done out of love and out of respect for his family? Besides, it had all happened so long ago. Surely they could leave it in the past and move on.

"Ms. Carlton?"

She looked up to see Malcolm Dandridge studying her with a concerned expression.

"Are you all right, ma'am?"

"I'm fine," she said wearily.

"I could give you a lift back to your office," he offered. "I don't think Mr. Harcourt would want you standing out here in the cold trying to find a taxi."

"I was going to walk," she said. "I need to clear my head."

"Then I'll walk with you," he said decisively.

"There's no need," she began, but let the protest die when it became evident that he wasn't going to take no for an answer. It was obvious his loyalty to William outweighed any antagonism he felt toward her. "Very well."

At least the man knew when to keep his own counsel, she concluded when he remained silent as they walked briskly through the midday crowd. She finally lifted her gaze and looked into his eyes. "Do you think he'll forgive me?"

Malcolm seemed startled by the question. "Why would he need to forgive you?"

"I made a very bad decision a long time ago," she explained. "I've just admitted it to him. He's not very happy with me at the moment."

Malcolm smiled and it softened his harsh features. "I don't think there's any question of him forgiving you, ma'am. He loves you."

"You believe that?" she asked, clinging to the lifeline he was tossing out. After all, it was evident that few people were closer to William than this man. In some ways, the bond between them seemed stronger than the ties William had felt toward his father.

"I've known how important you are to him for some time," Malcolm said. "I figured it out when he went to such lengths to get you back to London. It was never about business for him. It was always about you."

"Thank you for telling me that. I know your loyalty is to Mr. Harcourt."

He smiled. "Which is precisely why I told you. I think it's time you both put your cards on the table and grabbed this second chance, don't you?"

"I do, but it's gotten rather complicated."

"Because of your family?"

She nodded.

"And years ago, it was his family, if I'm not mistaken. Shouldn't you both have learned a lesson from that?"

Struck by the accuracy of his insight, Destiny regarded Malcolm with surprise. "How did you get to be so wise?"

"I've spent a rather long time with the Harcourts," he said. "You learn to read people, especially those you care about. I believe you have the same knack."

"I always thought I did. Perhaps it is time I started to trust my instincts again."

"Past time, I'd say."

"You wouldn't object to Mr. Harcourt getting involved with the competition?"

He laughed then. "I'd say he's been involved for years, wouldn't you? At least now, perhaps he'll be happy."

Outside of the Carlton Industries offices, Destiny impulsively stood on tiptoe and kissed Malcolm's weathered cheek. "Thank you."

He blushed furiously. "My pleasure, I'm sure."

Destiny stared after him as he turned and melted into the crowd. What an absolutely amazing morning!

"You saw that she got back to her office?" William asked Malcolm when he finally returned.

"Of course, sir."

"Is she okay?"

"I believe so, though she is worried that you might never forgive her for whatever it was she did years ago."

William sighed. He was struggling with that himself. He had been ever since Destiny had revealed that she'd all but deliberately cut him out of her life to force a reconciliation with his family.

"I can't imagine what she was thinking," he admitted to Malcolm. "She ripped our lives apart to get me to come back here."

"Would you have come otherwise, sir?"

"Probably not," William admitted. "My parents were being incredibly stubborn about Destiny and about what they expected from me. There seemed to be no room at all for compromise."

"Your father merely wanted you to take charge of your legacy, sir. It's not that unusual for a man to want that for his only son. His instincts were exactly right. You've done a bang-up job."

"Business isn't everything, Malcolm. Far from it."

"Neither is love," Malcolm countered. "It seems to me a balance is best all around. Perhaps you can find that now."

"In other words, forgive Destiny for being as foolish and stubborn as I was, and get on with things," William summed up.

"Precisely, sir."

William nodded slowly, seeing the wisdom in that. "What about her family, though?"

"A minor roadblock, sir. I'm sure you can deal with it."

"Your faith in me is sometimes blinded by affection, Malcolm."

"I'll deny it with my dying breath, sir. Now, I think it best if I get back to work and leave you to plan your strategy."

"I'm not going to war, Malcolm."

"Sometimes courtship can be just as complicated."

William chuckled. "I believe you're right...again. And I believe it's time I settled things with Fortnum Travel so that can't stand between us."

An hour later, William was sitting with David Fortnum and his board of directors. "Here's my one and only offer, gentlemen," he said. "I think you'll find it more than satisfactory and sufficient to put an end to the attempts by Carlton Industries to take over your company."

"We'll need time," David began, but William's scowl silenced him. He nodded slowly. "Perhaps, if you would give us a few moments, William, we'll be able to give you an answer."

William nodded. "I'll wait outside."

It took only five minutes for the board to reach its conclusion. David emerged from the meeting and grasped his hand.

"Thank you, old friend," David said. "I promise you won't regret this."

Knowing how infuriated Richard Carlton was likely to be, William wished he were half as certain of that.

Destiny sat in the lounge at Heathrow with Melanie, Beth and Kathleen and wondered if she shouldn't be getting on a plane with them. Maybe if she had a face-to-face confrontation with Richard they could settle this. But Melanie had promised to get Richard over here so he could meet William and, in the end, that would be the more sensible approach. Nothing she said on her own was likely to make a dent in the stubborn mind-set Richard had adopted where William was concerned.

"I wish you weren't leaving so soon," she told them. "You've barely gotten here. There's so much left that I want you to see."

"We'll be back," Melanie promised. "Soon."

"Absolutely," Beth agreed. "And we'll drag everyone else with us. Then we won't need to be on the phone half the time checking on the children and our husbands."

"We'll drag them all by the hair, if necessary," Kathleen added.

Destiny smiled at the image. "Yes, I believe you would. Thank you, darlings. I'm so glad you came. I've missed you."

"You could come back with us," Beth said. "Just for a visit."

"I considered that, but I think it would only give Richard false hope that I'm giving up over here. I think it's best if I stay right where I am and keep trying to get this division on solid footing. It's important to me to prove to myself that I have what it takes to do the job well. I'd like to hand him Fortnum Travel, if at all possible."

Just then their flight was announced. Destiny gave them each a fierce hug. "I love you. And despite my current exasperation with them, I love your husbands, too. Tell them that."

When it was Melanie's turn to say goodbye, she looked into Destiny's eyes. "Don't let them do anything to ruin this for you, okay? Grab every bit of happiness you can. You deserve it."

And then they were gone.

Destiny stared after the three women, who were so very different, yet uniquely suited to be Carlton wives. They understood the importance of love and family and brought a much-needed balance into their husbands' lives. She'd done well when she'd chosen them. If only she were half as successful at finding her own fulfillment.

She took a taxi back to her flat, though she dreaded

the silence that was going to greet her there. Even with such a short visit, they had brought noise and laughter into the place and made it feel like home. In the months she'd been in London, she'd almost forgotten how important that had become to her. She was no longer used to living on her own as she had so many years ago in Provence.

When she exited the elevator outside her apartment, she found William lounging against the wall. Her heart did a little somersault at the welcome sight of him, but she regarded him warily.

"I'm surprised to see you here," she said.

"I thought you might be feeling a bit low after seeing everyone off," he said.

"And that mattered to you because?"

He lifted a brow at her tart tone. "Because I love you, dammit!"

"How lovely of you to express it so sweetly," she said, barely managing to hide her amusement.

"It's because you tie me in knots," he said irritably. "I seldom know if I'm coming or going."

"Sorry."

"I doubt that. May I come in or do you intend to keep me standing out here in the hall? For all we know there are photographers lurking about in the shadows."

"If I let you in, will anything have changed?"

He frowned at the question. "What the devil is that supposed to mean?"

"We seem to keep dancing around the same old topics. I think it's time we move on or give it up."

William nodded slowly. "I see your point."

"And?"

"Let's talk about getting married," he proposed.

Destiny's chin dropped. "What?"

He laughed. "We haven't had that one on the table in a while. I think it's time we did."

"We... I..."

"Had I only known what it would take to render you speechless, I would have asked long ago," William taunted. "Come to think of it, I did, and you turned me down. Will you say no again?"

Now that the proposal was actually out there, hanging in the air between them, Destiny couldn't seem to gather her thoughts. It was oh-so-tempting to say yes this time and forget about all of the very real complications. But she couldn't seem to get the word past the lump in her throat or the fear in her heart.

"Married?" she echoed weakly.

"Is the idea so preposterous? I think we've waited long enough, don't you?"

"Perhaps too long," she said.

William stared at her. "Too long? What the hell is that supposed to mean?"

"We're not young anymore, William. We don't need to do things the traditional way."

"We've never done anything the traditional way," he countered impatiently. "I say it's time we did." He gave her a piercing look. "Do you love me, Destiny?"

"Yes," she said without hesitation.

"Then I think it's time we married and said to hell with the consequences. We'll deal with all the rest in time, but we'll do it together."

Destiny could just imagine Richard's reaction to such an announcement. He would be horrified. She needed time to prepare him, time to figure out if marriage was what she really wanted just when she was discovering what she was capable of accomplishing on her own.

"We can't do this now, William. Really we can't. In a few months, perhaps we can talk about it."

"What will be different in a few months?"

"My family…"

"Your family—and mine—are the reasons we've lost more than two decades out of our lives," he retorted. "I'm not prepared to let them cost us another minute. Years ago your nephews were young. They needed you. I accepted that. They're grown men now. They should want you to be happy. They need to deal with this."

"I can't expect them to do a complete one-eighty overnight," she said. "Richard, especially. He doesn't trust you. You saw to that."

William remained undaunted. "And my parents didn't trust you. We made the mistake of letting that keep us apart back then. If we hadn't, we would have been married before your brother and sister-in-law died and we would have raised those boys together. There would have been no question about it."

"You almost sound as if that's what you wanted," Destiny said, stunned.

"I did. It took me too damn long to see it. I admit that, but I would have given anything to be a part of that family you were creating with them."

"Oh, William," she said softly. "How foolish we've been."

"Yes, we have. Let's not make the same mistake now."

Destiny didn't know why she wasn't leaping straight into his arms, but she couldn't seem to bring herself to do it. She needed time to make everything right. It was her nature to want smooth sailing.

"A few weeks," she pleaded.

"What will change?" he asked again.

"I'll make them see how much you matter to me."

"And if they don't, if Richard still disapproves, what will you do then?"

She regarded him with dismay. It was something she hadn't considered, couldn't even permit herself to consider. Could she go against the wishes of her family, even one of them?

"I don't know," she said at last, her heart breaking.

William stared at her, his expression filled with despair. "Well, I assume you'll let me know when you figure it out."

"Of course I will," she said.

He touched her cheek. "I only hope it's not too late. Just so you know, though, I closed my acquisition of Fortnum Travel earlier today. I wanted you to know before the word got out. I've put an end to the competition once and for all, Destiny. Whatever happens now is just between us."

And then he was gone, leaving her openmouthed and silent with shock. The tears that had been threatening spilled down her cheeks and left her feeling empty inside and more alone than she had ever been in her life. He'd warned her of his intention to close that deal at any cost, but she'd been so sure that he'd relent in the end. Now whatever chance there had been of Richard accepting this man was gone forever.

20

Once again Destiny had chosen her family over him. At least that was how William saw it. And that was *before* she'd known about Fortnum Travel.

He left her apartment building with his heart heavier than it had been at any moment since the last time he'd set eyes on her in Provence so many years ago. He'd stood watching her plane take off and known in his heart that it was the end, despite her promises to keep in touch and let him know what was happening back in Virginia. He felt the same way now. It was impossible to imagine things changing for them, not for the better at any rate.

He knew she had her own share of regrets over the years they'd lost, but she still felt she'd been right. He was far more skeptical. Even with all he knew now about how conflicted her emotions had been when she'd gone back to the States to be with her family, even understanding why she'd felt it was best for both of them, he thought it had been the biggest, costliest mistake of either of their lives. He couldn't undo what had happened then, and he was far from certain he could fix things between them now, not with Richard and most likely his brothers standing squarely between them.

With his heart aching as he reached his house and poured himself a stiff drink, he settled in front of the fire and let the memories come as they had on so many other cold and lonely nights. Maybe there was an answer for him in the past, if only he could see it.

Provence, 1983

William hung up the phone slowly, his heart filled with anguish over what the Carlton family housekeeper had just told him. The news was going to devastate Destiny. He was glad in a way that he'd been the one to take the call. Perhaps he could soften the blow, but he doubted it. He knew how close she'd been to her brother, how often she spoke to him even now with years and distance separating them.

The Carlton housekeeper had been sparing with the details, in part because she'd been far too emotional herself. She'd said only that the Carltons' small plane had crashed in the fog-shrouded Blue Ridge Mountains and that there had been no survivors.

"These precious boys," she had said between sobs. "What's to become of them?"

"Don't worry," William had told her, knowing how futile the words were. How could anyone not worry under such sad circumstances?

"I'll speak to Destiny and I'm sure she'll be there on the first available flight," he reassured her. "She'll call you herself with the details."

By the time Destiny had come back from her

morning shopping, laden with bags of fruit, cheese and bread for the picnic they'd planned, he'd already booked her a flight. Seeing her coming up the path, he admired her lithe figure browned by the sun, her brown hair lit with golden streaks. She looked so incredibly happy and carefree. He ached knowing that he was about to destroy that.

She glanced toward the house and caught him watching. A smile broke across her face, lighting her eyes.

"Have you been waiting impatiently at the door all this time?" she called out in her low, musical voice.

William kept silent, not sure he had the strength to break her heart. Moreover, he was going to have to find the strength to let her go for however long it took to make things right for those three little lost souls, whose school pictures Destiny kept around the house and whom she bragged about constantly. For a woman so far from home, she'd kept up with each of their accomplishments. He almost felt as if he knew them himself, though he'd never set eyes on them.

Now as Destiny went into the kitchen to put away her purchases, she chattered a mile a minute about her trip into town and everyone she'd spoken to. William sat at the table, barely listening, gathering his thoughts, trying to find the right words to break the news. At last, she turned and looked at him.

"So somber," she said, her brow creasing with worry. "Is something wrong?"

"You need to sit down," he said quietly.

Caught by his tone, she sat at once. "What?"

He reached for her hand, felt her instinctively cling to him.

"It's your brother and his wife," he began, but even before he said the rest, her eyes filled with tears.

"Oh, no," she whispered.

"They were going on a trip today."

She nodded slowly. "To California on business. My brother mentioned it."

"It was a foggy morning," he said. "Your brother insisted on taking off, anyway. He was anxious to get there to close a business deal."

Her eyes filled with heartbreak even before he'd told her the rest. "Please don't tell me they're gone, William. Please don't say that."

"I'm sorry," he whispered.

"How…?" she began, but her voice trailed off, caught on a sob. "What happened?"

"Their plane crashed soon after takeoff."

"Oh, God, no." Horror washed over her face. "And the boys? Please tell me they weren't with them. Please tell me they're okay."

"They are. They're safe at home with the housekeeper. They hadn't even left for school yet, so she's kept them with her."

"That's good, then," she said, already trying to pull herself together. It was like watching a general prepare for battle, shrugging off all personal concerns to get the job done. "There are things I have to do, arrangements to be made. I have to get home."

"I've already booked a flight for you," he said.

"For me?" she said. "Not both of us?"

He studied her expression and concluded that she wasn't particularly surprised or dismayed. *Ask me to come*, his heart cried. When she said nothing more, he said, "This is a private time for you and your family.

You'll leave this afternoon. I can drive you to the airport as soon as you've packed a bag."

"Yes, I'm sure you're right. You're a marvel," she said, her voice brittle. "That's one less thing for me to do. I'll need to close up the house. You can do that, can't you, darling?"

"Of course," he said, his heart sinking at the realization that she'd already decided she wouldn't be coming back, at least not anytime soon.

As she began to spin away, William caught her. "Destiny, you don't have to be strong, not with me."

She gave him a defiant look. "I must be. There's no choice. There's no time for tears, not now."

He'd never seen her so emotionless. In that instant, a part of him knew that he'd lost her, but he didn't want to accept it. Not once had she suggested that he come along. Not once had she said she needed him. Not once had she leaned on him or asked for his comfort. He couldn't help feeling hurt by that.

Instead, she had turned inward for her strength. He'd always known that family meant the world to her and now hers needed her. For a woman like Destiny, there was no choice to be made. Her future was now in the States. In the blink of an eye she'd turned her back on Provence, on him and the life they'd built together.

William had no idea where his own future lay, not without her in his life. He supposed once she got on that plane, he would be forced to find out.

"Not this time," William said fiercely, finishing the last of his whisky.

He'd taken Destiny at her word back then, let her handle things on her own, and what had that accomplished? Nothing good for either of them. She'd had a fulfilling life with her nephews, but it was evident to him that she'd been just as lonely as he had been. He wouldn't let it turn out that way again. He wouldn't let her blindly choose family and sacrifice their love.

Earlier his proposal had been impulsive, tossed out too abruptly without nearly enough planning. Malcolm had been right, this was something that required a delicate, precise strategy. In an odd way, because they had fallen into lust, if not love, the night they met, they had never had a real courtship. Perhaps it was time they did.

Richard didn't like what he was hearing. He frowned at Melanie, who'd spent the past hour filling him in on the details of her visit with Destiny and her impressions of William. She was bubbling over with excitement about London and singing the man's praises.

"Those two are not in love," he said flatly.

Melanie gave him a tolerantly amused look. "You denying it isn't going to make it go away," she told him. "I've seen them together, Richard. I've talked to them." She gave him a pointed look. "I've *listened* to them. All you've done is spout off your opinions and get Destiny's back up. Even if William were the worst choice in the world for her, she'd be determined to defy you by now."

"She's not some adolescent," he insisted. "Sooner or later, she'll see I'm right. Family has always come first with her."

"And you would force her to choose?" Melanie asked, looking dismayed.

"Darling, what she sees is a man whom she once

loved with all her heart and now she has a second chance with him. The only thing standing in her way is the way you're reacting. She doesn't want to upset you."

"Do you blame me for being suspicious?"

"Not entirely, no, but you need to keep an open mind. Give him a chance."

Richard scowled at her. "It's crazy. People don't carry the torch for someone for twenty years."

"Apparently in Destiny and William's case, they do," Melanie responded evenly. "I suggest you get used to it. She chose you, Mack and Ben over William once. I don't think she'll do it again, not after the way she taught each of you about the importance of love."

"I will not get used to it," Richard retorted stubbornly. "I will destroy him before I let him use my aunt to steal our company bit by bit. Did you know he snatched Fortnum Travel right out from under us today?"

His wife gave him a look that normally would have made his blood run cold, but he was too furious to be daunted by it now.

"Forget about the damn company for once and pay attention to what Destiny needs," Melanie said. "She needs someone in her life. She deserves to have someone adore her the way William does. She deserves passion."

"Passion?" Richard stared at her, aghast. "They're sleeping together?"

Melanie regarded him impatiently. "What if they are? There's nothing wrong with it. They're both consenting adults. It would be perfectly natural for them to crave the intimacy they once had."

"How would you feel if she were your…?" His voice

trailed off before he could complete the thought. He knew he would sound either absurd or insulting and things were bad enough without that.

"Aunt?" Melanie supplied quietly, her tone like ice. "Destiny may not be directly related to me, but she is my friend. And based on the way you're reacting, I suspect she's going to need all the friends she can get. If you lose her over this, Richard, you've only yourself to blame. You'll have driven her away."

With that, she whirled around and left the room, leaving Richard to stew about the mess he'd made of things with his wife and most likely with Destiny, as well.

Still, he was right, dammit. There was far too much at stake to ignore his gut instinct. William Harcourt was using Destiny to ruin Carlton Industries. This underhanded business with David Fortnum proved that. Harcourt had used his old ties to the man to get him to accept a sweetheart deal that gave Fortnum little beyond the ability to fight off a Carlton takeover.

He picked up the phone and started to dial Destiny's number in London, even though he'd probably be waking her. Then an image of her being in bed with that no-good scoundrel made him replace the receiver. Time enough to speak to her in the morning. Maybe by then he'd be calmer and more in control, the way he was going to need to be to get through to her.

"Ms. Carlton, I think you need to come out here," Miriam said, a stunned squeak in her voice. She hung up without waiting for a response.

Destiny had never heard her assistant sound so completely undone. She raced across her office and threw open the door to find the outer office filled with flowers. It was a veritable sea of red poppies. Her eyes misted over at the sight of them.

"Is there a card?" she asked in a choked voice. Not that she needed one to know they'd come from William. No one else would have thought to send poppies.

Miriam handed the tiny white envelope to her. "I've never seen so many flowers at once," she told Destiny. "They kept coming and coming. Mr. Dandridge brought the first of them and gave me the card. I didn't know what to do."

"I'm sure the shock effect was exactly what William was going for," Destiny said wryly. She opened the card.

"Remind you of anything?" William had scrawled across it in his almost illegible handwriting.

Destiny smiled, instantly nostalgic. Of course they reminded her of something. She'd seen a field of poppies exactly like this too many mornings to count in Provence. She'd painted them in every light imaginable. As she thought about that, her fingers instinctively went to the tiny gold palette that William had given her for Christmas. She'd worn it every day since. More than once she'd been tempted to visit an art-supply dealer and buy paints and canvases, but there'd been too many other things to accomplish to spend a moment on what had become little more than an enjoyable hobby.

"What on earth?"

Chester's shocked exclamation interrupted her reverie. She laughed at his stunned expression. "A bit excessive, isn't it?" she asked him.

"William, I take it. Trying to make up for the Fortnum mess."

"Yes. That, and he's out to impress me."

Chester gave her a curious look. "Is it working?"

"He's never needed to impress me," she said honestly. "I love him."

"Oh, Destiny," Chester protested, clearly distressed. "That's impossible."

"You and my nephew," she said, unable to hide her dismay. "You're two of a kind." She regarded him fiercely. "And that is not a compliment."

"But William Harcourt?" he said worriedly. "You have to see that it's a dangerous mistake."

"I see nothing of the kind."

"Then how do you explain away his theft of Fortnum Travel?"

Destiny sighed. "It was hardly theft when it was the deal that David Fortnum wanted. He told me so himself when I spoke to him first thing this morning. He apologized to me, but said he had to do what he thought was best for his employees."

"And that was hooking up with Harcourt?" Chester scoffed.

"David and William are old friends. David trusts Harcourt & Sons. He doesn't trust us. That's the bottom line." She frowned at Chester. "Did you come in here for a reason?"

He opened his mouth, then snapped it shut again. "Never mind. I'll come back when I can have your full attention."

She gave him an impatient look. "Don't be insulting, Chester. Let's go into my office. Miriam, I'll send a response to William as soon as I'm through with Mr. Sandhurst."

Miriam's eyes were twinkling. "Yes, ma'am."

Inside her office, Destiny closed the door firmly. "Chester, let me make one thing perfectly clear. My personal life is none of your concern."

"It is if Harcourt's involved."

"No," she said emphatically. "That's the same mistake Richard is making. If I refuse to tolerate it from him, then you can be sure I won't tolerate it from you."

He seemed about to argue, then stopped himself. "If you insist."

"I do. Now, what brought you over here in the first place?"

"Edward Wildemon has turned in his resignation."

"Excellent," Destiny said with a sense of triumph. "That didn't take long."

"I beg your pardon."

"I'm all but certain he was our leak, Chester. I let him know that I was on to him, though I never made an outright accusation. I thought it would take much longer for him to get the message that he was no longer considered trustworthy."

"There's just one problem with that, Destiny. He's gone to work for the competition."

Destiny's jaw dropped. "Harcourt & Sons?"

"No, no," Chester said quickly. "Sorry. I didn't mean to imply that. He's been hired by Gleason and Mills. I believe he'll be in a position to do us a great deal of harm there. They've been wanting to make a serious move on us for some time now. They're a far more dangerous threat than Harcourt."

Destiny shrugged. "Can't be helped. We'll simply

have to outmaneuver them. Come back at three with David Perkins and let's go over every bit of information that Edward will be in a position to pass along. We should be able to see to it that they've wasted their money by hiring an insider."

Chester regarded her with grudging respect. "You surprise me."

"Because I'm not inclined to let that little weasel intimidate me?"

"No. Because I don't have the slightest doubt that you'll succeed in outmaneuvering anything they try. You're growing into this job, Destiny. There's no question about it. In fact, I'd say you're relishing this challenge."

She was taken aback by the compliment. "Thank you."

"It's not idle flattery, you know. I suspect you could have closed the deal on Fortnum Travel if you'd put your mind to it."

She scowled. "Meaning?"

"That you wanted an end to the hostilities more than you wanted that company under our umbrella," Chester suggested.

Destiny considered the suggestion and nodded. "You could be right."

"I think you should let Richard know about all of this," he told her. "Wildemon's resignation and the loss of Fortnum Travel."

She immediately bristled. "I thought you trusted me to get the job done. Isn't that what you just finished saying?"

Chester grinned. "Slow down. I wasn't turning right around and insulting you five seconds after complimenting you. I just meant that Richard ought to be aware that we might have to watch our backs for a while. I'm sure when you pass along that news, you'll be perfectly capable of reassuring him that everything is under control. By the end of the day, we'll have our strategy in place."

"Then that's when I'll notify Richard," she told Chester. "Actually, I think I'm looking forward to telling him that William is no longer our number one enemy."

No sooner had the words left her mouth, though, than she looked at Chester with alarm. "You don't suppose Gleason and Mills are doing this because they sense a weakness with me at the helm, do you?"

"If they are, they'll soon learn that they were very much mistaken to consider you weak in any way," Chester reassured her. "And I've told Edward to clear out his desk. Security should be escorting him off the premises about now."

Destiny nodded. "Excellent. We make a good team, don't we, Chester?"

"Yes, I believe we do."

After he'd gone, Destiny let out a sigh of satisfaction. She was slowly but surely beginning to prove her competence to those around her. She was even beginning to believe in herself. That left Richard. She knew that dealing with her nephew would be a lot easier if she gave up William, but it wasn't a sacrifice she was prepared to make. She simply had to trust that the man she'd raised would eventually see that love was more important than business.

Unfortunately, Richard wasn't the only one with doubts these days. She wasn't sure William believed that she hadn't already made her decision about the two of them, one that wasn't in his favor.

She pulled out a piece of her personal notepaper and jotted a note to William, thanking him for the grand gesture with the poppies, then buzzed for Miriam. "See that Mr. Harcourt gets this right away, will you?"

"Would you mind if I called Mr. Dandridge and asked him to come for it?" Miriam asked, then blushed furiously.

"You and Malcolm?" Destiny asked incredulously. "I didn't know you'd done much more than speak once or twice on the phone."

"We've only met once, just today in fact, but he's quite handsome, don't you think? Lives up to that lovely accent I enjoy so much."

"I hadn't given it any thought, but yes, he is quite distinguished-looking. And he's very kind, as well."

"I knew it!" Miriam said. "He has kind eyes."

Destiny shook her head. Would wonders never cease? Spring truly must be right around the corner, because love was definitely in the air.

"You and Miriam," William repeated, staring at his assistant. "The two of you are going on a date? We are talking about Destiny's personal assistant, correct?"

"Yes, sir," Malcolm said stiffly, looking decidedly uncomfortable at having his personal life dissected. "Is that a problem, sir?"

"No, no problem. I'm just surprised."

"As am I, sir. She's asked me to escort her to tea."

"Then by all means go," William said. "I don't suppose she had any message for me from Destiny, did she?"

Malcolm grew even more flustered. "Of course she did. That's why I saw her in the first place, to get this note for you." He pulled the envelope from his pocket and handed it to William. "Sorry, sir. I almost forgot."

"Yes, well, things tend to get a bit murky once women get involved in our lives, don't they?"

"You have no idea, sir," Malcolm said. "I don't believe anyone has ever asked me out on a date before. It's a bit disconcerting."

"Obviously Miriam has learned a few things from her boss," William replied with amusement. "Neither of them plays by the rules. Go along and enjoy your tea."

A rare smile tugged at Malcolm's lips. "I believe I will, sir."

Malcolm and Miriam. Who would have guessed it? William thought, bemused. Finally he dismissed the two of them from his mind to focus on Destiny. He tore open the note.

"The poppies are as pretty as a picture," she'd written. "It's something I never need reminding about, because the image is never far from my mind. Thank you for making it come to life again, though. With all my love, Destiny."

He leaned back, satisfied. Step one had gone rather well. Now to move on to step two. He picked up the phone and dialed a familiar number in Paris.

"Violetta, *ma che'rie,* how are you?" he asked the woman responsible for introducing him to Destiny all those years ago. He'd kept in close contact with Violetta Grégorie over the years, seeing her as a link to Destiny. They had maintained a casual correspondence, and in fact, Violetta was hosting a first European showing for Destiny's nephew, Ben Carlton, in her gallery sometime in the summer.

"Old and decrepit, as you perfectly well know," she responded in her low voice, made huskier by too many years of cigarettes. "When are you coming to see me again? It's been far too long."

"Actually, I was hoping to lure you to London," he told her. "I'll send you a ticket, if you say you'll come."

"Why would I want to come to dreary London when it's almost springtime in Paris?"

"To see Destiny Carlton again," he suggested casually.

"Destiny is there, with you? I knew I was right about the two of you," she said triumphantly. "What has taken so long for you to wake up?"

William laughed. "She's in London, but not with me. Not yet, anyway. I thought perhaps a visit with you would remind her of old times."

"Ah, so that's it," she said with understanding. "You are using nostalgia to win her heart all over again. Quite a clever tactic, *mon ami.*"

"Then you think it's a good plan?"

"If Destiny is as much the romantic as she once was, she'll be unable to resist," Violetta said confidently. "She was mad about you years ago."

"I hope you're right, but she's also a hardheaded businesswoman now."

"Once love enters the picture, few women will allow their head to overrule their heart," Violetta said. "So, then, for true love I will come to London."

"How soon can you be here?"

"So eager," she said, laughing. "Will tomorrow be soon enough?"

"Tomorrow will be excellent. Shall I meet your plane?"

"Too much bother. I will have someone drive me. I've been anxious to try that amazing tunnel they've dug under the English Channel. Look for me in the afternoon. Shall I come directly to your office?"

"To my house," he said. "You can settle in and have a bit of a nap before we put our plan into motion and surprise Destiny."

"Ever the considerate host," she said. "Why didn't I claim you for myself all those years ago? What difference does age make, after all?"

"I will adore you at any age," William told her. "You're timeless, Violetta, and next to Destiny, the greatest friend any man could have."

"You think of me so fondly only because I introduced you to the love of your life," she said.

He chuckled. "True enough, but there was a time after she'd broken my heart, when I could have hated you for that, but I didn't. Now, go and do your packing. I expect you to stay for a while once you're here."

"Au revoir, mon ami."

"Au revoir."

Slowly, William hung up the phone. He started to call out for Malcolm, then realized his assistant was off on a rendezvous of his own. Well, no matter. He could take it from here. In fact, for the first time, he was feeling astonishingly upbeat about the future—Richard Carlton, be damned.

21

Destiny wasn't sure what sort of feedback she'd expected once Melanie, Beth and Kathleen got home, but she'd assumed Richard would be the first one to call. Instead, to her dismay, it was Ben, her youngest nephew and the one she'd thought would inevitably be on her side if push came to shove.

"Destiny, I'm worried about you," Ben said the second she answered the phone.

"Why?"

"I think you know the answer to that."

"William," she said, with a sinking sensation in the pit of her stomach.

"Richard says—"

"I don't give two figs what Richard says," she retorted furiously. "He's got blinders on when it comes to this. What did your wife tell you? I assume Kathleen had quite a bit to say when she got back from her visit."

"The same thing Melanie apparently told Richard, that the two of you are in love."

She uttered a plaintive sigh. "Is that so impossible to believe?"

"Of course it's not impossible to believe that a man would fall head over heels in love with you," Ben said at once. "You're an amazing woman. I've spent most of my life watching some of the most intelligent, powerful men in Virginia become totally infatuated with you."

"Then I don't understand the problem. It can't be that you disapprove of William," she said sarcastically. "You don't even know him."

"Now, Destiny," he soothed.

"Don't take that patronizing tone with me," she retorted indignantly, cutting him off before he could offer some ridiculous platitude. "I thought I taught you never to judge someone without giving them a chance. Surely Kathleen had only good things to say about William. They took quite a shine to each other."

"Yes, but she's as much a romantic as you are."

"In other words, we're both fools."

"I never said that," he insisted, sounding shocked. "Come on, Destiny, be reasonable. Even though the man professes to love you, it didn't stop him from acquiring that company Richard was after."

"You don't know a thing about that. You're being just as unreasonable as you're accusing me of being," she snapped. "Never mind. I have to go. I'm meeting William in an hour and I have to get ready. I was thinking something wildly sexy would be appropriate."

"Destiny!"

Ben's protest sounded rather weak, as if she'd stunned him. Well, good. He deserved it. Obviously all of her nephews had gotten so used to thinking of her as their devoted aunt, they'd forgotten that she was also a woman in the prime of her life. Obviously she'd waited far too long to remind them of that. And, truth be told, she'd waited a bit too long to remember it herself.

"Got to go," she said, then automatically added, "Love you."

She hung up before he could say more. When the phone rang an instant later, she scowled at it, but picked it up, anyway, half prepared for it to be Ben, hoping to get the last word.

"Hi, Destiny," Mack said cheerfully.

"Not you, too," she muttered.

"Me, too, what?" he asked.

"If you called to tell me I'm an idiot or that William's not to be trusted, you can hang up now."

Mack's silence suggested she'd pegged his intention exactly right.

"Love you, darling, but I really don't want to hear it," she said blithely, and slammed the phone down in his ear.

The next time it rang, she ignored it. She was not going to allow her nephews to spoil this evening for her. William had hinted that he had a surprise in store for her tonight. After the outrageous extravagance of the poppies yesterday, she couldn't begin to imagine what he'd do next.

She grabbed her coat and headed out the door. She was meeting William at his place for a glass of wine before he revealed this surprise of his. Anticipation had her blood humming.

By the time she'd reached William's, she'd coaxed herself into a more optimistic frame of mind. She was in charge of her life now. If being with William was what she wanted, then her nephews would simply have to learn to live with it. Spending time worrying only about pleasing others never accomplished a blessed thing.

As soon as she alighted from the taxi, William opened his front door. Welcoming light spilled onto the street. She stood for a second at the foot of the steps admiring him.

Maybe tonight would be the night, she thought as her pulse skipped merrily. Through some sort of unspoken but tacit agreement, they'd avoided renewing their intimate relationship before now, but the heat had been simmering from the night of her party. Years ago there had been no question of waiting, but she was far more cautious now.

Tonight, however, she was eager to throw caution to the wind. Once they were lovers again, William would see that, married or not, she didn't intend to let anything come between them. Marriage would only complicate things unnecessarily. Perhaps in time, when she'd smoothed over her family's ruffled feathers… She let the thought trail off.

"Are you planning to come in or are you frozen in place by the sight of me?" he inquired with lazy amusement.

"You do take a woman's breath away," she said. "But you're all too aware of that, I'm afraid."

"It's only your reaction that matters to me," he insisted. "Now, come along before this cold air chills the entire house. It's drafty enough as it is."

When she reached the top of the steps, she placed her hands on his face and gazed into his eyes. "Have I told you that I love you?"

He smiled. "Not nearly often enough."

"It's true, you know."

She kissed him then, intending to prove to him that she was ready for anything. When they separated slowly, William gazed at her with dismay.

"What?" she asked. "Have I got this all wrong?"

"Not wrong at all," he insisted. "I want you more than I can say, but tonight's not the night. I told you I had a surprise for you. I have a guest who's waiting to see you again."

Thoroughly flustered, Destiny stared at him. "I hope I wasn't seen out here trying to seduce you."

He laughed. "It wouldn't matter a bit. I suspect she'd be all for it. She's always approved of us and she's definitely a huge proponent of seduction."

Her brow lifted. "She?"

He took her hand. "Come along and see."

Normally she was only moderately fond of surprises, but William was behaving so mysteriously, Destiny followed him eagerly. As they walked into the parlor, a thin, elegant woman rose from a chair. Even though she'd aged, there was no mistaking Violetta Grégorie with her dark, flashing eyes alive with intelligence and her vivid red lipstick outlining a full, generous mouth.

"Violetta," Destiny cried, and ran to her old friend, falling into a welcoming embrace that was as strong as ever, despite the more than twenty years that had passed. Violetta had to be in her seventies now, but she looked much younger.

"Ah, *ma petite*, you are as stunning as ever," Violetta proclaimed. "Let me look at you."

She held Destiny away from her and studied her intently. "More sophisticated," she declared eventually.

"But there is still that mischievous sparkle in your eyes. Have you brought me new paintings?"

Destiny laughed at the question, which Violetta had repeated in one variation or another every time they'd spoken through the years. "As you perfectly well know, I haven't painted anything worthwhile in years," Destiny said. "Isn't it enough that I sent my nephew to you? Ben's work will make you rich."

"But I have a special fondness in my heart for your paintings," Violetta insisted. She gestured to the one over the mantel. "It is wonderful to see William's collection. I almost regret selling them to him. I would like to have them in my own home. I have only the small portrait you did of me all those years ago."

"It was one of the few portraits I ever painted," Destiny recalled. "I was far better at landscapes."

"None of that false modesty," Violetta chided. "You did well with whatever subject you chose."

Destiny turned to William. "Thank you so much for this," she said, her arm still tucked through Violetta's. "Seeing my dear friend again is the best surprise you could have given me."

He grinned. "Then I shall have to work very hard to top myself next time. Now, then, I think there's time for a glass of wine before our dinner reservations. Will a Bordeaux suit you both?"

"Perfection," Violetta said. She looked into Destiny's eyes. "Now, tell me everything, *ma petite.* You've been well?"

"Very well."

"But lonely," Violetta guessed. "I can see it in your eyes. You must allow William to do something about that."

Destiny chuckled. "So that's why he brought you here, to sell him to me."

William frowned as he handed her the wine. "I wasn't aware that you needed to be sold on me."

"I'm aware of your many virtues, yes," Destiny agreed. "But I believe you're after more than my admiration."

"No question about that," he said. "I want everything this time, Destiny."

"I think perhaps that discussion ought to be put off till another time," she responded tartly.

"Why?" Violetta asked. "Not on my account, surely. Talk of love is never boring. Perhaps I can lend a fresh perspective to the discussion."

"Now, there's an idea," William said. "Destiny and I could definitely use a referee, actually. The conversations tend to get somewhat heated these days. We take different views of the future."

"Oh?" Violetta said. "How so?"

"William would like to go the traditional route," Destiny explained. "He's envisioning marriage and happily-ever-after, all that sort of thing."

"About time, don't you think?" William said.

Destiny frowned at him. "I think a less formal arrangement would suit the two of us much better."

"A romantic liaison?" Violetta suggested, her eyes alight. "Yes, I can see how that would appeal to you, Destiny. It would keep the excitement alive."

"And send Destiny's nephews into an absolute frenzy," William muttered.

She stared at him. "What on earth do you mean?"

"They don't approve of me now," William reminded

her. "How do you think they'll feel if they think I'm refusing to make an honest woman of you?"

"I never considered that," she admitted candidly. She'd feared they would be far more distraught if she announced an intention to wed him.

"Well, you might consider it," he said. "It could conceivably save me from winding up in a dark alley in dire straits."

"Don't be ridiculous," she said impatiently. "None of my nephews is inclined toward violence to solve problems."

"They've never faced this particular situation before, have they?" William countered.

Violetta suddenly laughed. "You two are exactly as you were all those years ago. So much passion. So much heat, I fear getting singed just being near you. Perhaps we should go to dinner before it explodes into something that shouldn't be witnessed by an outsider."

"You're hardly an outsider," Destiny told her. "It's because of you that we're together at all."

Violetta gave her a smug look. "You may thank me with a toast over dinner."

"Or not," Destiny retorted, giving William a withering look.

"Violetta, ignore her testiness. I will do the honors, if Destiny is too stubborn to admit the truth."

"Me?" Destiny protested. "I'm not the stubborn one."

William merely lifted a brow.

"Oh, all right, I am a tiny bit stubborn."

"Thank you." He gave her a hard kiss. "Actually it's one of the things I love about you."

"What an odd sort of compliment," she murmured.

"You're a rare sort of woman. The usual compliments are too pale and lifeless to suit you," he said.

Destiny chuckled at his glib tongue. She realized that it had been years and years since she'd laughed so much, since she'd felt this carefree. That was the true gift William was giving her tonight. Seeing Violetta again was reminding her of an irrepressible part of her that had been buried under the weight of too much responsibility for too many years now.

It wasn't that she wanted to go back again. Nor did she want to give up the excitement and challenges that lay ahead at Carlton Industries. But she did need to balance that, to find a fulfilling middle ground. And William, it seemed, was showing her the way.

Richard had spent a restless night and most of the day thinking about everything Melanie had told him. He'd even talked it over with his brothers the next morning. Nothing they had to say changed his opinion. The fact that she'd virtually hung up on both Ben and Mack said it all. He had to get Destiny away from that man's influence before he turned her against all of them. She might be furious with him in the short term, but in the long run she would thank him. He would simply have to make her see what a narrow escape she'd had.

The best way to accomplish that, of course, would be to get her back home, where she'd be away from Harcourt's influence. Then he, Mack and Ben could sit her down for a long heart-to-heart, the kind she used to have with them when she thought they were treading on dangerous turf. Of course, they'd been teenagers and Destiny was a mature woman, but the principle was the same. The straight talk would be based on love. Surely, she was reasonable enough to accept that.

To avoid another confrontation with his wife, he waited until he got to the office to place the overdue call that would set his scheme in motion. He caught up with Destiny at her desk.

"Yes?" she said, greeting him with far more caution than usual.

Richard frowned at her tone. "Is something wrong?"

"Why don't you tell me?"

Richard had the distinct impression that she'd been anticipating this call. "Were you expecting to hear from me this morning?"

"Actually I was expecting a call yesterday," she said. "That's when Mack and Ben chose to let me know that I was behaving like a silly old fool."

Richard winced. He should have considered that her reaction to Ben and Mack would make her even less open to whatever he had to say. Destiny was obviously braced for a fight. He decided to attempt another tactic altogether, though past efforts at subterfuge hadn't gone especially well.

"Actually I'm calling about something else entirely," he said, feeling his way carefully. "Nothing to do with Harcourt or the company, for that matter."

"Oh?"

"It's the baby, actually," he said, improvising. "She's sick."

"Oh? Your brothers didn't say anything about that," she said, sounding suspicious already.

"They don't know," he said. "This just came up overnight. I thought I should call you right away this morning. I'm really worried about her."

"What's wrong?" Destiny asked.

"She's spiking a really high fever."

"Children do that," Destiny said calmly. "If you're worried, call Beth. She can check it out."

"Actually, I was hoping you would come home."

The request was greeted with a long pause. "You want me to come home because your daughter has a fever?" she said slowly.

"It's more than that. She has this awful hacking cough," he added hurriedly, realizing that a fever wasn't nearly alarming enough. "She woke us up with it in the middle of the night. It was so bad I had to talk Melanie out of taking her straight to the emergency room. Now I'm thinking maybe I was wrong."

"Then call Beth," Destiny repeated. "She is a pediatrician. I'm sure she can put your mind at ease. If the baby really is as sick as you say, she could be much worse by the time I get there. Besides, what can I do really? I'm not a doctor."

"Can't you just come because I'm telling you we need you?" Just as he completed the question, he heard a soft gasp and looked up to see Melanie staring at him, her expression incredulous. That look was quickly replaced by dismay as she marched across his office, a scowl firmly in place.

Before Richard could prevent it, she'd grabbed the phone from him.

"Destiny, whatever he's telling you about our daughter, don't believe a word of it," Melanie said. "He's just being a pigheaded idiot." Her mouth slowly curved into a smile. "I should have known you'd see right through it."

Richard sank back in his chair. So much for sneaky

manipulation. Obviously it wasn't a lesson he'd learned all that well. Now he had both of the most important women in his life furious with him. Okay, *more* furious with him.

He turned and stared out his office window, studying the stark, wintry landscape, which wasn't yet showing the first sign of spring. It mirrored his mood. Only when he heard Melanie say goodbye to Destiny did he finally turn around to face the music.

"How could you?" she asked quietly. "How could you use our daughter as an excuse to try to get Destiny home? If Destiny had believed you even for a second, don't you realize how upsetting that would have been for her? If the baby were really sick, Destiny is too far away to get here in time to do anything. She would have felt miserable and scared and helpless. Is that what you wanted?"

"I wanted to get her away from Harcourt," he said defensively.

"By lying to her? You tell me which one of you treats Destiny with more respect? Right this second, I'd have to say William gets my vote."

She left his office and quietly, but emphatically, shut the door behind her. Richard groaned. He'd have felt better if she'd slammed it. That would have told him she was outraged. This, he thought, this was disappointment, and it cut straight through him, not just because it was Melanie, but because he suspected her disappointment was mild compared to what his aunt must be feeling.

When his private line rang, he was tempted to ignore it, but it didn't quit. It had to be a member of his family. They were the only ones who used that number.

"Yes, what?" he growled.

"Uh-oh," Ben said. "I guess you're in the doghouse, too."

"You could say that."

"Mack and I are having lunch to lick our wounds. Care to join us?"

"When and where?" When Ben named a restaurant in Old Town Alexandria not far from Carlton Industries, Richard responded tersely, "I'll be there."

Maybe one of his brothers would have some idea how he could make amends to his wife and Destiny. Neither one was likely to be a pushover.

"Can you believe he had the audacity to use his own child as a pretext to try to get me out of London and away from you?" Destiny asked William.

She was still seething over that one. She would never have believed Richard capable of doing such a thing. It was a good thing she'd been expecting some sort of ploy from him, thanks to those calls from his brothers. They'd merely cautioned her that she was courting disaster and pleaded with her to think twice. If only Richard had confined himself to the same sort of admonition. If only he'd ranted on and on about William's acquisition of Fortnum Travel.

When she finally met William's gaze, he was frowning. "Do you want to go home?"

"No, I do not want to go home. Why would I go running back there, when there's no crisis except whatever's going on in Richard's too vivid imagination."

"I thought perhaps you'd like to put his mind at rest."

"The only thing that would put his mind at rest

would be me quitting my job here and vowing never to set eyes on you again," she said candidly. "I'm thinking perfectly clearly about this, perhaps for the first time ever, and neither of those things is an option."

"They are your family. I know making peace with them is bound to be important to you," he said quietly.

She stopped her pacing and stared. "You're thinking of what I said to you about what happened with your family all those years ago, aren't you?"

He nodded. "You were willing to break us up so that I could make peace with them."

She heard the pain in his voice and knew that she'd been just as wrong then as he was now. "I'm sorry," she said. "You were right. Giving up one person for another is no solution. Now that the shoe is on the other foot, I finally get that."

"I certainly never thought it was," he agreed. "But it is what happened, isn't it? Though not entirely the way you'd originally envisioned it."

"Yes," she admitted slowly. "That is what happened. And now that I see all of the repercussions and unhappiness, I will regret it with my dying breath. I should have reached out to you. I certainly shouldn't have blamed you for not being a mind reader and not coming after me on your own, when I'd made it so clear that you should stay behind."

"Destiny, we can cover this ground again if you like, but I think we'd be far better off concentrating on the future."

"How can I?"

"It's simple enough. Just vow here and now to put the past behind us."

"But the past inevitably shapes who we are. It's impossible to ignore it."

"Not impossible," he insisted. "It's a choice."

She stared at him, not entirely comprehending. "In what way?"

"I could waste time and energy—in fact, I *did* waste time and energy—being angry over the unilateral decision you made to do what you thought was in my best interests. Now I choose not to think about that. All that matters to me is what we do about today and tomorrow. We still have control over that."

Destiny nodded slowly. "Yes, I see what you mean. So, if we control today, does that mean we can decide here and now to play hooky from work and take a walk in the park? It's the first truly lovely spring day we've had."

William laughed. "By jove, I think you've got it."

"I'll make you a promise here and now," she told him quietly, taking his hands in hers. "I will try my best to look forward and not back from now on."

He bent and kissed her gently. "Your promises have always been good enough for me."

"And yours for me," she said.

If only her nephews could see William the way she did, if only they could grasp that he was a man of integrity and honor, then all truly would be right with her world.

22

"If Destiny won't come home, even for a visit, then one of us needs to go to London and see firsthand what's going on with Harcourt," Ben said emphatically as he, Mack and Richard sat around a table nursing beers, their food mostly untouched, their expressions gloomy. "It was probably a mistake to send our wives. Women simply can't see things as clearly as men, not once they get some romantic fantasy going in their minds."

Mack stared at him with undisguised amusement. "I dare you to repeat that to Kathleen sometime. I figure that scene ought to be good for a laugh or two." His grin spread. "But only do it when I'm around to pick up the pieces."

Richard scowled at the pair of them. "I'm glad you two are taking this so lightly."

"Lightly?" Ben scoffed. "I just finished saying somebody needs to go to London. It's Mack who finds the idea preposterous."

"Not the idea, just your rationale," Mack corrected. "Aren't we here right now because we misjudged our wives? Let's not compound the problem by insulting them."

"Good point," Richard conceded. "Melanie's furious enough with me as it is."

"Then maybe you should be the one to visit Destiny," Ben said. "After all, you have the perfect excuse. She's running one of your major divisions. How's that going, by the way?"

"Far better than I expected, to be honest," Richard said bleakly. "If it weren't, I could fire her and she'd have to come home."

Mack hooted at that. "You are so delusional, big brother. Destiny doesn't have to do anything she doesn't want to do. It's not as if she's some kid who'd have no resources if you cut off her allowance. I'm not against you flying to London to see what's really going on, but I think you're going to be wasting your breath if you think you can persuade Destiny to change her mind where Harcourt's concerned. Every time one of us utters a word against him, she digs in her heels a little deeper. She slammed the phone down on me before I got so much as a word out about him. She just assumed she knew what I had to say."

"True," Ben said. "We're eventually going to drive her straight into his arms, if we don't lighten up."

"I suspect she's already in his arms," Richard admitted gloomily. "I'll settle for preventing her from marrying him."

"Maybe it's time we tried the reverse-psychology thing," Ben said.

"What reverse-psychology thing?" Richard asked blankly.

Mack rolled his eyes, as Ben explained with exaggerated patience, "The one where we pretend we're okay with it and take away the thrill of the forbidden. Maybe then she'll stop being so defensive and take a good long look at what the man is really after."

"Is there any dirt at all to be had on this guy?" Mack asked. "I assume you've looked into his background, big brother."

"Aside from his sneak attacks on Carlton Industries, he's considered a reputable businessman from a very fine family," Richard told them. "That's what made all those maneuvers so blasted annoying. I couldn't get a real handle on the guy or what he was up to."

"Could it have been exactly what our wives suggested, that he was merely trying to get Destiny's attention?" Mack asked.

"If he did, it was a damn risky tactic," Richard retorted. "It could have cost him a fortune and never gotten the slightest rise out of Destiny. And, of course, that doesn't take into account that Destiny is over there now and he still stole Fortnum Travel right out from under us. Would you tell me what the devil he needs with a travel company when all of his divisions are right in England? He had to have done it just to irk me."

"Or because he'd made a promise to Fortnum. Isn't that the way Destiny explained it?" Mack asked.

"Of course she'd believe him. That's precisely the problem," Richard said. "She's too trusting."

"You're forgetting one thing," Ben said, his expression thoughtful. "He supposedly knows Destiny very well. He obviously understands that when it comes to family, she'll do anything necessary to protect us and, by extension, the family business. Let's face it, if he understood all that, it was no risk at all."

Richard sighed. Ben was right. Other than paying some lawyer, who was probably on retainer or on the company payroll, anyway, almost none of Harcourt's schemes had cost him anything. He'd withdrawn from the bidding in the nick of time on most occasions… until Fortnum Travel. Had that been his target all along? Had the rest been mere diversions? Or had it always been about Destiny, just as he'd claimed?

It had all been rather cleverly concocted. Under other circumstances, Richard would have to admire the audacity of the man responsible.

"I'm going to London," he said decisively.

If he could convince Harcourt to back away from Destiny, he might not even have to see his aunt. Okay, that was something of a pipe dream, but he'd reached the stage when grasping at straws was the only thing left to him. He could hardly ground a fifty-three-year-old woman to prevent her from dating a man he didn't trust, though God knows he was willing to try.

The afternoon had been pleasantly lazy. The London sky was a brilliant blue with soft pillows of white clouds drifting overhead. The first daffodils were poking through the ground in the park. The air was balmy.

"Thank you for coming with me," Destiny said, gazing over at William, who was seated next to her on a park bench. With his collar loosened and his tie off, he reminded her of the man who'd lived with her in Provence, the man who'd been content with nothing more than her company.

"My pleasure," he responded. "What would you like to do now? It's nearly time for tea."

"I'd love tea," she said at once.

"Harrods? One of the elegant hotels? Or one of the Harcourt & Sons tea shops?"

She laughed. "If we were to go there, you'd only worry I was spying and trying to steal ideas."

"Where, then?"

"Would you consider taking me to your house?" she asked, her gaze steady on his.

William studied her intently. "Is it tea you're looking for now?"

"And perhaps a bit more," she admitted candidly. "What do you think?"

She had only to gaze into his eyes to know his response. There was a slow heat building there, an unmistakable eagerness. She remembered that expression from years ago.

"I think it's the most brilliant idea you've had since you came back to London," he said quietly. "But only if you're very sure."

Destiny smiled. "Have you ever known me not to know my own mind?"

"From time to time," he teased, "but very rarely."

"Then the odds are in your favor, aren't they?"

"Right. Then my place it is."

It was only a few minutes of brisk walking to William's home, but as if he feared even that might give her time to change her mind, he regarded her intently as he closed the door behind them. Knowing the question he hadn't yet asked, Destiny smiled at him.

"Let's skip the tea for now, shall we?" she suggested. "I'd like to see what you've done to bring your bedroom into the current century."

"How will you know?" he asked with a grin. "You refused to set foot in it the last time you stayed here. I believe you said a late-night visit would be inappropriate and quite likely to offend my parents."

She laughed. "I peeked in one morning after you and your parents were safely downstairs at breakfast. It was far drearier than the room I'd been assigned at the other end of the house. The location of that room, by the way, pretty much proved the sort of distance they intended to keep between us."

"I can assure you my room has improved vastly since then," he said, leading the way. He opened the door. "See for yourself."

Destiny stepped inside and admired the new sheer curtains at the windows, the rich shades of blue on the bed and the thick, cream-colored carpeting. Though the antique furniture was still dark and massive, the room was indeed far airier and brighter now.

"How's the bed?" she asked.

"You didn't bounce on it back then when you had your peek?" he asked, amusement glinting in his eyes.

"I didn't dare," she admitted. She had, however, buried her face in his pillow just to catch the familiar scent of him. Back then, even a single night spent out of his arms had been torture and they had been in London for a full week.

"Then, by all means, try it now," he told her.

She met his gaze, held it until her pulse scrambled and her breath caught in her throat. "Only if you'll join me."

"My darling Destiny, you couldn't possibly keep me away."

Destiny awoke at dawn filled with the kind of serenity she hadn't experienced in years. Being in William's arms again, the incredible magic of his touch had made her feel young and vibrantly alive. It had also reassured her that she was right to be fighting for what they had.

After all the weeks of caution, after all the years of separation, it was as if they'd never been apart. He was as fit, as virile and inventive as he'd always been. No man had ever known her body so well. No one had ever given her more pleasure.

She sighed and stretched, then gazed at the man lying next to her. "I love you," she whispered, stroking her hand across his stubbled cheek. The rough, totally masculine texture was something she'd missed for far too long now.

"I could use a shave," William murmured.

"Not on my account," she said. "Not just yet. I like the raffish way you look. It reminds me of the mornings you used to come looking for me in Provence, straight out of bed, all sexy and rumpled with just one thing on your mind."

"Would you be surprised to know it's on my mind right now?"

She smiled at him. "I was hoping you'd say that."

"We missed tea and supper," he said, regarding her worriedly. "Are you sure you're not starving for breakfast?"

"The only thing I've been starving for all these years is you," she insisted.

"Ah, Destiny, how did I ever let you go? I was such a fool not to chase you to the ends of the earth."

"It doesn't matter," she reminded him. "We're together now."

"Indeed, we are, in every way that matters."

This time when he made love to her, it was gentle and slow, each touch reverent. The flames built bit by bit, like tinder catching, until the heat exploded through her and then through him. She'd forgotten what it was like to experience all the degrees of passion, but it was coming back to her now. There were so many nuances yet to go, enough to last a lifetime.

"Now I *am* starving," she said eventually, when she could catch her breath again.

"Then grab a shower while I go and see what sort of delicacies I can rustle up to tempt you. Shall I bring a tray up here?"

"No, I think I'd better come down, if either of us expects to get to work today."

"Hooky's over?" he asked, looking vaguely disappointed.

"It's always best when it's not a habit," she told him, touching his dear face. "But there will be other nights and days, I'm sure of that."

"Ah, now you're looking toward the future. That's good. You've learned the lesson well."

"About time, wouldn't you say?"

"I'll see you downstairs. Grab a shirt or robe, if you like, after your shower. No need to dress."

"I'll be down in a few minutes, then."

After he'd gone, she stared after him for just a moment, counting her blessings. She loved her nephews and their families with all her heart, but William had just jumped to the top of the list. In his arms, she'd found herself again. She didn't think she could possibly bear to let him go.

When the doorbell rang, William muttered a harsh curse and put aside the eggs he'd been about to whisk.

When it rang again, the caller obviously impatient, he cut off the toaster and went to see who had the audacity to turn up on his doorstep at such an early hour.

To his complete shock, he discovered Richard Carlton looking thoroughly out of sorts.

"I ought to punch your nose in," Richard announced.

William took it as a good sign that Destiny's nephew seemed to have considered the idea and dismissed it. "A cup of tea, instead? I'll drink from the same pot to prove you have nothing to fear."

"No need. I have just two things to say and I can say them right here. Stay away from my company and stay away from my aunt."

"Sorry, I can't do that, at least not where Destiny's concerned. We could probably come to some agreement on the business aspect of things, eventually at any rate," William said, grateful that Destiny was taking her time upstairs. If she were to come down now, it could prove damn awkward.

Richard's scowl deepened. "Are you telling me you won't back off?"

"What kind of man would I be, if I did?"

"Dammit, Harcourt, be reasonable!"

William studied him with barely contained amusement. He doubted Richard would be pleased to know he was providing William with a certain amount of entertainment with his unrealistic demands.

"Do you fear a little healthy business competition?" he asked Richard.

"Of course not. I can handle a fair business fight any day of the week, just leave my aunt out of it."

"Hard to do since she's in charge of your operations over here. That puts her in the thick of it."

Richard paused at that. "Are you suggesting I fire her?"

William shrugged, taking momentary enjoyment in the idea of this young man digging his own grave. Destiny would have his hide if he tried to fire her, supposedly for her own protection. "Up to you, of course."

"Oh, you'd like that, wouldn't you?" Richard responded. "Does she have you running scared? Is that why you're anxious for me to call her back home? I'll be damned if I'll play right into your hands. Destiny stays right where she is."

"Your choice," William said blithely.

Richard raked a hand through his hair in obvious frustration. "Dammit, I knew I should have sent Mack over here. You wouldn't be quite so blasé if he were the one standing here."

"Neither you nor your ex-football-player brother are likely to intimidate me," William maintained.

Richard gave him a sharp look. "What are you really up to, Harcourt?"

"Running a business, same as you."

"And my aunt? How does she fit in?"

"I love her," William said simply. "Always have."

Richard looked completely taken aback by the candor of William's admission. William almost took pity on him and offered him the brandy he so obviously needed. Instead, he asked, "Are you sure you won't come in and have a cup of tea, maybe some eggs?" Perhaps seeing his face when Destiny joined them would be worth the risk. At least it would put everything into the open.

Richard blinked at the invitation. "No, thanks. I need to be going."

"A word of advice before you leave," William said mildly. "You might want to keep this visit quiet. I don't think Destiny would be particularly pleased about you meddling in her life."

"Destiny deserves whatever meddling I decide to do," Richard said grimly. "But you're right. I think we should keep this conversation between us."

"Maybe the three of us could have dinner while you're in town," William suggested, still trying to extend an olive branch to this man who meant so much to Destiny. He wanted to get to know all of the people who were important to her. He wanted—but didn't need—their approval. Destiny, however, quite likely did.

"I don't think so," Richard said.

"Your wife didn't seem to think I was such bad company or much of a threat, for that matter."

"My wife is a romantic. I'm not. I don't trust you, Harcourt. And when I'm through, Destiny won't, either."

"Fortunately for both of us Destiny tends to make up her own mind about things."

At least William hoped to hell that hadn't changed.

A gasp from the top of the stairs caught their attention at the same moment.

"Richard!" Destiny exclaimed with obvious dismay.

Richard stared into the shadows. "Destiny, is that you?"

Though she was dressed only in one of William's thick robes, Destiny descended the long staircase as regally as if she wore a ball gown. William had never been more proud of her. She met her nephew's shocked gaze without blinking, her chin held high. There was no question that she was a woman capable of facing down anything, even this awkward moment.

"What the devil are you doing here at this hour?" Richard demanded as if it weren't perfectly obvious.

A smile touched Destiny's lips, then vanished. "I should think even you could figure that out on your own. The more important question is what are you doing here?"

"He just stopped by for a chat," William said when Richard couldn't seem to find his tongue. "Nothing to get worked up over, darling."

Richard scowled at him. "She is not your darling."

William regarded him with amusement. "Destiny seems to find the notion agreeable enough."

Richard looked as if he might be reconsidering his earlier threat to punch William in the nose. Instead, he turned his attention to Destiny. "Get your clothes. We're getting out of here."

She stared at him as if he were speaking a foreign language. William waited for the explosion that was sure to follow such an order.

"I am not going anywhere," Destiny said coldly. "But you are leaving, Richard. Right now, as a matter of fact. I won't be bullied by you."

"Dammit, Destiny." Richard stared at her with obvious frustration.

"Go, Richard," she ordered, her gaze unrelenting. "We'll talk about all this later, when the timing is somewhat more appropriate."

"I doubt there's an appropriate time or place for this conversation," he retorted.

"Then we needn't have it at all," she replied, her tone icy. "I have never done you or your brothers the discourtesy of barging in on you and being insulting when you were with a friend. I thought I taught you better manners."

She was working herself into such a state that William felt compelled to step in before one of them said something they could never take back. A serious rift between Destiny and her family was the last thing he wanted to be responsible for.

"Darling, it's not a problem," he soothed. "Richard merely came because he's concerned about you. I can appreciate that he loves you and wants to protect you. I wouldn't have much respect for him if he didn't."

"I don't need you to defend me," Richard responded.

William sighed. "If I were you, I'd take assistance wherever I could find it. Can't you see that Destiny is about to lose patience with you entirely?"

"I'm already past that point," Destiny said. "If you won't leave, Richard, then I will." She swept past him and headed for the door.

Both men stared after her. It was Richard who grabbed her when she would have marched down the front steps, barefoot and wearing nothing but William's robe.

"You can't leave this house in a bathrobe," Richard protested, looking horrified. "Go back inside. I'll go. We'll talk later." His expression miserable, he met her gaze. "I'm sorry, Destiny."

A tear trailed down her cheek. "I know," she whispered. "So am I."

As soon as he'd gone, she flung herself into William's arms and burst into noisy sobs.

"It's okay," he soothed. "It will come out all right in the end."

"I know," she said, her voice muffled against his chest. "Why does he have to be so incredibly stubborn, though?"

William laughed. "Little question about that one, my dear. Look who he's had for a teacher."

She frowned up at him, her cheeks damp. "Now who's being insulting?"

"Just truthful, as you perfectly well know. Now, let's eat. Breakfast was almost ready before he arrived. It won't take but a minute to get it on the table. You're going to need all the strength you can get to face the rest of the day."

"Tell me about it. I don't suppose you'd like to play hooky again, after all. Being a business executive who reports to my pigheaded nephew has suddenly lost some of its appeal."

"No, I will not give you an excuse to avoid Richard. I think it's past time we got this settled once and for all."

Destiny regarded him with obvious regret. "I suppose you're right, but I have to say I'm not looking forward to this particular confrontation."

He chuckled. "Frankly, I'd like to be a fly on the wall. I think you can handle Richard."

"He's certainly not concerned about it," she said.

"He should be," William said. "You're a formidable woman, Destiny. It's about time Richard saw that for himself. Maybe then he'll stop worrying so much about my influence over you."

Though her eyes still shimmered with the sheen of tears, her lips quirked into a full-blown, satisfied smile. "Formidable?" she asked happily.

"No question about it."

"You know, no matter how things turn out, coming to London and seeing you again has been a wonderful boost to my self-confidence."

William studied her with alarm. She sounded almost as if she were ready to concede defeat. "What do you mean, no matter how things turn out? There's no question about that, Destiny. You're going to triumph, not just in business, but as a woman and as a wife."

She frowned at him. "I thought I told you how I felt about marriage," she said, ignoring all the rest of his praise.

"You mentioned it," he agreed. "But eventually you'll come around to my way of thinking."

"Now who's being stubborn?"

He laughed. "It's the only way I know to be any sort of match for you."

23

Destiny considered hopping on a plane and heading for Paris for a visit with Violetta, but cowardice had never been her way. She was clearly going to have to face Richard sooner or later. She might as well get it over with.

That didn't mean she didn't need to be fortified for the battle. One thing her nephew excelled at was spotting a weakness and taking advantage of it. She couldn't afford to show any hint of weakness.

Once she'd left William's, she went home, spent a half hour soaking out the delicious new kinks in her muscles, then dressed in a very tailored black suit, added her best pearls, her Italian leather pumps and the pin William had given her. The latter was meant as a reminder of what was at stake—not just her future with Carlton Industries, but her right to have the personal life she'd denied herself for too long in the misguided belief that her nephews required *all* of her devotion to make up for their terrible loss.

Surveying herself in a full-length mirror, she decided she looked every inch a no-nonsense, professional businesswoman. Maybe that would be enough to give Richard pause.

Striding confidently into the office a half hour later, she beckoned for Miriam to follow. "Close the door, please. I don't want anyone else to wander by and overhear this."

Miriam shut the door and regarded her with alarm. "Is there a problem?"

"You could say that," she responded wryly. "Richard is in town. He's clearly on a mission. I assume it's to break up my relationship with William, but if he can't accomplish that, he's likely to try to use my performance here in some way to insist that I come back to Virginia."

"But you've done a wonderful job here," Miriam protested loyally. "Everyone says so, even Chester, and you know what a skeptic he was at first."

There was no time to indulge in the pride Miriam's remark sparked in her. "Even so, I want you to pull together facts and figures on every single project we've been discussing around here. I want the itemized cost savings in every department along with the projections for the next two years. I'm going to bombard Richard with so much information, his head will spin. Maybe that will prevent him from getting into the matter that brought him charging across the Atlantic."

"You mean Mr. Harcourt?"

"Precisely."

"It's not that unusual that Richard would feel very protective toward you," Miriam said. "After all, you kept most men at arm's length for many years. Now when you've finally let down your guard, the man you've chosen deliberately set himself up as the enemy."

"Yes, well, we all know that William is not seriously intent on taking on Carlton Industries," Destiny said. "Richard seems to be the only one who can't accept that. It's unfortunate that William felt it necessary to acquire Fortnum Travel. That only solidified Richard's low opinion of him."

"Perhaps if they met…"

Destiny chuckled. "I'm afraid that's already happened," she admitted. "He caught me at William's this morning wearing his bathrobe."

Miriam's eyes widened. "Oh, my."

"Indeed. If only Richard's reaction had been mild shock."

"Was he outraged?"

"Pretty much, which is why I hope to forestall the discussion he's vowed to have the minute he walks through the door here. I refuse to be treated like a schoolgirl whose father caught her kissing some inappropriate boy on the front stoop."

"Richard might not be quite so upset if he'd merely caught you and William kissing," Miriam pointed out, struggling to hold back a smile.

"You're not helping," Destiny retorted, fighting a small smile of her own. "Besides, aren't I entitled to a life at this late date? A few weeks ago, I would have let Richard's opinion change things for me, but I've seen the folly of that. William and I have already lost too much time because I allowed his family's opinion to matter too much. I won't make that mistake twice."

"Of course not, but it's bound to be a shock to him, as well as to Mack and Ben. Essentially you've been a single parent whose entire world has revolved around them. They've had you to themselves for a very long time now. I suspect they're worried that they'll lose you, that you'll no longer have any time for them, especially since you've already chosen to move so far away."

Destiny stared at her. "You can't be serious."

"It's not that unusual for children to feel that way. I know mine will when they discover I've moved on now that their father's gone."

"But it's utterly absurd," Destiny protested. "Besides, they're not children. They're adults."

"Well, of course it's absurd," Miriam acknowledged. "No one ever said men were rational when it comes to this sort of thing."

Destiny was forced to acknowledge the validity of Miriam's observation. Something told her it was going to be a very long day.

"Just get all those reports together, would you?" she requested. "It's too bad I never learned yoga. Now seems like just the time for some nice, calming meditation."

"Or a good stiff drink," Miriam retorted merrily on her way out.

Destiny's gaze flew to the assortment of whiskey, sherry and other liquors on the credenza in her office. No, that definitely wasn't the answer. This conversation was going to be tricky enough without Richard coming in and discovering her sipping booze before lunchtime. He'd probably insist on having her committed.

No, the answer was to go on the attack the instant he walked through the door. If she'd learned nothing else from Mack and his attachment to football, it was that sometimes the best defense was a powerful offense.

Richard was dreading the confrontation that loomed with Destiny. It had gotten far more complicated when he'd discovered her in William's house, wearing the man's bathrobe. He shuddered every time he recalled the image. There had been no question at all in his mind that she'd merely been trapped at the man's house overnight by some calamity or another. No, the two of them were having an affair, and no matter how Richard broached the subject, he was going to come off looking like an interfering jerk.

Of course, there was a slim chance that Destiny had been thoroughly embarrassed by the incident and, having seen the way it looked through his eyes, would have ended it by now. Perhaps he'd never have to bring up the uncomfortable subject.

Okay, that was obviously a delusion, but it was enough to give him the courage to walk into her office.

She glanced up from the stack of reports on her desk and gave him a hard, unyielding look that destroyed whatever illusions he'd been clinging to. He felt like he'd been summoned to the principal's office after being caught cheating on an exam, when the shoe should have been on the other foot. Destiny was the one who was supposed to be squirming.

"Do you have a problem with the way I'm running things over here?" Destiny demanded before he could utter a word.

It was the second time this morning that someone had questioned his motives. He hadn't much liked it when Harcourt had done it. He liked it even less coming from his aunt. He was going to have to tread cautiously to keep her from blowing a gasket. Destiny in high dudgeon was something to fear and she was clearly on the brink of that now.

"No, of course not," he conceded, willing to give her that much. "To be honest, things have never run more smoothly. I expected you to get off to a much bumpier start."

"Then go back home and leave me alone." She gave him a piercing look. "Unless there's some other reason you're here."

"You know there is," he admitted, then grasped at the first straw he could come up with other than the obvious. "I've missed you."

"We talk almost every day," she said, regarding him with amusement.

"About business," he said, sticking to his story. If he failed at subtlety this time around, he was going to retire the tactic and go back to being his blunt, normal self.

"What else is there besides business?" Destiny inquired. "That's all you've ever wanted to talk about. You were never one to tolerate idle chitchat, not even as a boy. I've never known anyone more determined to stay on task. Not even your grandfather or your father had that kind of focus."

"Maybe I'd like to hear how you're doing," he suggested cautiously, because she had it exactly right. This was new turf for him.

"Never better," she said at once.

"I can see that. You're glowing." It irked him to no end that Harcourt was responsible for that. There had to be hundreds of more appropriate men in London.

Why was it necessary for her to become involved with a man who'd threatened their company, a man who'd obviously hurt her in some way years ago?

"Nothing like a good business battle to stir the blood," Destiny said. "I'm beginning to see why you've always enjoyed it so much. We haven't lost a contract since I got here, except for that travel company, but I've been considering some alternatives. I think we'll come out okay in the end."

"I wanted Fortnum."

"Flexibility is an important business trait."

Richard could see he wasn't going to win this round. He wasn't going to subtly steer the conversation in the direction he wanted it to go. She wasn't going to admit to anything on her own, not even after being caught on enemy turf. When a strategy failed so abysmally, it was time to retreat and regroup.

"I'm going to the hotel for a nap," he said finally, waiting to see whether or not she'd insist he stay at her flat. If she didn't, it was most likely because she didn't want him underfoot while she cavorted with Harcourt.

"You're not going to go around and greet everyone?" she said.

Irritated that he'd lost yet again, he snapped, "I'll do that tomorrow."

"Yes, I can see it would be best to do it when you're in a better mood," she said blithely. "Shall we have dinner tonight, then?"

The invitation was at least something. It suggested that she didn't have plans with Harcourt for the evening. "Yes," he said at once.

"Good. I'll call William and put him off until tomorrow." She beamed at him. "Unless you'd like to spend some time with him, of course. I know he's looking forward to seeing you again under less awkward circumstances."

Richard grimaced at the massive understatement. "No, I would not like to see him. Why are you having dinner with that man at all?" he asked, violating his own rule about not going on the attack where Harcourt was concerned until Destiny's temper had had time to cool down.

"I told you I intended to stick to him like glue."

"Don't you think you might be taking that to an extreme?" he inquired bitterly. "Do you have to sleep with him?"

She frowned at the question. "I'm not a young schoolgirl, Richard."

"But he's in love with you," Richard blurted without thinking.

Destiny's jaw dropped. Richard waited, not sure if her shock was due to the revelation or to the fact that he knew something so intimate about William's feelings for her.

"How do you know that?" she asked eventually.

"He might have mentioned it," Richard said numbly. His goose was definitely cooked now.

"When exactly did you two share this little tête-à-tête?" she asked, her voice like ice. "It must have been before I came downstairs."

"As a matter of fact, it was."

"Then you didn't come there looking for me at all. You came to warn William off. My appearance was a total surprise."

"More like a total shock," he conceded gloomily.

"You were the last person I expected to encounter there."

"I see. And you felt you had the right to interfere in my personal life because…?"

"Because I've been worried about you, dammit."

"Because you don't think I have a lick of sense? Because you think I'm capable of being disloyal to this family? Which is it, Richard?" She shook her head. "Never mind. I think I'll have dinner with William tonight, after all. You and I can talk again tomorrow when I'm not quite so enchanted by the notion of strangling you."

"You did this much meddling and worse behind my back," Richard said in his own defense.

"So I did," she said mildly. "Then you must recall how you hated it."

With that, she walked out of her own office and quietly shut the door behind her. Her demonstration of displeasure wouldn't have been any more emphatic if she'd slammed it and rattled the hinges.

Richard stared after her, knowing that he'd bungled the entire meeting. Destiny had been in charge from the moment he'd walked through the door.

Suddenly the wonder of that struck him and he found himself beginning to grin. He still didn't like Harcourt one damn bit. He definitely wasn't crazy about the man's influence over Destiny. But, by God, his aunt was amazing. If he didn't watch his backside, she'd take over the whole damn company one of these days and deserve to do it.

It would almost be worth sacrificing his own power and position to see her take on the business world.

There wasn't a corporate executive he'd ever met who'd be a match for her.

He laughed. One of these days, if she ever spoke to him again, he'd have to tell her that.

William frowned when Destiny appeared in his office looking flushed and furious.

"What's wrong?" he asked at once. "Come in here and sit down."

"I don't want to sit." Proving it, she began to pace. "I have never in all my life been so disappointed with anyone."

"Richard?"

"Yes."

William sighed. "What's he done now?"

"He's just being a completely bullheaded horse's behind."

"About me?"

"Yes."

"Then let me fix the problem," he suggested. "Tell me where to reach him. Let me invite him to my club. I'll sit him down with a cigar and a drink and tell him exactly how I feel about you."

"Apparently, he's already gotten that particular message. He says you shared it earlier today."

"Ah," William said, gathering that his revelation that he loved Destiny had upset her almost as much as it had her nephew. "Would you have preferred it if I'd lied to him? Told him that we were simply having a mad fling?"

She scowled at him. "There's nothing wrong with two adults having a madcap fling. We did it rather successfully for many years, in fact. There were no complications to that."

He bit back a grin. "Never said there were. I'm not sure Richard would take much comfort in it, though. I wouldn't if I were in his shoes."

"But if he concludes we're serious about each other, he'll assume that means marriage."

"A lot of people would leap to that conclusion," William agreed. Destiny was apparently the only female on earth to whom the idea seemed to be incongruous.

Destiny gave him an impatient look. "I'm sure in my nephew's view, a marriage between the two of us would be the very worst thing that could happen."

"Because I'm the enemy and likely to take you and the company for everything I can once I get my hooks into you," he concluded.

"Well, can you blame him?"

"Not entirely," William admitted. "That's all the more reason for me to sit down with him and explain exactly how things are. I could point out, in fact, that the last real skirmish was the one he himself initiated when he tried to buy that woolen manufacturer in Scotland."

"He doesn't want to see you," Destiny said glumly. "I suggested dinner and he blew a gasket. Even if he relented, he wouldn't be happy to be reminded of an incident that caused me to threaten to have him removed from his position. Besides, in his mind, it's the acquisition of Fortnum that proves you're still up to no good."

"Then what do you suggest we do? Stop seeing each other entirely?"

To his relief, alarm immediately registered on her face.

"No, absolutely not," she said at once. "I'm not sixteen, for goodness' sake. I won't let him dictate to me who my friends can be."

William frowned at her response. "Is that the only reason?"

She paused in her pacing and stared at him. "What do you mean?"

"Am I some bizarre form of midlife rebellion for you? Am I your way to prove your independence to your nephews?"

"Don't be ridiculous," she said.

"Pardon me, but I think you might take a look at this from my perspective," William said quietly. "It seems that everything you're saying and doing is a reaction to Richard. Shouldn't it be about what you truly want for the rest of your life? Once you've made up your mind about that, it might be a whole lot easier to convince your nephew to stop interfering. I have little doubt that right now he senses some sort of ambivalence on your part. I sure as hell do."

Destiny stared at him with obvious shock. "What are you suggesting?"

"That if you waved an engagement ring under his nose, he might begin to take us seriously."

"I thought we'd decided—"

William cut her off. "You decided. My offer's still on the table."

She sank onto a chair. "This has turned into such a muddle."

"It doesn't have to be," he told her more gently. "Make a decision, Destiny. Once you have, whatever it is, the rest of us will learn to live with it."

"I suppose you're right."

"You know I am. We're past the age for taking things by half measures." He went around his desk and extended his hand to help her up. "Get out of here and think about things, Destiny. What is it you truly want for the rest of your life? Once you've decided that, everything else will come easily enough."

He walked with her outside, then pressed a kiss to her forehead. "While you're thinking things through, don't forget that I love you with all my heart."

She gave him a small smile. "No last-minute pressure there," she chided.

"Just a reminder," he insisted. "I don't want it to slip your mind."

"As if it could," she said, her hand soft and warm against his cheek. "I'll be in touch."

And then she was gone, striding briskly and purposefully down the sidewalk, blending into the London crowd. William watched her go, his heart in his throat. He'd taken a huge chance by forcing the issue, but it was time. Whether she knew it or not, Destiny was ready to make this decision. She'd had more than twenty years to mull it over.

In the meantime, he had something he needed to do. He strode back to his office and tracked down Malcolm.

"I need you to find out where Richard Carlton is staying," he told his assistant.

"He's not at Ms. Carlton's flat?"

William smiled. "I gather there's been a bit of a falling-out between those two. I'm fairly certain he's been banished to a hotel. I'm sure you can find out which ones Carlton executives prefer when they're in town."

"Should I ring his room when I find him?"

William considered whether or not the man deserved a fair warning and decided against it. "No, but get the room number. I know it's something hotels prefer not to give out, but you should be able to manage it."

Malcolm nodded. "I don't believe that will be a problem, sir. Give me a few minutes."

What might have taken an extremely good private investigator a couple of hours minimum, Malcolm did, indeed, accomplish in minutes.

"He's at the Dorchester, sir. Here's the suite number. I believe he's in at the moment."

William took the piece of paper and grabbed his coat. "Then you know where to find me," he said.

"Will you be long, sir?"

"I suppose that depends on just how stubborn Carlton is inclined to be." He thought about Destiny's stubborn streak, then added, "It could take a while."

Malcolm gave him a rare grin. "Yes, sir. I imagine if Mr. Carlton takes after his aunt, I shouldn't expect you back this afternoon."

"Wish me luck."

"Always, sir, but you won't need it."

William appreciated Malcolm's display of confidence. If only Destiny had half as much faith in him.

Or in herself.

24

Destiny walked for hours, her head spinning. William had made it sound so simple. Just decide, he'd told her. The rest would follow naturally.

There was only one problem with that. Since coming to London, she'd discovered she wanted it all—a career, William and her family. No simple accomplishment, given the high emotions on all sides.

What if she couldn't have it all? she asked herself, trying to face reality. Was she willing to settle for less? And if so, what was she willing to sacrifice?

The job was something new. She supposed she could live without the challenge and excitement of it, but why should she have to? She was good at it. Damn good, in fact. No, she decided, she wouldn't give that up, not without a fight.

And William? What about him? She thought about what he meant to her, what he'd always meant to her. How could she sacrifice that again? She simply shouldn't have to. Neither of them deserved to spend another lonely year because of family pressures, first from his side and now from hers. They'd waited far too long for the happiness they deserved.

Which brought her to her family, or more precisely to Richard, who was the instigator of all the problems she was facing. Mack and Ben might be worried, but it was Richard who was stirring the pot and turning a tiny little molehill into a monumental mountain. If she could win him over, make him trust her judgment about William, it would solve everything.

Passing a tea shop, she realized she was starving and instinctively turned in, then realized it was one of the Harcourt & Sons shops. She smiled at the coincidence, then realized that it was a bit like being surprised to find a Starbucks back home just when the thought of coffee popped into her head. There seemed to be one on every block. Harcourt & Sons tea shops were almost as pervasive in London.

She found a vacant table, ordered a wonderfully strong Darjeeling and a scone with clotted cream, then resumed her musings. She was pretty much where she'd been at the outset. She still wanted it all. She simply had to figure out the way to do that.

Again, it came back to Richard. If she could bring him around, the rest would fall into place. Not an easy matter, but she could do it. She merely had to take the first step, and then the next, until he saw things her way. Hadn't she spent the past two decades molding him into the man he'd become? Surely she could still find some creative way to get through to him.

Sipping the last of her tea, she nodded decisively. That was it, then, and there was no time like the present to begin.

* * *

William rode the elevator straight up to Richard's floor, then knocked on his door. When there was no immediate response, he knocked a little harder. More than likely, the man was sleeping off his jet lag. That could work in William's favor. Richard wouldn't be so quick to argue over every little thing William said.

At last, the door to the suite swung open and Richard stared at him, his eyes bleary, his face lined with fatigue and evident dismay.

"You!" he said, sounding cranky and inhospitable.

"May I come in?" William inquired, then walked right past him without waiting for a response.

Richard didn't argue. He merely shut the door and stood with his arms folded across his chest, glowering. "Make it quick."

"I don't think that will be possible. Why don't you shower and I'll order up coffee?"

"Dammit, man, you can't come in here and take over. I didn't even invite you in."

"No, but you won't be rude enough to toss me out, so let's handle this as pleasantly as possible," he said mildly. "Want some eggs with your coffee? Or perhaps a sandwich?"

Richard looked as if he wanted to argue—or perhaps tear William limb from limb—but he finally shrugged. "Order whatever the hell you want," he grumbled, and left the room.

William took it as a good sign when he heard the water come on in the shower. He called room service and was about to order a hearty lunch for two when someone knocked on the door. He took it upon himself to open it and found Destiny on the threshold, mouth gaping.

"I gather you concluded Richard was the key to things, as well," William said.

"I thought I told you he didn't want to see you," Destiny said, brushing past him.

"We don't always get what we want. It's a lesson your nephew needs to learn."

"Where is he? Why are you answering the door?"

"He's taking a shower and probably trying to wake up sufficiently to toss me out. I was about to order lunch. Care for something?"

She regarded him with a bemused expression. "Have you won him over already?"

"Hardly," William admitted ruefully. "The only agreement we've reached so far is that I wouldn't be leaving till we'd talked."

"Amazing."

William picked up the phone again and dialed. "Destiny, what can I get you?"

"Nothing. I just had tea in one of your shops. The scone was dry."

He laughed. "I'll make a point of passing the word along to the bakery." He ordered a large pot of coffee for himself and Richard, then added two club sandwiches. He doubted either of them would feel much like eating, but it would give them both something to pull apart when things got tense, which they were bound to do once Richard discovered his aunt was also on the scene.

When he'd hung up, he turned to Destiny. "What did you come here to tell Richard?"

"That he's not going to bully me into giving up either you or my job," she said at once. "That I want him to accept my decision and make peace with it."

"Think he'll go for it?"

"Not at first," she admitted. "But I think I can make him see that I know my own mind and that I'm entitled to do things my own way." She gave him a curious look. "Why are you here?"

"For much the same reason. I wanted to get my cards on the table, ask for your hand, that sort of thing."

Destiny's jaw dropped for the second time in less than ten minutes. "Ask for my hand?"

"I know it's a bit old-fashioned," he admitted. "But I thought it would be a nice touch. Thought it might show that I respect his role in your life. Bit tricky to pull off with you sitting right here, though."

"You want me to leave?" she asked incredulously.

"Might be best."

"Not till I've said my piece," she insisted, her hands folded in her lap.

Silence fell for several minutes, then she glanced at him. "Do you happen to have a ring?"

William's heart took an unexpected leap, probably a dangerous thing at his age. "An engagement ring?"

She nodded.

"Of course," he admitted.

"Could I see it?"

"Want to see if it's big enough to impress him?"

"No, I thought if I waved it under his nose as you suggested earlier, it might get his attention and make him take us both seriously."

William shook his head. "I've revised the plan. I think we'll go about this in a more traditional way. Richard strikes me as a traditional kind of man."

"Stuffy, you mean."

He grinned. "Your word, not mine."

"Yes, I suppose you're right about that. Okay, we'll do that much your way."

"Lovely of you to agree. Every successful business-person understands the art of compromise."

She smiled. "Only one of the skills I've mastered since coming here."

Richard walked into the room just then and stared at the two of them. "Ganging up on me?" he inquired tightly.

"Actually, no," William said emphatically with a pointed glance in Destiny's direction.

"William's right. I'll only be here a moment. I just came by to tell you that I love you, that I respect you and want your approval when it comes to William, but I'm prepared to live without it if that's the way it needs to be." She stood up and headed for the door, then glanced back over her shoulder. "Oh, and one more thing. I am not giving up my job, no matter how annoyed you get with me over all of this. One thing has absolutely nothing to do with the other, and I won't allow you to get them all twisted up."

Richard stared at her. "You amaze me."

She beamed at him. "I'm not surprised. Lately, I seem to be amazing myself. Now, listen to what William has to say, darling. I think you'll be pleasantly surprised."

"I doubt that," Richard muttered. "Where's that blasted coffee?"

"On its way," William assured him. "Should be here any minute. I think we'll wait for it. No sense in getting into things and ruining our appetites."

Richard gave him a sour look but didn't disagree. He did look relieved, though, when there was an almost immediate knock on the door.

"I'll let him in on my way out," Destiny said.

The waiter wheeled in their food and coffee, then left as well, leaving William and Richard in awkward silence. Richard poured two cups of coffee and picked up a section of the sandwich only to set it down again.

"Just get on with it, Harcourt. Say whatever you have to say and get out."

William heard the impatience in his voice and concluded the atmosphere wasn't likely to get any friendlier than this.

"I told you earlier today that I love your aunt," he began.

Richard's frown deepened. "Not what I want to hear."

"No, I'm sure of that. You'll be even less likely to be happy with the rest. I intend to marry her."

"Over my dead body!" Richard retorted.

William regarded him with a level look. "If need be."

Richard faltered a bit at that. "You're serious?"

"As a train wreck," William confirmed. "Now, before you get all riled up and defensive, hear me out. I've loved your aunt from the moment we met more than twenty years ago. Had it not been for your parents' deaths, we would have been married long before now."

"Oh, really?" Richard said skeptically. "I don't recall you ever coming to Virginia, standing by her side while we were all grieving. You abandoned her then, didn't you?"

"Yes," William said honestly. "But not exactly in the

way you mean. You see, I'd had a rift with my family over her. She concluded on her own that that rift could only be mended if she broke things off with me. I didn't realize that at the time, but she used your family's tragedy to make the break. I should never have allowed that to succeed, but I had too much pride and not enough sense. I picked up on all the signals and stayed away. In hindsight, I see what a huge mistake that was, but at the time I thought I was doing what she wanted."

"You expect me to believe that she broke up with you and broke your heart and not the other way around?"

"That's exactly what I'm telling you, though I can't deny that I bore some of the blame," William said. "You can ask her yourself. I won't make the same mistake again, though. This time I will fight to keep her. You, your brothers and your wives can stand in our way, if you feel you must, but I intend to marry her. I'd like your blessing because I know how important it is to Destiny that you not be unhappy about this, but I don't need to have it."

Richard stared at him mutely.

"Well?" William prompted. "Are you going to fight me on this? You know it's what Destiny wants, too."

"I need to think about what you've said," Richard said finally. "It's a lot to absorb."

"In other words, you want time to call for backup," William guessed. "Go ahead. I'd probably do the same in your shoes, but I will tell your brothers exactly what I told you. Your wives already believe in me. So does Destiny. They can't all be wrong, can they?"

He nodded when Richard said nothing. "I didn't think you'd risk calling them fools. That's the most promising thing that's happened since I arrived."

Richard gave him a wry look. "Saying things like that has already cost me," he admitted. "I may be stubborn, but I'm not stupid."

William grinned at him. "Never thought you were. A smart man always sees the handwriting on the wall."

He left to give Richard time enough to read it for himself.

The minute Harcourt left his suite, Richard did in fact call for reinforcements. He figured if he was going to have even half a chance of keeping Destiny and Harcourt apart, he was going to need Mack and Ben by his side, united in their opposition to this liaison. Nothing William had said had swayed him in the slightest, but he could see that it was going to be trickier than ever to convince Destiny that she was wrong about the man. If he was smooth enough to almost win over Richard with all that talk of missed opportunities, then Destiny had never stood a chance.

Unfortunately, Richard hadn't counted on Mack and Ben's wives coming along, as well. The next day, he opened the door to his suite to find the entire Carlton clan on his doorstep, babies and all. Even Melanie had turned up, looking decidedly displeased with his plan to disrupt Destiny's romance. The presence of the women was going to make it a lot more difficult to reach consensus on what needed to be done to save their aunt from William's untrustworthy clutches.

"Why exactly are we here?" Ben asked.

"To save Destiny," Richard said, his expression grim.

"From a man who's loved her forever and wants to

marry her?" Melanie scoffed. "Why am I sure that she won't thank us?"

"She's not thinking clearly at the moment," Richard said. "Harcourt has her believing they're some kind of star-crossed lovers. Hell, he almost had me believing it."

"Really?" Ben said. "What did he say?"

Richard repeated the conversation he'd had with William.

"Oh, my," Beth and Kathleen whispered in unison. "How sad."

Richard scowled at them.

"I think we need to give it up and start listening to Destiny," Mack said, casting a pointed look at Richard. "If she was able to look into our hearts and see exactly who and what we needed in our lives, then why should we think she's incapable of seeing what she wants for herself?"

"Amen," Melanie said, glowering at Richard.

"You want to just give up and accept this?" Richard asked, feeling the first stirring of defeat.

"If we don't want to lose Destiny, then yes, that's exactly what we need to do," Ben said. "We've fought this for months now and nothing's changed, except that she and Harcourt are closer than ever. If it turns out our doubts are right and he hurts her, then we can be there to pick up the pieces, but preventing her from marrying him doesn't seem to be in the cards."

Richard stared from him to Mack and back again. "Traitors," he said, but it was only a mildly muttered accusation.

"Pragmatists," Ben insisted. "We've lost, bro. Let's cut our losses before it's too late."

Richard sank down on the sofa beside his wife. She took his hand and brought it to her lips.

"It's going to be okay, Richard," Melanie soothed. "Look at how right Destiny was about us."

"And us," Mack said, winking at Beth.

"And us," Ben added, his hand on Kathleen's gently rounded belly. "I want Destiny to be a part of my baby's life."

Richard knew it was over then. There was a whole new generation of Carltons that deserved to have Destiny's magnificent influence. If accepting Harcourt was necessary to accomplish that, he supposed he could swallow his pride and keep his doubts to himself.

"But I'm going to keep my eye on him," he vowed.

Mack and Ben laughed. "Never thought otherwise."

The entire Carlton clan was holed up in a London hotel plotting and scheming against her. Destiny knew they thought otherwise. She knew they'd come because they loved her, but their lack of faith in her judgment was beyond annoying.

What had she done since coming to London, after all? She'd shored up the European division so that it was healthier than it had been in decades. She'd fought off one assault after another from William's company and others. She'd discovered that she not only had the Carlton genes for business, but the social and diplomatic skills necessary to turn deals into a win-win situation for all parties. Her employees—even Chester—were happy and highly motivated. Her tenure at the helm had been a raging success by all standards.

"I think it's clear what they've decided. They're not going to be happy until I've been replaced and come back home," she told William glumly when they hadn't heard from them two days after William's visit to Richard and a full day after the others had arrived en masse. "I hate making them so unhappy."

"They're unhappy because they think I'm going to take advantage of you sooner or later," William said.

"Oh, fiddle, you're not going to do that," she said with certainty. "Not that you could, anyway. I'm not young and naive."

He regarded her with amusement. "You never were. You had the upper hand from the moment we met, and you knew it. I believe I mentioned that to Richard, but he might not have passed it on. Shall I tell the rest of them that?"

"I doubt they'd listen. I'm not sure even I believe that."

"Perhaps this will help." He held out a small jeweler's box. "I was going to wait until things were more settled with your family, but maybe this is the time."

Destiny stared at it warily. "What's that?"

"Wouldn't you rather open it and see for yourself than listen to my inadequate description?"

"I'm not sure," she said honestly, her heart pounding.

"You're not a coward, Destiny. Just look at how you faced the overwhelming responsibility of raising those three boys without batting an eye."

She sighed. "If only that were true. I was terrified."

"But you didn't run away like I half expected you to do. You didn't beg me or anyone else to step in and share the burden. You're a strong woman, Destiny. I loved you then. I still do. But I also admire you more than I can say."

She was genuinely surprised and touched by his admission. She was humbled by it. She'd never felt she had done anything extraordinary. She'd simply done what she'd had to do.

She studied his dear face. "You do?"

"Surely you know that there's nothing ordinary about you," he chided. "I was counting on that when I started going after bits and pieces of Carlton Industries. I knew you'd come to fight me to protect what was yours."

She sat back, stunned. "I knew all along that you'd planned this, but I'm still surprised that you went to such lengths. Are you still plotting and scheming?"

He nodded. "Of course. I had to say a few provocative things to Richard to assure he would call those protective nephews of yours to congregate over here to save you," he said.

"You don't feel as if they're here to gang up on us?"

"No. I prefer to view it as a smart way to save time when we plan the wedding. I think Melanie, Beth and Kathleen intend to finish the job I'd begun."

She wanted to be angry about the scheming, but how could she be? Wasn't this exactly what she had hoped for when she'd come barreling over to London to save the day? She could have left the whole business crisis for Richard to handle, if some part of her hadn't wanted to see William again to see if he was the man she'd remembered or merely a foolish fantasy that had lingered in her heart for far too long.

"Will you open this now?" he asked, again holding out the small velvet box. "I've had it for a long time."

She opened the box and stared at the square-cut emerald.

"Diamonds are too tame for you," he told her. "I wanted something that captured your light, your fire."

She noted the name of a famous French jeweler inside the box. "When did you buy this?"

"The day after you left France. I'd planned to give it to you the moment you came back." He touched her cheek. "I'll have to work at forgiving you for making me wait so long."

Her eyes shimmered with tears. "But it's been worth the wait, hasn't it, to be here now, older and wiser and more certain of what we have?"

"And with half a dozen Carltons nipping at my heels to make sure I do the right thing," he said with a grin. "Yes, it's been worth it. So, Destiny, will you marry me?"

"I should make you ask Richard for my hand," she teased, envisioning the scene with some enjoyment.

"I've already done that," he reminded her. "He's been withholding his approval."

She laughed. "In that case I think a quick elopement might be our wisest course of action. Let them sit around at the hotel and stew, wondering where we've gone. A Paris wedding would be lovely this time of year. Violetta could be there," she added, warming to the idea.

"Never," he said. "I kept a safe distance between myself and your family once. I'll never do it again. We'll tell them together, my darling, and damn the consequences. They can't stop us. They can only slow us down a bit. And if you want a Paris wedding, we'll take them all along with us."

Destiny thought of the formidable group waiting across town. They would accept this—eventually, anyway—because they loved her and because William made her happy.

And if they didn't? Well, it wouldn't be the first time she'd run away from family and followed her heart.

But she would do everything in her power to see that it didn't come to that. She'd postponed her own happiness for a lot of years. Now she intended to grab it and hang on with everything in her, and that meant keeping her nephews—her beloved *children*—in her life, along with this man who meant the world to her.

She regarded William with shining eyes. "I think two excellent negotiators like us should be able to convince them that this merger is in our best interests, don't you?"

He grinned. "You bet, but if you don't mind, I think I'll let you do most of the talking. You seem to have developed a fine knack for getting your way."

"Not really. I wanted a fascinating liaison with you. You were the one dead-set on marriage from the beginning."

He laughed. "You have to let me win one once in a while. Otherwise, where's the sport in arguing?"

"Do you think we'll bring this much passion to our relationship when we're eighty?" she asked wistfully.

"And longer," he said confidently. "In fact, I'm counting on it."

Epilogue

Feeling rather smug, all things considered, Richard left the fancy dining room where they'd all had dinner with William and Destiny. Ben and Mack stepped into place beside him as they strolled back toward their hotel.

"Why the devil didn't you just tell them that you approved of this wedding?" Mack asked.

Richard grinned. "I wanted to make the old man sweat a bit longer, just to see what he's made of."

"And?" Ben prodded. "What was your conclusion?"

"No question that he loves Destiny," Richard conceded. "Not that I'm convinced he's not some sort of business shark, but the prenup he agreed to sign even over Destiny's objections pretty much settled that worry."

"I still say you gave him a rough time for no reason," Ben scolded mildly. "It wouldn't surprise me a bit if they decided to elope and leave us out of it."

Richard regarded his brother with alarm. "You don't really think they'd do that, do you?"

"I'm with Ben. I think they might," Mack said. "You were awfully tough on him."

"But I relented in the end," Richard protested. "Did you miss that?"

"Oh, I caught your grudging concession that you wouldn't stand in their way," Mack agreed. "Made me feel all warm and fluttery inside."

Richard stared from one to the other. "Hell, you can't be serious. We can't let them elope. Destiny deserves better than that from us."

"I agree," Ben said. "Mack?"

Mack nodded at once. "Let's head back over there and smooth this out once and for all."

Richard turned to find that Melanie, Beth and Kathleen were grinning.

"What?" he demanded.

"It's about time the three of you came to your senses. Now, let's go plan a wedding," Melanie said, tucking her arm through Richard's. "Just try to remember one thing."

"What's that?" Richard asked.

"It is Destiny's wedding. You don't get to micromanage it."

"Me?" Richard asked indignantly.

"Yes, you!" five voices chorused emphatically.

He laughed. "Okay, okay." He turned to his brothers. "Think our wives can keep their noses out of it, too?"

"Not a chance," Mack said.

"No way," Ben agreed.

Melanie, Beth and Kathleen merely shrugged. "Destiny already asked for our help," Melanie said.

Richard frowned. "They were never going to elope?"

"Well, they would have if you hadn't come around,"

Melanie told him. "But I convinced them to give us five or ten minutes to work on you."

He stared hard at his brothers. "And you were in on this scheme, too?"

"Scheming and manipulation," Mack said cheerfully. "It's the Carlton way."

Richard tried to maintain his indignation, but he couldn't pull it off. "Damn straight," he said at last.

In the end, the wedding was held in Provence in the middle of a field of poppies. All of the Carltons attended, as did Violetta and most of the people from the village, old friends it seemed to Destiny that she'd left only days, rather than decades, ago.

There was no aisle for Destiny to walk down, but when the minister asked who was giving her away, Richard, Mack and Ben stepped forward. "We do," they said in unison. "With our love and our blessing."

Tears streamed down Destiny's face as she kissed each one of them in turn, then faced William, her heart lighter than it had been in years.

The vows came easily. She'd loved and cherished William for most of her life now. Never again would they have to face whatever challenges came along alone. He would be her strength and, as she'd only recently realized, she was capable of being his. Together they were a formidable team.

In fact, if she had her way, there would be a Carlton Industries and Harcourt & Sons merger one of these days that would be just as invincible as the two of them.

But that was getting ahead of herself, she thought as she gazed into her new husband's eyes. Right now there was a honeymoon to savor, right here in the farmhouse where it had all begun. All she had to do was get this meddlesome family of hers out from underfoot by sunset. Given the way they'd fallen in love with the farmhouse and with Provence, that didn't seem likely.

Ah, well, a honeymoon with the family she adored wasn't such a bad way to begin her new life, either. After all, very little on earth meant more to her than family…and now William was a part of hers. Sometimes fate simply couldn't be ignored, no matter how long it took.

* * * * *

Turn the page for a sneak peek at
MENDING FENCES
by #1 New York Times *bestselling author*
Sherryl Woods,
available soon for the first time in trade paperback
from MIRA Books.

1

Present

Grady Rodriguez had been a police officer for nearly twenty years, but he'd never gotten used to interviewing young women who'd been the victims of date rape. It wasn't quite the same as talking to those who'd been assaulted by strangers. For those women, there was little ambiguity about the attack. It was usually random, unexpected, violent and degrading. It could happen to any woman at any age who happened to be in the wrong place at the wrong time.

Date rape tended to happen to young, often inexperienced women who knew their attacker. They were left with a million and one questions about what they might have done differently, how their judgment about the guy could have been so wrong, why saying no hadn't been enough. He'd responded to too damn many of those calls, listened to too many brokenhearted sobs, seen too many injuries.

In either case, the women questioned everything about themselves. They dealt with unwarranted shame, sometimes made a thousand times worse by the well-meaning reactions of the people who loved them. In all instances, it changed who they were, made them more cautious, less trusting. Sometimes it destroyed relationships or even marriages.

From everything he could see as he and his partner, Naomi Lansing, walked into the off-campus Coral Gables apartment where tonight's attack had happened, Lauren Brown was typical. A pretty college student with shiny, long blond hair, she barely looked old enough to date. A kid that young shouldn't have had her innocence stripped away in a manner that left her eyes glazed with pain and disillusionment. Seeing her huddled in a corner of the bed in her room in tears, Grady wanted to punch his fist through a wall, but Naomi was cool and calm, the kind of soothing presence the situation required.

Naomi's compassion allowed him to remain in the background, to study the scene in a coldly analytical way. They were the perfect team for this kind of investigation, something he'd never have predicted back when they'd first been assigned to work together and every encounter had been a test of wills.

"She was like that when I came in," Lauren's roommate, Jenny Ryan, told them in an undertone. "Just rocking back and forth and crying. She said her date had hurt her, but she wouldn't say anything else. She asked me not to, but I called nine-one-one anyway. The creep shouldn't get away with this. I don't care who he is."

Something in her words gave Grady a chill, the hint that Lauren's attacker was well-known, perhaps well-respected in the University of Miami campus community.

"You did the right thing," Naomi assured her. "We'll take it from here. Could you wait in the other room?"

For a moment, Jenny hesitated. "I'm not sure I should leave her."

Naomi sat on the edge of the bed, careful not to crowd Lauren. "You'll be okay, right? You're up to talking to me?"

Lauren's head bobbed once, but she didn't look up.

As Naomi began murmuring the most intrusive questions in her quiet, matter-of-fact voice, Grady studied the bedroom. Painted and carpeted in the bland beige of inexpensive rentals, it was decorated in a style that was too shabby to be chic. There were mismatched pieces of furniture, a few snapshots—family pictures, it looked like—stuck into the dresser mirror, a laptop computer next to a stack of textbooks and an antique rocker he would bet had been a prized possession from home.

Other than the tangled spread and sheets on the bed and a few pieces of clothing that had been tossed on the floor, the room was neater than most coed rooms he'd seen. Carefully gathering the clothes she'd apparently been wearing, he noted the buttons missing from her blouse, the torn strap of her bra and a rip in her panties, all consistent with someone intent on having sex, perhaps with an unwilling partner. He found three buttons scattered around the carpet and added those to the evidence.

Leaving it to Naomi to retrieve the sheets and spread and whatever trace evidence they might contain, Grady walked into the living room to join the roommate. "Any idea who Lauren was out with tonight?" he asked her.

"Evan Carter," she said without hesitation. "You know who he is, right?"

"Yeah, I've heard of him," he said, struggling to maintain a neutral expression.

Carter was a star football player at the University of Miami. Only a sophomore, there was already speculation about him becoming a top NFL draft choice before graduation. News reports, however, also cited his excellent grades, good enough for the career he hoped to have in the legal field representing professional athletes. He had brains, talent and charm—the kind of trifecta that made it easy for people to miss any hints of a darker side, the sense of entitlement and immunity that came with being a celebrity of sorts.

A local boy, Carter was already used to the spotlight by the time he entered UM. He'd been courted by both the Florida Gators and by Florida State Seminoles, top UM rivals. When he'd opted to stay close to home, there'd been a sigh of relief from the Miami fans, who'd followed his stellar high school career.

"Is that the crowd Lauren hangs out with—the jocks?" he asked Jenny.

"No way. To tell you the truth, Lauren's never dated much. She's basically pretty shy and quiet. She's here on a scholarship, so she studies a lot. Evan's the first guy she's really talked much about. They're in the same biology class—I'm in it, too—and they've been working on this project together for a couple of weeks now. When he suggested dinner and a movie, she couldn't believe this superjock had asked her out. She was so excited." Her lower lip quivered and her expressive dark eyes filled with anger. "Damn him for doing this to her!"

"Were you here when they left? Did you see them together?"

Jenny shook her head. "I had to go to the library to do some research for a paper that's due on Monday. I didn't get back till about two minutes before I called you."

"So you can't be sure they actually got together tonight," he suggested.

Jenny practically quivered with indignation. "Are you trying to say she made it all up or something?" she demanded. "Lauren would *never* lie about who she had a date with or about what happened. Lauren doesn't lie. Period."

"Maybe a girl who doesn't date much developed a crush on this unattainable guy, built herself a whole fantasy scenario," he suggested.

"No, absolutely not!" Jenny said emphatically. "She's the most honest, grounded person I know. Her dad's a minister, for goodness' sakes. She has this whole moral code she lives by. Most of the time the rest of us fall way short of meeting her standards, but she never judges any of us for that."

Satisfied, Grady backed off on any suggestion that Lauren could have exaggerated anything that happened with the Carter kid. Instead, he focused on what Jenny herself knew firsthand. "But you yourself didn't witness any part of the date, correct?"

She sighed. "No. I never saw them together, but I imagine there are plenty of witnesses in the building or on the block. It's mostly college kids living in this area, so there's always somebody going in or out, especially on a Friday night. And Evan's the kind of guy who attracts attention. He makes sure of it."

Grady knew the type. They thrived on being the center of attention, being recognized. They also thought they were above the law. Maybe tonight Grady would get lucky and that tendency would seal the case against Evan Carter.

"If Detective Lansing looks for me, tell her I'm going to knock on a few doors, see what I can find out from the neighbors," he told Jenny. "I'll be back in a few minutes. You'll stay put, right?"

"Of course. I'm not leaving Lauren."

The white stucco building on the fringe of the UM campus only had four units, two upstairs, two down. He tried the downstairs doors to no avail, then loped back upstairs and knocked on the door across the hall from Lauren's. When it swung open, the sound of classic jazz flowed through the air. The long-haired kid wearing boxers, a T-shirt and flip-flops stared at him with blurry eyes and a bewildered expression.

"Is the music too loud or something?" he asked Grady. "I try to keep it low."

"The music's not a problem," Grady assured him. He showed him his ID. "Mind if I ask you a couple of questions?"

"Am I in trouble?"

The kid sounded nervous, which made Grady wonder what he was up to. Then he caught a whiff of marijuana and knew. That, however, was a problem for another night.

"No, no trouble," he assured him. "This is your apartment?"

"I have a roommate, but he's out on a date."

Grady made a note. “What’s your name?”

“Joe Haas.”

“And your roommate’s?”

“Dante Mitchell.”

“He plays football, doesn’t he?” Grady asked, trying to envision the huge defensive tackle sharing a place with this skinny, unassuming kid.

“We’re from the same hometown. His folks think I’m a good influence on him.” He shrugged, his grin self-deprecating. “As if he’d ever listen to me. Still, we get along okay.”

“Have you been home all night?”

“It’s Friday night,” he said as if that was answer enough. “I’ve been here just chilling out.”

“Seen anybody? Heard anything unusual?”

He stared at Grady with a blank expression. “Like what?”

“Anything that seemed out of the ordinary?”

“Did one of the apartments get robbed? Is that why you’re asking all these questions?”

“No. I’m just trying to get a feel for what was going on around here tonight.”

“I think everybody’s out, except me. Dante left around seven. Jenny headed out about the same time with a bunch of books. She always goes to the library on Friday night. She says it’s quieter then. The guys downstairs, they always head straight for happy hour after their last class on Friday. I don’t think they’ve come in yet. They’re usually pretty noisy, so I would have heard them if they’d come back.”

“What about Lauren? Have you seen her?”

He shook his head. “I know she had a date with some jock, a friend of Dante’s.”

"Did she tell you that?"

"No, Dante mentioned it. He thought it was pretty hilarious for some reason."

"Why was that?"

"I guess because Lauren's really shy and this guy thinks he's some big hotshot."

"You know a name?"

Joe shook his head. "I'm not that into football. Dante probably said, but it didn't stick."

"And you never saw Lauren with this guy?"

He shook his head, then frowned. "Lauren's okay, isn't she? Nothing happened to her tonight, did it?"

Grady ignored the questions. "Thanks. If you think of anything else, give me a call." He handed him his business card.

Joe followed him back into the hall, his expression filled with concern. He bypassed Grady and headed straight for Lauren's door. Grady intercepted him. "Not tonight."

Alarm shadowed the boy's eyes. "I just want to check on Lauren. She's a sweet kid, you know?"

"Talk to her tomorrow, okay? She'll need a friend then." He leveled a look at the kid. "And you might want to lose the weed before I come around again. Next time I won't look the other way."

"Shit!" Joe said, his expression immediately guilt ridden. He all but ran back to his own apartment and shut the door.

Grady shook his head. For a fraction of an instant he was grateful he didn't have teenagers, but then he thought of his beautiful little Megan and his heart ached. She would have been sixteen now and he would give every last breath in his body to have his daughter back, no matter what sort of foolish mistakes she might make.

Tonight wasn't the night to travel down that dark path, though. Another young girl needed him.

Inside Lauren's apartment, Jenny was exactly where he'd left her, blindly thumbing through a magazine, her attention directed toward the room where Naomi was still questioning Lauren.

"Did anybody see anything?" she asked when she realized he was back.

"The kid across the hall was the only one home, and he confirmed she was supposed to go out with some jock tonight, but he didn't see him and didn't have a name. He says his roommate had told him that."

Jenny smiled. "Joe's a little spacey most of the time, but he's a good guy. It might not seem like it, but he's practically a genius. He's studying physics, but most of the time he's bored, because he knows as much as the professors. He puts up with a lot from Dante, who thinks he's God's gift to the universe. Will it help that Dante knew about the date, too?"

"It might," Grady conceded.

"What happens next?"

"We'll need to get Lauren to the hospital, get her checked out," he said. "Can you come along? It might make her feel better to have a familiar face around."

"If she needs me, I'm there," Jenny told him.

A few minutes later, Naomi emerged with Lauren and the four of them made the trip to the Rape Treatment Center at Jackson Memorial Hospital for the necessary indignity of a physical examination.

As they waited outside while a physician gathered evidence and offered counseling to Lauren with Jenny at her side, Grady sat beside Naomi and compared notes. "You think she'll go through with this? Will she press charges against the Carter kid?" he asked. "It's a tough road, especially with his high profile. The publicity could be pretty devastating, even if her name's kept out of it."

"She's scared," Naomi said. "But she's starting to get angry. If she weakens, something tells me her roommate will make sure she fights back."

He nodded. "Jenny's mad enough for both of them. I wish all the girls we come across had someone in their corner like that."

Naomi nodded. "Me, too."

"We need to do this one by the book," Grady said wearily. "I want an arrest warrant in hand before we go anywhere near that kid."

"That could take time," Naomi warned. "It's almost morning now and half the judges are going to be on the golf course and the rest are probably out on their boats."

"We'll call the state attorney's office and leave that problem up to them. I don't care how long it takes, I want that warrant before we say boo to that kid. The media's going to be all over this case and I'm not losing it because we didn't cross every *t* and dot every *i*."

Just then the weary-looking physician who handled far too many of these cases emerged from the treatment area.

"How's it going, Doc?" Grady asked Amanda Benitez.

"I'm starting to have a very jaded outlook on life in general and men in particular," Amanda said. "This guy roughed her up pretty good. He was smart about it, almost as if he knew how to go about it without leaving the kind of obvious visible marks that would call attention to what he'd done. Her stomach, her upper thighs have some nasty bruises, though. He was strong and he was mean."

Grady read between the lines. "He's done this before?"

"I'd say yes. You know the pattern as well as I do. It's not just about the sex. This is a guy who gets off on hurting women, the more innocent and defenseless the better. You have a name?"

Grady nodded. "And when this goes public, the shit is going to hit the fan."

It was well past midnight on Saturday and Marcie had just finished cleaning up the kitchen, putting every dish and glass back into place, polishing every piece of chrome and mopping the floor for the second time that day, when the doorbell rang.

Worried that it would wake Ken and the kids, she hurried into the living room to answer the door. Startled to see two uniformed officers and two other people in plain clothes outside at this hour of the night, she was tempted not to open the door, but weighed her caution against the possibility that they'd wind up waking her family by continuing to ring the bell. She finally opened the door a crack, the security chain still in place.

"Can I help you?"

"Pinecrest police, ma'am," one of the uniformed officers said. "We have two detectives from Coral Gables who'd like to speak to your son. Since they're out of their jurisdiction, we came along."

"I don't understand," Marcie said.

"You're Mrs. Carter?" the female detective asked. "Evan Carter's mother?"

Marcie's breath lodged in her throat. "Yes, why?"

"We need to speak to your son," she repeated. "Is he here?"

"He's asleep. What is this about?"

"I'm Detective Lansing," the woman told her. "And this is Detective Rodriguez. We need to talk to Evan. Would you get him, please?"

Though it was phrased as a question, Marcie recognized a command when she heard one. She tried to think what Ken would do. He'd probably tell them to go away and come back at a civilized hour, but Marcie had been brought up to respect authority. Four very somber police officers from two jurisdictions were more than enough to intimidate her.

"You'll have to give me a few minutes," she said at last. "He's a sound sleeper."

"No problem. We'll wait," the woman told her.

Reluctantly Marcie let them inside, then started to climb the stairs. After only a couple of steps, she turned back. "Maybe I should..." she began, her tone apologetic. "Could I see some identification?" She'd read stories about fake police officers, even in uniform, and home-invasion robberies. Even though she recognized the Pinecrest logo on the uniform and saw the marked car in the driveway, it was smart to be absolutely sure.

Without comment all four of them held out badges and ID, removing any doubt that they were exactly who they'd said they were. She almost wished she hadn't asked. Until that instant, she'd been able to hold out a slim hope that this was all some hoax or maybe a case of mistaken identity.

Evan was a good kid. He always had been. Oh, he had a mouth on him. He was like his father that way, but he'd never given them any trouble. He'd never so much as put a ding or dent in the car, never gotten into mischief the way some of the other boys in the neighborhood had. His dad had seen to that. Ken was a stern disciplinarian and both her kids showed him a healthy amount of respect.

Thinking about that made this whole scene feel surreal. Once again she hesitated. "Why do you need to see Evan at this hour? Is he in trouble?"

For the first time, Detective Rodriguez spoke. "Ma'am, could you just get him? We'll explain everything then."

Filled with a sense of dread, she climbed the stairs. At the top she debated waking Ken but decided against it. Who knew what he would do or say? He had a quick temper and a sharp tongue. He tended to act first and think later. He might wind up making a bad situation worse. If Evan needed him, there would be time enough to wake him then.

Inside Evan's room, she found him sprawled facedown across his bed with a sheet barely covering him. Sometimes when she saw him like this, it caught her by surprise. In her heart, he was still her little boy, not a full-grown man with broad shoulders and muscles toned by hours of training at the gym. His cheeks were stubbled with a day's growth of beard and his blond hair, usually so carefully groomed, stuck out every which way. Seeing him reminded her of the way Ken had looked when they'd first met, way too handsome for his own good.

"Evan," she murmured, her hand on his shoulder. "Wake up! Evan!"

He only moaned and buried his head under the pillow, just as he had for years when she'd tried to wake him for school. Marcie knew the routine. She yanked the pillow away and then the sheet, averting her gaze from his naked body as she did so.

"Wake up!" she commanded, shaking him.

"Wha...? Go 'way."

"Get up now," she said urgently. "There's someone here to see you."

He blinked up at her. "What? Who?"

"They're police officers, four of them. Two local and two from the Gables."

"Shit, oh shit," he muttered, raking his hand through his hair.

Something in the panicked expression that flitted across his face terrified Marcie. Had there been an accident? Had he left the scene? Or drugs? She knew there were kids at college who used them, but Evan had always been smart enough to steer clear. He'd wanted his football career too much to risk messing it up by experimenting with drugs or steroids. Ken had hammered that lesson home years ago.

"Do you know what this is about?" she asked. "Should I get your dad?"

"I'll handle it," he said, grabbing a pair of jeans and yanking them on, then snatching up a T-shirt from the end of the bed and pulling it over his head. "Don't come downstairs, Mom, okay? I'll take care of this."

Marcie fought to stay calm. "I don't like the sound

of this, Evan. I think someone should be with you. Do I need to call a lawyer?"

"I said I'd handle it," he snapped. "Go to bed."

Marcie winced at his tone. She should have been used to it by now. Ken used that exact same tone when he spoke to her, but it was relatively new coming from Evan.

"You're not going down there alone," she insisted. "Now either I come with you or I get your father."

"Whatever," he said belligerently.

Marcie followed him downstairs. At the bottom of the steps, the two detectives stood in his path.

"Evan Carter?" Detective Rodriguez asked.

"Yes. What the hell is this about?" he demanded, his voice radiating antagonism.

Again, he sounded so much like his father, it gave Marcie goose bumps. Instinct kicked in. She was about to try to smooth things over with the detectives, but realized they were oblivious to his attitude and totally focused on their own mission.

"You're under arrest for the rape of Lauren Brown," the woman said quietly. "Anything you say can and will be used against you…"

Rape! Marcie was incredulous. This simply couldn't be happening. As the detective read Evan his rights, Marcie fought back the bile rising in her throat and ran upstairs to wake her husband. She couldn't shake the sound of the word *rape*. It kept echoing in her head.

"Ken, get up now! The police are arresting Evan. They say he raped somebody."

She didn't have to say it twice. Ken bolted out of bed with a curse and ran for the stairs, Marcie right on his heels. She heard Caitlyn's door open and knew that her daughter had been wakened by the commotion as well.

"Mom, what's going on? Why is there a police car outside?"

Marcie couldn't bring herself to explain. "It's all a terrible misunderstanding," she said. "I'm sure that's all it is. Your father will straighten everything out, but I need to go with him."

"Go with him where?" Caitlyn asked, her eyes wide. "It's the middle of the night."

"To the police station. I'm going to call Emily and see if you can go over and spend the night at their house, okay? I don't want you here alone."

"Who's been arrested? Is it Dad?"

"No, sweetie, it's your brother, but like I said, it has to be a mistake." Her hand shook as she picked up the phone and hit the number on the speed dial for Emily.

Her friend and neighbor answered on the first ring, instantly wide awake. "Marcie, is everything okay? I saw the flashing lights on a police car turning onto your street, but I never heard a siren. What's going on?"

"I can't explain now. Can Caitlyn stay with you?"

"Of course," she said at once. "Send her over. Is there anything else I can do?"

"Pray," Marcie said, her voice catching on a sob. "Pray that the police have made some horrible mistake. My boy..." She couldn't even finish the sentence.

"They came for Evan?" Emily said, sounding as shocked as Marcie felt.

"Yes. Please, just watch out for Caitlyn. She's on her way. I don't know how long we'll be gone. I'll tell you everything tomorrow."

"Go. Don't worry about anything here. Just promise that you'll call me if there's anything else I can do."

Marcie sighed as she hung up. She wondered if Emily would sound half as supportive once she found out what Evan had been accused of doing. There were some things even a best friend could never understand or forgive.

And if there was any truth, any truth at all to the charges, Marcie wasn't entirely certain she'd ever understand it, either.